Gas

A novel by
Bill Kelley

The following is historical fiction, as such it depicts characters and events which may appear superficially related to actual characters and events, however it is entirely fictional.

Dramatis Personae

The Artist. . . . . Tommy Cobb. Our man. Son of a famous Cape Cod painter.

The Scientist. . . . . Apple Piehl. Works for the EPA.

The Witch. . . . . Goody Hallet. Samuel Bellamy's girlfriend.

The Woodcutter. . . . . . . Jack Bellamy. Proprietor of the gas station. Father of Samuel.

The Pirate. . . . . Samuel Bellamy. Jack's son. Goody's boyfriend.

The Artist

Tommy Cobb was an artist. One had to admit that. He had taken the leap. Whether or not he was any good was another question. Fortunately, for him, that he was only twenty-eight was why the question was totally irrelevant. Unfortunately, on the other hand, being that he *was* only twenty-eight, he was unable to grasp that particular irrelevance and so, as young men often did, he suffered needlessly. If the truth be told he wasn't very good anyway, not yet. As it happened Tommy was the illegitimate son of the well known American regionalist painter Richard Cobb of the New York Ash Can School. He was a skilled draftsman and astute observer of a lonely landscape in the early days of what would become a uniquely American twentieth century style of oil painting. Richard Cobb was perhaps the only legitimate protégé of Thomas Hart Benton (Tommy's namesake and the greatest expressionistic American painter, regionalist or otherwise). Like Benton before him Richard Cobb was seen as a stubborn hold-out. With his traditional methods and subjects he confounded the modernist art of his day and was dismissed as a sentimental rustic. Awash in New York abstract expressionism he persisted in painting lighthouses and dune shacks. He painted gas stations and all night diners. In New York at that time (the forties and the fifties) one didn't paint a gas station, let alone a sunset or a lighthouse. In fact, depicting an object or a subject of any kind was seen not merely as taboo, but worse, it was seen as embarrassingly plebeian. It was seen as uneducated and rural. Better not to even use a brush or an easel or to even paint something that could actually fit into a typical American household.

These paintings didn't fit figuratively or literally. Even if one liked it he couldn't get it through the front door. The idea was to radicalize the situation. To take art back from those who wanted to buy it and put it in their homes. Thankfully this malicious plan backfired so completely as to justify paying upwards of six figures for a painting of a single stripe across a uniform background color. Sometimes you didn't even get a stripe. You got a uniform background color and that's it. Artists splashed aluminum oxide industrial pigments over giant canvases which were to be stretched across the side of an old barn or over a concrete floor in an abandoned factory. As in any artistic movement, no matter how silly, mean-spirited, or misguided, some drawn into it end up being very good indeed (geniuses even) but they are the rare few. More than likely the mob in their wake overwhelms their contribution. Still, for whatever reason, Richard Cobb was in New York in the forties and fifties and yet somehow he was not an abstract expressionist. This begs the question: How did he get away with it? The answer is simple. He got away with it in the only way one ever did when it mattered, by being earnest and by being good. That has always overridden popular sentiment. And so, as is often the case in the appreciation of art, we acknowledge that Richard Cobb was indeed an American master, retroactively.

Richard Cobb was fascinated with women. True most men are, but he really seemed to like them. He painted them with skin as white as a marshmallow. They had raven hair and big legs and shapely bosoms bathed in sunlight. Some would say that in certain respects he had failed at being a man, but there was no doubt that as an artist he had succeeded.

Richard Cobb died in nineteen-sixty-nine, two years after Tommy was born and, sadly, Tommy was something of a secret as his father was already married and moderately famous. Tommy's mother was a kind and humble woman. She never made a fuss. This didn't sit well with Tommy, but due to the pain and shame of it all he had usually repressed the urge to think about it. Though Tommy had become a painter himself, he honestly felt this was a coincidence and he couldn't see how his father had any influence over him. After all, he had never met him.

Tommy stabbed a hot dog with a fork and held it over the flame of his little gas stove. He was the kind of guy who would camp in an apartment. Not that this was an apartment per se. He liked to think of it as an art space. In this way he was relieved of the responsibility of having mundane domestic accouterments such as frying pans, alarm clocks and towels. On this particular morning, he had in fact needed a towel but instead used a pair of pajamas to dry off. That he had pajamas was in itself odd, though he had never slept in them, he kept them because they were a gift from his mother and he planned to use them as painting rags, which he always needed.

It was ten a.m. He wore plaid boxer shorts and stared bleary-eyed into the flickering blue gas flame. One would be remiss to assume Tommy was merely vacuous. Though he was perhaps the epitome of his generation, a Gen-X slacker, he usually managed to convince those who knew him that he was a deep and sensitive person. He accomplished this for the most part by being deep and sensitive. He'd gladly give you the smelly paint-speckled shirt off his back.

Tommy was nothing if not impractical and given to flights of nostalgia. His contemplative mood this morning was triggered by the smell of the burning hot dog which reminded him of summers at the beach when he was a boy. Those were memories he cherished. He hadn't had such a bad childhood, thanks to his mother. He reminded himself that he should probably call her, and that he should probably go to the beach this summer. Why couldn't he do that? He felt it was unlikely given that he had no money, no job and no girl. But why did he need money, or a job, or a girl, to call his mother or to go to the beach? It all made perfect sense to him. You don't want to call your mother when you're doing badly because it will just make her feel worse. His life was a train wreck no matter how he sliced it.

But all this negative thinking would get him nowhere and so he resolved to relax and cheer up. He reminded himself that he had a talent for seeing the good side of a thing when he put his mind to it. After all, today he might get some good work done.

He went to his easel and saw a clean canvas. The clean canvas was a sacred thing. It was empty, yet laden with gravity and solemnity. Like the proverbial fool who had not yet opened his mouth, it too was potentially perfect. He would revel in that moment and take time to mix the paint. He had to get the colors just right. He had to mull over his collection of damar varnish, linseed oil, and turpentine, the ingredients which when properly administered produced the smell of a freshly cut Christmas tree. He used an eyedropper, dispensing the tinctures with precision. The consistency had to be just right. He knew he was ready when the paint was creamy and buttery and looked good enough to eat. This took effort. Sometimes it never came. Often he mixed the paint until it was putrid and he would have to scrap the whole batch and start over.

This morning however he got some decent colors going and so he began, carefully. It was slow, but he persisted. He was content to chip away at the thing. He couldn't expect every day to be inspired. Occasionally he'd lose faith. Sure he had some good stuff but he had been lucky. Maybe he'd never get it back? Maybe all his best work was behind him?

Tommy walked away from the canvas and surveyed what he had done. It wasn't a pretty sight. In fact it sucked. He backed off another ten feet and looked again. It still sucked. He picked up the hot dog fork, went back to his easel, closed his eyes, took a deep breath, and stabbed at the canvas repeatedly. This made him feel better and he laughed.

He sat on the couch, with the fork still stabbed in the center of the canvas, when there was a knock at the door. He considered not opening it, but he knew it would be Antonio. Antonio Azule was a good guy, and he did after all own the place, and had given Tommy the benefit of the doubt more than once.

Tommy opened the door. "Hey Tony Blue, what's shakin'?" Antonio entered the room and went straight for the canvas. Tommy fell back into the couch, put his feet up on the coffee table and awaited Antonio's judgment. Antonio took his time. As usual he was generous with Tommy.

"What's this, the portrait of Dorian Gray?" Antonio gestured toward the fork stuck in the canvas.

"Dorian used a knife but I had to make do," said Tommy.

"That's just as well," said Antonio. "One shouldn't keep sharp objects around you when you're working." Antonio stepped a few paces back and looked at the painting again. He closed one eye and squinted. "The Portrait of Dorian Gray," he repeated.

"We can't all be clever Antonio."

"No," said Antonio.

"Basil was a good painter,"

"Was he? Or was Dorian just a really good subject?"

"Both," Tommy answered. "Regardless, the portrait of Dorian Gray was supposed to be a good painting whereas that there is a hideous piece of shit."

"Hideous?"

"It's the worst piece of crap I've ever done."

"You've done worse," said Antonio. "I've sold worse. Besides, Dorian started out beautifully and then ended terribly, wouldn't you say?"

"Yes," said Tommy. "But that painting on the other hand ended terribly *and* started terribly."

Antonio gestured toward the fork. "May I?" He pulled it out. "Some people let them dry and paint over them. You know? To be fiscally conservative?"

"No you're right," said Tommy. "I could save you a few bucks." Antonio recoiled at this last comment. He flopped on the couch beside Tommy and frowned.

"I'm just fucking around," said Tommy.

"I know you are," said Antonio.

Tommy suddenly felt ashamed and he was right to. Antonio had sold some of Tommy's paintings and granted he had taken a small fee but still he was always focused on what was best for Tommy as an artist. He had arranged Tommy's first one man show, and he had given him a place to stay. He was a genuine patron of the arts and not some self-serving impresario like most art dealers. Antonio didn't care about money, it was beneath him.

"So anyway Antonio how are things with you?"

Antonio and Tommy sat and talked for a while. As usual they enjoyed each other's company. Within an hour they had covered politics, philosophy and science.

"You know Tommy, few people really know how to have a decent conversation. I don't know who I'll talk to when you're gone."

"Am I going somewhere?" Tommy asked.

Antonio smiled and then decided to have a beer, which worried Tommy a bit. Tommy had a beer as well though it was barely eleven-thirty. They lapsed back into conversation. They mused about the Dalai Lama, Nietzsche, and the possibility of space colonization. They discussed the relative merits of Marc Chagall and Salvador Dali. Antonio explained that Chagall was a true Surrealist who painted from his subconscious while Dali merely postured for effect.

"He was a poser," said Antonio. "He was sensationalistic and shallow." Tommy agreed but interjected that Dali was a good draftsman while Chagall really couldn't draw all that well. Antonio balked at this. "He drew fish with wings for Christ sake! What more do you want?"

"You make a good point," Tommy admitted. "Were you aware that Salvador Dali had a pathological fear of grasshoppers?"

"I wasn't," said Antonio.

And so it went, back and forth, until Antonio decided to come to the point of his visit.

"So Tommy." He appeared apologetic. Tommy braced himself. "I've got a girl coming over to look at the place."

"A girl?"

"Yeah."

"All right," said Tommy. "Is she good-looking?"

"I would say so," said Antonio. "She's like Janine Garaphalo with red hair."

"I know the type," said Tommy. "That's a good type. Can she paint at least? Please tell me she can so I won't feel so bad."

"She does great pottery."

"Of course she does," said Tommy.

"Right," said Antonio. "Which means she's not an artist? '

"Is she?"

"I can sell her work and that has to count for something don't you think?"

"And you'll get laid maybe," said Tommy.

"It is what it is. I mean what the fuck? Am I right? But seriously Tommy it's not about that. I'm thinking of what's best for you in all of this. You're ready for something else man. Anyone can see that."

"You're right. How am I going to stay here?"

"The change will be good for you. You've said it yourself."

"I know."

"Go and get laid. That's what people do."

"I see your point Antonio. You make a point. How am I going to be an *enfant terrible* or whatever it's called when I'm in my thirties?"

"I didn't actually say that."

"No, but I get it. You can't be the new kid when you're in your thirties. I get that, I do. I get it. I totally get it."

"You're only twenty-eight."

"Right," said Tommy. "Still my days are numbered."

"So that's it? You're done? You're all washed up at twenty-eight? Your father was thirty-five before he had his first one man show. Barnet Newman was forty. Motherwell never dipped his brush until he was fifty." Antonio usually knew better than to bring up Tommy's father or even his peers but at this moment he felt the context justified it. He was right. Tommy thought about this awhile.

"He was better than me."

"Newman and Motherwell weren't that good," said Antonio.

"He was," said Tommy. He didn't even like to mention his father by name.

"Yeah well he's dead and we're alive."

"I guess that's something."

"You better believe that's something," said Antonio. "And that's my point Tommy. You need to get out of here and have some fun."

"Ok Antonio. I don't disagree."

Antonio smiled. "You know, like go to the beach or something."

Tommy laughed. "You know I haven't gone swimming in like three years?"

"It's probably been longer than that," said Antonio.

"Tony Blue, you make a damn good point. I'll be out in a week."

"Don't be so dramatic," said Antonio. "Take two."

Tommy Cobb walked the streets of New York. He walked ten blocks all the way to the museum of modern art. It was Sunday so it was free, but you had to give a donation. Tommy put a penny on the counter. The young woman across from him was slightly amused. "Cute," she said and handed him a map.

"I don't need it."

"Me either." She was the kind of girl he liked. She had thick black frames, a pierced eyebrow and pulled back hair, probably an artist, definitely a grad student. He imagined kissing her and then he walked away.

Of course they would have his father's paintings, but first Tommy would look around. As always he ended up in front of Van Gogh. No matter how many times he saw one he couldn't get over it. When he looked closely he could see where Van Gogh had touched it. He pictured it hanging in Vincent's grimy hovel as he prepared his meager diner and went to bed. He imagined him seeing it again with new eyes when he awoke as Tommy did when he awoke and looked at his own paintings hanging in whatever grimy little hovel he happened to be living in at the time. This was how he liked to think of Van Gogh. As a man outside of his own time but trapped in a certain period in history. This was how Tommy felt. He was as fascinated by the idea of Van Gogh as a man as he was by Van Gogh as a painter. In fact sometimes he asked himself whether it was really the paintings that made him like Van Gogh so much. He had read a book of Van Gogh's letters to his brother Theo, which totally impressed him and had supplied him with endless reflections on his own philosophy of life and art. The impression that Tommy took away from this book was that Van Gogh was very smart and well spoken and that contrary to conventional wisdom he wasn't even the slightest bit crazy. In fact, in his writing he came across as unusually sane. Van Gogh was a great writer on top of everything else. Tommy was of the opinion that to be a writer one had to be observant and sensitive and above all, one had to be rational. You could definitely say that Tommy was prone to idolizing certain men in history. That was just the way he was born. He had always idolized people. He knew that in general he tended to give people too much credit but surely some of these historical figures were worthy. He got a Van Gogh self portrait tattooed on his chest. It was big and beautiful and took three months to complete. It cost him nearly a thousand dollars and this in spite of the fact that he could in no way afford it. Not to mention the fact that he had managed to go twenty-seven and a half years without a single tattoo and he always said that he would never get one. He paid dearly for it. It went over his collar bone, pectoral muscle and sternum. He found that the sternum was in particular among the most painful places to have needles stabbed repeatedly into one's flesh. It was torturous. When he came across the very same self portrait in the museum he felt a deep spiritual connection standing there in front of it. When a woman stopped to take a picture of the painting Tommy wanted to unbutton his shirt, but he didn't. He realized that would've been stupid and yet he still wanted to do it.

Eventually Tommy made it around to the gallery of his father's paintings. He knew that his father must have been a disciplined and orderly man. A master to be sure, but totally different than Van Gogh. His work was studied and austere. He had the temperance and foresight of an older man. He saw his work through to its logical conclusion. Unlike Van Gogh, Richard Cobb was lucky enough to have a mature major phase. As inspiring as Van Gogh was he would always have that painful James Dean quality. It broke your heart and that was its appeal. Cobb on the other hand impressed Tommy for an entirely different reason. There was nothing tragic and full of potential in his work. It was realized sufficiently and not at all tragically cut short. Yet Tommy preferred the fleeting and painful Van Gogh. He was the patron saint of all suffering young men. Tommy thought there might be something to the fact that they both committed suicide, and they both seemed to do it in a way that lacked conviction. In fact, Van Gogh wasn't even trying to commit suicide technically. He just wanted to shoot himself in the stomach and suffer; the fact that he died a couple of weeks later was like an afterthought. Tommy had certain suicidal tendencies that he was keeping in check.

He was pleased to see that they had brought some of his father's earlier work into the rotation. He looked at them carefully. He had seen some of them before but not all of them, not in person. He saw two statuesque women looking at each other placidly over bowls of copy suey in an old time New York automat. It was a mesmerizing scene. The women were captured in a pregnant pause, where both appear to have a lot on their minds but nothing they are willing to talk about. He saw the Truro dune shacks and the lower Cape Cod seascape paintings. These were sometimes called the "Salt Box Paintings." He found them beautiful, austere and serene. He saw the stately Victorian architecture paintings from Provincetown and Gloucester. They weren't mere houses but rather studies in the effects of light. In particular, they were studies in a certain kind of light, usually early in the morning or late in the afternoon when the effects are stark yet complex. They were about what houses do to light and what light does to houses. As such the paintings were mainly about contrasts and contrast in and of itself. In other words these particular paintings were about nothing less than the difference between good and evil.

He saw the lighthouse painted in Maine on a stormy rocky coast, and then a lighthouse on a placid Massachusetts Bay. How does one do lighthouses without being cliché? By treating them fairly and with fresh eyes. They were beacons of spiritual power. Power points, like the standing stones in Scotland and Ireland. He saw the paintings from Brooklyn, done in the thirties with women looking out windows. They had white skin and were muscular and erotic, but in an understated way. Richard Cobb knew exactly what to paint, but, more importantly, he knew exactly what *not* to paint. If he painted a woman looking sexy he did it so you thought you weren't supposed to notice even though you did. It was a trick of course, but one artfully played.

There was one painting in particular which really blew Tommy away. It was perhaps the first time he had been surprised by something he hadn't noticed in his father's work. The painting was entitled simply: "Gas" , painted in nineteen forty-seven, twenty years before Tommy was born. It was an unusually long horizontal canvas, saturated with rich, deep hues and it depicted an old time gas station in the middle of the night, with antique pumps and flickering neon bulbs. Tommy knew the conventional wisdom on this painting was that it conveyed loneliness, but he felt this was not right. It conveyed the opposite to Tommy. It was cozy. Apparently everyone had, until now, gotten it all wrong. It was a beacon of respite on an otherwise murky wooded road, in essence a "lighthouse" on the road.

Most fascinating of all to Tommy was the man tending the gas pumps. The man looked more or less exactly like Tommy himself. It was a strange feeling to be standing there looking at himself in this beautiful old painting. How had he ended up there? And why hadn't he noticed it before? Tommy realized it was his father. Apparently his father had chosen to paint himself as the attendant, and now, as Tommy had begun to age, he had taken on the look of his father. It was unnerving. He stood by the painting and ruminated for a while. He wanted to know why his father had been so inspired by this scene. He lamented that he could not seem to find such inspiration for himself. It was then that Tommy had an epiphany. The painting was entitled "GAS" and that said it all. That was exactly what Tommy needed. He needed to find his own gas.

On the way out of the museum Tommy saw an interesting young woman. She was painfully beautiful. She had freckles and shiny hair and two braids like a farmer's wife. She was like an artist Pippy Longstockings-type. He followed her into the gift shop. She was so perfect that just watching her made him feel very sad, like he was now aware of exactly what he was missing. Why couldn't he be with a girl like that? He stood beside her and prepared to say something but never got his chance. Just then a young man came up and kissed her on her cheek. Tommy sighed, but he was relieved. He would have embarrassed himself if he had said anything. He was at least glad for having avoided that.

It was just then that Tommy saw, on the shelf in front of him in the gift shop, a box set of Richard Cobb postcards entitled: "The Outer Cape Series. The Early Years." On the cover was the painting "Gas." It was fifteen dollars. He had barely twenty dollars to his name. He reminded himself that he wasn't a practical man. He decided he would buy them rather than eat dinner that night.

Outside Tommy sat on a park bench and went through the post cards. He looked at them a while and thought long and hard about his life. "That's it," he thought. "I'm going to the fucking beach this summer."

The next day Tommy left all his paintings with Antonio Azule, borrowed two hundred dollars from him, and then piled everything else he might need into his junky Toyota 4runner and hit the road for Cape Cod.

The Scientist

Apple Piehl was a scientist to the core. She had a different lab coat for every day of the week. She lived for microtubule assembly dynamics. Some would say she may have sacrificed a few things along the way, but what did they know? Indeed, she *had* fallen in love, twice in fact, but in both cases it never seemed to gel. She was not yet aware of regrets in that regard, being only twenty-eight. Of course she was the first to admit that she was ambitious. She liked to think of herself as a woman in a poem by Anais Ninn. She saw herself as self-assured, driven, and noble. A commitment to biological research was for the betterment of the world after all. And, as if that weren't enough, she was also politically uppity and socially conscious. She was a feminist, and a vegetarian.

By most measures Apple had lived a charmed and fortunate life. She came from a well-off, sophisticated family. Her father was a surgeon and her mother a psychologist. She drove an Audi A4 that her grandmother had given her on her birthday. She grew up in West Newton Massachusetts, a swanky, safe and idyllic suburb of Boston. Still, Apple never felt privileged or entitled. She never squandered her opportunities. She had been disciplined and focused in her studies, earning a degree from Wesley before going to Harvard for a PhD in biology.

Given that she was a biologist it was somewhat unusual that Apple had ended up working for the Environmental Protection Agency, but she was intrigued by an opportunity to publish in toxicology, and so far it had been working out well for her. Though she had only been on the job a year she had already earned the respect of her co-workers and was viewed as a potential up-and-comer in the Agency.

Apple pulled back her hair, put on her lab coat, latex gloves and plastic goggles and went to work. She liked Mondays because she would get to run a new pig eye assay. Running a new pig eye assay was like a whole new beginning. She removed a tray of pig eyes from the incubator and placed them under a ventilated hood. She unwrapped a sterile pipette and dosed the eyes with trichloroacetic acid. She then administered a glowing purple dye and placed the dish over a lighted table under a microscopic camera. She photographed the glowing pig eyes, which she thought looked beautiful.

Frank came up behind her. "Nice assay."

"That never gets old," said Apple. Frank was in his street clothes and wasn't wearing gloves or goggles.

"Come on, stand back. You're not sterile."

"Sorry Apple Cheeks." Frank tucked in his shirt.

"You know that could come across as informal don't you think?" She went back to her microscope.

"Sorry A.C."

"Yeah. I should be used to it by now anyway." She peered into the eyepiece and fiddled with the knobs.

"Is that thing equipped for epi-illumination?" Frank asked. Apple decided not to dignify such a stupid question with a response. "You got a green interference filter there? You know that things supposed to be cold. What are you at? Like really cold or what?"

Apple looked up for a moment. "How did you even end up here Frank?"

"I told you. I bombed out of law school."

"And you're supposed to be my boss? 'Cause I'm still a little foggy on that one."

"That's what they tell me." Frank tried to look into Apple's microscope but she shoved him away.

"Listen," said Frank. "How are you anyway Apple? You seem tense. Things going ok at home?"

Apple picked up her clipboard and began filling out her data. "Aren't you supposed to synchronize the clocks or something like that?" Asked Apple.

"Oh we've got people for that," said Frank.

"Right. Thank God for that."

"You better believe it," said Frank. "So anyway listen, can you give it a rest for a minute?"

"I'm busy Frank."

"Ok, so acid is bad for pig eyes! We get it!" Frank stormed out of the lab.

Moments later, while Apple was deeply immersed in her work, Frank stuck his head through the door. "All right," said Frank. "I'll let you go. I've got something I've got to take care of right now anyway. But later we'll talk ok? I've got a couple things I need to run by you. You know, important shit. I'm serious. We'll talk later, huh?"

"Yeah sure Frank, later." She never even looked up from her work.

At four-thirty Apple carefully avoided Frank and slipped out unnoticed. She was always happy to see Kalessin at the end of a hard day. Kalessin was her little red Audi A4. She named her after a red dragon from a fantasy novel by Ursula K. LeGuin. She just started to back out when Frank jogged up waving like he had something important to tell her, which she knew he probably didn't. She rolled down her window.

"Ok so you're leaving, that's cool."

"Yeah I gotta go feed my cats Frank. They're kind of high strung, you know?"

"I'll bet," said Frank. "Listen, anyway Apple, some of the guys are getting together on Friday night. What do you think? It'll be fun. I'll buy you a cosmo, Grey Goose just like you like. You know they have that trivia tournament over at the Irish pub? We could really use somebody besides me that's not a total idiot."

"Stiff competition down there at the pub huh?"

"Oh we've got a whole interagency rivalry thing going on. It's really starting to heat up. We're going up against the guys from *in vivo* this week. Those guys think their shit don't stink."

"Oh I'm sure that it does," said Apple.

"So you're in?"

"It sounds tempting Frank, but I've got to tell you, I don't relish the idea of hanging out with those people all night. They'll probably want to talk to me or something."

"So now that you're *in vitro* study director you're too good for *in vivo* guys?"

"It's not just the guys. I don't like the women either."

"They're not all bad. You guys can swap stories about immunofluorescence over martinis. I'll bet you have more in common with those eggheads than you realize."

"Frank, you do understand that they're scumbags don't you? It's a commonly known fact. Have you even been in one of their labs?"

"I've been down there," said Frank.

"They torture bunnies Frank. They do shit to ferrets with electrodes."

"Maybe so," said Frank. "But they get the job done."

Apple closed her window half way and put Kalessin in gear. "Yeah anyway I have yoga on Friday," she told him.

"You have yoga on Friday night?"

"That's right. Is there something odd about that?"

"Well now that you mention it Apple, there is. I mean I know you're all into your chi and your chakras and all your fucking granola tofu bullshit, but I mean come on. People should go to yoga on like a Wednesday or a Sunday or something, not Friday night for Christ sake."

Apple smiled and thought about this for a moment.

"You make a well reasoned argument Frank. You really do. Nonetheless I have yoga on Friday. So I'll see you tomorrow, ok?" She started to close her window the rest of the way but Frank stopped her before it was completely shut.

"Don't get me wrong Apple. I didn't mean anything by that. I mean of course I know that you're a scientist. A good scientist in fact."

Apple opened the window a little bit.

"Okay."

"No I'm serious; you're a damn good scientist Apple."

"Thank you Frank. I appreciate your saying that. I really do."

"No Apple, I'll be the first one to admit that you know more about pig eyes than anyone in this place."

"Thank you Frank."

"You're Miss Piggy."

"Right."

"You're like the frikin' Goddess of pig eyes."

Apple let that one go and drove off.

On Friday, on a whim, Apple skipped her yoga class and went to the Irish pub with Frank. Needless to say he was thrilled. With her help they beat the *in vivo* people handily at trivia and they all won gift certificates to The Olive Garden.

"I suppose they might have something I could eat," said Apple.

"I'm all about the chicken parm," said Frank. Now he would have another excuse to hang out with Apple outside of work. She had to admit she had a good time, and he had bought her that Grey Goose Cosmo just like he said he would. He wasn't such a bad guy outside work. She really shouldn't have encouraged him though. She knew that was dicey. He was obviously attracted to her and she had no intention of ever dating him or anything. Not that she had scruples about dating her boss; it was just that he wasn't physically appealing to her. He was out of shape and for some reason he always smelled like Lysol. Somewhere in the back of her mind she understood that her actions could be construed as playing Frank to get ahead in the agency. If the truth be told she could be rather manipulative. After all she had her priorities. The more she thought about it the less it bothered her. And it worked too. Frank thought about it all weekend and by Monday morning he had come up with a plan to help her.

On Monday morning Frank brought in coffee and donuts and wore his lab coat for some reason. He had rolled up maps and manila folders under his arm when he ambushed Apple in the corridor outside the lab.

"What's all this?"

"Coffee in my office in ten minutes?"

"What's the occasion?" She asked.

"Serious stuff," said Frank.

"Yeah?"

"Science stuff Apple. Right up your alley."

"You don't say?" She wasn't actually the slightest bit interested.

"And I got you a donut too."

"Blueberry?" She asked.

"Of course." Now she was slightly interested.

"All right Frank. Ten minutes. Just let me check my eyes first."

"They look great from here." He smiled.

"Very funny," said Apple. "Ten minutes."

"Make it nine. I'm a busy Apple man."

Frank spread the maps across the conference table in his office. He was surveying them while holding two cups of coffee in his hands when she walked in.

"This better be good," she said.

"Oh it's good," he assured her. "It's French Roast." He handed her a cup.

She looked at the cup disapprovingly. "Styrofoam? This is the E.P.A. isn't it Frank?"

He sighed. "You want me to go down to the kitchen and get you a mug?"

She took a sip. "No it's good, thank you." Frank shoved a donut in his mouth. Apple picked up a donut. "So what's this about?"

"Lower Cape gas stations," said Frank. He gestured toward the map.

"Gas huh?" Apple looked at the map. Frank had circled all the gas stations on lower Cape Cod with red ink.

"They have to get gas somewhere." She sipped her coffee.

"I guess," said Frank," but that's not my problem. "Look here." He pointed to the section of the map that covered the last three towns of the Outer Cape. "In nineteen eighty-four there were fourteen gas stations between north Wellfleet and south Truro. Guess how many there are now."

"I haven't the slightest idea," said Apple.

"Only three."

"Interesting. I suppose that's because of the nineteen-eighty-five legislation which revisited the wisdom of having underground storage tanks in a highly corrosive context within less than a hundred feet to the groundwater."

"Precisely," said Frank.

"So what's the problem? Obviously they were in compliance or they wouldn't still be in operation."

"One would think not," said Frank. "Except for this one right here, Jack's Gas — the oldest gas station on Cape Cod." Frank pointed to the last gas station in north Truro just before the Provincetown line. "As you can see it's just barely inside the recently revised National Seashore property area," said Frank. "The tanks were fourteen and a half years old when the National Seashore enveloped the property and their hard cut-off included only underground storage which exceeded fifteen years. Basically this one was grandfathered in by the skin of its teeth."

"Pre-existing nonconforming," said Apple.

"Exactly," said Frank. "That old chestnut. They're operating under a temporary suspension of condemnation loop-hole."

"How temporary?" Asked Apple.

"That's my point," said Frank. "How temporary indeed? For all we know that place could be leaking like a sieve already."

"Then again maybe it isn't," said Apple.

"Yeah well I'm not willing to take that chance, are you Apple? We're talking about the environment here. I mean that's what it's all about, am I right? We need to be proactive here Apple. We need to think outside the box." Frank shoved a powdered doughnut into his mouth.

"Are you proactive Frank?" Asked Apple.

"Sure," said Frank. "I got you doughnuts didn't I?"

"True," said Apple. "You have management skills, I'll give you that."

"You know pig eyes Apple, but I know people. Besides, you're proactive enough for the both of us. This could be a real feather in our cap if we did something about it now before anybody else."

"Something?" asked Apple.

"Sure why not? You're not the only one with ideas Apple. I mean think about it. That's one of the last underground storage tanks on the lower Cape. Sooner or later someone's going to get the credit for digging it up. Why not us? There are people in the agency who haven't been too happy about it. People who could throw us a bone now and then. I mean look at this place." Frank gestured toward his relatively humble office space. "Do you think I want to stay in this dump forever? You've seen the offices downtown, they're much bigger. Look at this desk. It's an embarrassment. It's practically falling apart. You're not the only one with ambition Apple."

"I know Frank."

"And what about you?" continued Frank. "You're going to need funding soon enough. Pig eyes don't grow on trees you know."

"They grow on pigs," said Apple.

"You're a good scientist Apple but sometimes you're so caught up in your minute details and data that you miss the bigger picture. If I were to criticize you, which I'm not, I would say you need to learn to open up and collaborate."

"So you're not saying that," Apple clarified.

"No," said Frank. "But if I were, that's what I would say. You see, I'm privy to certain information. I've been hearing things. Agency people like you Apple, but they see you as a lone wolf, maybe even as a bit of a rogue. They're half expecting you to do something crazy, but they're hoping it's crazy in a useful way. Why not prove them right? They like to be proven right. Let's make the guys upstairs stand up and take notice."

"Upstairs?" asked Apple.

"Well figuratively. They're not actually upstairs per se."

"Right," said Apple. "And they think I'm a rogue? Why would they say that?"

"Because you're ambitious and unpredictable Apple."

"Really? That's kind of exciting."

"Sure, why not?" Said Frank. Apple grabbed another doughnut and thought about this. "But I don't do field work Frank. I wouldn't know what to do. You know me. I do research."

"So do research. Just think of the National Seashore as a giant pig eye and think of that old piece of shit gas station as trichloroacetic acid."

"You know Frank that actually makes sense in a really stupid kind of way."

"Yeah and it would be a little easier to secure funds for your eyes if I could demonstrate that you were useful in some other way."

"That sucks that I have to be useful," said Apple.

"I could initiate an investigation on Outer Cape ground water. I could make you primary investigator."

"P.I?" asked Apple.

"Sure, why not?" said Frank.

"But I'm really busy."

"Oh right, cause you have cats," said Frank.

"Among other things," said Apple.

"Right, the pig eyes," said Frank. "And yoga on Friday nights."

"You know I'm really close to a breakthrough Frank."

"On the eyes? Yeah I know you are. But nobody else does. Why would they? What the hell do they know? Besides, you could investigate here and there, like on weekends and after hours if you wanted to, so it wouldn't take away from your research. It might help you out a little. You'd get time and a half."

Apple wasn't completely disinterested. "A lone wolf huh? They really said that?"

"Sure, why not?" said Frank. "Just see what you can dig up."

The Witch

Goody Hallet had no real friends other than her one-eyed dog Seamus and her cruel but ruggedly handsome fisherman boyfriend Samuel Bellamy, and so she spent most of her time working at the health food store in Wellfleet or walking Seamus in the woods along the back beach of Cape Cod.

Goody stood on a breezy hilltop overlooking the dunes and the ocean. The wind tossed her hair and the land rolled down before her like a scene out of Anne of Green Gables. Seamus darted through the tall grass, excited by the familiar odors on the air. He could smell fish, clam, rabbit, fox and the many birds all around him. The sway of the beach grass with its subtle gray hues mesmerized Goody. It was spring and everywhere clover and primrose dotted the hillside. She wore a loose fitting dark sweater and jeans, both of which were slightly tattered and she had tied bits of broken seashells and fish bones into her hair. She was only twenty-four and indeed beautiful, though in an unconventional sense.

She loved to wander alone in the dunes in search of driftwood, stone, herbs, bones and anything else interesting. She could find these things even when others could not. She had it down to a science. She knew the driftwood was better on the back beach because it was older and came from farther away, she knew the shells and pebbles were better on the bayside. She understood the difference between the bones in the dunes in Provincetown and Truro compared to the bones in say Wellfleet or Eastham. In Provincetown it was coyotes and fox, but in Truro and Wellfleet it was deer and groundhogs. Eastham was for the birds, literally. In the late spring and early summer there was a greater diversity of birds in the salt marshes of Eastham than anywhere in America with the possible exception of the Florida Everglades. Goody also knew that the Pamet river on the harbor side in Truro was where tired old fish came to die. They beached themselves in the half salt water swamp where nothing ever rotted away but instead stayed put until something ate it or hauled it away, or until it was overcome in the mud. Goody pulled them out of the mud and brought them home where she'd dry them out and decorate them with feathers and sea glass. Her motivation was either artistic or spiritual, but of course there is very little difference between the two.

Goody was sometimes referred to as a follower of the philosophy and lifestyle of Wicca, but she was the type of person who disliked rigid categories, especially regarding one's personal beliefs. If she hadn't found Wicca, she would have followed nature and her heart anyway eventually, which would have amounted to the same thing. Still one had to admit Goody was definitely a type. She wore old-school black Converse All Stars, a silver pentagram medallion, and heavy eye-liner. A perceptive observer might say she had a definite Celtic, neo-pagan quality, but Goody never used terms like "Celtic" or "neo-pagan" . She didn't have to know what they were to be them. In fact it was better that she didn't. If you didn't know any better you would have thought that she was a punk rock girl, but she wasn't a punk rock girl. She was Goody Hallet, the Witch of Wellfleet.

It was on this particular morning on the first day of spring when Goody proved to herself that sometimes her magic spells actually did work. She ground up a nautilus shell to a fine powder, mixed it with lemongrass and ferret urine and covered her sneakers with the mixture. She had in mind to find something special for her collection and sure enough she found something very special indeed. She found a dead sea turtle, full grown and not at all decomposed, in the Sandy Neck marsh in north Eastham. When she came upon it her heart skipped a beat. She stood and cried softly as Seamus paced, wagging his tail and sniffing the air. It wasn't that Goody was saddened or even necessarily happy at that moment, she shed tears because she was moved. She felt saddened for the passing of a beautiful creature but she felt happy that her spell had worked and that she would return home with such a magnificent find. Seamus was obviously moved as well. He loved the smell of a good seaside find. He lived for such smells and loved Goody for bringing him to them. He waited for her to do something. She did nothing. After a while she gave Seamus a nod and he jumped into action. First he smelled the turtle joyously then he licked it and rubbed the fur on his neck into it. He then ground the whole side of his face into it. He lost himself in the moment and began to roll all over it. "That'll do," said Goody and she put her hand on Seamus. He regained his composure and backed off. He crouched in the grass, looking at her expectantly. She laughed. "It doesn't smell that good does it?" She reached down and grabbed the turtle's foot and then rubbed the smell into her neck and breasts. "All right," she said to Seamus. "Let's take it home."

The turtle was about the size and weight of a spare tire but Goody managed it easily enough. She was wiry and strong for her size. She took off her baggy sweater and wrapped the turtle up in it just in case anyone happened by before she could get it up to the road and into the trunk of her car.

Goody lived in a small rented cottage in Wellfleet overlooking the harbor. It was a cozy little place which she enjoyed very much. Her boyfriend Sam slept over frequently and used the place whenever he liked, still it was her place, not his, and she liked it that way. Incidentally, Sam liked it that way as well since he avoided any responsibility of upkeep or rent. Sam was the kind of guy who knew all the angles. Whenever Goody returned home the first thing she had to do was feed the two cats on her porch. They never went inside and so Goody didn't feel they were her pets necessarily. They just happen to live on her porch. She laughed when she saw them as they always seemed to be in a perpetual state of waiting. Apparently they were waiting for Goody to do something.

"You guys really need to get a life," she said as she got the turtle out of the trunk of her car and carried it out to the back yard. The cats darted back and forth under her feet, whining and taking swipes at each other as they went.

"Marisa! Leave Spot alone," she said. Spot was the bigger younger male and Marisa, who was named after Marisa Tome, was the smaller older female. The two didn't exactly get along but they tolerated each other for Goody's sake, and for the sake of the food she provided. On this particular day there was a mysterious third cat waiting for Goody in the backyard.

"Well look at you!" said Goody. "Where did you come from?" She was small and thin but was all fluffed up around the neck and was very beautiful. One didn't expect a long haired Persian-type cat to be a stray, but she appeared very thin, she had no collar, and her long black hair was tangled and unkempt. Her hair was black indeed. It was black as Seamus' gums. Goody assumed she was female because she appeared mature despite being small and frail under all that fluff. WheneverGoody tried to get close to her she would move away, but then she'd stop and wait again just out of reach.

"Have it your way," said Goody. She put a bowl of food on the edge of the yard where she could feel safer. As soon as Goody retreated she would creep up sneakily and eat. She ate quickly and then went to hide in the bushes and watch Goody as she prepared her backyard fire pit. Goody sang softly to herself as she gathered wood.

Once the fire burned a while she put a large lobster pot over the flames, filled it with a hose and then shoved the dead sea turtle head first into the pot.

"All right then," said Goody. "Now we're cookin'." The black cat gave Goody a funny look from under the bushes.

"I'm not going to eat it silly!" said Goody. "It's for the shrine."

Goody had assembled her pagan shrine on the wall inside her cottage. It was a work in progress and the sea turtle would be the perfect addition. Nearly the whole wall was covered with bones, crystals, feathers, seashells, pebbles and bits of sea glass, many pieces of which were wrapped in copper wire and hung decoratively from chunks of driftwood. She had skulls from just about every species found on Cape Cod, everything from tiny plover sandpipers with their fragile little skulls, all the way up to a clunky horse head and even a dolphin skull and a few choice pieces of whale vertebra. The horse, which she dug up in the dunes by Herring Cove, appeared to be very old and had a bullet hole between the eyes in which she had placed a feather from a red tail hawk. When she began her shrine it was an act of pure intuition. She had no idea what she was building but she couldn't help herself. It evolved as its importance became increasingly obvious. She burnt sage and candles and left offerings under it. She had never been an obsessive person or even much of a collector before, but now this collection occupied most of her energy. It had taken on a life all its own. She saw herself as a steward to this collection and reminded herself it was her responsibility now to see it through.

Goody went to the cabinet over the sink in her humble kitchen and removed a bag of sea salt from within. She sprinkled the salt on the floor, drawing a circle about five feet in diameter. She sat on the floor in the middle of the salt ring, closed her eyes and began to pray. She no longer prayed, as she had in her childhood, to God. She prayed to Mother Nature.

The Woodcutter

Jack's Gas looked more like a cottage than a gas station. It had wood shingles, a red brick chimney, big stacks of firewood, and flower boxes in the windows. Route Six was the main road on the lower Cape but this patch in Truro was particularly rural. Around Jack's there was only the empty road and the forest.

Jack Bellamy slept in a small room in the back of his gas station which he called "the bunk house" . On this particular morning he had trouble sleeping and awoke restless and tense. It was still dark when he got up and looked out the window. It was spring and just before dawn and the birds were making a racket, which he didn't mind. He liked to hear the blue jays in particular. Not that they were a pretty sounding bird, but he respected them because they were dignified and resilient.

He peered into the darkness at his wood lot. Only twenty cord out there, maybe less. He would need ten or twenty times that by the summer. Perhaps he could do five hundred cord by the fall if he set his mind to it? At that moment he had an epiphany of sorts. He would cut and split wood this summer. Perhaps this didn't seem like such an epiphany but it came to him as a kind of antidote to a creeping sense of dread that was looming somewhere deep in his spirit. He had always cut and split wood but this time he would really cut and split wood. He would cut and split wood like nobody ever had or like nobody ever would again. He would split a shit load of wood. That was his master plan. That was how he would save himself and purge the anxiety from his mind once and for all. At his age one didn't normally suffer from self delusion. Jack knew himself well enough to know it would definitely work.

He went into the station and turned on the lights. There were two rooms. A small office with a cash register and then another, which he called "the sitting room" with a pot belly stove, couch, tv and kitchenette. He stood at the sink and filled a glass of water. He smelled it, shuttered, and then downed it and shuttered again. He then opened the cabinet above the sink where he had a bottle of vodka. He poured the vodka into a coffee mug.

Jack the woodcutter stepped outside into the fresh morning air and smiled. He wore shiny green aviator sunglasses, red sneakers and a floppy white canvas Gilligan-style sailor's cap. He was in his sixties but had aged well. He was tall and straight like good oak. He held a chainsaw in each hand and his oil stained tee-shirt read "Save a Tree." Jack was not usually an ironic man but he had his moments.

He headed for the woodlot out back. He wouldn't open the gas station officially for a few more hours and so he could work uninterrupted until then. He climbed atop a large pyramid of horizontally stacked tree trunks which formed a kind of staircase on either side of the pile. Along the way he had shoved smaller tree limbs into the cracks between the logs sticking out perpendicular to the pile. This was to prevent the logs from rolling while he stood at the top and cut the lengths into roughly fifteen to eighteen inch sections. He fired up the saw and you could hear it rattle through the empty forest just as the sun was coming up over the sea.

Once he had cut most of the trees under his feet and he could no longer safely get to those underneath he would put aside his saw and begin to toss the cut sections down from atop his pile. This was a particularly strenuous part of the job but Jack wasn't afraid of a little hard work. Hard work was in fact all he had in life. His wife had died many years ago and, though nearly everyone on the lower Cape knew of him, he had no really close friends. He had no hobbies or interests to speak of other than the occasional Red Sox game on TV. He did have an adult son who lived in the same town and occasionally worked with him but their relationship was not a particularly healthy one. This was not due to any fault of Jack's. Sam was like his mother he supposed, a dreamer and an artist. Jack had no use for a romantic or artistic view of life. He was a true old school Cape Codder in that sense. He was no "wash-ashore" as the newcomers were called, but an old Yankee Protestant of English stock, a self reliant hard ass pick yourself up by your own bootstraps kind of guy. Sam's mother on the other hand had been an Irish Catholic schoolgirl from south Boston. In other words, according to Jack, she had her head in the clouds. She had a poetic soul and cared nothing for hard work and that was just how Sam had turned out. Or at least this was how Jack rationalized Sam's lazy and immoral behavior. Jack may have been deluding himself just a touch. The fact of the matter was Sam was not a particularly artistic person, though he was indeed a self proclaimed artist. More to the point he just wasn't that good of a son to Jack. Not that Jack was complaining. Maybe he wasn't such a good father either? He wasn't a very social person anyway. He liked to work. Sam, on the other hand, did not.

And that, thought Jack, was the crux of their difficulty. They just didn't see eye to eye, he would say.

Once Jack had tossed all the cut sections down to the base of his wood pile he would then pour another coffee mug full of vodka before gassing up his splitter. Sometimes he would mix it with orange juice or Kool Aid, or whatever he had lying around, but lately he had taken to drinking it straight, or mixed with a little gassy water from the tap. After all, who was he trying to impress? He reminded himself that at his age all that crap starts to fall away and you start to see things for what they really are and in his case that meant cheap vodka disguised in a coffee mug. Then again he would cut and split a cord of wood before most folks had even gotten out of bed. You couldn't argue with results.

Occasionally he would split by hand — he could split a half a cord in forty minutes as he liked to remind people, but that just wasn't practical. He had two hydraulic splitters and anyone who used one would tell you it required plenty of hard work to operate. He would hold the cut log section in one hand and hold the splitter handle in the other. He would then toss the split sections into a pile. Once the pile got fairly large he would take a breather and then stack the split pieces all around the property of the gas station. The way in which he stacked the pieces was an art in itself. First he would lay logs like a railroad track around the perimeter of his wood lot and then he would run pieces perpendicular to those so they became the foundation of a wall. He would then wall in his woodlot and eventually the entire property of the gas station. It was only possible to stack a wall about five or six feet tall before he ran the risk of it toppling, but if he made two five foot walls beside each other he could then build another five feet up above spanning those two walls. Likewise he could build two such ten foot walls alongside each other and build yet another five feet over that by spanning those two. And so like both the ancient Egyptians and the ancient Mayans Jack found that one could go as high as one liked provided that one always made the base a good deal wider than the top. Why not just throw the wood in a disorderly pile one might ask? Because wood seasons when it is exposed to air flow. It wasn't the heat that seasoned a piece of firewood, it was the wind. A pile of wood in the hot sun would not season in half the time as a neatly stacked pile exposed to a good air flow, even if that air was cold. Furthermore, firewood stacked neatly occupies less space than wood in a pile. He knew that if he stacked it well he might get five hundred cord by the fall. Firewood was expensive on the lower Cape. There really weren't that many suppliers. You could always pick up a couple of cord in November but by late February you had few options if any. If he had enough seasoned wood he would monopolize the supply by late winter. Jack had no interest in money. He just wanted to cut and split more than anyone on Cape Cod. It was purely a matter of personal excellence, of setting a goal and sticking to it. He only had twenty cord so far. He had over four hundred to go. He decided to look into buying another chainsaw.

Once Jack had stacked the split pieces he went back to work cutting. By now the sun was high and the wind had picked up. He stood atop his wood pile and he sent a shower of saw dust showering into the salty wind. An arc of tiny fragrant chips shot out from behind him as he worked and it drifted through the sunlight. He had accomplished his goal for the first part of the day but he persisted and told himself he would cut just a little bit more. Soon he would have cut more than he had ever done in a single morning. He was driven by some new enthusiasm which he could only attribute to this morning's epiphany and to the arrival of spring. It was then, just at that moment of utter determination to cut and split more than ever before, that he slipped for the first time. In twenty years or more of working on his wood pile he had never fallen, but on this day something was different. He had pushed himself a little farther. A little too far perhaps and it was just then that it happened. It happened as though in slow motion. The saw bucked. He shifted his weight. He stepped back. He looked up at the clear spring morning sunlight. He saw the sawdust showering in a beautiful arc through the sunlight and he felt himself drifting backward through the air. He fell, with the saw still in his hands, backward off the woodpile and he floated ten feet or more through the air down to the soft pine needle floor of the woodlot. He landed on his back and choked, more from astonishment than anything else. He had fallen from his wood pile. He threw his saw off to the side, still rattling and sputtering in the cool spring air. Was he seriously hurt? He couldn't tell. He looked up at the sky through the branches and he closed his eyes. He was at peace. If he was to die like this it would be a perfect end. He knew he should die like this. He felt an overwhelming sense of peace and solitude as he closed his eyes and relaxed. Jack the woodcutter had, for the first time, and perhaps the last time, fallen from his woodpile. He was enveloped in a black empty peaceful solitude. The chain saw beside him stalled and went quiet as he let out a sigh and fell asleep.

The Pirate

With his black hair dancing on the wind and his dark eyes cutting the spray Samuel Bellamy stood on the pitching deck of his rusty iron boat, the sturdy stroller affectionately called "Whydah" . He had a joint in his mouth and a beer in his bloodied, calloused hand. The blood was not his own. The wind was against him now as he tried to light the joint, and, though he was alone, he laughed. At least for the moment he was happy, having just landed a big bluefin horse mackerel off the Windowpane Bank. He was now well northeast of the Nauset Bluff and had towed the fish for the past twenty minutes, "playing tag" as he called it, but in the end he prevailed by gaffing it nicely through the eye. He dragged it thrashing onto the deck where he beat it to death with a three pound flashlight. The giant Cape Cod bluefin horse mackerel was not a tasty fish but Sam knew that it was a noble beast with a heart striking in mass and musculature for its size. On the spot he cut the heart out and held it up to the pale sun and smiled. He'd pound it flat, slice it into strips, marinate it in A1 steak sauce, and eat it all week with boiled potatoes, carrots and corn. Having no use for the rest he tossed the mutilated heap into the waves and the swarm of gulls following Whydah appeared very thankful indeed. "You're welcome!" he shouted.

Sam placed some fish guts on the edge of Whydah's low gunwale to tease birds. The Herring gulls were good to eat if you could get a hold of one of the younger hens, but they were crafty and too hard to catch. He turned his back, only for a moment, and the fish guts were gone. "You bastards!"

He retired to his wheelhouse to get out of the wind and to smoke while contemplating his next move. He'd go around the point, into the cove, and then head for the Pamet where his pots had been down since the middle of the previous afternoon. He'd see what was what before mooring in Wellfleet for the night. If he could manage a couple of lobsters he'd unload them at one of the local restaurants and then go out for a couple of beers.

Once in the harbor he located his green and black buoy, gaffed his toggle float marked with his initials "SB" and hauled it in. He could reasonably assume to get at least something out of a twenty hour soak. He pulled the wire trap on deck. The traditional tar-dipped wooden half cylinders were no longer used. Sam's pots were steel wire cages coated in green and orange plastic. He was momentarily enthused to see something flopping around inside but his encouragement quickly turned to frustration.

He had three lobsters, but technically he had nothing. Two of them were "tinkers" (sub-legal size — keepers had to be one and a quarter pound and at least three and a quarter inches from the eye socket to the beginning of the tail). These little guys were border line, maybe two pounds between them, close but not quite right, and the third was big enough — easily three pounds — but she was a breeder and had a belly full of eggs.Sam held her up and examined her underside. "God damn it you fuckin' slut!" He tossed her on the deck and sat down for a cigarette. Sam liked to think of himself as iconoclastic and philosophical, and though indeed he was, in his case these tendencies may have amounted to little more than a disdain for any kind of rules or regulations. If he had been a political man, which he wasn't, he would have been a libertarian, if not an outright anarchist. And he was a thirsty libertarian at that and wasn't about to throw back thirty-five dollars worth of perfectly good lobster. Whydah didn't have a proper scupper but she did have an old beer cooler and that did the trick. Sam tossed the two tinkers in the scup and tucked it away in the wheelhouse under a grimy wool blanket. He took out a rag and a jug of bleach and went out on deck where he left the old hen.

"Don't worry old girl. This won't hurt a bit." Sam then proceeded to soak the rag in bleach and then he used it to wipe away the clusters of tiny black eggs from under the lobster's tail. "There you go. Good as new. If I didn't have the horse mackerel heart I'd eat you myself."

In the span of two short minutes Sam had thus wiped out ten or twenty thousand baby lobsters. No one had ever accused Samuel Bellamy of being a compassionate or forward looking person. In fact he didn't enjoy a very good reputation most of the time, but he had his moments — after all he was a born and raised Wellfletian smackman and that went a long way on the Outer Cape. Also he was Jack Bellamy's son and that went even farther. Jack was easily one of the more respected old-timers on the twelve mile stretch between south Wellfleet and north Truro. Jack was even an ordained Protestant Reverend once upon a time, but it was well known that none of that had rubbed off on Sam. Still people tended to cut Sam a break based on his father's good name.

Just as Sam had put away his bleach and rag and tossed the hen into the scup he was surprised to see a small sailboat silently crossing his bow. He recognized it as "Sultana" , Lawrence Prince's rig out of Provincetown. Lawrence was not a friend and Sam was a bit alarmed. Had Lawrence seen anything? He waved and Sam gave him the finger. Lawrence laughed and kept going. Sam knew Lawrence wasn't too bright anyhow. His big claim to fame was that he drank a lot because his father had killed himself by jumping off the Sagamore Bridge. He fell a hundred and fifty feet and shattered every bone in his body. When he hit the water it may as well have been solid rock. Sam knew that wasn't exactly true. It was true that his father had taken the leap, but Lawrence probably would have drank a lot anyway. The only other notable thing about him was that he lost a toe a few years back to a thirty pound blue boy out at Wing's Neck.

Later that afternoon while Sam was having a beer at the Bomb Shelter, a divey fisherman bar in Wellfleet harbor, he noticed Lawrence Prince slightly drunk and apparently running his mouth. He was telling Nate Nickerson something, discreetly, and they were looking over at Sam smiling. Later when Lawrence had wandered off to the cigarette machine Nate, who was a friend of Sam's, came over and put his hand on Sam's shoulder.

"Listen Sam," he said. "I got seven grand under the mattress and I'm ready to go."

"You ain't ready yet," said Sam. "You're half ready. Can you double that by the fall?"

"I got it covered."

"Then you'll be skipper on Whydah in time for hittin' the striper."

"I can't wait," said Nate. "I'm on it. My old lady is suing her boss. Did I tell you? She's getting a big pay out 'cause she got hit in the face with a table that fell off a fifteen foot high stack of boxes in the store room. She broke her nose and fucked up her back."

"Lucky for you," said Sam.

"Yeah well, she still looks pretty good."

"She always did, especially from behind."

"Damn straight," said Nate. "But Goody Hallet, now she's pretty damn cute."

"Yeah well that goes without saying."

"Definitely," said Nate.

"No I mean it." Sam's face got serious.

"No, right," said Nate. "I had a couple of beers. You know what I meant."

"I do," said Sam. "You're all right. I wouldn't hand over Whydah to just anybody ya know."

"You can't put a price on that," said Nate.

"Fourteen grand," said Sam. "She's the sturdiest stroller in Wellfleet."

"You got the title?"

"Don't worry about it," said Sam. "What's the old man gonna do with her? He hasn't been asea in fifteen years."

Lawrence Prince stumbled out of the bathroom and found a seat alone in the back of the room. Sam and Nate watched him with disapproval.

"What was that all about anyway?" asked Sam.

"What?"

"I saw you guys looking over here before. What's his problem?"

"Listen Sam," said Nate. "That little toe-less prick said he thought he saw you out in the bay scrubbin'. I told him he better keep his mouth shut."

"You kiddin' me?"

"I shit you not. He knows better too. I mean he's lucky I'm a friend of yours or you'd have to kill him, am I right?"

"I might have to anyway. You know that's bullshit Nate. I don't do that."

"Of course not."

"Not in the harbor in broad daylight for Christ's sake."

"You know better than that," said Nate. "You know that toeless piece of shit is married to the Harbor Master's cousin?"

"No shit?"

"That fucker better not run his mouth am I right?"

"The Harbor Master's cousin huh?"

"Yeah," said Nate. "You remember Molly Ryder out of Eastham. She's Bobby Silva's cousin I think. Aint she?"

"How the hell do I know?

"Remember? She had a nice ass."

"Yeah now that you mention it."

"It's like a ripe peach."

"What's she doin' with that skinny piece of shit?"

"Whataya think? His mothers got that hotel in West Dennis Port. She'll be dead before you know it."

"So will he if he don't watch his lip," said Sam.

"I know you don't do that shit," said Nate. "Scrubbin' I mean."

"Of course."

"Not in broad daylight," added Nate.

In the early evening as the sun began to set Lawrence Prince headed for his car. Sam was waiting for him.

"Hey Lawrence. How's it going? You got a smoke?" Lawrence gave Sam a cigarette. "You got a light?" Lawrence fumbled for a light and lit Sam up. "What's this, like a chick cigarette?" Sam took a deep drag and spit at Lawrence's feet.

"Menthol," said Lawrence. "It was buy one get one free."

"Menthol huh?"

"Yeah, buy one get one free."

"That's what black guys smoke."

"Yeah," said Lawrence. "The price is right."

"You like black guys Lawrence?"

"Sure, they're all right. I like black girls better though."

"I'll give you that," said Sam. "I hear your wife has a nice ass like a black chick. Is that true Lawrence?" Sam took a deep drag on his cigarette and blew the smoke in his face.

"That's not right Sam. You shouldn't talk about Molly like that."

"No huh?" Sam smacked Lawrence across the face. "Nate told me what you said. You said I was scrubbing?"

"No Sam it wasn't like that. I was just fucking around I swear! I just told him I thought I saw you. It was foggy out there. I was only kidding around anyway. I didn't mean nothing by it. I shouldn't have said that. I know you wouldn't do that. "

"You're damn right I wouldn't, said Sam.

"Especially not in broad daylight," said Lawrence.

"So you're gonna let me go?" He was now trembling.

"Close your eyes," said Sam.

"Come on man. I learned my lesson. I won't say nothing." Lawrence lit a cigarette and took a drag. Sam let him relax for a moment.

"Close your eyes," said Sam. Lawrence closed his eyes and clenched his jaw. Sam punched him square in the face. Lawrence fell to the ground and went into a fetal position. Blood spurted from his nose.

"You're a real piece of shit you know that?"

"I know," said Lawrence.

Chapter Six

It seemed to Tommy Cobb that being an artist was a good explanation for any sort of irrational or even antisocial behavior. Indeed, if one were producing good art, it might even be advisable. For example, Tommy's own homelessness and his habitual new beginnings. If one didn't know any better one would think such an abrupt departure was maybe a little nutty, or at least reckless. Actually, for him, it was neither, not unless he was prepared to admit that his entire adult life had been nutty and reckless. That he had managed to spend an entire year in Antonio's studio was unusual. He had been drifting without direction for the better part of twelve years and, in spite of this, it was always difficult and emotionally unsettling whenever he had to start over again.

He drove all afternoon and throughout the evening. He was still in shock and hadn't begun to process the gravity of what he had done. Where would he go? What if he couldn't find a job? How long could he live out of the back of his truck? Rather than answer these questions he went into an emotional lock down. He had done this sort of thing before and it had always seemed to work out. After all he had no girlfriend or job in New York and so what was he worried about? At this point he had very little to lose. He sure wasn't getting any painting done. He hadn't finished one in months. He had always been a slow painter, but now he was so slow it was ridiculous. Antonio was a nice guy but even his patience and generosity had its limits.

Tommy arrived at the Cape Cod Canal at about ten o'clock at night. It was windy and raining and he was exhausted. He pulled into a rest area overlooking the canal and the Sagamore Bridge. He parked beside some RVs where he knew it would be safe to spend the night. He got out into the rain and walked down to take a look at the canal when he was struck by a sense of eerie familiarity. Just why he felt this way took a moment to register. The scene looked different at night in the rain. He went back to the truck, flipped through the stack of postcards and there it was. His father had painted the very same view forty-eight years earlier, twenty years before Tommy was born. He had, in fact, painted most of the Outer Cape series in only two and a half years, from forty-seven to forty-nine. He had averaged twenty good paintings a year at that point, which Tommy knew from experience was impressive. During that period he must have been at the height of his creative powers and here Tommy was nearly the same age and in the same place and yet he was already washed up. Tommy had a flare for melodrama at such moments. Deep down he knew that he would probably paint well again. But believing it and doing it were two different things. Tommy took the post card and walked outside. He stood there in the wind and the rain and started to cry. He cried so hard he surprised himself. He hadn't cried like that in years. He didn't cry because he was frustrated or unsatisfied with himself as an artist, though he was, but for some other reason, perhaps something far less meaningful and interesting. He had come to the realization that he was ashamed of himself and he was afraid. He was afraid of failure. What if he couldn't find a job? Would he go back to New York? What was he even doing? What were his intentions? He couldn't say. He told himself it was just because he was so tired. He would feel differently in the morning.

He climbed into the back of his eighty four Toyota 4runner (a real piece of crap actually, but it was perfect for just such an adventure). He got into his sleeping bag without even bothering to take off his shoes. Maybe it was the sound of the rain on the cap, or that fact that he was emotionally drained, or even that somewhere in the back of his mind he was satisfied with himself for finally making a bold move, but whatever the reason Tommy slept very well that night. He usually slept pretty well. Maybe that was his problem? Maybe Tommy slept too well? He averaged ten hours a night when circumstances allowed it. He was a good sleeper. His mother, who had a degree in psychology, used to say that Tommy was into "avoidance". That was why he liked to sleep so much. This made sense to Tommy. It also probably explained why he loved movies and books so much, and painting.

Tommy was all about "avoidance", which was a good way to be for an artist. After all it depended on what you were avoiding. He liked to think that he avoided all the bullshit in life, but not the good parts. He wanted to focus on the quality of the time he spent awake, not the quantity.

The following morning Tommy awoke and felt slightly less depressed if not optimistic. The sky had cleared and the view of the canal was inspiring. Tommy could see why his father had chosen it as a subject. People walked their dogs, played Frisbee, and biked along the canal. The sun sparkled on the water and sail boats skipped on the waves. There were gulls all around and he could smell the fresh ocean air.

"I'm going to the fucking beach this summer!" Tommy said to himself in what now had become a mantra. He laughed, and then he added: "I might even call my mother... eventually." That was perhaps a bit ambitious. He wasn't ready to call her just yet. He loved his mother dearly and respected her but he was intimidated by her. He felt like she judged him and underestimated him. He wanted to prove her wrong. He wanted to show her that he wasn't a fuck up, but until now he hadn't been able to pull it off.

He never for a moment actually thought he was a fuckup, only that he might be mistakenly perceived that way and this was an important distinction for him. He decided he would write his mother a short message on the first of the Richard Cobb Outer Cape Series postcards. He chose the Sagamore Bridge painting of course. It read simply: "Hey Mom. Recognize this painting? Now I do too! I'm looking at the real thing right now. He did it the year you were born! Left New York yesterday. I'm going to the beach this summer! Love ya, Tommy." Tommy had said "*he* did it" , not "*Dad* did it." That was deliberate. Tommy never spoke of his father in a familiar tone with his mother. It was rare indeed that he would even mention him to her. She never liked to talk about him with Tommy.

Tommy drove across the Sagamore Bridge and then officially onto Cape Cod. He had driven through Massachusetts a number of times and he had been to Boston on more than one occasion but this was his first time on the Cape. Even from the highway he thought it seemed different than anywhere he had ever been. It reminded him of Scotland or Wales. The trees were different. They were scraggly, twisted and stunted. The air was different too. It smelled unusually fresh. He had a good feeling about it all but he wasn't sure why. For one thing it just felt good to get out of the city. Tommy understood that the city was intellectually stimulating, but, on the other hand, it was hard to deny that it was also a polluted and congested shit hole. He had been in New York for years without ever really becoming a city person. He also never felt like a suburbanite or a country person for that matter either. He knew that he would probably never fit in anywhere. He didn't necessarily lament this fact, but instead romanticized it as a useful condition for being an artist. Ideally one had to be an outsider to see things with a critical eye. Still it did seem a little odd, even to him, to be an outsider forever.

Tommy had grown up in an utterly nondescript community in northeast Pennsylvania in a half-assed little town known as East Stroudsburg. When he graduated high school (by the skin of his teeth) he lived alone with his mother and didn't really have much to hold him back and so he immediately hit the road "Jack Kerouac style" — -actually in Tommy's case it was more of a "mid-eighties Grateful Dead camping in a parking lot style" but in any event he had romanticized his wandering deadhead lifestyle and spent the past twelve years doing very little other than roaming around indulging himself. He had spent most of that time partying and sleeping and "not looking back" as it were. When on occasion he did "look back" it was with embarrassment and disdain for his ordinary, middle class, plebeian upbringing. This of course was unfair to his mother and more than a little melodramatic. One is always better off having had a safe and uneventful childhood in just such a community and it was to Tommy's mother's credit that she had managed to pull that off.

And so Tommy was a spoiled young man, entirely without a sense of responsibility, and furthermore he had no meaningful relationships to speak of other than with his mother with whom he rarely spoke and with certain old friends who had since married and had children and moved on with their lives, which is to say he only had relationships with people he didn't actually ever have to see. It wasn't that he was a cold person or that he didn't want to have close ties, in fact quite the opposite was true; he craved such relationships, it was just that apparently until now he had fallen through the cracks. One couldn't discount fate in these sorts of things. He could have just as easily got married and had a family but maybe it just wasn't in the cards? People acted as though those sorts of things were the result of one's own choices, but maybe sometimes they weren't? Still, he probably shouldn't have spent the past twelve years partying and sleeping.

Chapter Seven

On the previous Friday Apple missed yoga in order to hang out with Frank and the work people and so when the next yoga night came around she was ready for a good session. She could feel the tension in her limbs. She had a lot on her mind, especially with work. Yoga was her personal down time, her time to relax and let all that work stuff go. Originally she liked Ashtanga which was a very physical fast paced yoga style, a lot like an aerobic cardio workout, but now she had found the Kundalini style and it had opened up a new world for her, a world of mental and physical relaxation.

On this Friday evening Apple had an interesting thing happen to her. At the end of a long and productive session, during her final pose, she had perhaps for the first time in her life a genuine spiritual epiphany, which came to her in the form of a vision. In Kundalini yoga one always closes with a certain exercise known as Shivasana, the so-called "corpse pose," so called because one lays on one's back, closes one's eyes and attempts to meditate with a complete stillness of mind and body. The Shavasana corpse pose is always done at the end of a Kundalini session because it seals in the benefit one received from the previous exercises. Often at this point of relaxation and stillness the instructor would speak softly and guide the class into a deeper meditative state. In this way it was somewhat like hypnosis, except that as a scientist Apple understood that hypnosis was usually a fake, while this was, for her, totally real.

Deep in her Shavasana corpse pose, Apple was overwhelmed with a feeling of peace and contentment. She felt herself melting into her surroundings, which is to say she had the sensation of completely losing her identity. Her personality was a mask and now she felt relieved and even giddy at the idea of removing that mask if only for a moment. It was then that she ceased to be herself and instead became a formless field of energy without desire or attachment to anything in the world. At this point the instructor had stopped speaking and let his class drift into silence. All was still, calm and quiet when the vision came to Apple. She had her eyes closed. Her breathing was shallow. She saw a beautiful, blue skinned, shirtless young man, adored with golden jewelry and flowing colorful silks and long curly black hair. He was somehow both plump and fit simultaneously. He had a look of happiness and contentment on his face. He played a golden flute and had a small animal crawling around on his shoulder. At one point the animal pecked at his cheek as if to give him a kiss. It was then that Apple could see that it was a tiny white and brown ferret. From her studies in college she knew that this apparition was the Hindu deity known as Krishna. She had taken a class on Eastern mysticism as an undergraduate in order to satisfy a philosophy prerequisite and though she had enjoyed it she never truly took it seriously. She wondered about the ferret. She had never seen Krishna depicted with a ferret. She decided she would have to look into it.

At the end of class Apple was totally energized and full of a renewed enthusiasm for her work and her life. She asked her instructor if having a vision during Shavasana was unusual. The instructor told her that it was something which happens occasionally but that it wasn't commonplace and certainly not something one should take lightly. He told her that one should think long and hard about what that vision might mean and always treat the memory of it with the appropriate gravity and solemnity.

On the way home Apple felt great. She felt totally relaxed. Once home she fed her cats, had a cup of herbal tea and went to bed. She slept wonderfully as she always did after yoga.

Apple awoke refreshed and excited to start her day. She had a fried egg sandwich with ketchup, and a soy milk smoothie with protein powder, and then she worked out for forty minutes while listening to a books on tape lecture series entitled: "Books That Have Changed The World" . She listened to a detailed synopsis and explanation of Goethe's "Faust" . The tapes were a gift from her father who thought that Apple should expand her intellectual horizons beyond biology and toxicology. Later in the day she was planning to visit her parents who were having a late lunch at her father's yacht club in Yarmouth Port, but first she had to go to work briefly to feed her eyes. She wasn't expected to go in on Saturday's but her enthusiasm and ambition were such that she couldn't help herself from starting a new experiment on Friday. The pig eyes could not make it through the weekend on their own. No longer attached to a pig, they were kept alive in a special solution which provided them with the necessary oxygen and nutrients. The solution only lasted about thirty-five hours though, and had to be replenished, which is why one didn't usually initiate such a procedure on a Friday. Apple couldn't help herself, even if that meant going in on the weekend.

All was well with the eyes and so Apple decided to run a few errands before heading out to Yarmouth Port. She stopped by a local bookstore and, quite serendipitously, she found a nice big book on Krishna with lots of pictures. She was so excited about her yoga vision that she sat in her car in the parking lot for a good while looking at the pictures of Krishna. She found that there were many very old beautiful paintings of Krishna, and some of them were quite famous. He was an especially good subject for artists in that he was meant to symbolize all that is romantic, fun, and sexual. One might even say that Krishna was infused with a kind of rock and roll carnal sensuality. As such, in the paintings, he was often depicted dancing and playing the flute, or among peaceful and playful animals. Sometimes he was depicted among attractive topless women. Apple found these images compelling. Perhaps she was getting ahead of herself but she thought that maybe she might like to convert to Hinduism. It was as if she had the feeling that she had finally found religion. She had been raised in a Protestant family and both her parents and her two sisters were still church goers but Apple had given it up when she became a scientist. For the past few years she had considered herself an atheist. The prospect of maybe not being an atheist after all was exciting for her. She decided to learn all she could about Krishna and the other Hindu deities. She reminded herself of her instructor's advice that she should carefully contemplate the meaning of her vision. Was it some kind of revelation? Why the ferret? Many of the paintings depicted him with animals, usually a white cow, but none with a ferret. She thought about the ferrets in the *in vivo* lab at work and how she had objected to their treatment. Maybe that was it? If she could make the pig eye assay work it would spare a lot of animals from live testing. Maybe the ferret kissing Krishna on the cheek was a gesture of thanks? But Apple's assay wouldn't spare ferrets, it would spare rabbits. The pig eyes were intended to be an alternative to the Draize rabbit test. Still there had to be a connection, the *in vivo* lab was the only place she associated with ferrets.

Apple was so caught up with her work and then her Krishna book that she had arrived a half an hour late for lunch with her parents. It was a lovely afternoon and her parents, Pebbles and

Scooter, had taken an outdoor table at the club. It was an exclusive club and their table was on a sprawling wooden deck overlooking the harbor. Apple rushed up, apologizing for her lateness. She kissed them both on the cheek before taking her seat.

"I had to swing by the lab this morning and I got a little behind schedule," she told them. "I'm really getting close with my experiment, it's very exciting."

"I'm sure that it is," said Pebbles.

"You don't have to get snippy about it Mom. Would you rather I said I got held up because of traffic?"

"She would," said Scooter grinning.

"Actually the traffic was kind of bad," said Apple.

"Too late," said Scooter. "She already knows it was your fault." He winked at Apple and smiled.

"Sorry."

"It's nice to see you," said Pebbles. "I like that top. It's cute."

"Thanks Mom. Remember you gave it to me?"

"She just shops blindly," said Scooter. "She has no idea what she's buying. It's a problem. We're working on it."

"Well it looks good on you," said Pebbles.

"You look cute too Mom."

"You're working on a Saturday?" asked her Mother.

"No," said Apple. "I just had to stop by for a half hour to feed the eyes."

"It seems like you're working a lot doesn't it? Don't forget to stop and smell the roses now and then."

"I smell the roses," said Apple. "I smell them all the time. I went out to a pub last week and had three martinis. And this morning I had a nice workout and listened to Dad's lecture tapes. I listened to Goethe's Faust. It was actually quite inspiring." Apple reached across the table and stole a strawberry off her father's plate.

"And you find that inspiring do you?" he asked.

"Sure, why not?" said Apple. "I've got to hand it to you Germans Dad, you're a real barrel of laughs."

"Well you're German too," said her father.

"No," said Apple. "I'm just a regular boring American like Mom." She laughed and took her mother's hand.

"We weren't sure what to order for you," said Pebbles. "Do you want a grilled brie sandwich with mustard and pickles and a side of edamame?"

"Who wouldn't?" asked Apple. "That sounds so good right now."

"I have no idea what you two are talking about half the time," said Scooter. "Remember you used to like the Cajun blackened chicken sandwich here?"

"That was like ten years ago Dad, get a grip."

"She's a vegetarian, you know that," said Pebbles.

"Some vegetarians eat chicken don't they?" Scooter asked.

"Dad how can you be a surgeon and be so dense?"

"I'm retired," said Scooter. And then he added, "You know Apple 'Faust' is an apropos story for you. I hope the parallels weren't lost on you." He winked again.

"A scientist's ambition running amuck huh?" Said Apple.

"That's my girl," said Scooter.

"Honestly," said Pebbles. "I have no idea what you two are talking about half the time."

Apple ordered a grilled brie sandwich with mustard, pickles and a side of edamame and had a pleasant conversation with Pebbles and Scooter. In fact she had such a relaxed and fun conversation with her parents that she almost told them about her yoga vision and her new found interest in Hinduism. Upon reflection she decided her mother wasn't quite ready to hear about it. There were some things one just didn't need to share with one's parents. She was having such a lovely afternoon. Why introduce controversy?

After they had coffee and just as Apple was about to get going a young man approached their table.

"Well hello Mr. and Mrs. Piehl. Nice day huh?"

"Hey Oliver. How are you?" Said Scooter. The two shook hands.

"Oliver this is our Apple," added Pebbles. Pebbles put her hand on Oliver's arm, which Apple thought seemed a little weird.

"Hello Apple," he shook her hand.

"Hi, nice to meet you," said Apple.

"A pleasure," said Oliver. "You parents have told me about you."

"Oh really?" said Apple. "Well I guess I'm at a disadvantage," said Apple. She smiled at him and tried to pretend that she didn't suspect her mother of arranging this totally accidental meeting. He wasn't a bad looking guy and he was about her age. She wasn't completely disinterested. She noticed he was wearing leather shoes with no socks. Apple knew that was a thing with these preppie guys at the club. She thought it was creepy but she might be able to let it slide if he was nice.

"Your mother tells me you're a doctor?" asked Oliver.

"No," said Apple.

"Really?" asked Oliver. He laughed and put his hand on Pebbles' shoulder.

"She's modest," said Pebbles.

"I'm a biologist," said Apple. "There's a slight difference."

"I'm sure there is," said Oliver. "Though I'm sure I wouldn't know about it. I'm just a hack investment guy like my dad, huh Scooter?"

"Your father isn't just a broker Oliver, he's an artist in my book." Oliver laughed.

"Don't let the FCC hear about that," he quipped.

"Well I'll bet that's interesting," said Apple insincerely.

"No it isn't really," said Oliver. "But you gotta eat." Apple faked a smile.

"Well I guess somebody has to do it," said Apple.

"Apple!" Pebbles' was embarrassed by Apple's bluntness. "She's kidding," said Pebbles.

"She's a barrel of laughs," Scooter chimed in.

"It's quite alright," said Oliver. "I appreciate your candor. I imagine your own work must be fascinating."

"Well to me it is," said Apple. "But no, most people's eyes glaze over the moment I try to explain it."

"People are idiots," said Oliver.

"Really?" asked Apple. She smiled at him, this time with sincerity and he picked up on it.

"Well I've always liked your father and I understand you're a chip off the old block."

"I've been called worse," said Apple. At that Oliver simply smiled. Apple felt he did have a sincere smile for an "investment guy" , whatever that was. Oliver had a few more polite words for Apple and her parents and then he excused himself and was off.

"He's such a nice young man, wouldn't you say Apple?" asked Pebbles. "And I understand he's single."

"Oh, you don't say? What a coincidence. Nice try Mom."

"Just think about it Honey," said Pebbles. "Would it kill you to think about it?"

Apple got up, kissed them both. "Thanks guys," she said and then she was off.

Chapter Eight

A red sun set on the bay and Goody's fire burned low until all that was left were glowing coals. Her turtle had been boiling for hours when Sam arrived but it would have to go all night before she could separate the body from the shell. She was inside when Sam smelled the fire so he went around back to check it out. He found her big pot simmering on the coals and a long wooden spoon sitting on a rock beside it. He staggered up to the fire and nearly fell in before catching himself. He leaned over and took a smell.

"Damn that's some strong shit right there."

He picked up the spoon, dipped it into the pot and took a taste. He choked it down with difficulty. "You've got to be kidding me. I gotta get a girlfriend who can cook."

Goody stuck her head out the window, "Baby don't eat that! I found it in the marsh at Sandy Neck!" She laughed when she saw that he had already tried it.

Sam coughed and spit on the ground. "What the hell is it?"

"A turtle," said Goody. "A real beauty too, wait till you see it. You know, for the wall."

Sam took another sip and shuttered.

"Don't do that Baby!" Goody laughed. "You're gonna get sick!"

"I've heard the Japanese love this stuff."

"You're a nut, you know that?"

"I've got presents." Sam held up a bag and waved it around. Goody pulled her head inside and ran out into the yard. She threw her arms around Sam and gave him a kiss.

"Whew! Boy you stink Baby!"

"That's 'cause I've been working all day," said Sam.

"You don't smell like you've been working all day. You smell like you've been smoking pot and drinking all day."

"Do you want your presents or what? 'Cause I'll give them to one of my other girlfriends if you don't want them." He dangled the bag in front of her face. She grabbed it but he pulled it away.

"What did you get me?"

"Five things," said Sam. "Each one cooler than the next." He reached into the bag and removed the items one at a time to heighten their impact. "A giant bluefin horse mackerel heart, a pack of cigarettes, two lob chicks, and last but not least... your favorite, a box of soft sugar cookies."

"Thanks Baby!" Goody was genuinely pleased. Sam was usually cruel hearted but in many ways he was a contradiction. Those cookies were her favorite. She picked up the two tiny lobsters, which were still alive, and examined them. "Are you sure they're chicks 'cause they look kind of like tinkers Sam."

"You think I don't know a tinker? I've been culling chicks since you were sitting on a shag carpet watching Mighty Mouse in your mother's double wide in bumfuck western Mass. Give me a goddamn break would ya!" He grabbed the lobsters before she could look at them more closely and threw them back in the bag. "A lot of women would be happy if their boyfriend brought home lobsters, but not you. You gotta bust my balls."

Goody kissed him on the cheek. "Come on Sam, I didn't mean anything by it." She took the bag. "I'll put them in the fridge. Let me see that blue fin. I'll marinate it overnight just like you like it." Goody took her presents inside. Sam followed her.

"Tonight at the Bomb Shelter I hear a brother-in-law of the Harbor Master was talkin' shit about me and so I had to straighten that out, then I gotta come home to the Marine Fisheries Oversight Commission over here."

"I know baby. Take your shoes off and have a cookie."

"Gimme one of those cigarettes," said Sam. "Got any beer?"

"Maybe you should have got me some beer too." she said.

"You got a lip."

"I'm kidding."

"Yeah I know. You're always kidding."

"Why should things have to be serious all the time?"

"You're lucky I'm so tired," said Sam.

"Have a cookie," said Goody.

Sam and Goody went to bed and made love. As usual it was good for both of them and they were both satisfied at least with that aspect of their relationship. After they lay quietly and reflected on things.

"My dad's getting pretty bad," said Sam.

"What makes you say that?"

"It just popped into my head I guess."

"Have you talked?"

"Not really."

"You probably should." She kissed Sam on the cheek and then rolled away from him. "I don't think I want to go to Oregon Sam. It's so far away."

"That's the whole point," said Sam. "It's far away for a reason."

"I want to go to school Sam. Remember?"

"So go out there. They have more financial aid out there anyway."

"In some shack in the middle of nowhere?"

"What the hell are you gonna learn in college anyway? Think about it. You barely made it out of high school. You don't even read. I gave you those books and you didn't even read them."

"I hate history," said Goody.

"Yeah. And you don't like science, or math, or English, or any of that shit."

"I like science."

"Oh you do? And what do you like about it?"

"I like the ocean," said Goody. "And I like bones and seashells."

"That's not science, that's beachcombing."

"Do they have the beach out in Oregon?" Asked Goody.

"They have a little something out there," said Sam. "Maybe you've heard of it, it's called the Pacific Ocean."

Later when Sam had fallen asleep Goody took the two baby lobsters down to the beach and let them go. She was quite moved to see them swim away in the moonlight.

Chapter Nine

Tommy Cobb drove straight from Hyannis to Eastham without stopping. Once in Eastham he got an Italian sub and a six pack of Guinness. He poured a beer into a paper cup so he could drink it while driving around looking for the old Thomas Paine windmill. He found it in Eastham precisely where his father had painted it forty years before. In fact it had been there for three hundred years, which made it all the more unlikely that anybody would want to change anything about it. Except for the red door, and the wrought iron door hinges and window latches, it was made completely of unpainted wood. Like all Outer Cape architecture it was left unpainted and had weathered to a silvery gray. The park was lined with scrub oak and locust. Tommy sat on a bench and enjoyed his lunch. Once again he wrote his mother a short note on the back of a postcard. This one depicted the Eastham windmill and it read: "Which way to the beach? I haven't been swimming in like two years. Love Tommy. P.S. This thing is over three hundred years old and the most famous thing about it is that you know who painted it."

Actually Tommy wasn't crazy about the painting. It had no people in it and was plain, though of course Tommy understood that that was the point of it. His father planned those kinds of things. Obviously he intended to make a point about solitude. Even so it was kind of boring Tommy thought. What he really wanted to see was the old gas station from the painting "Gas" . That was practically his father's masterpiece. He wasn't sure whether or not the place was still around and he had no idea how to find it. He knew it must have been on the lower Cape because of the year it was painted.

He drove through Eastham and Wellfleet. Now that he was far down Cape the atmosphere took on a different quality. The architecture was strictly traditional; there were no fast food places or ugly buildings of any kind. The houses were nicer and farther apart and the roads became narrower and less developed. He drove east and looked out over the bay to Provincetown, which was a beautiful view, and then he drove west until he reached the open ocean on a beach called Head of The Meadow. Usually names like that were hyperbolic but this beach was truly at the head of a meadow. Tommy had never seen anything like it, and he had been all over the U.S., the U.K. and parts of Europe. The closest thing he could compare it to was Conemarra on the west coast of Ireland. It was the idea of having pastures and forests that ran right up to the sea without anything messing them up. One didn't encounter that in many places in the U.S. Maybe Oregon or Main, but in those places it was a lot more rocky, here you got the dunes and the tall grass running right up to the shore. Before Tommy thought Cape Cod might be something like Long Island or the Jersey Shore, but he could see that it wasn't. It was way better. There were hardly any big hotels or nightclubs or anything. Sure the Cape had its commercialism but that mainly took the form of overpriced little Inns and B and B's and art galleries and places like that. And of course the restaurants were the big thing on the Cape. Nice little restaurants on a whole lot of winding roads. They wound to the ocean, the bay, or Provincetown. There wasn't a single set of traffic lights on the nine miles between south Wellfleet and north Truro.

The beach at the head of the meadow was huge and totally empty. There were no concession stands or gift shops or anything — just one big stretch of beach with dunes and cliffs and beautiful grassy hills. Tommy sat and looked out at the ocean and had a Guinness in a paper cup. He decided if he couldn't find anywhere else to go for the night he'd come back and sleep in the parking lot overlooking the head of the meadow.

There was one place his father had painted that was on Tommy's road atlas, the Highland Light in north Truro, and so Tommy decided to check that out before heading for Provincetown. He drove down a long twisted road through the forest where most of the trees were stunted and peculiar. The land itself was somehow small, twisted and peculiar as well. The hills and valleys were small, the rivers and stones were small, even the sky was small. If Montana was big sky country then the Outer Cape was small sky country. It was as if Tommy were looking out across miles of rolling hills and mountains when in fact he was looking out over five hundred yards or so of miniaturized landscape. There was scraggly bramble, blueberry and raspberry. The trees were locust, cedar, maple, scrub oak and pine. It was apparent that the trees had a tough time with the sandy soil and the salty wind and therefore one had the sensation of looking out over a forest of bonsai.

Tommy Drove along the winding road through the forest until he came to a small parking area on a windy bluff. From there he could see the Highland Light. When he got out of the truck it was extremely windy. He walked out to the lighthouse to get a good look. This was no tourist prop, but a necessary lighthouse in full working order. Actually it did have a small museum and gift shop but they were closed. Tommy was glad they were closed. He would not have paid to go inside. He wanted it to be quiet and solitary, just as a real lighthouse should be. He wondered how his father had painted in such a harsh environment; he must have done sketches outside and then done the bulk of the work in his studio. No one could do a large oil painting on that windy bluff, not even a determined painter like Richard Cobb. He stood and looked at the light for a while and tried to get nostalgic but he could only get so nostalgic while standing in such a wind. He sat in his truck and compared the painting on the postcard to the actual scene. He thought about how his father had highlighted certain aspects and played down others for maximum effect. He would paint the Highland Light if he could find a job and stick around awhile. Maybe in Provincetown he'd get something going. He knew it was a tourist trap in the summer and there were probably lots of retail and restaurant jobs. Tommy was a dismal salesman but he was a hell of a dishwasher. He washed dishes in a dozen states, not to mention Ireland and England. He had even done a stint in Hollywood where everyone kept telling him "white boys don't wash dishes in L.A" . But Tommy did. He washed dishes in L.A. no problem. And so that was his new plan. He'd become a Provincetown dishwasher for the summer, no matter what they were paying. How much money did he really need if he slept in his truck? Then he would paint. He'd paint the Thomas Paine windmill and the Highland light just as his father had. If he couldn't get inspired he'd fake it. This summer was going to be different. He would hang out at the beach and get laid just like Antonio Azule had suggested.

That night Tommy drove out to Provincetown, left his truck in a legal residential spot on the outskirts of town, and walked around. He thought it seemed very interesting. It was small, he walked from one end of town to the other in less than an hour, but he found that there were lots of good galleries on the east end of Commercial Street. Mostly he just looked in the windows and kept moving. Provincetown was among other things a gay resort, but Tommy was used to that. Having just left New York, and before that having bummed around in many so-called "artist's havens" he knew the feel of those places. They all had a certain gay quality, whether it was Hollywood, Amsterdam, Cambridge, the South End in Boston,

South Street in Philly, Boulder Colorado, Key West, or Galway. He understood that all the art colonies were gay. But they weren't only gay. Provincetown was diverse. It was a Portuguese fishing town. It was a historical port and an intellectual and philosophical writer's colony. Provincetown was known to be the oldest art colony in America in fact. Even without knowing anything about the town Tommy knew it was the kind of place he liked. In fact, nearly immediately upon being exposed to Provincetown, for some inexplicable reason, Tommy completely got it. He understood that Provincetown was a beautiful paradox and that it was not at all what it appeared to be. Most people never got that, but some people got it ten minutes after rolling in, and that was the thing about Provincetown.

He finished off his six-pack and walked around all night. He walked from one end to the other and back. He went into a couple of the smaller quiet bars and sat alone. He wanted to soak it all in.

He never made it back to the head of the meadow that night as he had planned. Instead he drove out to the west end where the tip of the Cape terminates at a long stone jetty called Long Point. From there he walked along the shore out to a spot just before where the Cape starts to bend back on itself and then to the back beach in a small inlet known as Herring Cove and then out to Race Point, where he could see Boston twinkling 25 miles away across the bay. He sat on a blanket and smoked cigarettes all night and contemplated his life and everything, and his next move, until finally he fell asleep under the stars. He listened to the waves and the gulls and he slept as soundly as he usually did.

In the morning Tommy awoke to the sound of a fog horn echoing across the bay and he had only one thought in his head, coffee. He would go into town and get some coffee. He found a little gourmet café on the west end where he bought a good cup of coffee and a blueberry muffin. He showed the girl working at the cafe the postcard painting of Richard Cobb's "Gas" and asked if she had any idea where it might have been painted. She had no idea but told him to go to the Provincetown Art Association in the east end.

The Provincetown Art Association was a homely little place with a good artistic vibe. It was more than just a museum, it was a genuine art space and Tommy felt instantly at home. He poked around for an hour or so until a woman appeared who was obviously the one he was looking for. She was a colorful older woman with freckles, red hair and a flowing green scarf by the name of Jan Kelly and her historical gravitas and artistic countenance were such that it was obvious to him that she knew a little bit about everything he was searching for. She was unusually attractive for an old woman and she had a clever air about her. Tommy explained what he was after and she told him that she had been hanging around painters on the outer Cape for most of her life and that she was very much aware of the fact that there had been some controversy about the actual inspiration for Richard Cobb's painting "Gas" . She explained that Cobb sometimes used a combination of sources and places to create a setting and so while one couldn't therefore say with certainty that any one place was the actual place in the painting she personally believed that the inspiration for the painting "Gas" had come from a place called Jack's Gas, a gas station in Truro.

"Is it still there?" Tommy asked.

"Sure it is," said Jan. "I don't think they do much business though. It's just a little place in Truro on Route six. I don't think there's another business closer than a couple of miles on either side."

Tommy had come that way the night before. He must have driven right by it in the dark. He thanked her and quickly headed back into Truro.

Chapter Ten

There was no telling how long Jack had been passed out or knocked unconscious at the foot of his woodpile when Tommy arrived. Tommy pulled up to the pumps but the place appeared closed. He could tell right away this was the place. It looked like the old filling station in the painting. It had been slightly modernized. The old glass bulb topped gas pumps were gone, though the ones that were there were rusted and looked by no means up to date. One of the pumps even had duct tape where the nozzle connected to the hose. There was a modern soda machine beside the front door but aside from that it looked just like a nineteen thirties service station. Even for the thirties it was rustic. It was all whitewashed clapboard with window shutters and pane glass. Not fake panes, real ones. It wasn't even paved; it had a sandy dirt lot. There was a lot of firewood around the place, stacked out back and along the sides which seemed to double as a fence marking off the edges of the property. Tommy could tell the place was intended to look folksy for the tourists. There were messy, hand painted, signs with uneven red block letters. Over a rack of portioned out firewood cribs the sign said: "Help yourself. Put ten bucks in the mail slot in the front door." Another sign over the air compressor read: "Free Cape Cod Air" . One sign said: "Oldest Gas Station On Cape Cod (oldest Attendant too!)".

Tommy went inside, and though the door was unlocked no one was inside. Outside he noticed a truck and a wood splitter out back so he took a look around the woodlot. He then saw Jack still unconscious, on his back, in a pile of pine needles and saw dust with his chainsaw lying beside him. Tommy ran up to Jack, got on his hands and knees and put his hand on Jack's shoulder. He carefully removed Jack's sunglasses to see if he was dead. His eyes were closed. Tommy could see that he was breathing and that he had plenty of color in his face. In fact he was smiling and looked as if he were completely comfortable and just taking a nap. Tommy gently shook Jack's shoulder.

"Hello? Are you ok?" Jack opened his eyes.

"You?" Said Jack. He tried to sit up before he realized he was hurt. He groaned and propped himself up on one shoulder.

"Just take a minute," said Tommy. "I'll help you get up when you're ready."

"I don't understand," said Jack. "What year is this? I must be asleep."

"It's nineteen ninety seven."

"Well all right then," said Jack. "Help me up." With Tommy's help Jack got up and stumbled into his gas station sitting room. Once inside Jack lay across the sofa and Tommy took a seat in the easy chair beside him.

"You must have fainted or something," said Tommy.

"I'll be alright," said Jack. "I just need a breather."

Tommy just smiled and sat quietly wondering what to say. "So you're Jack?" he asked.

"I've been called worse," Jack replied. "And what's your name son?"

"Tommy Cobb."

"Tommy Cobb? That's a good Cape Cod name."

"I've never even been here before," said Tommy. "I'm from Pennsylvania."

"Well I imagine it's a good Pennsylvania name as well."

"No," said Tommy. "It's mostly Pa Dutch out there."

"I went to The Netherlands when I was in the Navy," said Jack. "Didn't care for it. Found it rather gloomy."

"Pa Dutch isn't Dutch, it's German," said Tommy.

"You don't say?"

"Yup. Hey Jack, why did you say 'You' like that when you opened your eyes and saw me?"

"No reason."

"It just seemed kind of weird," said Tommy.

"I guess I thought you looked like someone but now I can't remember who anymore. I don't know. I guess the fall kind of shook me up."

"Are you going to be ok?" Asked Tommy. "Do you want me to call someone for you?"

"I'll be fine," said Jack. He tried to get up but fell back on the couch. "Do me a favor son. Could you get me a glass of water? There's a glass in the cabinet over the sink right there."

Tommy stood at Jack's little kitchenette sink and filled him a glass from the tap. Tommy smelled the water and made a face. "I don't think you can drink this. There's something wrong with it."

"Nonsense," said Jack. He took the water and gulped it down.

Tommy looked around the room to take it all in. It was an interesting little room. It had a pot belly stove and a collection of twenty-five or so hats hanging all around on the walls.

"This is a really cool place," he said. "Have you been here all your life?"

"Not yet," said Jack.

"You know," said Tommy. "My father was an artist and he painted a picture of this gas station a long time ago. Like forty five years ago. That's why I wanted to come see the place."

"You don't say?" said Jack.

"It's a famous painting in a museum in New York. Have you ever heard of it?"

"I'm afraid I don't know much about art," said Jack. "You'll have to talk to my son Sam. He'll tell you all about it. A lot of famous artists and writers used to hang around here in the old days."

"Really?" asked Tommy.

"Sure," said Jack. Eugene O'Neil, Jackson Pollock, Motherwell, even Hemingway had a picture taken out front with the painter Barnett Newman in the fifties."

"Wow," said Tommy. "Barnet Newman? I thought you said you didn't know about art?"

"I know enough about it to know I don't understand most of it," said Jack. "I once saw Barnett Newman brought to tears explaining one of his pictures to my late wife Marie. I'll be damned if it wasn't just a single straight line down the middle of a canvas and the man was crying like a baby about it, seriously."

"Wow, that is so cool."

"Is it?" said Jack. "Like I said, I don't pretend to know about art. Oh they all came through here back in the day. All kinds of bohemians and wing nuts. We had the only gas station just outside Provincetown so they all had to stop here if they wanted to make it into town. They were all headin' to Provincetown for some reason I never figured out. You couldn't swing a cat without hitting some famous artist or writer back then."

"Really?" said Tommy. "My mother used to come down here a long time ago. She was into that stuff. I guess that's how I ended up an artist."

"You ever hear of Jack Kerouac?" asked Jack.

"Of course," said Tommy. "He changed my life even though he died when I was like two years old."

"I could never read him," said Jack. "I'm more of a Jack London guy"

"I can see that," said Tommy.

"Anyway," said Jack. "That's his hat up there over the door — the cowboy hat."

"Kerouac's hat? Right there? The cowboy hat?" Tommy jumped out of his seat.

"He stopped here in sixty-two I believe it was. Anyway, he was drunk and he left that hat on the back of the toilet."

Tommy stood under the hat looking up at it amazed. "This is Jack Kerouac's hat? You've got to be kidding me. But he didn't wear a cowboy hat did he?"

"That's 'cause he left it here," said Jack. "That may have been how we started the hat collection, come to think of it. After that everyone wanted to leave a hat. Now I have more damn hats than I know what to do with."

Jack had a small black and white TV in the corner of the room and he asked Tommy to put on the ball game. They sat and watched baseball and Tommy decided he would just sit there and not say another thing until Jack did. After a while Jack spoke.

"You know something? I may have hurt myself worse than I thought. I don't think I can get up.'

"Do you need to go to the hospital or something?" Asked Tommy.

"Hell no," said Jack. "The closest hospital is an hour and a half away. But I know you probably want to be on your way and I don't think I can make it to the phone. Do me a favor and call my boy for me. There's a phone in the office beside the cash register."

Tommy made the call and about a half hour later Samuel Bellamy arrived in a Jeep J10 pickup with a chrome skull mounted on the front of the hood. The truck was hand spray painted with black primer and had a tattered and faded American flag in the cracked rear window. He had a stack of lobster traps bungeed in the back. Tommy thought Sam looked like a rock star. He had a choppy black beard, long hair and he wore scuffed up boots, oily Carhartt pants and a tan Dickies canvas, flannel lined, work jacket. He had green mirror sunglasses (like Jack's) and a cigarette hanging out of his mouth. He looked about five years older than Tommy, maybe more. He had a skull and crossbones tattooed on the side of his neck.

Tommy stood out front to greet him. The two shook hands.

"How's it going?" said Tommy.

"I'm Samuel Bellamy out of Wellfleet," said Sam.

"Tommy Cobb out of nowhere," said Tommy.

"Thanks for helping out. Where's the old man? What's he drunk or something?"

"He fell off his woodpile," said Tommy. "He seems ok but he says he can't get off the couch."

"There's a lot of that going around," said Sam. Sam went inside and went straight for the cabinet over the sink. He took out Jack's vodka and poured two glasses and handed one to Jack.

"Hey Pop. Your man here tells me you fell off the woodpile. Since when do you fall off your woodpile?" Jack and Sam both shot their vodka quickly. Sam poured another and handed it to Tommy who was now standing in the doorway. Tommy took it and tossed it down.

"What'd the saw buck up on ya?" Asked Sam.

"Maybe," said Jack. "I think I must have been out an hour or more when he found me. For all I know the kid saved my life."

"You saved my Pop's life," Sam poured another shot for Tommy.

"I'm getting kind of hammered," said Tommy. "It's like ten o'clock in the morning."

"Is it already? I've been up all night."

"You can't get up?" Sam asked Jack.

"My back is out. And I think maybe I broke a couple ribs."

"Jesus Pop. I can't sit in for you right now. I got a lot of shit going on."

"I'll be back on my feet in a day or two," said Jack. "You said you were going to man the pumps this week didn't you?"

"Yeah but I was planning on bailing on that. I figured you could pick up my slack. The blues are running off the bank. The Cove is a goddamn lollapalooza this week. I can't afford not to go. You know how it goes. You can't plan that shit. Strike when it's hot. That's what you taught me Pop. I gotta eat am I right? You think I can feed Goody on the scraps you throw me around here? Look at me, I'm skin and bones over here."

"You look pretty solid around the waist if you ask me," said Jack.

"This coming from a guy who gets all his vitamins from coffee and booze," Sam said to Tommy.

"I could take or leave the coffee," said Jack. Jack then tried to stand up. His face contorted with pain. Sam grabbed him under his arm.

"Help me get him in the truck," he said to Tommy. With some difficulty Tommy and Sam got Jack into the passenger seat of Sam's truck. "Listen Tommy I appreciate your help like this. Are you gonna be around for a while?"

"Yeah I guess, I mean I don't really know what I'm doing to tell you the truth. I just got into town from New York a couple of days ago."

"Ok 'cause I really want to buy you a beer, you know to show you my appreciation and all," said Sam.

"Buy me a beer?"

"Sure," said Sam. "I'll show you around town, whataya say?"

"Ok," said Tommy.

"But you're not like a criminal are ya Tommy? I mean no offense if you are."

"I'm an artist," said Tommy.

Sam took a twenty out of his wallet, handed it to Tommy and then got into his truck. "Look Tommy you gotta do me and Pop a favor. Just hang around and make sure no one robs us blind while we're gone."

"Yeah?"

"Nobody's gonna come by anyway and I'll be back as soon as I get Pop squared away at the clinic in Wellfleet. I just want to make sure he's not bleeding internally, you know anymore than usual I mean."

"Just lock the place up," said Jack.

"Nah, fuck it," said Sam. "If it takes longer than an hour or so I'll give him some more when we get back."

"It's not the money," said Tommy. "I just never did a cash register before."

"It probably doesn't have anything in it anyway. If anyone comes, just pump whatever exact change they have."

"I should pump for them?"

"This is a service station Tommy. We don't dick around. We check the oil; wash the windshield, the whole nine yards. Don't worry you'll be fine," and with that they were off and Tommy was left standing at the pumps dizzy from the two shots of Jack's vodka. The first thing Tommy did was to go inside and try on Kerouac's cowboy hat.

Over the next hour and half only a few cars came through and Tommy had fun checking the oil and washing the windshields. He found a rag in Jack's utility room and hung it from his back pocket in what he imagined made him look like an old time filling station attendant. Though he was alone he laughed out loud when he remembered just where it was that he had seen someone do that, it was the attendant in his dad's painting.

The health clinic was in South Wellfleet so it took Jack over ten miles away from his gas station. "I hope you brought your passport," said Sam. They had to wait nearly an hour before the doctor could see them. Sam fidgeted around in the room and occasionally he paced. Jack had a clipboard on his knee and wore his reading glasses.
"Why in the hell do you have to write your name and address in four different places on these things? I mean once they have it they have it." Sam was standing in front of a painting on the wall. It was a sentimental floral scene with lots of pink and purple.
"Can you believe this piece of crap?" Said Sam.
"It's not that bad."
"The hell it isn't. I mean look at it. It's handmade, with real paint and everything and yet it's not even a real painting."
"You lost me." Jack went back to the forms in his lap.
"Pop, have you ever thought about retiring? I mean I know you don't want to now but you're gonna have to retire some day aren't you? Don't you ever think about what you might like to do when you're done splitting wood?"
"I'm too young to retire," said Jack. "And I have nowhere to go and nothing to do. We can't afford to retire." Sam understood why Jack had said "we" rather than "I".
"You used to say I'd get a little piece of it, remember? Remember when I was a kid and you said you would eventually give the place to me?"

"That's true," said Jack. "You want the place? It's yours. You can start tomorrow."

"You know what I mean Pop."

"Oh right. You want money. I'm afraid we don't have any of that."

"Why not sell the place? We could both go our own ways and start living a whole new life."

"And that's what you want is it?"

"Pop do whatever you're gonna do I don't give a shit. Me, I'm getting out one way or the other. I'm sick of the Cape. I think this is gonna be my last season."

"Well I'm not going anywhere Sam."

"Ok so you're just gonna keep pumping gas and chopping wood until you die? Good luck with that. Pretty soon you're not even going to be able to stay afloat anyway. How are you gonna fix the pumps? When are you gonna pay the seventy-five grand to get new tanks?"

"The tanks are fine," said Jack.

Jack sat on the examining table and the doctor listened to his heart with a stethoscope. "What is this Doogie Houser M.D.?"

"I've heard of that," said the doctor. "It was a popular TV show before I was born."

"I don't get out much," said Jack. Dr. Pena was a very young little woman with glasses and a ponytail.

"I'm hearing a murmur," she said.

"The good kind?" asked Jack.

"I'm afraid there aren't any good kinds. Your rib cage is bruised which is causing your heart to beat irregularly. I can't be sure whether your heart was already slightly off beat or not but it's more than likely the trauma caused by the fall. We'll just have to wait a few days so I can listen to it after you've calmed down and we'll take it from there."

"Thanks Doc."

"Mr. Bellamy you're going to have to take it easy. Have you considered that you may have fallen because you're pushing yourself a little too hard? I have to say, it's a little early to have alcohol on your breath on a weekday."

"Ok Doc I get what you're saying. Maybe I should try to stop and smell the roses once in a while huh?"

"Or not so much as the case may be," said the doctor.

Jack and Sam got in the truck and headed home. "What'd they say?" Asked Sam.

"Nothing?" said Jack. "I have to go back in a few days."

"Yeah huh?" said Sam. "Well they gotta make a buck too. That doctor was pretty cute though huh? I wouldn't mind fucking her."

"What do you think of Tommy?" asked Jack. "He seems like a nice enough guy don't you think?"

"What the hell was he doing poking around out back anyway?" Asked Sam.

"He's Richard Cobb's son," said Jack.

"The hell he is."

"That's what he said."

"What'd he say?"

"He said he was from Pennsylvania and he was Richard Cobb's son."

"No shit?"

It was less than two hours when Sam and Jack returned.

"How'd you make out," asked Tommy.

"He'll live," said Sam. "How'd you make out?"

"Fine," he handed Sam the fifty dollars he had sold in gas. Sam nonchalantly gave Tommy another ten and put the rest in his own pocket.

"Jesus Tommy Pop tells me you're Richard Cobb's son?"

"Yup," said Tommy.

"Well holy frickin' Mary. I'm impressed. I wish my dad was a famous painter," and then he looked over at Jack who was still sitting in the truck. "No offense Pop."

"None taken," said Jack

Tommy pulled the post card of "Gas" out of his pocket and handed it to Sam. "That's why I'm here. I just had to see the place for myself. You know, to see what had inspired him to do his masterpiece, well in my opinion anyway."

"Look at this shit," said Sam. "You look just like him." He showed Jack the postcard but Jack didn't even look at it.

"Help me inside," said Jack. Sam looked at the picture some more. I've heard of this painting but I don't think I ever saw it."

"I saw it a few days ago in the Guggenheim collection in Manhattan," said Tommy. "That postcard doesn't do it justice."

"Man that's cool," said Sam. He held the picture up so he could compare the painting to the real thing with Tommy standing just as in the painting. "That's eerie," said Sam. Sam stuck the postcard in his back pocket and opened the door of the truck to help Jack out. "Give me a hand," he said to Tommy. They Helped Jack into his sitting room. Sam took a small bottle of pills out of his pocket and read the label. "It says here you're not supposed to drink or operate heavy machinery with these so that pretty much rules you out Pop."

"I don't want them," said Jack. "Just leave me a couple." Sam took three pills and put them on the table and then pocketed the rest. He sat down beside Jack and he gestured to Tommy to take a seat.

"All right look," he said. "We have to have a business meeting right now. This is important."

"Can't it wait?" Asked Jack.

"No it can't," said Sam. Sam then took out another three pills and gave one to Jack, took one for himself and offered one to Tommy.

"I'm good," said Tommy.

"Suit yourself," said Sam. "But when they're gone they're gone." Sam and Jack both swallowed the pills. "All right so listen. Pop you're bustin' my balls all the time 'cause I don't have the time like I used to help around here."

"I don't ever remember you helping around here," said Jack.

"Yeah well your memory ain't what it used to be, that's my point," said Sam. "You don't even know half the shit I do around here 'cause you're always half in the bag out back on your woodpile. And now I gotta worry about you falling off the damn thing on top of everything else."

"That's not likely to happen again," said Jack.

"Regardless," said Sam. "I gotta get out on the bank as soon as possible. The blues are running and god knows what else is hot right now with the water heating up and you're clearly gonna need some help around here. Now your man here is clearly a stand-up guy and he's new in town and by the looks of him he's been sleeping in his truck for at least a week so let's work something out that's mutually beneficial. You need a job, am I right to assume that Tommy? It doesn't have to be permanent or anything."

"Sure," said Tommy. "I was planning on washing dishes in Provincetown."

"How old are you Tommy?"

"Twenty-eight."

"And you're not a Mexican or a Jamaican, am I correct in assuming that?"

"That's right."

"Well I'm sorry to burst your bubble but twenty-eight year old American guys don't wash dishes down here. Just hang out here today and keep an eye on the place while Pop rests up. If you have any questions he'll tell you what to do. I'll be back tonight at closing time and we'll go have a beer in P-town. Sound good? And seeing as how you're Richard Cobb's son I'm prepared to say ten bucks an hour plus all the frozen milky ways you can eat. But for that price we may want you to split and stack some wood once and a while."

"You'll have to teach me," said Tommy.

"Jack will teach you, I gotta run. See you tonight Tommy."

Tommy followed Sam out to his truck and then said almost apologetically, "Hey Sam I changed my mind about that codeine. I'll take one if it's all the same to you."

"We're gonna get along fine," said Sam. He took out the vial and dumped two in Tommy's hand. "Save one for tonight," he said as he drove away.

Jack stayed in his sitting room all afternoon watching baseball. At one point he got up and cooked a frozen dinner in his microwave which Tommy took as a sign that he really wasn't that badly injured. Once or twice Tommy sat and watched the game awhile but Jack didn't seem interested in speaking and the few times that Tommy made a comment Jack just nodded and smiled.

Every once in a while a car would pull in and Tommy would spring into action. "What can I get ya?" he'd say and then put the nozzle in the tank. While he washed the windshield he'd offer to check the oil. At first he thought this was merely a folksy way of being nice but he soon realized it was a ploy to sell more oil. Very few people were likely to say no and almost everyone was down at least a little bit. Even if it were less than half a quart he'd sell them a quart and give them the rest to take with them. Many of the customers were regulars and old friends of Jack's and were allowed to carry a tab until the end of the month. Tommy would write what they had spent in a ledger book and have them sign for it. Some people came by just to get cigarettes and put it on their tab. Tommy could see that Jack's was not run like any gas station he had ever been to. It really was something special and the customers seemed to appreciate it. Whenever someone asked where Jack was Tommy replied, "he's inside taking a breather."

Maybe it was the vodka and codeine talking but Tommy felt relaxed and happy for the first time in months. He was excited that he had found Jack's Gas and excited to spend some time on the Cape and maybe to get to know a new art scene and most of all he was relieved that he had found a job. And not just any job but somehow the perfect job for him at that moment in his life. It was like fate had intervened. He felt that if he were to try to paint now he would finally be inspired, but that remained to be seen. He knew from experience that his artistic motivation was fickle. In a few hours the drugs would wear off and he might think to himself: "I used to be a successful artist in a Manhattan loft and now I work at a gas station and sleep in a truck." He thought it seemed funny how subjective those things could be. In any event, for the moment he was happy.

Sam showed up around eight-thirty. He told Tommy he had a few things to do at the station before they went out. Jack was passed out on the couch. Sam locked the pump handles with padlocks and put the oil and various other items into the utility room before locking it as well.

"Keep an eye on what I'm doing," he told Tommy. "You're gonna have to do this whenever the old man fades before closing up."

Sam took out a long wooden rod fifteen feet long marked on the side with numbers like a giant wooden yard stick. He opened a metal cap on the driveway and dropped the rod down into the hole. "You won't ever be doing this though. I'll take care of it," said Sam. He pulled the rod out and based on where the rod was wet with gas he could tell how much was left in the underground storage tanks under the pumps. He then went into the office and recorded that amount in a green leather bound ledger. Tommy noticed that while he was recording this figure he looked to see if Jack was still asleep before he erased and then changed some of the figures in the ledger. He took twenty dollars from the till before locking it up, and then he took a pack of cigarettes from the rack above the register. "All right," Sam said. "Lets hit it."

Chapter Eleven

Sam took Tommy over to Goody's cottage in Wellfleet so Tommy could take a shower. Tommy was embarrassed to use a total stranger's shower but he needed it and it did feel great. Sam had a way of putting Tommy at ease. He was the kind of guy you just immediately knew. Maybe a lot of people disliked him right away as well, but either way you knew him quickly. Sam was also an artist and he didn't waste any time before telling Tommy he had a lot of ideas he wanted to run by him, ideas for putting together shows for the coming season. Unlike Tommy Sam was not concerned with inspiration. Apparently he had enough inspiration for both of them. Tommy was all ears.

Goody's cottage was cozy and full of life, and death. Seamus the one-eyed dog greeted them at the door. He was always happy to see guests. Goody's cats hung around on the porch and inside Tommy saw the animal skulls and the driftwood hanging on the wall and he smelled the pungent odor of the place. It reminded him of a pet shop. Sam informed him that the smell was from Goody's ferret Artemis. Artemis came out to greet them and playfully nibbled at Tommy's feet.

"Artemis be good!" Said Goody.

"Let me guess," said Tommy. "He's named after the nineteenth century vaudevillian comedian and satirical poet?"

"Close," said Sam. "Artemis Pile from Lynard Skynard, right Baby?"

"Very funny," said Goody.

"Well it's a cool name for a ferret," said Tommy.

"Was he funny?" Goody asked. "The comedian I mean."

"Supposedly," Tommy said. "He did vaudeville pantomime; it was popular at the time."

"That sounds interesting," said Goody. "But I don't think I know what vaudeville means, or pantomime." Tommy laughed.

"You think she's kidding?" Sam said. "She's never heard of the nineteenth century either." Again Tommy laughed. "It's not funny," said Sam. "I have to live with this shit."

"I have too heard of that," said Goody. "I have as much education as you do."

"Which is none," said Sam. "But at least I try to expand my mind."

"Oh sure you do," said Goody. "That makes you sound like a druggie or something, you know that?"

"Let me ask you something Tommy," said Sam. "Where do you stand on psychedelics? I mean do you think they can make you smarter?"

"Actually I do," said Tommy. "I mean if a person is already dumb they probably won't work but I do believe they can make smart people smarter."

"This guy is an intellectual from New York City," said Sam to Goody. "Just shut up and get my dinner would you?"

"I'm just saying I have too heard of the nineteenth century. That's all I'm saying. I don't know why you have to embarrass me. That's all I'm saying."

"Ok, name one thing from the nineteenth century," said Sam. "One fucking thing."

"Actually Tommy Artemis is named after Apollo's sister. The Greek goddess of the hunt and wildlife 'cause ferrets are good hunters. But I'm not into history or anything. I just thought it was a pretty name."

"Well you're only off by a couple thousand years," said Sam.

"That's pretty clever if you ask me," said Tommy. Artemis bit Tommy's boot lace and then ran and hid under the couch.

"When it comes to religion and hocus pocus bullshit like that, Goody's all over it," said Sam.

"Thank you," said Goody. "I take that as a complement."

"You would," said Sam. "Regardless it's a glorified rat if you ask me."

"Rat's aren't all bad," said Goody. "I think they're kind of cute. And they're much more intelligent than most people realize. Tommy did you know that a rat is smarter than a cat?"

"No I didn't know that," said Tommy.

"Right 'cause everyone knows how smart cats are," said Sam. "They're right up there with sharks and goldfish."

"Anyway, rats aren't all bad," said Goody.

"You're probably right," said Tommy.

"You don't have to agree with her just because you're a guest," said Sam. "Don't encourage her. Goody, I'll tell you something about rats. You ever hear of the Black Plague?"

Goody let that one go and put dinner on the table. "I hope you like fish Tommy," she said. She gave Tommy a plate of horse mackerel heart and vegetables. Tommy took a bite and complemented her cooking. The three of them ate quietly for a few minutes.

"You're a painter Tommy?" Tommy nodded and kept eating. "We love painters around here, don't we Sam?"

"We like good ones," said Sam. "There are a lot of pussy artists around here painting flowers and shit."

"Oh but I'll bet you're a good one aren't you?" Asked Goody.

"Tommy is Richard Cobb's son," said Sam.

"I don't know who that is," said Goody.

"He's only like one of the most important American painters of the twentieth century," said Sam.

"Well that's pretty cool," said Goody.

"Anyway," said Tommy. "I don't usually paint flowers."

"What do you paint?" asked Goody.

"Women and the moon and trees mostly," said Tommy. "I've got slides in my backpack if you want to check them out." Tommy spread out a box of slides, a magnifying glass and a small battery powered light box on the table. Sam and Goody went through them as Tommy ate. They were both very interested and took plenty of time looking at them and commenting on the different aspects of Tommy's style that caught their interest.

"Well you're good," said Sam.

"Thanks," said Tommy.

"And not really at all like your father either," added Sam.

"Yeah, about that Sam. If you don't mind I'd rather you not bring up my father. He wasn't really my father anyway. I mean you probably know as much about him as I do."

"I understand Tommy. You want to make it on your own. I get that. You know a lot of people around here compare me to my father and I don't like it one bit."

"What are you talking about?" Asked Goody. "Jack is one of the sweetest guys you'll ever meet."

"That's just it," said Sam. "You think I want people thinking I'm sweet?"

"Fat chance," said Goody under her breath.

"The guy is a one trick pony. Okay he likes firewood. We get it. But what else is there? He doesn't do anything. He doesn't go anywhere. He's got no fucking life. He hasn't gotten laid in like twenty years. He wouldn't know art if it came up and bit him in the ass. I don't know. I just don't want to end up like that. You know what I'm saying Tommy?"

"Yeah I think I do," said Tommy. Sam went back to Tommy's slides.

"Looks like you've been busy," said Sam, referring to the fact that there were at least fifty slides.

"Unfortunately not lately, said Tommy. "Actually I'm a slow painter. Basically it took me my whole life to produce that many slides. And lately it's been getting worse. I've been having kind of a block for awhile now. I can't seem to get anything done anymore."

"Well don't force it," said Goody. "You're obviously talented. You just have to wait and it will come I'm sure. Maybe you're trying too hard to control it. You have to just step back and get out of its way."

"That is such bullshit," said Sam. "The man is attempting actual fine art Goody not some touchy feely new age arts and crafts bullshit. The man is an artist."

"I'm just giving an opinion," said Goody.

"Yeah well men are talking here so do me a favor and give more food and less opinion would ya?" And then he said to Tommy quietly. "Stick with me Tommy and I'll have you cranking the shit out. You'll paint circles around all these assholes around here. Do you know how long the art scene around here has been waiting for some real artists?" Sam shoveled fish into his mouth and grinned at Tommy. "You and I are gonna piss some people off and make some money."

"Yeah?" said Tommy. Tommy was conflicted. Part of him wanted to believe Sam and part of him was unconvinced. Still everything that had been happening to him since he arrived on Cape Cod was somehow perfect and kind of dreamy and odd. If something were to get his juices flowing again it would be something like this. It would be someone like Sam. And Sam didn't seem to have the slightest question in his mind that what he had just said was absolutely true. It was funny that he and Sam had hit it off so well since it seemed to Tommy that Sam was basically the exact opposite personality type. He had no self doubt, no lack of inspiration. None that Tommy could detect anyway.

Tommy decided he would give Sam the chance to make good on his claim. He would try to take Sam's lead and see what happened, including even forcing himself to eat every bit of food from his plate. At that moment the food itself symbolized to Tommy Sam's harsh and strange world. It was like nothing he had eaten before. It was savory and exotic and not at all easy to get down but Tommy was determined to eat it and furthermore to enjoy it. He felt as though he were acquiring a taste for it even as he slowly finished it off.

Sam cleaned his plate and then went into Goody's bedroom and returned with a painting of his own. He put it on the floor and leaned it up against the refrigerator and waited for Tommy's appraisal. Tommy stood up and looked at it closely. He wasn't sure what to make of it. It was clearly primitive. He thought it looked like a folk painting, but it definitely had something different about it.

It was about twenty-four inches across painted in bright acrylics. It depicted two men and a dog in a beach forest under a starry sky. The men were apparently digging up a grave and one man held a skull in one hand and a lantern in the other in what looked like a scene out of Hamlet. Sam's drawing style was messy but interesting and his unusual use of color and his ambitious subject matter were clearly a sign of potential, though his draftsmanship and color technique were on the messy and reckless side. Like most artists Tommy's immediate reaction was to ascertain whether or not it was as good as his own work. He quickly decided that it was in fact not quite as good as his own.

"Pretty fucking good huh?" said Sam.

"I love it," said Goody.

"What do you know?" said Sam. "Let the man speak."

"Very cool," said Tommy.

"Yeah huh?" said Sam. "Do you like the dog?"

"I do," said Tommy. "It reminds me of Picasso's Guernica horse, like the way his mouth is elongated."

"That's exactly what I was going for," said Sam.

"You said you were going for Chagall," said Goody.

"I love Chagall," said Tommy.

"You don't even know who Marc Chagall is," Sam said to Goody. "I was the one who told you about Chagall. Tommy is an artist. Don't embarrass yourself and act like you know about Chagall."

"I know what I like," said Goody.

"Just shut the fuck up and let the man think would ya? Picasso's Guernica huh Tommy? You totally nailed it. I was going for that with the dog, like the horse in Guernica. That's what I was thinking, the way his tongue is hanging out like that. I was going for that with the elongated snout too. You know what I mean?"

"I can see that," said Tommy.

Goody cleared away the dishes and poured Sam and Tommy rum and cokes and she poured herself a glass of water and they went outside on the front porch for cigarettes.

Tommy looked through the screen door at Goody's skulls and driftwood on the wall.

"I gotta tell ya that's really very cool Goody. That stuff on the wall is awesome."

"It's my Wicca shrine," said Goody. "It's not done yet but it's getting there. Do you like it?"

"I love it," said Tommy. "Did you find all the stuff around here?"

"Yeah in the beach forest and the dunes," said Goody. "That's what I do."

"Why do you call it a Wicca shrine?" Asked Tommy.

"Don't get her started," said Sam.

"That's what it is," said Goody. "It's all the things that are important to me. I'm into witchcraft and these are the things that I feel spiritual about, it's my art."

"Witchcraft. Really? That's cool." Said Tommy.

"Not like most people think of it," said Goody. "It's really just a philosophy of being in touch with the forces of nature and the weather and the trees and the ocean and stuff like that."

"No," said Tommy. "I know what you mean. I've heard of that. That's cool. Your collection here is really beautiful."

"You guys are painters," said Goody. "And that's great and that's your art, but this is my art. This is what I do." Goody showed Tommy her new sea turtle shell.

"It is cool, I'll give you that," said Sam. "But technically it's not art."

"But look at how beautiful it is," said Goody.

"Your tits are beautiful too but that doesn't make them art," said Sam. "You're an old time shore wrecker, and a damn good one; probably the best in fact, but does that make you an artist? I don't know. There's a difference."

"Everyone is an artist in a way," said Goody.

"Then no one is," said Sam.

"I don't know why you say that," said Goody.

"That's because you're not an artist," said Sam. "Tommy knows what I mean. Right Tommy?"

"I do," said Tommy. "Not about Goody, but I know what you mean about art. It's a subtle distinction, one that people don't usually make."

"It isn't that subtle," said Sam. "Art is man made and it has content. It says something. And it isn't real. It has to be fake. That way it's symbolic or allegorical. The real world isn't symbolic or allegorical because it's the real world. A symbol is not literally the thing it symbolizes. It's a representation of the thing which it then sheds light on."

"I totally get that," said Tommy. "Like an object or whatever can't literally be the thing that it's metaphorically compared to because then it wouldn't be what it is. Otherwise it wouldn't be a metaphor, it would be just what it is in the first place, which is real life and not a metaphor for real life."

"That is exactly what I'm saying," said Sam. "The fact that you get that proves to me that you might be as smart as I am."

"Well I have no idea what you two are talking about," said Goody.

"You know," said Tommy. "Picasso said art is a lie that tricks you into seeing the truth."

"Exactly," said Sam. "That's my point." Sam put his hand on Tommy's shoulder.

"But look at this." Goody picked up a small piece of driftwood and showed it to Tommy. "Look at these lines Tommy. Look at how subtle they are. Is this art or am I crazy?"

"She doesn't get it," said Sam.

"It's beautiful," said Tommy.

"Come here baby," Said Sam. "Now look at this ass." Sam put his hands on Goody's ass. "It's fucking beautiful am I right?"

Tommy didn't say anything though he did think Goody's ass was beautiful.

"Don't be a pig," said Goody.

"You get my point?"

"Of course, but I think I get Goody's point too. I mean this thing is like an installation ya know?"

"I've always thought installations were stupid," said Sam.

"You lost me," said Goody.

"I know," said Tommy. "But as an installation it's pretty good."

"Thanks," said Goody.

"Don't even bother," Sam said to Tommy.

They finished their drinks and Tommy thanked Goody for her hospitality and then Sam and Tommy jumped in Sam's truck and headed for the harbor. Sam decided they should skip town for the night and instead head out on Whydah. Sam parked in the lot at the head of the Pamet River on the bay in Truro and he borrowed a dinghy from the pier to get them out to Whydah. He made Tommy row. Sam could have done a much better job but it was a question of tradition and protocol. He wanted to start teaching Tommy as soon as possible. Once aboard Sam showed Tommy the ropes. Tommy observed the name "Whydah" painted across the stern and enquired as to its meaning.

"Don't know," said Sam. "She's a good deal older than I am. It's pronounced "wida" like widow with a Cape accent. Like if I ever get married she's gonna make a "wida" out of my wife."

"It sure is cool," said Tommy as he looked around.

"She," said Sam, "is a classic. A thirty-two foot Monterey diesel troller. Sam showed him around the deck. He brought him inside the little wheelhouse cockpit.

"This here is my chair," said Sam. "Whatever you do don't ever fucking sit in it." Tommy could see that Sam was not joking.

"No problem, I can understand that," said Tommy. "Why would I sit there? That would be totally stupid." Sam showed Tommy down into the tiny cabin in the V-berth under the wheelhouse. It was about ten feet square and six feet high.

"This here is where I eat and sleep," said Sam.

"Awesome," said Tommy without even a hint of sarcasm. The fact of the matter was that Tommy was totally enjoying himself. Sam then showed him the inboard engine installed under the deck.

"She's got a 330 horsepower Volvo diesel motor," said Sam.

"Sweet," said Tommy. They went back out on deck and sat down and put their feet up and had beers as the sun set on the harbor. It was a beautiful spring evening with very little wind and a calm sea.

"Cape Cod is one of the only places in the U.S. where you can watch the sun rise and set over the water every day," said Sam.

"And Florida," said Tommy.

"Yeah but in Florida you would have to drive three hours to do it, here it's in the same fucking town."

"You know something Sam? I'm really glad I met you. This is really fucking cool, thanks."

"When we're asea you gotta call me Skipper," said Sam.

"Seriously?" asked Tommy.

"You see somebody else here?" Asked Sam. "Somebody's gotta know what's what out here or it can get bad real fucking fast. It's not always this calm out here. When it isn't you'll be glad you've got a skipper."

"Ok," said Tommy. "Skipper it is." Sam took out a bag of pot and began rolling a joint. Tommy noticed that Sam rolled unusually large joints. He rolled it like a cone, European style, thin on the smoking end and wide on the other and he put a little piece of a rolled up match book cover in the tip like they do in Jamaica.

"You don't fuck around do you Skipper?" Said Tommy. Sam lit it up and took multiple hits before passing it to Tommy.

"You're a real city boy, I can see that," said Sam.

"Not really," said Tommy. "But I guess compared to you I am."

"You like to fish?" Asked Sam.

"Sure," said Tommy. "But I don't know shit about it. Maybe you can teach me?"

"Well I'm a Wellfletian smackman it's true," said Sam. "But I don't want to teach you about that."

"I don't know what that means."

"A Smackman is an old time Cape lobster fisherman."

"See I'm learning already."

"You ain't learning shit. I'll tell you when you're learning."

"Cool," said Tommy. And then he added: "Skipper." Sam took out a couple of fishing rods and handed one to Tommy. He opened his tackle box and set up Tommy with an unusually large hook and a very heavy sinker. Sam then went into his cooler and got a fish which he cut up with a knife.

"I'm gonna give you the deep bait fish," said Sam. "That way you don't have to do shit but sit and wait. They're gonna love it. That's what we call an idiot jig. No offense."

"None taken. Who the fuck am I? "

"Nice and deep," said Sam. "Just let it fall."

"Got it."

"You're looking for flat fish, or maybe shark if you're lucky."

"I was born lucky," said Tommy. "But if I get something you gotta tell me what to do."

"All you have to do is crank it in and I'll beat the shit out of it with my Louisville slugger over there."

"Got it."

Sam put a big hunk of the fish on Tommy's hook and tossed it into the sea. He looked up at the sky with reverence and then made the sign of the cross with his thumb on his forehead. "Don't underestimate the importance of ritual."

"That was a pretty big hook Skipper."

"Yeah, I always make em a little too big. That way you don't get anything, unless it's something interesting." Sam then took a weathered and seasoned looking hand carved wood lure from his tackle box and kissed it. "Maybe if you're good I'll let you try one of these," he said.

"Somehow I doubt it," said Tommy.

"For now you can fish deep," said Sam, "Deep is fun. You never know what you're gonna get. This baby is for skimming on the top side where you know damn well what you're gonna get."
"And what is that?" Asked Tommy.

"Usually nothing," said Sam. "I'm looking for a blue or a striper. They like a chase across the surface. That's what they do. It takes a bit of finesse to wear'em down." Sam cast far out into the calm green sea and then reeled his lure in slowly. "Now we're fishing," he said. He flicked at his lure as it skipped across waves.

"What do I have to do?" Asked Tommy as he played with his long heavy rod.

"You don't have to do shit," said Sam.

"I'm on it," said Tommy.

The sun had gone down and darkness surrounded Whydah as the two men quietly looked out to sea. Tommy was giddy but he knew it was best not to speak. An hour or so passed before he felt a tug on his line. He jumped into action and reeled it in. It took a good while to get to the surface. His bait had been sitting on the ocean floor at least a hundred feet down. He was thinking of Sam's words that you never know what you're going to get when fishing that deep when he first saw what looked like a human face emerge from the murky depths. About two feet under the surface he clearly saw a white face with big lips and a flat nose.

"It's a skate," said Sam.

"Like a stingray?" Asked Tommy, as he pulled it into the boat.

"Yeah except it's a skate." Sam grabbed the hook with a needle nose pliers and hung the skate over the side of Whydah until it wiggled and thrashed its way off and plunged back into the sea. Sam explained that while it was not unusual to eat the fins of a skate it was not really worth the trouble.

"It's like eating a baby shark." Tommy put fresh bait on his hook and tossed out into the waves. "What if I catch a shark?"

"Then we catch a shark."

"Can we use the Louisville Slugger?"

"Yeah," said Sam. "If I'm feeling humane. Otherwise I just use this." Sam reached under his chair and pulled out an enormous black knife. "This is the bayonet they used in hand to hand combat in Korea in the fifties. See it has this hole in the handle where they would slide it over the barrel of a rifle? I usually stick it on the end of my gaff and it makes a good harpoon."

"Sweet," said Tommy.

The two men fished awhile and enjoyed the serene peace and calm of the sea and then Tommy remembered something he wanted to ask Sam.

"Skipper," he began. "This morning when I found Jack behind the station he said some things that I thought seemed kind of strange. When he first opened his eyes he looked at me as though he already knew me and he said "what are you doing here?" or something along those lines. It was kind of freaky. Do you think he could have known my father?"

"I thought you didn't want to talk about that," said Sam.

"Well I just don't want you to bring it up. You know in front of other people to impress them or whatever. But I'm just wondering why did Jack think he knew me? Maybe he thought I was him. You saw the way he looked when he did the painting. He looked just like me."

"If he did ever meet Cobb he never mentioned it. Shit I'd be surprised if he could remember that far back. He would have had to have been in his early twenties. That was right around the time he started working for Jack Snow, the first Jack."

"There was another Jack?"

"Yeah my dad's real name isn't Jack it's Robert. The name kind of came with the gas station."

"That's why when I asked him if he was Jack he said 'I've been called worse'?"

"Yeah," said Sam. "That's one of the stupid folksy things he always likes to say. It was funny like the first twenty times I heard it."

"Actually I'm supposed to become the next Jack," said Sam.

"You should."

"Yeah but I ain't gonna do it. I got other plans for the place."

"Like what?" Asked Tommy.

"Lets' just relax and fish awhile," said Sam.

Chapter Twelve

Tommy and Sam stayed up all night fishing. In the morning Sam dropped Tommy off at Jack's where Tommy slept in the back of his truck for a few hours before starting work. Sam was then off to Hyannis where he had an important secret meeting with a big gas company representative. He wore his new black Timberland work shoes and a tucked in flannel shirt. It was the closest thing he had to formal business attire.

Sam sat in a little office across the desk from a rather large imposing figure of a man by the name of Mr. Ben Horegold. Mr. Horegold's beard was even thicker and blacker than Sam's but Sam was hardly impressed, mainly because of the tacky pastel-hued Cape Cod prints which Mr. Horegold had displayed on the walls of his office. "You know Ben — can I call you Ben?"

"Of course," said Mr. Horegold. Sam continued.

"Anyway Ben I could help you get some real paintings for your office if you want instead of this crap."

"Are they that bad?" he laughed. "I hadn't noticed."

"That sort of thing matters," said Sam. "I mean what is this anyway? They look like you got them at KMart or something." Ben was not put off by Sam's candor.

"I guess you're right. They're pretty lame huh?"

"I'm just sayin'," said Sam.

"Right," said Ben. "So how's your father?"

"Drinking' like a fish," said Sam.

"You think he's ready to retire?"

"Oh I know he is Ben. But I don't think he knows it just yet."

"You explained our proposal, did you?"

"Just in broad strokes. I'm working on him gradually. He'll come around."

"Well we appreciate that Sam. I hope you know that."

"Yeah I know you do. Let's just say for the sake of argument that my Pop is still gonna need a job. Have you thought about that?"

"Of course Sam. I understand that completely. Even if we decide to buy you out your father could still basically run the place."

"Basically?"

"Well of course he'd have to be willing to defer to some of our suggestions. Is that something you think he'd be amenable to?"

"If the price is right," said Sam. "What kinds of suggestions?"

"Well as you know the place needs some work. I mean don't get me wrong we love the folksy character that Jack has given the place over the years but we're talking about laying out some serious money here and so obviously we'd have to, you know, get the place up to speed a little bit. Nothing too severe I don't think."

"Yeah well I'll be honest with you," said Sam. "My Pop doesn't like change and it's not going to be easy for him. You guys are really gonna have to make it worth our while."

"Well that's what we're here to discuss isn't it?"

"Exactly," said Sam.

"Ok so let's talk numbers." Ben leaned back and crossed his arms.

"I'm thinking like one point five gazillion," said Sam. Ben laughed.

"And for that you'll throw in a painting or two?"

"No doubt," said Sam. "You ever heard of Tommy Cobb from New York?"

When Tommy awoke and reported for duty Jack teased him a little. "Keeping Banker's hours are ya?" Jack was already on the mend and had been up early, ready for another hard day's work. Tommy got up around eight and only had a few hours of sleep at that. Needless to say he was still quite sleepy but he found that he didn't have much to do other than to listen to Jack explain how to open the gas station for business. Jack called it his 'two penny lecture' for some reason. Tommy found that Jack had many of these cute little sayings; the humor of which was usually lost on everyone other than Jack. Jack showed him how to unlock the office, the gas pumps and the utility room in the garage. He showed him how to display quarts of oil stacked in pyramids by the pumps. He showed him where all the relevant keys, locks and light switches were located and finally he handed Tommy a wad of bills and then went to his wood pile. Mostly Tommy sat around all day in a lawn chair out front. If a car pulled up he would have to greet them, pump their gas and check the oil. Even in nineteen-ninety-five this seemed excessive and Tommy suspected that it may have driven away as many people as it attracted. In any case it seemed there were very few customers and those few they did have all seemed to have permission to run a tab, evidentially the only requirement for this was that they know Jack even slightly. Jack wasn't worried about it. He told Tommy how he only made about two cents a gallon on the gas anyway. Tommy thought this was crazy but Jack explained that even the big gas stations only got maybe twice that. The profit margin was in the volume and in the peripherals. Jack's peripheral was ostensibly in firewood, cigarettes and frozen Milky ways. As far as Tommy could see Jack's had very little sales either way which he was happy about since he was beginning to find that he really disliked greeting strangers and making small talk. Tommy would never pass as even a decent salesman. He thought maybe the one exception to this would be if he were selling art. He liked to talk art, even with strangers.

A few days went by and Tommy fell into a rhythm, offbeat as it was. Jack offered Tommy the cot built into the wall in the sitting room. It was like something you would expect to find on a boat. Jack had hidden, and forgot about it seemed, a bottle of cheap vodka in the blankets on this cot. Tommy said to himself: "When in Rome..." and then discretely polished off the bottle over the next three days. Jack slept out back in the bunkhouse (which actually had only one bunk). The station would usually close pretty early, Jack said once the tourist started coming in all the time he would have to stay open until nine. Tommy wasn't looking forward to that and was already plotting a way to get out of working for Jack all summer. On those first few nights Tommy drove around, and walked around, all over Wellfleet, Truro and Provincetown just to see what was out there and to kill time so Jack could have his privacy in his sitting room before going to bed.

After a week or so of working for Jack Tommy met Apple. She pulled up in Kalesin, her sexy little red Audi A4. Tommy went to work pumping her gas and checking her oil. He was embarrassed by not being able to locate the dipstick. Apple got out of the car and helped him while offering a few impressive remarks about German engineering. He surmised that this woman was probably smarter than he was. He was also taken with her looks, but this hardly bears mentioning, romantically and sexually deprived as he was.

"Are you Jack?" she asked. Tommy thought about Jack's reply 'I've been called worse', but didn't want to come across as trying too hard.

"He's out back on the woodpile," said Tommy. Apple took out a very nice camera from her car and asked if Tommy minded if she look around.

"I'm a bit of an amateur photographer," she explained.

"Cool," said Tommy. The more he thought about this reply the better he felt about it. He almost said 'aren't we all', which would sound cool at first, but then seem pithy and stupid once he thought about it awhile.

"Cool," said Apple. She took pictures of the whole place from out front. She then got some shots of Jack working out back with his chainsaw. He acted as though he didn't see her but, as most people would be, he was flattered. He may have been reluctant to admit it but he wasn't completely unaware that he was indeed cultivating an image, perhaps even more so than most people. He knew that his image, in some small way, was potentially iconic to tourists and enthusiasts of Cape Cod history. In this sense he was aware of playing a role. He was destined to be old Jack the woodcutter, the last proprietor of the oldest gas station on Cape Cod and it did instill in him a sense of responsibility. He was well aware of his unique stewardship to a tiny piece of Americana, but to admit that, seemed, to him, not a little uncouth.

Apple took a picture of Tommy at the pumps as well. He knew this was merely to make him feel good. She bought a frozen Milky Way and then told him her name. He shook her hand and told him his own. Her hand was warm and soft, he thought. Pretty girl's hands were always like that.

"These are killers on your teeth," said Apple as she chomped on the frozen Milky Way.

"I get to eat as many as I want," Tommy told her. "I've been living on them all week."

"That may not be so nutritious," said Apple.

"No," said Tommy. "But the price is right." Apple laughed which Tommy enjoyed very much. He imagined kissing her. It was all he could do to keep from reaching out and running his fingers through her hair, which was wild and wavy and easily ten different shades of yellow and brown. He noticed that she had very fine hairs on her cheeks, like soft girl sideburns which he found compelling.

He imagined kissing her again. Apple was already busy poking around. She noticed how run down and rusted the gas pumps were and she noticed the pump handle repaired with duct tape. Obviously the place was barely legal when it came to the pumps. She asked if she could look inside and so Tommy showed her the office and Jack's sitting room.

"It's so cute in here," she said.

"Yeah," said Tommy. "This place is like in a time warp or something."

"Are you in a time warp?" asked Apple.

"No," said Tommy. "I just started here."

"You look like you're in a time warp," Apple teased him. She looked at his shirt disapprovingly. It was an army shirt, not a real army shirt. He got it at a department store in the mall.

"I'm just trying to fit it," said Tommy.

Apple noticed the small bathroom behind the office with a sign on the door which read: "Sorry, Employees Only."

"I really have to go," she said. "Do you think it would be ok?" Being a new employee Tommy was reluctant to break the rules.

"Well, make it quick he said." Just as Apple was about to go into the bathroom Jack appeared.

"Sorry Ma'am," he said. "I'm afraid it's out of order." Tommy knew it wasn't. He had been using it. It even had a shower which Jack used regularly but Tommy hadn't yet due to the gasoline smell in the water. Jack swore he couldn't smell it, or taste it. Tommy couldn't believe that Jack had been drinking it, but then again Jack got nearly all his hydration from coffee, cheap wine and vodka, sometimes he drank ice tea with vodka.

Apple was surprised Jack wouldn't make an exception.

"It's kind of an emergency," she said. Jack led her outside into the woodlot. He told her it would be no problem if she wanted to go behind the woodpile. He assured her that he would keep an eye out. She thanked him and went behind the woodpile for a couple of minutes. She had no intention of peeing but instead just had a look around while she was out there. Once she was done she came around front and tried to wash her hands under the outdoor spigot beside the utility room, but was disappointed to find that it had been disabled. Jack went back to his woodpile and Tommy took a seat out front. Apple nodded to Tommy and smiled as she got into Kalesin and drove away. Tommy was glad that he hadn't come on too strong. He had definitely played it cool. As long as she came back one more time he'd get his chance to make his move. This was his new theory. You never go for it on the first meeting, you just lay the groundwork and play it cool. If you get a second chance then you go for it. He had a feeling she'd be back.

Later that night Jack told Tommy that it was very important that he not let any customers use the restroom, no matter how pretty they were. Tommy apologized and assured Jack that it wouldn't happen again.

The following day Apple met with Frank to tell him that she had stopped by Jack's just to check it out.

"Anything suspicious or out of the ordinary?" Asked Frank.

"Maybe," said Apple. "I tried to get a water sample discreetly but they wouldn't let me use the bathroom. So then I tried the hose outside but apparently it was disabled."

"I knew it!" said Frank.

"We don't know anything just yet," said Apple. "The place is pretty run down though."

"A little too run down wouldn't you say? The place is an abomination."

"I wouldn't say that. They seem very nice actually."

"Then why not let you use the restroom? What have they got to hide?"

"They said it was out of order."

"Yeah right," said Frank. "And the hose outside?"

"I guess that seems a little suspicious," admitted Apple.

"Those dirt bags! You have to keep trying."

"I don't know what else I can do Frank. Why can't we just tell them we want to check the water?"

"We don't want to arouse suspicion just yet," said Frank. "Technically we're supposed to have a reasonable suspicion before we initiate an investigation. I mean we do have reasonable suspicion but we're supposed to have something beyond what we have."

"Right," said Apple. "Because we don't have anything."

"So we're supposed to sit and wait until it's too late?" Asked Frank.

"The water table flows toward the Pamet River. Why not drill a well somewhere down stream? I could probably tell from there."

"Exactly," said Frank. "You're always thinking. I like that."

"Ok then let's do it," said Apple.

"It's a damn good idea. Really it is. But unfortunately we're going to have to back burner that for the time being."

"Back burner?"

"Oh we'll do it," said Frank. "Eventually, but we can't spend that kind of money just yet. Do you know how much it would cost to drill a hundred and twenty feet under the Pamet?"

"Five thousand?" Offered Apple, she really had no idea.

"Try fifteen," said Frank. "And that's before we pay you to test it."

"That's a rip off," said Apple. "I mean before the part about paying me."

"We can't throw money around just yet unless we're damn sure we're going to find something."

"We can't be sure if we don't drill," said Apple.

"I guess it's kind of a catch twenty-two," said Frank.

"You know, snooping around there makes me feel a little bit like a scumbag. I don't know if I'm up to it."

"Well that's something you'll just have to get over. After all we're talking about protecting the environment here Apple, that's our sworn duty isn't it?"

"I guess." Apple knew Frank didn't give a shit about the environment, but worse she knew her own motives were suspect.

"And of course there's the pig eyes," said Frank. He seemed to always know what she was thinking.

"The pig eyes are important to me."

"You think I don't know that?" Said Frank. "The pig eyes are everything. I know that. When you pull it off I intend to ride your coattails as far as I can. I backed you all the way didn't I? When did I ever not let you do your pig eyes? When you publish your findings, maybe this fall, and some big company buys your assay, you better not forget who helped you along the way. That's all I ask."

"This fall?" Asked Apple. "Do you think I'll really get enough backing to make it by the fall?"

"You have to help me so I can help you," said Frank. Apple was encouraged.

"Frank, you've been a tremendous ally for me in the agency really, and I'm going to make you a minor co-author on the paper when it's done, really, you deserve it. You'll have a piece of the patent and everything. We just have to make sure it gets done whatever it takes."

"Well all right then," said Frank. He seemed genuinely moved. "You better."

Chapter Thirteen

It was early on a Friday night, shortly after Tommy's first encounter with Apple, when Sam arrived at Jack's, just after closing, to take Tommy out for a beer. Tommy was going a bit stir crazy and he welcomed the offer. Sam arrived in Goody's truck with Goody in the passenger seat.

"I blew a head gasket in mine," he explained. "I had to bum a ride. Maybe we could take yours?"

"Ok," said Tommy. With that Sam jumped out of the truck and Goody got in the driver's seat. She said hello to Tommy, Sam kissed her on the cheek and then she was off.

"Thank God," said Sam. "Taking a girl to a bar is like taking sand to the beach."

"I was just thinking I need to get a girl," said Tommy. "So I can take her to the beach."

"Well then you better go to a bar without a girl," said Sam.

"That actually makes sense," said Tommy and then he added: "But then is taking a girl to the beach like taking sand to a bar?"

"Well anyhow we're going," said Sam.

Before they left Sam went inside to check on the old man. "He's not dead yet or anything is he?" Sam detoured into the office, borrowed some cash from the till, took a pack of cigarettes and then went into Jack's sitting room to say hello. Tommy waited outside. A minute or so later Sam returned and said: "Lets hit it!" he then punched Tommy in the arm and jumped into the truck.

First he wanted to take Tommy to the Bomb Shelter in Wellfleet for a quick one and then they'd go to Provincetown so Sam could show him around.

"Sound good?" Asked Sam.

"Very good," said Tommy. "Especially that beer."

"The first ones on you," said Sam.

The 'quick one' quickly turned into a couple of quick ones and then a quick few. After that there was no point in calling them 'quick' anymore. Tommy and Sam sat in the dimly lit, dank space paying for each other's beers and lighting each other's cigarettes. It occurred to Tommy that for the exact same amount of time and money they could buy their own beers and light their own cigarettes, but he had to admit it had a certain worldly cordiality to it. It also made it so you had to drink and smoke as fast as the other guy. In that respect Tommy was no slouch but Sam was ambitious. Tommy had a look around the room and decided this may have been the shitiest bar he had ever been in.

"You know Sam," he said. "You kind of implied there would be girls here but this doesn't seem like the kind of place that girls go to."

"Yeah?" said Sam. "I guess that's true. I come here to just think, or to talk. It's hard to talk about shit when there's women around you know? I mean you can't bring up politics or religion or anything like that you know what I mean? Not that I want to bring those things up right now. I'm just saying I'd like to be able to if I wanted to."

"That's true," said Tommy.

"So anyway," said Sam. "There is something I want to talk with you about. I want to talk business. I need to make you a serious offer."

"Ok," said Tommy.

"If you make a decent painting right away I can sell it for you for a lot of money."

"How can you be sure?" Asked Tommy.

"I've already got it lined up. I got the hook-up."

"The hook up?"

"Yeah the hook-up. I got it. Have you ever read Norman Mailer?" Asked Sam.

"No," said Tommy.

"You ever heard of him?"

"Sure I've heard of him. He's a famous writer who lives in Provincetown."

"Yeah well he's a friend of mine," said Sam.

"Really?"

"Well sort of," said Sam. "Anyway I told him about you. You know he's got one of your father's paintings and he wouldn't mind rounding out the set with one of yours. He's a rich motherfucker too. You should see his house. He's got like all the classic Outer Cape painters in there."

"What painting of my father's does he have?"

"It's just some small piece of shit really. Not even as good as the slides of your shit you showed me."

"I doubt that," said Sam.

"I saw it myself, it's nothing really. It's like a small Truro landscape with a house in it. I was thinking maybe you could do something like that too so he would have to have it, like to complete the set you know? It would be pretty smart on our part if we did something like that. Then we could get some other sales off the idea that we sold to Mailer. You know how these guys operate. Once one has something they all want it."

"You know Sam I've always resisted cashing in on my father's reputation. I want to make it on my own."

"Fuck that," said Sam. "That's just pride talking. You want to work at a gas station all summer or do you want to spend the summer drinking and getting laid?"

"Well if those are my only two choices," said Tommy.

"Well then that's what we need to talk about," Sam put his hand on Tommy's shoulder. "You need management my friend and I got the hook-up down here. I know all kinds of rich P'town art fags, some of them with good taste too. They're not all posers, most are and we couldn't discriminate but I just want you to know we could actually make a difference. We could get involved and shake things up if we wanted to. And I know some other famous guys besides him."

"Like who?" Asked Tommy.

"You ever hear of Noam Chomsky?" Asked Sam.

"Nope."

"Well he's famous," said Sam. "And Jack cuts and delivers his firewood. He's got a nice little place out in the woods in Wellfleet."

"What's he famous for?"

"Linguistics," said Sam. "You ready for another beer?"

"You can get famous in Linguistics?" Asked Tommy.

"Sure," said Sam. "Somebody's gotta do it. He's like world fucking famous in linguistics. He teaches at MIT I'm pretty sure. Anyway P-town's a small town but there's a lot of heavy hitters in the art scene if you have the hook-up."

"And you have it? '

"That's right," said Sam. "I'm totally hooked up. I'll be your manager. I could set up some shows for us, like two man shows where we both show. That way you wouldn't need as much stuff."

"I don't know if I could come up with anything right away Sam. I've been going through a dry spell."

"Fuck it," said Sam. "You got your paints and shit with you?"

"I got everything in my truck," said Tommy. "I was hoping to maybe get started again but I'm a little worried about it lately. I kind of hit a wall right before I left New York."

"We could drive down to New York and get some of your old paintings," suggested Sam.

"No, I can't do that. I mean I could but I don't want to. It was pretty hard for me to get out of there and I don't want to go back any time soon. You know it's like when you leave a girl or a job and you just can't bear the idea of showing your face for a while, you know?"

"I can help with that," said Sam. "You'll find that I can be very motivational. Besides I'm a fast painter — not as good as you necessarily, but I'm fast. I can tell already by your slides that your problem is psychological, or philosophical or whatever, and not a matter of technique. You're obviously good. What's the most you ever sold a painting for in New York?"

"I don't know, usually around five hundred bucks I guess. I sold a couple for more when I was hot, but in New York that isn't saying much. Anything less than a grand is like an embarrassment."

"See that's what I'm talking about," said Sam. "We could teach each other. You teach me how to be slow and good and I'll teach you how to be fast. Whataya say? !" Sam held up his beer bottle and waited for Tommy to tap his own against it. Reluctantly Tommy did so.

"Fuck yeah. We're gonna paint tonight!"

"Tonight?"

"You said you're slow right? So we gotta start as soon as possible. I'll take you over to my studio in P'town." Tommy was surprised to hear that Sam had a studio but he was quickly learning that Sam was full of surprises.

Having got that bit of business out of the way Sam decided they didn't have to stay at the Bomb Shelter any longer. They jumped in the truck and headed for Provincetown.

"You mind if I twist one up?" Sam pulled a baggie of pot out of the front of his pants. "We gotta celebrate."

"You know Sam I already had a manager in New York. That's the other reason I can't get my paintings from New York. After all my friend Antonio Azule financed those paintings, he put me up and bought the materials and everything. I mean when he sells them he'll send me most of the money but I really can't bring myself to take them back just yet. He deserves at least the chance to sell them for a while."

"Antonio Azule?" asked Sam. "What the fuck kind of name is that?"

"That's a perfectly normal name in New York."

"What, you mean he's Spanish?"

"Well he's not Spanish," said Tommy. "But he speaks Spanish sometimes. He's Puerto Rican." Sam smirked and shook his head. "What?" asked Tommy. "Is that funny?"

"You gotta loosen up man I'm just bustin' your balls," said Sam. "Anyway Antonette Aziz might know New York but I know Norman Mailer and Noam Chomsky." With that Sam lit up the joint, took a deep drag and passed it to Tommy, who happened to be driving at the time.

"You know Sam I don't usually smoke weed in my truck while I'm driving."

"Right," said Sam. "But if I'm going to be your manager you're gonna have to defer to my judgment on these sorts of things from now on. You might think you know how to be a New York artist but you don't know Jack about being an Outer Cape one." Tommy took the joint and hit it.

"I don't want to find out about being an Outer Cape felon either."

"I know all the cops down here," said Sam.

"That I believe."

They drove for about ten miles until they reached Provincetown. Sam had Tommy take the smaller roads along the bay. They saw the harbor in Truro, and then, across the bay, the Provincetown skyline sparkling on the water like Van Gogh's "Starry Night".

They arrived in Provincetown by way of the beach on the east end of Commercial. One never went to the north or the south in Provincetown, only to the east or the west. They went east, which would bring them by a few places Sam wanted Tommy to see. They passed Norman Mailer's house, a red brick tomb of a house, partially obscured behind a hedge. From the east it overlooked the bay and the breakwater behind Provincetown center. Sam told Tommy how he had been an extra in Mailer's movie "Tough Guys Don't Dance" . They needed some guys to look like real year-rounders and so they gave Sam ninety bucks an hour just to show up.

"I didn't need a wardrobe or make-up," said Sam. "That was how I met Mailer for the first time. It was like me and some drag queens and movie stars hanging around Mailer's piano smoking a joint. You can't make that shit up. That's when I first saw your Dad's painting. It was in the living room over his fireplace."

"What movie stars?" Asked Tommy.

"Ryan O'Neal, Farah Faucet, and some other people. I even did coke with Ryan O'Neal."

"Really?" said Tommy.

"Oh he's cool. And then I partied with some other guy, Wings Howser. He was famous, on BayWatch and some other shit. The scene I did had a hot chick with her tits out. Man she was good-looking."

"Really?"

"I kid you not. I was thinking about going out to Hollywood to see what would happen, but can you picture me in L.A.?"

"No" said Tommy. "Not really."

"Exactly," said Sam. "Besides I've always felt I should stay around to help Jack. He probably made it sound like I don't care but I'm always looking out for him you know?"

"I can see that," said Tommy. "So Norman Mailer's a pretty cool guy though huh?"

"He's alright," said Sam. "He might be too cute by half."

"No."

"He's an awesome writer."

"Is he?"

"You gotta read The Naked and The Dead and The Deer Park Tommy. No guy down here can claim to be educated if he hasn't read at least that much."

Not more than ten houses or so after passing Mailer's they passed the former home of John Dos Passos. "I don't know who that is," Tommy admitted.

"You will," said Sam.

"I suppose no one can claim to be educated without knowing about him either?"

"Well if you must know," said Sam. "He's fucking huge. Everybody knows about Dos Passos. I mean basically I'm embarrassed for you that you don't know about him. He's like bigger than Mailer really."

"Really?" Asked Tommy.

"What the fuck do you read anyway?"

"I read Kerouac," offered. Tommy.

"Of course," said Sam. "And Henry Miller?"

"Henry Miller changed my life," said Tommy.

"Everyone says that," said Sam.

"No, seriously, I'm not kidding. After I read Black Spring, when I was like twenty-one, I quit my job and hit the road just like that. Just to be a real artist, ya know?"

"I know what you mean," said Sam. "I wanted to do that too but I think Miller just ended up making me use the word "cunt" a lot more. He kind of liberated that word you know? He made it seem respectable and literary."

"I'm still afraid to use it," said Tommy.

"Well at least I know I'm not wasting my time," said Sam. "Miller, really? That's something."

They continued through the center of town where Sam pointed to a few places they might like to have a show once they got some paintings together and then they drove into the far West End where there were beautiful little houses with gardens on tiny narrow roads. Sam showed Tommy a shack on a wooden pier overlooking Lands End. "That was the original workshop for the Provincetown Players and the first place that Eugene O'Neal's plays were performed. Do you know how important Eugene O'Neal is to American theater, or even to the world theater?" Asked Sam.

"I think so," said Tommy.

"No," said Sam. "You couldn't possibly. He's like Shakespeare. Jack Kerouac is like a pimple on his ass."

"What about painters?" Asked Tommy. "Weren't there a lot of big painters down here?"

"Surprisingly not," said Sam. "I mean there were a ton of painters, and there still are but not as many important ones as you might think. I'd say there were as many painters down here as anywhere in the states, but only a few greats. Robert Motherwell lived in Provincetown. He was one of the "Irascible Eighteen." Among the eighteen were some good artists. New York guys like Pollock, de Kooning and Rauschenberg. Your father was probably friends with all those guys. Now that the dust has settled it's pretty well known that unlike those other guys Motherwell couldn't paint his way out of a wet paper bag. You ever see "Elegy to the Spanish Republic No. 34?"

"I've seen it in person."

"It sucked, am I right?" said Sam. "His deal was that he was a philosophy professor who never painted anything before the heroic big breakthrough fad hit in America. Apparently his literary and philosophical background convinced him that painting was no longer about talent. It was about where you fit in art history and so you had to have a radically new way of painting to be important. It was all about the next big breakthrough. If people didn't get it, well that was even better since it was all about confounding expectations of what a painting was supposed to be doing anyway. They had reached the end of the line for the old-fashioned draftsmen. Traditional art was pronounced dead. In that sense it was kind of like punk rock, only it happened forty years earlier. In the history of art, painting has always been ahead of music, just like music has always been ahead of the novel. They all go through the same inevitable movements, and, interestingly, even in the same order, but not at the same time. Painting is the canary in the coal mine. Motherwell was the perfect example of that. He painted a giant black blob on a twenty foot canvas but at the time people thought they were looking at the next Mona Lisa."

"And people fell for it?" Asked Tommy. "I mean they liked it?"

"Oh they loved it," said Sam. "They couldn't get enough of it. Basically it was an emperor with no clothes type of thing.. Even now the temptation to be heroic and misunderstood at all costs hasn't completely worn off. Sometimes I'm tempted to crank out a few Abstract Expressionism ditties myself just to cash in on it if you know what I mean. But I can't do it. I can't paint something that I know is bullshit, even if I know it will impress people and sell. That's why ultimately I'm an idealist, if you can believe it."

"Oh I believe it," said Tommy. "What other painters were around here back in the day?"

"Well there was Hawthorne," said Sam. "He started a school down here, kind of an American version of the French Impressionists. He was actually really good. I'd say more so than anyone he basically set the tone for the way all the Provincetown painters have been ever since. It's like that whole blotchy, brightly colored, purple and orange, landscape style that you see all over the place in the galleries down here. If you could pull that style off Tommy we could make a fortune. Me, I can't really paint that way, but I do respect it."

"That's a little bit more like my father's style I think."

"Exactly," said Sam. "Obviously he was awesome. But I don't think of him as a P'town painter. He was a New Yorker who just happened to end up in Truro."

"Some of his best work was down here," said Tommy.

"No doubt," said Sam. "Even so, if anything I'd say he was a Truro, or a Wellfleet, artist, not a P'town artist."

"There's a difference?"

"Oh it's huge," said Sam. "Truro and Wellfleet are real. My studio may be in P'town but I'm a Wellfleetian without a doubt. I think your father knew that difference as well. He never went in for P'town crap. While everyone painted seascapes and boats he looked inward and painted the streets in town and the woods and the dunes. He never took the easy way out.

"You should teach a class on this shit," said Tommy. "It seems like you're really into the history of it all."

"History being the key word," said Sam. "The Cape is gone now. It used to be a place for the outcasts but that was too good to last I guess. I'm just glad I got a taste of it before it died out. Everyone wanted to get in on the fun, and who could blame them? But that killed it. Now it's just a place for rich yuppies. In my own short life I've seen this place go from a genuine artist colony to a bastardized parody of itself.

"It still seems pretty cool to me," said Tommy.

"You didn't see it before," said Sam. "Besides, just wait until after Memorial Day. By then this place will be overrun with tourists and you'll be hiding out in Truro."

"Well at least you can sell them paintings maybe?" Offered Tommy.

"You think tourists buy paintings? They buy tee shirts, bumper stickers and lobster ashtrays. You watch. I'll sell your paintings, but I'll sell them to nostalgic year-rounders who can barely afford them."

Tommy and Sam drove around town and Sam showed him such notable places as "The A House" , a cool, ivy covered, haunt on a dead end alley behind Commercial Street, where Henry David Thoreau wrote, among other things, a famous letter to Ralph Waldo Emerson in 1857. A century later the cozy vibe was as strong as ever when Billie Holiday and Charlie Parker did heroin and kissed by the fire. Sam explained how the A-House had now evolved into the ultimate oxymoron: "a rustic discothèque".

Sam took Tommy by the old graveyard behind Bradford Street, off Shank Painter Road. They had to jump a chain link fence and brave their way through a briar patch just to get inside. The thin, weathered, lichen-covered slate headstones, had skulls with wings on them and some were three hundred years old. Amazingly, this was not a tourist spot, or even open to the public. Some of the graves were scattered through a patch of dunes and forest so overgrown and inhospitable that tombs were actually partially exposed and sticking out from the side of an eroded hillside. "These are the crypts of the original witches, rakes, and rogues of P'town," said Sam. Tommy was totally impressed. Sam told him that if he wanted to know more about the cool old forgotten graves on the lower Cape he should ask Goody about it.

"She knows where all the secret bone yards are down here. Some of them, out in the woods in Truro, are so secret she hasn't even shown me where they are yet."

"That's awesome," said Tommy. "I'm surprised to hear you pay Goody a compliment."

"How so?" Sam seemed perturbed. Tommy laughed nervously.

"No, I didn't mean anything."

"So what are you saying?" Asked Sam.

"Nothing," said Tommy. "I guess I just got the impression that you were kind of hard on her, but what do I know?" Sam took his time and thought about it.

"She's pretty cute though, right? I mean she's good looking, wouldn't you say?"

"Sure," said Tommy. "She's pretty."

"Just do me a favor and don't even think about it," said Sam. "I like you Tommy and I don't want anything to come between us."

"Shit of course not. It never even crossed my mind."

"Fair enough," said Sam. "I'm just giving you a heads up. That's where I draw the line." Tommy tried to laugh.

"Of course. What do you think? I'm not some kind of asshole."

"Cool," said Sam. "But I don't want to hear about how I give her a hard time or anything like that if it's all the same to you."

"Right," said Tommy. "I get it." Sam put his hand on Tommy's shoulder.

"I'll get you laid this summer, don't worry about it."

"Awesome," said Tommy.

They hit the packie on the corner of Bradford and Shank Painter where they got beer and papers before heading to Sam's studio in Pablo Golokovsky's garage. Pablo was a local young poet, and a Cape Cod Community College student, who lived with his parents, and had been, at least until Tommy's recent arrival, Sam's most promising protégé. Sam had set up shop in Pablo's father's garage, in a swanky west end house overlooking the ocean. He had been painting there for the better part of six months.

Tommy took his fold-up easel and followed Sam inside. Clearly he had been busy. There were several easels, quite a few with half done paintings on them and everywhere there were piles of paints and brushes. The room was nearly buried in magazines and books and littered with dirty clothes, cigarette butts and empty beer bottles. Apparently Sam was not picky about materials or methods; as well as canvases he had painted all sorts of plywood, bricks, rocks, seashells, not to mention the walls and the furniture.

"Sometimes I do folk art," said Sam referring to a small end table decorated with boats and clouds. "I know it's looked down on but I'm trying to make folk art cool again you know?"

"I get that," said Tommy. "I mean what is folk art really? Those kinds of distinctions don't mean a thing."

"That's my point," said Sam. "You gotta paint something' so why not a table?"

"This place is awesome Sam. It feels like you could get a lot done here doesn't it?"

"It does have a good vibe doesn't it?" Sam turned on a number of lamps and lights all over the room. He had aluminum work lamps clamped over the tops of all the easels, as well as a wide assortment of desk lamps and even several bare bulbs hanging around the room.

"Got enough light?" Asked Tommy.

"Ok here's the thing," said Sam. "You're probably one of these guys that think painting outside in the perfect light and all that is key. Am I right?"

"I guess," said Tommy. "I mean I don't usually do that but I assume it must be better."

"Wrong," said Sam. "You gotta be able to paint anywhere and anytime, which is, if you think about it, usually in the middle of the night. You can't wait around for optimum conditions. Painting outside with a floppy hat and a French easel is for old ladies and tourists. If I had a dime for every piece of shit down here posing on the side of the road with a floppy hat and a three-hundred dollar field easel." Sam looked at Tommy's Van Gogh-style fold-up easel. "No offense," he added.

"No of course. Painting outside is cool like just to stay in touch with the way some really good people paint you know? I mean the fresh air and all that. But ultimately you need privacy. Besides, painting inside makes you look inside. When you don't look at things you tend to paint more from the way they look inside. I think that's important. I don't want to paint the way things really look, that's what cameras are for."

"That's what I'm saying!" Said Sam. "And then when you do paint outside and look at shit you end up painting it the way you imagine it anyway, at least I do."

"Yeah me too," said Tommy. "One time I painted all day out in the woods for like ten hours and I did this really cool painting of trees and it was great to be outside in the woods and everything but when it was all said and done it looked exactly like what I would have done in the middle of the night in my apartment, and let's face it there's no wind, no bugs, no rain, and no people. You can control the environment inside and that's way better."

"Exactly," said Sam. "You gotta control the environment. And for that you gotta have a shit load of lights."

"Ok," said Tommy. "The brighter the better, I got it."

"Very bright," said Sam. "Everybody down here is all about big windows with north light you know?" Sam's studio had no windows. "I say there's nothing like a sealed up space with a few 120 watt bulbs in the middle of the night to get you in the mood."

"It's like how they don't have windows and clocks in Vegas casinos," offered Tommy.

"Right," said Sam. "Once you're in here working on a painting the rest of the world ceases to exist. Now don't get me wrong. I know it would be great to be a painter like Monet or Van Gogh and to not have a job or anything so you can just sit around all day and wait for the perfect sunset or whatever, but that just ain't realistic in our modern lives."

"Definitely not," said Tommy. "And then when the light is just right outside it changes like ten minutes later."

"Right," said Sam. "But the real point is that you just have to do it whenever you can, which for me is usually at night anyway." Sam put in a Muddy Waters CD. "You like Blues?"

"I do," said Tommy. "What about bluegrass? '

"Sure," said Sam. "I like the real country too. Not pop, but like real country, like George Jones and Hank Williams and shit like that."

"Me too," said Tommy. "You like Tom Waits? I listen to him when I'm painting."

"I like Waits," said Sam.

"Really?" Tommy was impressed. People didn't usually know about Tom Waits.

"He's a goddamn national treasure like Jerry Garcia or Bob Dylan," said Sam as he fumbled through his pile of plywood. He picked out two pieces, one for himself and one for Tommy. "You ever paint on plywood?"

"What are you kidding?" He laughed. "Well actually no, not really. But I'll give it a shot"

"Well get used to it," said Sam. "I got a lot of plywood. Canvas is for art school guys with French easels."

"It's kind of rough and lumpy," said Tommy.

"Life is rough and lumpy," said Sam. "You just gotta put the paint on it thick." Sam was busy setting up his easel and assembling his supplies. Tommy started setting up as well.

"I'm thinking of fish," said Sam. "I'm gonna paint some fish."

"That sounds good. I don't know what to do. Do you mind if I paint fish too?"

"I insist," said Sam. "You can't go wrong with fish. And you gotta have plenty of beer too. That's key." He took a swig. "Don't you find that to be true?"

"I do," said Tommy. "Bright light, tunes and beer. Is that your formula for a good painting?"

"They don't teach you that in art school," said Sam. They both began to paint. It felt odd for Tommy to paint on cue like that and even more so with somebody else there painting as well. Sam scrutinized Tommy's supplies. He picked up one of his brushes.

"You use these tiny little things? No wonder it takes you forever." Sam showed Tommy one of his big course brushes. "Now that's a man's brush."

"You could sweep the floor with that thing," said Tommy.

"I just might," said Sam. "What do you use for a medium?" He picked up, and then smelled, each of the little vials in Tommy's collection.

"Just a bunch of stuff. You know, dammar, linseed, turp, stuff like that."

"I use gasoline, beer, and black Sharpies." Sam wasn't kidding. He guzzled his beer, dipped the tip of a Sharpie in a small saucer of gas and proceeded to scribble all over the plywood. He scribbled until it created a complex mass of blurs and net-like effects which took about a half hour or so to really get going. He then looked for the fish randomly suggested by the scribbles in the way one might look for them in the clouds, once isolated they were reinforced and then colored in. Tommy was interested in this technique. It was completely different than the way he usually got started. Normally he spent a long time planning a subject but he could see that that wasn't going to go over well with Sam. He just grabbed a brush and some paint straight from the tube and jumped in. They painted for a while without talking.

After an hour or so when they were both totally into what they were doing Pablo Golokovsky showed up. He was a good-looking, tall, blue-eyed blond guy in his early twenties with an expensive looking polo shirt and a slight Spanish accent.

"Well all right," said Pablo. "A little action in the studio." Sam introduced them and they shook hands.

"Pablo, this is my buddy Tommy Cobb. He just started working for Jack. He's a New York painter so do me a favor and don't be a pain in the ass and embarrass yourself."

"Right on," said Pablo. They continued to paint while Tommy and Pablo chatted. Pablo told him how he was Argentinean but had spent most of his life in Provincetown and how he was a student and an aspiring poet. He explained that his father had a lot of money for some reason and how he sometimes lamented that fact because it kept people from taking him seriously as a poet, and this was something which he was obviously very into. Sam then interjected that it was probably hard for people to take him seriously because he was such a spoiled pretty boy who still lived off his parents. Tommy told Pablo that he could relate in that his father had also been a successful artist.

"Yeah except you don't have any money," added Sam.

"True," said Tommy.

"Why is that?" Asked Pablo. "I mean if you don't mind my asking." Sam stopped painting for a moment. He was curious as well but had enough class and maturity not to ask.

"Yeah my father kind of fucked over my Mom in that sense," said Tommy. "He was already married when he met her and they never really got together even though my Mom wanted to. The whole thing was a big family secret. Anyway my Mom ended up trying to put the whole thing out of her mind I guess. He was like thirty years older than her and he died when I was just a baby. Still I can't seem to live it down."

"Life is tough," said Sam sarcastically.

"Speaking of prick fathers," said Pablo to Sam. "My dad wants to know if you have anything for him." Sam rolled his eyes and pulled a small bag of pot from his shirt pocket.

"Here, give him this."

"That's it?" Asked Pablo.

"Tell him it's really good. That's some serious stuff." Pablo took it and smelled it before putting it in his pocket.

"No he'll be psyched," said Pablo. "Moms out at her sisters and he's got his chips and cheese steak all ready and the game on. This will make his night. I'd better go give it to him right now." Pablo excused himself and stepped out.

Once he was gone Sam explained to Tommy that Pablo was a bit lost but still a good kid and that he had taken him under his wing so to speak.

"He's a punk poet," explained Sam.

"Is he any good?"

"Actually he's not bad," said Sam. "But don't tell him I said that. He's got a long way to go and the last thing he needs is encouragement." They continued to paint a while and eventually Pablo returned with a beer and a laptop computer.

"He was psyched," said Pablo.

"Of course he was," said Sam. "Your father is not such an asshole really when you think about it."

"No he is," said Pablo. "He's a total dick believe me."

Sam was already almost done with his painting and Tommy thought it looked pretty good. Tommy on the other hand had barely started. He tried to paint faster.

"What about me?" Asked Pablo. "You gonna twist one up or what?" Sam handed him his bag.

"Don't go crazy," he said. "That's all I got and me and Tommy have a lot of work to do tonight."

"I'm all right," said Tommy.

"I'll tell you when you're all right," said Sam. "Just keep painting."

Pablo snatched the bag from Sam's hand and flopped down on the couch. He pulled his big glass bong out from behind the couch, packed it and did a couple of hits. He melted into the couch. Tommy and Sam kept painting. Pablo opened his computer and reread his latest poem to himself. He fidgeted around and occasionally laughed quietly to himself.

"All right," said Sam. "Read one of your poems to Tommy and get it over with."

"You don't mind?" Asked Pablo.

"Just do it before I change my mind," said Sam.

"This one is really good," said Pablo. "I mean this might be the best one yet. I was up all last night working on it."

"Of course you were," said Sam. "Just go ahead already." Sam hit pause on the CD player. Pablo stood up and cleared his throat. He put the computer on the table so he could read from it while standing.

"Ok," he said. "It's called Huck Finn is the New Buddha."

"Of course it is," said Sam. "That sounds about right. Wait a minute, let me get a beer before we do this." Sam cracked a beer and went back to work on his painting. Tommy stopped painting and waited.

"Ok here we go. It's called "Huck Finn is the New Buddha."

"Got it," said Sam. Pablo carefully read aloud from the computer screen:

HUCK FINN IS THE NEW BUDDHA by Pablo Golokovsky.

Morning swam by dreaming of nothing
But coffee and french-fries.
In the streets I noticed only the posers
The pretty people.
Pasty faced art fags,
How I love their meaty red lips.
Heavy boots help them to remember
With blue black mops.
Some are breeders like myself
And are unexpectedly bright.
Many of these mops become so bright
They can't even smoke a cigarette
Without having an anxiety attack.
Smell the low tide.
Provincial towns are paragons of duplicity,
A dreamy abstraction.
Elegance is a cautious celebration indeed.
Smell fried clams, homemade fudge.
Street music from lesbian crooners.
Overheard a hunchbacked woman ask
If her friend was a bottom.
I knew she was a top,
An aggressor.
I told her happiness is chaos .
Love is easy ostrich pop culture.
Life is cyclical and it turns into soup.
I've heard only vegetable soup is ethical.
Empirical jelly beans swept into pyramids of ash.
River boats of good will carry the new Buddha.
I met the new Buddha at community college
And I killed him on the spot.
I tried to explain Buddha to a stranger at a bar.
He knew who he was.
Slow and sure, not like Gary Cooper,

More like Spencer Tracy.
Old man beside me at the bar
Is defeated in advance.
Shot of brandy, glass of wine.
He lights a cigarette and the weighty fluid in his eyes
Sparkles beside the flame.
Embarrassed by his silence I walk away.
I have no time for this unpromising old man.

Pablo paused dramatically and then shut his laptop and flopped into the couch and lit a cigarette. Tommy waited for Sam's reaction. Sam kept painting. "Well that was pretty good if you ask me," said Tommy. "It's a damn good poem Pablo." Pablo smiled. Of course Tommy would say that. Tommy was right, it was pretty good but he also knew that technically it wasn't really good either. Sam would know that. It had certain problems. It was too sentimental, too derivative. Sam continued to paint for a few more minutes in silence.

"You don't have to say that Tommy just because you're new around here," said Sam. "He needs to hear the truth."

"No I liked it," said Tommy. "That shit was deep."

"He knows it's bullshit," said Sam.

"Maybe he just likes it," said Pablo.

"So now you're a Buddhist? I thought you were a Catholic. Since when are you a Buddhist?"

"I didn't say I was a Buddhist or a Catholic. You know art is a religion in a way."

"So you're a pagan like Goody and Jack?"

"Isn't Jack a Reverend?"

"He worships his wood pile," said Sam. "And anyway what the fuck do you know about the Buddha? And who the fuck are you to talk about Garry Cooper and Spencer Tracy? I should kick your ass talking about Gary Cooper and Spencer Tracy. Name one movie Garry Cooper was in. Can you do that for me at least? Tracy wasn't even slow and sure anyway, he was a fag, did you know that?"

"He was fucking Katherine Hepburn for like twenty-five years," said Tommy. "And he was married the whole time. Also he drank a lot. And he was very cool."

"See now this guy knows what he's talking about," said Sam to Pablo.

"But Cooper on the other hand," said Tommy. "He was fucking Ingrid Bergman, that's even better. Man she was so hot."

"He may have been fucking Ingrid but when it came to acting he was kind of stiff," said Sam. "You couldn't compare him to Spencer Tracy. There's no comparison."

"That's my point," said Pablo. "That's Buddhist."

"You wish that was the point," said Sam. "But it isn't. The point of the poem has to do with how Huck Finn is the new Buddha. By that I assume you mean that because Huck was a morally right boy who nonetheless got into trouble with his spontaneity and intuition that he was in fact a kind of modern Buddha, a uniquely American Buddha at that. That's the point of the poem. I'm not saying it pulls that off, I'm just saying that would be the point of the poem if it actually did have a point. That's what it wants to be about."

"I agree," said Pablo. "That's it exactly. Sam you're a fucking genius. That's what I was saying."

"Well almost," said Sam.

"I think I see what you're saying," said Tommy.

"You don't have to agree with him," said Pablo. "He knows he's right."

"I used to be a Catholic but now I'm agnostic," said Tommy.

"Art is my religion," said Pablo.

"The hell it is," said Sam. "Community College is your religion."

"I met the Buddha at community college and I killed him on the spot," said Pablo. "You have to admit that's a cool line. It's totally deep. You know because enlightenment comes from within? The saying goes "if you meet the Buddha out on the road kill him on the spot." You know like I learned about him in community college and I killed him there? Come on, that's cool right?"

"That's cool," said Tommy. "I get it."

"Yeah but you didn't kill him," said Sam. "You ate that shit up. You know nothing about Buddha, Huck Finn or Cooper and Tracy yet you write about them because you think it sounds like Ginsburg or Bukowski. You're just aping the stuff they told you in community college."

" No, I just really want to write like Bukowski."

"Bukowski didn't write about Buddhism," said Sam. "He just was a Budhha himself."

"Like Huck Finn," said Tommy.

"Yeah except Huck Finn was kind of stupid and he was made to believe. Bukoski was real. And he didn't have time for Buddha. He didn't have time for religion or politics or even metaphors in a poem. He just cut away all that and went straight to the bone. To write like him you basically have to do the exact opposite of what you did with that poem. But other than that it sounds just like him."

"So what do I have to do?" Asked Pablo.

"That's easy," said Sam. "All you have to do is be an ugly motherfucker. You can't underestimate the effect that has on a person. Then get abused by your father for your entire childhood and then work a humiliating and monotonous job at the post office for ten years. Then come talk to me about sounding like Bukowski."

"Was he really that ugly?" Asked Tommy, while he continued to paint. Sam was also painting away furiously.

"He had a face that would make a freight train take a left turn up a dirt road," said Sam. "He had severe debilitating acne."

"Debilitating?" Asked Tommy.

"He had to go to a doctor every couple of weeks just to have that shit lanced and drained. He had backne and assne too. He had it all over him all his life. That's what made him such a good writer."

"Interesting," said Pablo.

"So just to clarify," said Tommy. "You're saying Bukowski had a pimply ass?"

"That's common knowledge," said Sam.

"Man that's tough," said Tommy.

"Yeah well we can't all be that lucky," said Pablo. "We have to work with whatever we've been given in life."

"And he didn't go to college," said Sam. "I fucking hate people who went to college."

"I didn't go to college," said Tommy.

"You dodged a bullet there," said Sam.

"So you hate me?" Asked Pablo.

"Community college doesn't count," said Sam.

"Bukowski didn't have to read Shakespeare and all that shit," said Pablo. "He wrote from his heart."

"Oh he read Shakespeare," said Sam. "And Joyce and Dostoyevsky and all that stuff. You better believe he read all that and he could tell you what it was about too. He could probably even tell you what Finnegan's Wake was about."

"Nobody knows what Finnegan's Wake is about," said Tommy. "That's kind of the point of I think."

"Sure they do," said Sam. "I read it. It's about a father who's dying and about his two sons and how they each react differently to his impending doom. In the beginning Finnegan falls and the entire story takes place before he hits the ground. It all happens like in a dream and the fact that it's his wake is like a play on the word. Like will he wake from his dream or will he die? Or like, is he already dead and they're having his wake?"

"Well anyway," said Pablo. I may not be a poor ugly drunk but I want to be like Bukowski minus all that."

"He drank all day just to relieve the pain of his shitty life," said Sam.

"Just think of how good he would have been if he weren't an alcoholic," said Pablo.

"And if a frog had wings," said Sam "he wouldn't bump his ass from hopping all the time."

"If you know half as much about fish as you do about art you must be one hell of a fisherman," said Tommy.

"Oh I know fish. I know where fish are gonna be before they even get there. I know what they're thinking."

"He's not kidding," said Pablo.

"I mean look at this thing? Do I know fish or what?" Sam held up his painting. It was a complex interwoven mess of fish. Is that beautiful or what?"

By the end of the night Sam had completed two paintings and started on a third. Tommy's first painting was barely started. "It's all up in my head," he explained.

"A lot of good it's doin' up there," said Sam.

Chapter Fourteen

After her discussion with Frank about the possibility of publishing her pig eye research in the fall, Apple was full of a renewed enthusiasm for her work and so she decided she had better take another crack at Jack's Gas. She got Kalensin washed and she was all shiny and sparkling in the sun as she pulled up to the pumps. Tommy was excited to see Apple's car and he jumped into action. "Hey Apple! How's it going? Fill'er up huh?"

"Why not," said Apple smiling. This time she looked at Tommy a little closer. Would she be able to go through with it? She had been preparing herself for the worst. Actually he wasn't that bad, a little rough around the edges maybe, a definite fixer-upper but not without potential. She liked that he had kind eyes and nice teeth. She found his lack of style and refinement oddly compelling. He looked like he had grown up in the woods, like he had been raised by wolves. If he had anything going for him at all it was that he was practically dressed in rags. He wasn't the type she went out with in the past that was for sure. He probably hadn't even gone to college. Apple liked to think that wasn't the kind of thing that would influence her appraisal of him either way.

"It only took a couple of gallons," said Tommy. He removed the pump nozzle. "You barely used any since the last time you were here."

"Well I suppose I just wanted a frozen Milky Way," said Apple. "You haven't eaten them all yet I hope."

"Not yet." She handed him the money and he took it. "You should start a tab," he said as he went inside to get the candy. When he returned Apple was standing outside. She wore her hair down with sunglasses, sandals, tight jeans and a light summery top. She looked damn good and she knew it. Guys were easy that way anyway. Still she had taken a few extra steps to make sure that she looked good for this second meeting. She didn't wear makeup however, that was where she drew the line. If he didn't like the way her face looked naturally then tough shit for him. She would only wear makeup and a dress if somebody died or got married, she had her priorities. She didn't want him to think she was trying to look good for him, not any better than usual anyway. That would have clearly ruined the effect that she was going for. Tommy was indeed impressed by her looks as he handed her the candy. He appeared distracted and nervous. His hands were slightly shaking. She thought maybe he didn't take meeting a pretty girl lightly. It was obvious to Apple that he would be lucky to go out with her and that he knew this and that he would therefore handle the situation with the proper respect and gravity that she felt it deserved. Needless to say it was ironic that she felt this way given the fact that her main reason for trying to meet him was only to get a better look at the gas station. Still she was conflicted and wanted to have her cake and eat it too. She wanted to manipulate Tommy and play him toward her own nefarious goal while simultaneously keeping the possibility open that maybe she actually did like him. Tommy's own motives were less complex. He wanted to touch her and kiss her, and possibly if things went really well, to sleep with her. He looked at her very closely and decided that he probably hadn't ever kissed anybody quite as pretty, certainly not lately.

"Enjoy," said Tommy referring to the candy bar.

"Any change?" Asked Apple.

"Change only comes from within," said Tommy. He thought that sounded clever enough. Apple smiled; maybe he was clever after all? Perhaps he had gone to college? But he didn't look like a guy that went to college. He looked like a guy that spent the past ten years sleeping. He looked like a guy that worked at a gas station. This was something Apple would have to see about. When you went to a school like Harvard you don't bring it up. She didn't want to set up a situation where she came across looking conceited. That was her cross to bear. She needed to learn to be less revealing and more mysterious. Her primary concern in this regard was not so much not to be a conceited person as it was to not appear to be one.

"Let me ask you something Tommy," she said. "Do you know anything about the Hindu god Krishna?" Tommy shook his head. "I mean I've heard of him, but no not really."

"What have you heard about him?" She asked.

"Well I know that he was a real historical figure and not completely made up like most of the other Hindu gods. And I know that he wasn't actually blue, but I'll bet he did play the flute. And I know that as a religion it's not as hokey as people think it is."

"No? I don't think so either," said Apple.

"People get the wrong idea from American Hare Krishnas. In India it's not a cult or anything. It's a mainstream religion."

Me, I'm more of a Buddha guy. I like to think of myself as half Catholic, half Buddhist." At this point Tommy realized that he may have been laying it on a bit thick.

"Interesting," said Apple. "And you don't find that to be any kind of a contradiction or an oxymoron or anything like that?"

"Not at all," said Tommy. "Why do you ask?"

"No reason," said Apple. "Anyway what is it that you like about Buddhism Tommy?"

"Well I like the idea that the whole world as we know it doesn't actually exist. I find that kind of reassuring," said Tommy. Apple laughed.

"And how in the world could that possibly be reassuring?"

"Well that opens up a whole can of worms doesn't it?" Said Tommy. "You know with like Bukowski and Henry Miller and Allen Ginsburg and all that stuff?" Tommy was clearly treading on thin ice here but he thought he was doing so well he might like to try out some of his new Sam and Pablo ideas on her.

"I'm not into writers that promote drug use," said Apple.

"No me either," said Tommy. "But those books aren't about that."

"Are you sure?"

"Yes I'm sure," said Tommy. "You know Henry Miller was pretty smart."

"I've heard," said Apple.

"He was like an American sage, ya know? Anyway one of my friends tells me that Huckleberry Finn is the new Buddha?"

"How so?" Asked Apple.

"You know on account of his moral spontaneity and all that."

"You mean Huckleberry Finn's?"

"Yeah."

"Interesting," said Apple. "I guess I can understand that. You know I once had a boyfriend whose favorite book was Tropic of Cancer, me I couldn't get past the first ten pages of it. "

"He must have been very smart," said Tommy. Apple laughed.

"He was kind of an ass. My old boyfriend I mean, not Miller."

"Well if he liked that book he couldn't have been too bad," said Tommy.

"Ok so Henry Miller was smart," said Apple. "He clearly knew about something to fill up all those books, but did he really have to use the word 'cunt' so much? I mean as a woman that's got to make you wonder. I mean what was his problem anyway? Who uses the word "cunt" that much?"

"It was just a gimmick," said Tommy. "But you have a point. I guess there aren't a whole lot of women who like Henry Miller are there? Come to think of it, I'm pretty sure I've never met a woman who actually did like him."

"Maybe that should tell you something," said Apple.

They heard Jack's chain sawing out back. Apple looked at the woodpile which was now starting to spill around from the back wood lot and had begun to envelop the sides of the gas station as well. "Is it my imagination or did that wood pile get bigger already?"

"He's a man on a mission," said Tommy. "I have to hand it to Jack. He's a hard worker and he knows exactly what he wants out of life."

"And what's that exactly?" Asked Apple.

"More wood," said Tommy. "Jack figures you can never have too much wood."

"And so that's his name, Jack?"

"No, but he's been called worse," said Tommy. Apple smiled and there was a little bit of an awkward pause. "How are the pictures?" Asked Tommy.

"The pictures?"

"Your photography?"

"Oh right. Not very good I guess. I'm working on it."

"I'll bet they're great," said Tommy. "Especially the ones you took of Jack. It seems to me he's a good subject. I'll bet he photographs like Abraham Lincoln. He just has that intense look you know?"

"He looks like Samuel Becket," said Apple.

"Right," said Tommy. He knew that Sam would know what Becket looked like. "Well anyway I'd like to see them sometime."

"Oh I'd be too embarrassed I think."

"Well I'd be a sympathetic viewer," said Tommy. "I'm an artist myself and so I know how exposed it makes you feel."

"I'm no artist," said Apple. Again there was a bit of a pregnant pause while Tommy tried to think of what to say next.

"What kind of art do you do Tommy?"

"I'm a painter. I mean I'm not saying I'm good or anything like that, just that I'm a painter because that's what I like to do."

"That's very cool," said Apple.

"You think?"

"I do," said Apple. "I have respect for anyone with that kind of patience. I can't sit still for that long. Maybe you could show me your paintings some time?"

"I'll show you my slides," said Tommy.

"Slides?"

"I photographed some of the paintings I did in New York."

"Well I'd like to see them," said Apple.

"I'll make you a deal," said Tommy. "I'll meet you for coffee tonight early. I'll bring my slides and you'll bring some pictures."

Apple agreed but said it would have to be later because she had to go to yoga first. This was a lie. She knew if it were late enough Jack would be asleep and she might get a chance to get inside the gas station again. Also she needed some time to maybe dig up a picture or two which might make it appear that she was at least interested in photography. Indeed she had always intended to get into photography, but until now she just hadn't got around to it.

For the rest of the day Tommy was happy and thought of nothing else other than Apple. He replayed the things they had said to each other over in his mind. He thought maybe he shouldn't have told her he was a painter. He reminded himself that it would be better if he could remain somewhat mysterious and not put his cards on the table so quickly. Still he had to tell her he was a painter. After all, he had to find some way to impress her, otherwise why would a girl like her go out with a gas station attendant? She was obviously sophisticated and intellectual, she knew about Samuel Becket and Krishna and she drove an Audi. She was what he and some of his old friends in New York used to call a "teasock" . She definitely had an ace or two up her sleeve. He suddenly realized that he hadn't even asked her what she did for a living. That was a mistake. Clearly she was an accomplished person and probably quite proud of whatever it is that she did for a living. He reproached himself for not asking. "She probably thinks I'm self absorbed. I gotta remember to not talk so much about myself."

Later when they had closed up and Jack retired to his sitting room Tommy decided that he had better take a shower. It was not a good shower but Tommy had no choice. The water was cold and smelled like gasoline. The shower walls and the curtain were covered in black mold.

"You know," said Tommy. "I'm gonna clean that shower for you at some point."

"Be my guest," said Jack.

"I mean not right now because I have a date."

Tommy met Apple at ten o'clock in front of The Bomb Shelter in Wellfleet. "Are you serious with this place? I almost got raped out here." Tommy laughed.

"It's not that bad," said Tommy. "This is where my friends hang out".

"Well you're new around here so I'll cut you a break," said Apple. "Your friends must be interesting."

"You know," said Tommy. "Artists, poets and fishermen. That sort of thing."

They took a seat in a booth in the back of the room. There were some rough characters playing pool and a group of women sat cackling and smoking at the bar. For all of her obvious sophistication and refinement Apple was anything but a snob and she was relieved and happy to see that there were other women around who were clearly safe and having a good time. "I guess it's a little late for coffee. Do you think they could make me a Grey Goose Cosmo?"

"I don't see why not," said Tommy and he got up and headed for the bar. He returned with a pink martini and a pint of Guinness. "For a divey place these guys really know their cocktails." Apple clinked her martini glass against Tommy's pint glass and took a sip. She looked at her drink suspiciously.

"Did you see if he used Goose? It tastes a little funny. I don't think he used Goose."

"The price was right," said Tommy. "It's probably just the dirty glass. So what's up with your photographs? You got them."

"I chickened out," said Apple. "You're the artist Tommy, not me."

"What is it that you do anyway Apple? You've obviously got your shit together whatever it is."

"I'm a scientist," she said.

"That makes sense. You look like a scientist I think. What kind of science?"

"I'm a biologist," said Apple. "Mostly I do toxicology."

"No shit?" Said Tommy. "I'll bet you don't smoke pot either do you? I mean if you don't mind my asking."

"No I don't," said Apple. "Do you?"

"Not really," said Tommy. "I mean not if you don't."

"That wasn't very convincing," said Apple. "Besides, you already admitted you like Henry Miller. You can't take that back."

"Tell me about biology," said Tommy. Apple told him all about the pig eyes. She was having a good time in spite of herself. Was she really interested in this guy? She told herself as long as she's out she might as well try to have a good time. She still had the gas station in the back of her mind.

"So the pig cornea is very similar to the human cornea?" Asked Tommy.

"Precisely," said Apple. "But the really important part is that they can be used post mortem so we wouldn't have to use live animals for eye irritant testing. It could be quite revolutionary."

"That's a very noble cause," said Tommy. "I mean that. Just think about all those rabbits all over the word being subject to torture just so we can test cosmetics and cleaning products. That's one thing about a career in science. You must feel like you're doing something that can really make a difference. It's just so damn noble."

"Not always," said Apple. "Science is like anything else, sometimes you have to get your hands a little dirty."

"I guess that's the irony of being an artist," said Tommy. "You get your hands dirty literally but not figuratively. It's like the one thing in life where you never have to compromise you know? It's pure in that way."

"I'll bet you get your hands dirty working for Jack," said Apple. Tommy pondered that for a moment. "I do," he said.

"So tell me about that Tommy," said Apple. "How did you come to work for him?" Tommy remembered what he decided earlier, that he should remain mysterious and keep her talking about herself, but now that he was pretty sure that she was interested in him he became bold and reckless. He told her all about Richard Cobb as a painter, what kind of a painter he was and about the kinds of subjects he liked. Tommy explained that he had come to Cape

Cod as a pilgrimage to find inspiration in the places that his father had painted.

"My father painted Jack's Gas a very long time ago, well before I was born." He told her about the painting of Jack's done in the forties. "I never even met him," said Tommy.

"That's sad," said Apple. "But I think that sounds like a very sweet idea."

Apple had never heard of Tommy's father but explained that she knew very little about art anyway except that she did enjoy looking at paintings quite a bit more than looking at photography or sculptures. She told Tommy how she loved the impressionist painter Claude Monet and how she had once visited the Orsay museum in Paris and how ever since then she had collected Monet prints for her apartment. Tommy told her that he too had been to the Orsay and had been greatly impressed by it. Apple was surprised that Tommy had been to Paris.

"Twice," said Tommy. "I went Kerouac style. I slept on park benches and in subways and redundant chapels."

"I just did it the regular tourist way," said Apple.

"Oh I was a tourist," said Tommy. But I had to do it on a shoestring. I did Paris on like a couple hundred bucks if you can believe it. Not including the flight."

"That's unheard of," said Apple. "I suppose it's different for men. Women can't just wander around in a place without accommodations and bum around like a young guy can."

"I did the Champs Elysee, The Louver, The Eiffel, Notre Dame, and the Pere Lachaise cemetery. That graveyard was one of the best parts. That's where Balzac and Voltaire are buried, and Jim Morrison. Morrison's grave was beautiful. From there I took a bus all the way to Amsterdam. It was like a fifteen hour drive but it only cost fifty bucks and I got to see Belgium on the way. In Amsterdam I slept for a week in the park under a bush in the rain but it was worth it to see the Van Gogh museum." Apple was impressed. Tommy then lifted up his shit and showed her the very large and colorful Van Gogh portrait he had tattooed on his chest. Apple was embarrassed by Tommy's informality but she was not completely unimpressed by his bare chest and flat stomach.

"Please put that away," she said. She looked around to see if anyone had noticed.

"Sorry," said Tommy. "I'm just really into Van Gogh."

"Well I'm not going to lift up my shirt," said Apple

"You don't have any tattoos," said Tommy. "Do you?"

"Maybe I do but can we change the subject please?"

"Well now I'm excited," said Tommy. "Something to look forward to!" Apple blushed. "But of course Monet is awesome," said Tommy. "He's one of my heroes no doubt"

"He's my favorite," said Apple. "Do you ever paint like Monet?"

"I try," said Tommy. "I mean who wouldn't?"

"Well that would impress me," said Apple.

"Me too," said Tommy. "What about those old black and white photographs of Monet working in his studio and in his garden? Have you ever seen those? I think they would impress you as a photographer." Apple admitted she hadn't seen them. "They're beautiful," said Tommy. "Talk about a guy who photographed intensely like Abe Lincoln. He looked like he was chiseled out of hickory with that brow and that long crazy beard and a cigarette hanging out of his mouth and he had like a navy p-coat jacket and wool pants with brass buttons and those old fashioned leather boots with those big brass buckles like a pirate. Man he was cool. He was like Abraham Lincoln and Jerry Garcia rolled into one."

"I'd like to see them," said Apple. "Have you found all the places yet?" She asked. "The places in your father's postcards?"

"Let me show you," said Tommy. He jumped up. "I'll be right back." He went out to his truck and quickly returned with the postcard book. Apple had a look at them. Tommy showed her the few places he had managed to find so far. Apple lingered over the painting "Gas" . It had the same effect on her that it had on everybody who saw it. She was drawn into it. She found it mesmerizing.

"You look just like him," she said. "It's kind of eerie."

"Yeah," said Tommy. "I do." Apple had a look at the rest of the post cards. She picked out another card and held it under the light.

"I think I know where this one is." She handed Tommy the card. It was a painting of a pharmacy store front, closed and empty in the middle of the night. "This doorway looks familiar," she said. "I think it's right down the street. The pharmacy isn't there anymore but I'm pretty sure this doorway is in Wellfleet by the library. It looks just like it."

"We have to go see it," said Tommy. "This is gonna be awesome."

"We'll go in a little bit," said Apple. "I'm enjoying this place right now."

Tommy never got around to showing Apple his slides. He decided to turn the conversation away from himself. She told him how she had gone to Harvard and that she had a PhD and how she didn't usually admit that. He teased her that it only took her about twenty minutes to get around to it. She told him it was because she trusted him for some reason.

"Your secret is safe with me," he told her. She then told him how her upbringing was embarrassingly bourgeoisie and how her parents were shameless yacht club types and that their names were actually Scooter and Pebbles.

"Let me get this straight," said Tommy. "Your mother's real name is Pebbles?"

"That's right."

"Seriously?" He was teasing her.

"I know," said Apple. "It's embarrassing. Pebbles and Apple. That's like a thing with Cape Cod preppies. See you're still learning all this because you're from off Cape but that's like a thing down here. My aunt's name is Kitty, and I've got an Uncle Junnie Winterbottom if you can believe it and another uncle named Skipper Merryweather believe it or not."

"Wow," said Tommy. "It's like you were born in a Henry James Novel."

"We need help," said Apple. "It's pathetic."

"I know exactly what type you are," said Tommy. "I could tell as soon as I met you. You're a tea sock!"

"A tea sock?"

"Oh you're a classic tea sock," said Tommy. "That's what you are. We have them in New York, though not as many as up here I don't think."

"What's a tea sock?"

"It's a phrase I learned from a German girl in Ireland named Maren Worke. Maren wasn't a tea sock but she told me about what tea socks are like. As soon as she explained it to me I understood and I wished that Maren was a tea sock but she wasn't. She was just a beautiful German milkmaid who liked to party."

"I don't like to party," said Apple. "In fact I never use the word "party" as a verb unless I'm making fun of someone."

"I know," said Tommy. "That's because you're a tea sock."

"Was she really a milkmaid?" Asked Apple.

"She was to me," said Tommy. "She was a real Hardy type of girl with two braids and like overalls and fat red cheeks. We hooked up and hitch hiked together for two weeks and it was like a fantasy for me you know? She was like Tess of the D'Urbervilles, you know?"

"You lost me," said Apple.

"You know, like a tough hitchhiking farmer's daughter type," said Tommy.

"And she told you about tea socks?"

"Right."

"Why am I one?" Asked Apple.

"You're a vegetarian right?" Asked Tommy.

"As a matter of fact I am."

"And you're a liberal democrat of course," said Tommy.

"Who isn't?" Said Apple.

"And you go to work with like your lab coat and your glasses and your ponytail, am I right?"

"I have to tie my hair back. I'm working with toxic chemicals."

"You're totally a tea sock," said Tommy. "I've always liked tea socks but I could never get one to go out with me 'cause I didn't go to college. A tea sock is like a pretty, studious, hippie type girl, or like an alternative rock type girl, you know with the rectangular black framed glasses and the Birkenstocks. They drive like a sensible yet expensive car like a BMW or a Volvo or a Subaru Outback, or in your case a sharp little Audi A4. They're crunchy granola types but totally sober and from rich families and even though they have hippie leanings they never admit it because they're totally against smoking pot even though they listen to like Radiohead and REM and National Public Radio. Also they're pretty even though they don't wear makeup and they never have painted fingernails or heels or nylons or anything prissy like that."

"Nobody wears nylons," said Apple. "This is nineteen ninety-three."

"But you have short fingernails and you never wear makeup do you? You're a tea sock, admit it."

"So you've got me all figured out then?" Apple was clearly amused by Tommy's characterization.

"And they do yoga," said Tommy.

"Well I guess that clinches it then," said Apple. "I'm a tea sock." She reached across the table and put her hand into his. At that moment Tommy knew he had her exactly where he wanted her, he had charmed her into a corner. There was nothing left to do or say other than kiss her. This was his moment. He'd have to take it now or risk not getting it back. He stood up and leaned over the table and kissed her. He kissed her very slowly and carefully and she kissed him back, there was no question about it. They were both good kissers as it turned out, or to put it another way they had similar kissing styles, very careful and very slow and neat. He returned to his seat and they both sat quietly for a moment.

"Do you want another Cosmo?" He asked.

Apple got in Kalesin and followed Tommy back to Jack's. She left Kalesin at Jack's and got into Tommy's piece of shit Toyota 4Runner and they headed back out on the road. She laughed quietly to herself as she remembered what one of her girlfriends from school had once said to her. She said: Whatever you do, never follow a hippie to a second location.

"What's so funny," Tommy asked.

"You wouldn't characterize yourself as a hippie would you Tommy?" Tommy laughed.

"Definitely not." He looked at the quartz crystal he had hanging from the rear view mirror. He fondled it. I just keep this for good luck," he explained.

"Of course you do," said Apple. "That's very non-hippieish."

"I have no idea where I'm going," said Tommy.

"Just keep going," said Apple. "I'm having fun."

Tommy found a parking spot in Wellfleet center behind a church and they walked around and window shopped some of the galleries and boutiques, all of which were closed, before Apple brought him to the doorway from his father's painting. It was an old wooden recessed doorway with big bay windows on both sides of the door which would have served as display areas had it not been vacant.

"That's it," said Tommy. "That's totally it." Tommy held the post card in his hand as he stood in the doorway. "He must have been standing right here where we're standing now when he painted it."

"It's a good painting," said Apple.

"Yup, it's good," said Tommy. For a moment he lost himself and a tear ran down his cheek.

"You're a really sweet guy," said Apple. "I mean that. Don't be embarrassed." Tommy wiped his eyes.

"It looks like it doesn't it?"

"Oh this is definitely the place," said Apple. "He must have done it just before sunrise. It has that pre-dawn stillness to it you know?"

"That was his thing," said Tommy. "He didn't want daylight or any people around in his paintings fucking them up."

There was a bench in front of the place so Tommy and Apple sat awhile. He put his arm around her and she cuddled up to him and he felt as though they were totally bonding as they sat there in silence enjoying the moment.

Tommy took Apple back to Jack's. It was late and Jack would definitely be soundly asleep by now. Tommy figured if he could get Apple on the couch in Jack's sitting room he'd have a fairly good chance of sleeping with her. At this point that was all he could really think of, however Apple seemed to be now backing off a bit and playing it cool and so he decided he'd be ok with some heavy kissing instead and then he'd say good night. He was totally in the mood for that anyway. Why go for the kill on the first night? She clearly liked him and he was more than happy about that even if she wouldn't sleep with him. Not that he would necessarily rule that out.

He showed her into the gas station and they sat in the sitting room on Jack's grimy little couch. They kissed for a couple of minutes and Tommy was completely happy and at peace when Apple suddenly stood up, excused herself, and walked out of the room. She went into the office and then into the bathroom. Tommy waited quietly.

Apple locked the door behind her. She had a small glass vial in her pocket, which she took out and then unscrewed the cap. She knew that if she turned on the faucet Tommy would hear her and so she just stood there frozen for a moment. She looked at the toilet which was clearly not clean and she shuttered when she realized what she'd have to do. She thought maybe she could take the back off the toilet and scoop some water from there but she was afraid that he'd hear her. She decided she had better just stick her hand into the toilet and fill up her glass vial, which is what she did. She then put the cover on the vial, stuck it in her pocket and then flushed the toilet just so he would hear her and then she unlocked the door and went back to Tommy.

"I'm sorry about that, I just couldn't hold it," she said.

She sat down and kissed Tommy for a little while longer, partly just to make it look good and partly because he was a good kisser and she did kind of like him. Just as things started to get hot and heavy she got up quickly, said good night, and was gone. Tommy was giddy and disoriented as he thought about what had just happened. He was slightly disappointed but not at all surprised. After all she would have to leave abruptly like that, either that or she would have slept with him but he couldn't have expected that on their first date. All things considered he knew it went well. He sat there for a long while thinking about everything and he felt happy. He went outside and had a cigarette and listened to the crickets and the spring peepers. Eventually he climbed into his little cot and fell asleep. He slept soundly as usual. Apple, on the other hand, didn't feel so well. When she got home she found it difficult to sleep.

Chapter Fifteen

Tommy's father, the famous painter Richard Cobb, was in his early sixties when he met Tommy's mother and died abruptly, only a few years later, under slightly mysterious circumstances. At that point Jack was in his late thirties but he had known Cobb for over fifteen years. They were friends, though they saw each other very infrequently, and Jack, more so than Cobb, was influenced by their friendship. Cobb spent most of his time in New York but he took a summer home in Truro and he befriended Jack when he made his masterpiece painting of the gas station. At that time Jack was in his twenties. Manning the pumps daily and learning the business, Robert Bellamy (he was not yet known as "Jack"), had the opportunity to watch Cobb create his masterpiece. He observed Cobb working from the early charcoal and pencil sketches made in the spring to the actual painting and then the endless restarts and revisions throughout the height of the season, and then into the fall when it was finally completed. Cobb was older and seemed accomplished and wealthy to the young Robert and so he looked up to Cobb. Though, even then, Robert had come to the idea that he had little understanding, or even sympathy for artists, but he saw in Cobb something different. He was driven and he was a hard worker. The part that Robert didn't understand was that Cobb was obviously depressed and grumpy and that he seemed to require a lot of brooding before he could paint something that he felt good about. Robert decided that Cobb was disciplined and a hard worker but unfortunately much of that hard work was often wasted in the end. These observations were the beginnings of his view that art was ultimately self indulgent and reckless, an opinion which he would carry on, and chastise Sam with, for the rest of his life. The circumstances under which Cobb ended up dying cemented this view in Robert's mind. At the time that he met Cobb, Robert (or "Jack" as he was now called) was still known as little Robert Bellamy, the kid who worked for Old Pop Snow at the filling station. Pop's real name was Jack Snow and he was the original "Jack" when he first opened the place in the twenties. Old Pop Snow had his own share of scandal. It seemed that originally he had had a partner in the station, an ambitious young man by the name of Richard Aiken. Dick, as he was known, had put up most of the money and therefore had a lot of ideas about how to run the place and for whatever reason these ideas were apparently at odds with Pop Snow's vision for the place. As it happened one night Dick and Pop went out fishing on Dick's new boat "Whydah" and in the morning only Pop returned. Dick was never heard of or seen again. Pop Snow swore Dick had fallen overboard and that he had tried desperately to save him but that tragically he was unsuccessful. Dick had no strong family ties and so as it happened Pop ended up owning both Whydah and the gas station and that was officially the beginning of Jack's Gas. There were whispers and innuendoes regarding this suspicious beginning in the early days when Robert Bellamy first started to work for Jack but by the time Cobb came around years later those rumors were all but forgotten. Cobb completed his painting and moved on to other local subjects and other adventures and as the years passed old Jack Snow outlived the rumors and became a beloved local character before dying and leaving both the station and Whydah to his dedicated young protégé Robert Bellamy. Thus Robert Bellamy became the new "Jack" in Truro in the late nineteen sixties right around the time that Tommy was born. By then the painting "Gas" was already considered an important work and had been purchased for a very high price by the most famous young New York art impresario at the time Peggy Guggenheim. It may well have been with that money that Cobb purchased his little Cape Codder overlooking the Pamet nestled in the bayside dunes of Truro, and it was there on the heels of that accomplishment that he met Tommy's mother and briefly fell in love with her while his wife and children were safely ensconced in a respectable brownstone in Brooklyn.

Taking all of that into consideration it was unusually eerie for Jack when he awoke early one morning in the spring of ninety ninety-three and saw a young Richard Cobb once again working at his easel out in front of the gas station just as he had all summer nearly thirty years ago. It was very early and not having quite recovered from his fall Jack was feeling a bit wobbly when he stepped outside to take a closer look. He noticed that his hands were shaking. He had never had tremors before. He intended to approach the man standing behind his easel when he was overwhelmed with dizziness and nausea and he suddenly fainted. Jack lay unconscious on the ground outside the front door of his utility room for quite some time when he awoke bleary and confused. He had no idea how long he had been out but he could see that it was still morning and he heard Tommy shuffling around inside. He got up, regained his composure and went inside. Tommy was apparently unaware that he had fainted.

"I guess I'm still keeping banker's hours," said Tommy, wiping the sleep from his eyes and putting on a fresh tee-shirt.

"You and me both," said Jack as he headed for his vodka in the little cabinet above the sink. Jack filled his coffee mug about a quarter of the way with vodka and then put in an ice cube and filled it the rest of the way up with water from the tap.

"I wasn't sure about that water," said Tommy. Tommy was preparing to make coffee and he had a jug of spring water beside the sink. "You can use this if you like." Jack took a sip from his mug and shuttered.

"The water is fine," he said. "I've been drinking it since before you were born; besides the vodka will kill anything in it."

"Yeah, including you," thought Tommy. "Suit yourself," he said. "Me, I'm having a good strong cup of coffee. You want one?"

"Maybe later," said Jack. He was still confused. He looked out the window where he had seen the apparition of a young Richard Cobb painting and then he looked at Tommy who had clearly just rolled out of bed. "You were up earlier outside weren't you?"

"Not today," said Tommy. "I had a great night last night on my date. I slept like a baby. What time is it anyway?" Jack looked perplexed. He had no idea what time it was. He decided he had better go back to the doctor soon.

"I've got to get some wood cut," he said and went back outside. Tommy was disappointed. He wanted to tell Jack that he had kissed a girl, a pretty and sophisticated tea sock scientist no less. All day Tommy had a skip in his step and a glide in his stride and the time flew by as he rehashed in his mind all the witty and revealing conversation of the night before. He had come across well he thought, sensitive and artistic and she clearly went for that sort of thing, after all she loved Monet. The kissing was intense and passionate too, not at all awkward he thought. He imagined what it would be like having her as a girlfriend and spending the summer with her. He imagined telling his mother about her and introducing her to Sam and Goody and Jack and he anticipated painting as well. He would use a new style to paint her, one that was quick and impressionistic like Sam's. She would like that. Perhaps she would be his muse? That was probably just what he needed to start painting well again. He looked forward to telling that to Sam, to assuage Sam's concerns as well as his own that despite his temporary block he could paint well this summer after all. In his mind he saw Apple at the beach in her bikini laughing, and yelling happily, playing in the surf on the back beach by the Highland Light and then they would walk together along the shore and tell each other their most intimate thoughts and dreams and their aspirations and goals for the future. The silly sentimentality of all this revelry wasn't completely lost on Tommy, certainly not in retrospect, but he felt one could allow such emotional recklessness on the morning after kissing a girl for the first time in over a year. Not kissing a girl for that long when you're in your late twenties was unnatural and it was bound to have some negative effects, not the least of which was Tommy's already borderline self esteem, not to mention his being so horny and desperate. He liked to think that the reason he hadn't been with a girl for so long was that ironically he was actually very picky. Ironically in that he knew he'd gladly sleep with nearly any woman, and he'd enjoy it too, and so he wasn't picky in that sense but he was picky about the kind of women he pictured himself with in the long run. He felt that a girl should be smart, maybe even a little smarter than himself, for some reason he found that appealing, maybe even necessary. Unfortunately such a disposition was likely to set him up for disappointment since normally any woman that smart wouldn't go for a guy who never even went to college, and certainly not for a guy who ended up working at a gas station. This was why it was so important to Tommy that he was an artist. He believed that was the one way he could impress women, at least those types of women. Once again this was his excuse for everything. Art was like a substance abuse problem for Tommy, a compulsive coping mechanism. Like a substance abuse addiction, art was for him always the cause of all his current problems and yet simultaneously it was also, in his mind, potentially the answer to all his future problems as well. Once again he would prove this by hanging his hat on the fact that by coming across as a serious artist he could perhaps impress Apple even though she was a scientist and he worked at a gas station. Tommy was still too young to admit, even to himself, that maybe this attitude was an indication that he had some serious self esteem issues to work out.

In the afternoon while Jack was taking a breather in his sitting room Tommy came in and put a frozen pizza in the microwave. Tommy fiddled around in the kitchenette waiting for his pizza while Jack sat on the couch and read the paper. Early in the morning before either of them had gotten up Goody had dropped off some home grown radishes and basil from her garden. Tommy sliced some of it up and covered it with salt and pepper and put it on his pizza. He popped a chunk of the radish in his mouth and was amazed by how good it was. "This is like the best thing I ever tasted," he told Jack. Jack flipped through the pages of the paper.

"She's a good kid," said Jack. "She's got a real green thumb that's for sure." Tommy was still giddy from the night before and decided to confront Jack out right.

"Jack you knew my father didn't you? I know you did. I can tell by the way you look at me." He stood in front of Jack defiantly. Jack waited a moment before folding his newspaper and looking at Tommy for a moment.

"Come here," he said. Tommy moved closer and Jack reached out and put his hand on Tommy's chin. He turned Tommy's face into the sunlight of the window so he could examine it more closely. He turned Tommy's face another way so he could look at his profile. He let go of his chin and Tommy stepped away.

"It's in the eyes," said Jack. "And in your brow. I did know him."

"Were you friends?" Asked Tommy.

"Not really," said Jack. "He didn't have any friends I don't think, not at the time anyway. He was a busy man and I was just a dumb kid getting in his way."

"Why didn't you tell me?" Asked Tommy. He took a bite of his pizza and sat on the arm of the couch beside Jack.

"I'm an old man," said Jack. "I've forgotten more than you already know."

Chapter Sixteen

Goody stocked the shelves at the little health food store in Wellfleet center called Lembas. It was named after the ultimate health food, the elvish bread from the Lord of The Rings. Goody had read the Lord of The Rings and loved it. It was in fact the only literary work she had ever been affected by. It had taken her so long to read, nearly five years, and she had liked it so much, that she decided she would never have to read another book again to regard herself as a lover of literature. If she ever felt the need to read something like that again, which she doubted, she would just read The Lord of The Rings again, and try to pay attention a little more. She knew there was plenty in it she hadn't gotten the first time. Occasionally she fantasized about walking into the forest down some deep lovely trail and suddenly finding herself lost in middle earth. If she could do that she'd leave it all behind and wouldn't look back. Though having said that, short of going to middle earth, there wasn't any other place Goody would rather be than the outer Cape. She had, in fact, a deep spiritual connection with the Cape. Half the people who lived there year round felt the same way. The lower Cape was actually kind of like a middle earth in some people's minds. You could live there, especially in the off season, as a way of escaping into fantasy. This was a contradiction for Goody given some of her goals. In one sense she definitely reveled in the isolation and alternative lifestyle the Cape offered, and yet on the other hand, she sometimes imagined herself as a traveler and an independent career minded woman. Sometimes she visualized becoming a marine biologist and helping to save the whales. Why couldn't she do that? She knew more about sea shells and fish bones than Sam and he was a genius in some ways. She knew more about that stuff than anyone in fact. Eventually she would come back down to earth and delve into her real world where there were compromises and disappointments and where she would think about money and work and paying her bills. That was where Lembas fit into her plan. If she had to work it wasn't such a bad place all things considered. At least she got to be around things she was interested in. Things like crystals and incense and plants and vegetables and vitamins and good whole foods and homeopathic tinctures and herbal supplements. As she stocked the shelves she went through all these items and read the labels and smelled them and tasted them and thought about what she might like to try and what kinds of things she needed for her magic potions and spells. Between the stuff she collected in the dunes and the stuff she got at an employee discount that was all she really needed.

Apple came into Lembas to have a look around. Apple liked health food stores. Being that she was a vegetarian, she needed to buy whey powder to supplement her protein, which she usually mixed with soy milk or occasionally organic skim milk. Along with the whey she had tofu and granola in her basket when she shopped the aromatherapy aisle, where she had in mind to maybe find something that might help her with her yoga meditation. She was hoping she might have another Krishna vision.

"Are you interested in aromatherapy?" Asked Goody.

"Well you know I haven't been until now but I've been experimenting with yoga and I'd like to use some kind of incense to help me get in the mood but I'm not sure if I can because of my asthma. I've never been able to use any kind of burning candle or incense because it inhibits my breathing."

"I see," said Goody. "I think we may have a few things you might like around here somewhere." Goody looked through the shelves and took down a couple of small bottles and read the labels. "You know what you should do? You should use like a steam pot. It's much less harsh than a burning type of thing. She handed Goody a small vial of tea tree oil and another of echinacea. "Have you tried these?" Apple read the labels on the bottles and then opened them and smelled them.

"No I haven't. Do you think they might be what I'm looking for?"

"I do," said Goody. "What you do is you boil purified water and you put in a few drops and inhale the steam. It will fill the room with a nice aroma but it's subtle and shouldn't be hard to take like incense. I know what you mean about most of this cheap incense. It's overwhelming, even for me, and I don't have asthma. What a lot of people do to get the full effect is you drape a towel over your head and put your face over the water and let the steam build up under the towel. Tea tree oil is a natural antibiotic. It has all kinds of uses, it reduces swelling and inflammation in the lungs and it helps with all kinds of stuff. It's good for acne. Not that you would need that, but I do. Your skin is very clear and pale."

"A little too pale," said Apple.

"No pale is good."

"Well thank you," said Apple. "But I have my days like anyone else."

"Anyway," said Goody. "The tea tree has a powerful and clean aroma like spearmint which opens up your airways. I do it whenever I have a cold and it works great."

"I see," said Apple. "Thank you."

"No problem," said Goody.

"And what's the story with echinacea?" Apple put the tea tree oil in her basket.

"Oh well that's a whole other thing altogether. It's not really an aromatherapy thing but I think you should try it if you have asthma. It's a fantastic supplement for all kinds of things, especially breathing and airway constriction type things." Goody noticed that April, her boss, had overheard her and was now frowning at her from behind the counter by the cash register. Goody knew what April was thinking but she decided April was just kind of a bitch.

"Are you taking anything for your asthma?"

"Yes," said Apple. "I take Claritin when my allergies get bad because that affects my asthma, and I have a regular inhaler too which I use maybe a couple of times a day. It's a bronchial dilator I guess they call it. Actually it's related to adrenalin, which I know is probably not the greatest thing in the world for me but it does help. Also I take a once a day Advair inhaler in the morning. It's like a powder that you inhale from a disc shaped thing. Have you ever heard of it?"

"Sure," said Goody. "I think so." In fact she hadn't.

"It costs like a million dollars a week," said Apple, "even with insurance. I'd really like to try to wean myself off of it."

"I definitely think you should try the echinacea," said Goody. "You just put a few drops in some fruit juice or tea or whatever a few times a day. Also throw a few drops into the boiling water when you do your tea tree oil. It works as an inhaler as well."

"Sounds good," said Apple as she tossed the tiny vial into her basket.

"Have you heard the joke about the woman who was taking echinacea?" Goody asked. "One day she forgot to take her medicine and died of an overdose." Goody laughed nervously. Apple thought about this for a moment but she didn't get it.

"How so?" She asked.

"When you first start out with echinacea you have to use a lot," said Goody. "But then after a while it starts to work and you have to use less. The less you use it the stronger it gets and after a while you only use like a half a drop to feel the complete effects. It has a reverse tolerance I guess you'd call it. The more you water it down the stronger it gets. That's the funny thing about echinacea," said Goody.

"She died of an overdose because she didn't take it." Apple laughed. "I get it."

"It's pretty funny," said Goody and she laughed again.

"Though I wonder if that's scientifically valid," said Apple.

"I'm pretty sure it is," said Goody. "But you never know with that sort of thing anyway." Apple found Goody's reply endearing. She had a cute way of putting things.

"I suppose you don't," said Apple.

"Well then you know what I mean." Goody smiled awkwardly and looked over Apple's shoulder at April who was still watching, and frowning. Why did she have to be such a bitch? Apple reached out and touched one of the bits of bone that Goody had tied into her long matted hair.

"This is interesting," said Apple. "It's very rare. Do you know what it is?"

"It's a sea feather," said Goody.

"That's right. That's exactly what they call it down here don't they? It is a sea feather. A keyhole limpet in fact, and I think they're pretty rare." Said Apple.

"They're around," said Goody. "I know where to find them."

"Where?" Asked Apple.

"It's a secret." Goody smiled coyly.

"You can tell me," said Apple. "I'm a scientist, a biologist actually and I'm quite interested."

"Sorry," said Goody. "It's a secret."

"Of course," said Apple. "You know some people think they're plants but they're not. It's actually a Hydrozon, which seems very much like a plant but it's actually an invertebrate animal."

"Interesting," said Apple. Actually she knew that. She wouldn't have put it that way but she did know that a sea feather wasn't a plant. Apple thanked her and went up to the cash register. Goody looked at April and smirked. As soon as Apple left, April approached Goody as Goody continued to stock the shelves and avoid eye contact.

"Goody I don't want you giving out medical advice you know that. If someone has a question please send them over to me. I do have a degree in homeopathic healing after all."

"I'm sorry," said Goody. "It was really no big deal."

"You've been warned," said April and she walked away. Goody felt ashamed. Who was she to be giving medical advice to a biologist? She could be such a jerk sometimes.

Later April seemed to lighten up and Goody started to feel better. Just before closing Sam's friend Pablo Golokovsky showed up and Goody could see that he was nervous and that he had something for her. He had a packet hidden under his arm as he paced in front of her, a large manila folder. The fact of the matter was he was attracted to her and he knew it and he knew that she knew it. He also was pretty sure that she thought he was good-looking since after all he was, everybody always told him so. He also knew Sam would kill him if he ever even thought about Goody in that way and so he had better not think about it and she knew that as well.

"Did you get it?" She asked excitedly. "Come on, give it to me." Pablo looked around to make sure no one was watching before handing her the envelope. She opened it up and looked at the papers. "Thank you; you're a real nice guy Pablo. Thank you for doing it so quickly." Pablo immediately chastised himself for doing it so quickly. Obviously he came across as too willing.

"You have to get that in the mail pretty soon," he said. "If you want to get in for the fall semester." He looked around over his shoulder. "Ok I gotta go." Goody grabbed him and kissed him on the cheek.

"I've got something for you too, just something I made." Goody ran off into the back room and then returned with a gift for Pablo. It was a small macramé wall hanging she made with coarse hemp twine and birch branches. She showed it to him before rolling it up and handing it to him. "It will give you good luck," she said and winked. He smiled and ran off.

Pablo walked through Wellfleet center toward the public library where he parked his car. Along the way he passed a touristy outdoor clam shack where he stuffed Goody's wall hanging into the trash. Obviously Sam would kill him if he found it. Pablo got about a block away before his interest in Goody got the better of him and he returned to dig it out of the trash can. When he got home he hung it on the wall in the studio where he thought it looked cool under a poster of Val Kilmer as Jim Morrison and then he called the Bomb Shelter and asked for Sam.

"This better be good," said Sam. "I'm a busy man."

"Hey how's it going?" Said Pablo. "So anyway I was just in the studio hanging up this cool macramé wall hanging with hemp and birch tree sticks that Goody gave me and I wanted to tell you so you wouldn't think there was anything weird about it or anything."

"Why would I think there was anything weird about it?"

"No reason, I just wanted to tell you."

"Why the fuck would Goody give you a present? What are you saying here Pablo? What the fuck are you talking about?"

"No it's nothing bad or anything," said Pablo. "It's just that she asked me to pick her up an application for Community College in Hyannis and since I was up there anyway, and out of respect for you — I mean I didn't want to say no, ya know? Anyway I did and so she gave me a present. It was no big deal." Sam didn't say anything which made Pablo even more nervous. "I mean I don't know if it was a secret or what but if she does tell you you have to back me up and act like I didn't tell you. Is that cool? I mean I don't know, maybe I got the impression that it was kind of a secret, and so I just wanted to tell you but don't tell her I told you or I'd feel like an asshole ok? You're not mad are you? I just figured I better tell you."

"No you did the right thing," said Sam.

"So when are we gonna hang out?" Asked Pablo. "How's Tommy? You know I have a good feeling about that guy. He liked my poem didn't he?"

"I just don't know why my girlfriend is confiding in you," said Sam. "That's gotta make me think."

"It was nothing," said Pablo. "That's why I told you, out of respect."

"Ok," said Sam. "You're a good shit."

"Thanks Sam. So anyway…" Sam hung up.

Goody didn't tell Sam about the college application. She took a couple of days to secretly fill it out. The main thing was financial aid. She had to convince them she was worthy. She had barely enough time if she wanted to make it for the fall semester.

The next day Goody sat at her kitchen table and did the bills. Sam knew she'd be sending out her mail the following morning and so the next day he got up early and said he was going fishing, but instead he went to a small place down the street to kill time where he had a Bloody Mary. He returned to the cottage shortly after ten when he knew Goody would be out walking with Seamus. Luckily the postal carrier had not yet arrived and so Sam rifled through Goody's mailbox and found the application. Maybe he'd throw it out? He'd have to think about it awhile.

Chapter Seventeen

That night Sam called Jack's and told Tommy to pick him up at Goody's late so they could go fishing. Tommy arrived and found him with his gear all piled up out front ready to go.

"You call this late?" Said Sam.

"It's nearly eleven. I gotta work in the morning. I don't want to piss Jack off."

"He doesn't give a shit, believe me."

Tommy put Sam's gear in the back of his truck. He had five rods, ten-footers with huge hooks and heavy sinkers, and he had some sections of pvc pipe, each cut with a sharp point on one end. Sam had a sledge hammer and a case of beer. Tommy picked up the rods and admired them. "Are these things big enough?"

"You got any money?" Asked Sam. "We need bait."

"Like fifteen bucks," said Tommy.

"You wanna buy a codeine?"

"I'm good," said Tommy. "I still got that other one."

"You wanna sell it?"

"I'm gonna need it I think," said Tommy.

"Oh man," said Sam. It's really good for fishing, especially with beer. I hope you're ready 'cause we're gonna catch some fish."

"On the boat?"

"No, on the beach. I got a feeling the striper are coming in close. The tide is midnight."

"Sweet," said Tommy. They drove to the bait shop in Wellfleet harbor. Sam was hoping to get there before closing but by the time they arrived it was too late. "These dicks are never open!" Tommy thought this was funny since it was now after eleven. "We gotta go to P-town," said Sam. "And make it quick. I think they close at midnight." Tommy drove very quickly and along the way Sam rolled a joint and lit it up. When they arrived at the supermarket in town they had less than three minutes 'till closing and the front door was already locked. Sam tried the exit door and it was still open so they rushed in, ignoring the disapproval of the guy at the register. It felt very odd to Tommy to be rushing around in a supermarket, totally high, in the middle of the night. They rushed to the fish market counter, which of course was already shut down and so they had to get the frozen stuff instead. Sam found two styrofoam quart containers of squid and a vacuum packed mackerel. At the check-out he grabbed three Slim Jims and a bag of chips. It came to just over twenty dollars. Tommy gave Sam his fifteen and Sam covered the rest. "I got the beer," he explained.

"I'm just glad we made it on time," said Tommy.

"Just under the wire," said Sam. "The story of my life."

They parked in the public lot at Herring Cove and carried the gear down to the beach. It was a beautiful out and the sea was calm, though there were some small waves coming in.

Sam hammered the pvc pipes into the sand about ten feet from the water. Tommy then understood that they were to hold the rods upright. Sam opened one of the frozen squid containers and smashed it with the butt of his knife. He cut off a piece and gave half to Tommy. "We'll save the mackerel.." They baited up and cast into the surf. Tommy didn't cast nearly as far as Sam.

"That's far enough, don't worry about it."

"But that was lame," said Tommy. He reeled it in and tried again. This time he got it out a little farther.

"You gotta leave it alone or you're gonna waste bait," said Sam. "Sometimes it's better to be closer anyway. This way we got all our bases covered."

"Yeah?"

"Big striper," said Sam. "I've seen them come right up to like ten feet of water. Are you hungry? Cause if we get one I'm making Goody cook it. I don't give a fuck how late it is."

"I'll eat it," said Tommy.

"Oh it's good," said Sam. "You don't gotta do shit to it either. It's good just plain with salt and pepper."

"Sounds good?"

"I eat striper every day of the week."

They fished quietly for a while and enjoyed the peace and quiet.

"Well I made it," said Tommy. "I'm at the beach just like Antonio said and it's not even summer yet."

"And not just any beach," added Sam. "This is a good beach."

"It is," said Tommy looking around. "I can't believe how empty it is around here."

"That's the thing," said Sam. "Pretty soon the tourist will be here, but right now it's still good. In the fall it's even better if you can believe it."

"Yeah? How so?"

"Well Fall is beautiful on the Cape. That's probably the one thing I'm gonna miss when I go."

"Where are you gonna go?" Asked Tommy.

"If I tell you you can't tell anyone."

"Of course not," said Tommy.

"No, I'm serious," said Sam. "If Jack finds out it's gonna be bad."

"Ok," said Tommy. Sam remained quiet. He reeled in his line and checked his bait.

"I've been putting away money," he said. "For a long time now and I got some serious plans worked out, and I haven't told anyone other than Goody. I bought a shack on five acres deep in the woods of central Oregon. I've been researching it for awhile and I think I got a seriously good deal. It's totally prime undeveloped land with lots of woods and freshwater."

"That's awesome," said Tommy.

"I'm gonna go out there and build a log cabin and just get off the grid once and for all. That's what my whole life has been leading up to anyway so who am I kidding? I just need to do it and get it over with you know?"

"That sounds great. Where exactly in Oregon?"

"Between Corvallis and Eugene way out in the middle of nowhere in this place called McKinley Pass in the Cascade Mountains about fifty miles off route 100."

"I've been there," said Tommy.

"Fuck you you have," said Sam.

"No really. I spent a summer bumming around Oregon five years ago on my way out to California. I took the long way. I went through Washington and Idaho and then down into Oregon. In fact I camped in a state park near McKinley Pass for a couple of weeks. It's totally one of the best parts of Oregon no doubt. Shit it's one of the best parts of the world I'll bet. There's some hard core people living out there too, but nothing you can't handle. Actually, now that I think about it, you'd fit in perfectly. I met some serious hippie chicks out there. That's where I learned how to pick mushrooms, you know like the real shrooms. They're like fifty bucks an eighth around here, but out there they're totally free. Man, I had such a good time out there. I hooked up with this one girl who spent half her life running around in the forest dressed up like an elf. She had red dreadlocks and a mandolin and she sang German folk songs around the fire. That was one of the best times of my life. It was like a dream really. I'm surprised I ever left but after a few months I ran out of money and so I drove down to L.A. and ended up washing dishes in Hollywood for a couple of years. It all went downhill from there but finally I got enough money together to go to New York and try to be a painter."

"See that's why I like you," said Sam. "You know what you're talking about. Tell me about Oregon. I need to know."

"Oh it's fucking ridiculous," said Tommy. "The first thing you notice when you arrive is the smell of the trees. You just drive around with the windows down and you can smell the trees everywhere you go. The whole place smells like dammar varnish and turpentine. It smells awesome. And then when you get deep in the woods you can't believe how beautiful it is. It's so dramatic it looks like a movie set or something, with like giant mushrooms and old growth trees and everywhere you go it's deep and dank and covered with moss. You see like a giant sequoia lying across a river, like a bridge that you can walk out across, and fish off of. You can catch rainbow trout, brookies and brown trout everywhere no problem just with worms and a little hook. And they're good too. You're gonna love them. You can live on them and just get like a big bag of rice or whatever to go with it and that's all you really need. It's like the land of the lost out there. It's like Middle Earth. Everything is moist and pungent and dank. It's so good that you wonder how does everybody not know about it, but they don't for some reason. It's like everyone out there knows they're in on this great secret but apparently everyone else is just too lame to know about it. Like everyone else in the country is just so tied up in the urban, and the suburban, rat race that they never realize how awesome it is out there in the truly natural parts of our country like Oregon."

"Well I'm going," said Sam. "I'm gonna hunt and fish and grow vegetables and just give up on the whole American air-conditioned nightmare. I'm totally ready for it." Sam took a hit off his joint and looked out over the ocean. "That's what I'm gonna do Tommy, what do you think about that?"

"Man that's hard core," said Tommy. "That's totally hard core."

"Yeah well I'm a hard core guy," said Sam.

Eventually they got a couple of bites. Sam had something pretty big and he fought it for a while but it got away at the last second. It was definitely a blue, he told Tommy. He could tell by the way it fought and by the way it bit through the line and escaped at the last second. "Blues always do that," he explained. "They're crafty that way."

Tommy caught something small and spiny and ugly which Sam called a George Burns fish. Tommy didn't see the resemblance. "I thought you said we would only catch big fish on a hook like this?"

"That's why it's a George Burns fish," said Sam. "It's small, but it's got a big mouth." Sam took the fish from Tommy and drop-kicked it back into the ocean.

"That ain't right," said Tommy.

"He'll be fine," said Sam. "They're made out of rubber." They fished a while longer and had a few more beers and Sam smoked some more pot, but Tommy took a pass. He could barely see straight as it was. Compared to Sam he was a lightweight. "See I can take or leave the booze," said Sam. "But I'm never gonna stop smoking weed. That's something I've come to know about myself. You get to a certain age and you just know that. I guess what I'm saying is that I just really like pot Tommy, you know what I mean? I just really fucking like it."

"I think I know what you mean," said Tommy. "That's why I know you're gonna love Oregon. Dude it's like the pot is practically free out there and it's ridiculously good."

"Indeed," said Sam as he dragged deeply. "We'll see about that."

"Are you going alone?"

"I haven't decided yet. Goody wants to go but I'm not sure. I mean I love her to death and everything but you know I'm just kind of torn about the whole thing."

"Yeah huh?" Tommy didn't want to say anything about Goody.

"On the one hand, she's got great tits and ass, but then on the other I don't know, she can be such an idiot sometimes you know? I don't think she gets me. Is that so much to ask? Why couldn't I have

a girl that gets me? Besides, I think she might be getting a little fat."
Tommy waited and didn't say anything. As far as he was concerned
Goody was totally hot.

"You know I met a woman recently. I took her to the Bomb
Shelter. I was hoping you'd be there. I ended up taking her to Jack's
sitting room to make out. It was sweet."

"You didn't fuck her?"

"Next time," said Tommy. "I'm working up to it."

"That's bullshit," said Sam. "What's her name?"

"Apple. She's from up Cape I guess, not down here anyway.
She's like a preppie scientist Harvard teasock and she drives an Audi
A4 and has tits that are really rockin'. I mean they're not too big or
anything but they're firm and pointy you know? I really like her."

"Harvard? What's her angle? Slumming with an artist? I
know the type. Don't wear your heart on your sleeve I'm telling you
right now. She's gonna eat you up. What is she Jewish? I'll bet she's
Jewish. I know the type. Fuck Harvard. You need a P'town chick."

"I like Jewish girls," said Tommy. "But she's not. She wants
to convert to Hinduism. She's into Krishna and yoga."

"Of course," said Sam. "I know the type, believe me. Tell her
you can't convert to Hinduism, you just have to be one. Doesn't she
know that? She went to Harvard and she doesn't even know that?
She's probably one of these yuppie girls from West Dennis or
Yarmouth Port, am I right?"

"Actually I think she is, but she's cool. She seems really
smart."

"I'm sure she is, probably too smart."

"I think we hit it off."

"Don't get me wrong Tommy, just keep it in perspective.
Girls like that don't stick around."

Tommy caught two more George Burns fish which Sam
found amusing. Sam didn't catch any George Burns fish and this he
explained was no accident, apparently it had to do with knowing
what you were doing. This seemed a subtle distinction to Tommy.
Sam decided it was time to cut up the mackerel and then the fish
really started hitting. The next forty-five minutes or so were very
exciting as they fished with the mackerel They were getting hits left
and right, often fighting with them and only losing them at the last
minute as they got close to the shore. Sam showed Tommy how you

could tell they were striper or blues by the way they skipped around on the surface and by the way they hit the bait hard and took off running. The striper took the mackerel without swallowing the hook and so you had to be patient and wait for just the right moment to go for it and give it a good yank.

"Striper are ambush feeders. They sneak up on that shit quick. They look for bait fish in the rocks, but the tide keeps shifting so they have to keep moving where they hunt. This is a good spot though; there are a lot of rocks out there. They're like fifty feet from where we're standing. I got a twenty-five pound monster out there last fall. That's when they really hit."

"No shit? Man I hope I get one."

"This thing was as long as your leg."

"A twenty-five pound monster huh? That's huge."

"Oh they get bigger," said Sam. "I've seen'em get close to forty pounds just before winter. You'd be eating that thing for a month."

"Man, now I'm getting hungry!" Tommy cast a good fifty feet into the surf.

"Not bad," said Sam and then cast fifteen feet further.

They ended up having a pretty good night and they both fought with many fish over the next couple of hours. When it was all said and done they had three fish. Of the three fish that Sam deemed keepers he decided they would let one go. "One for you," he said. "And one for me and one we let go to tell the tale." Tommy was moved by Sam's compassion which he thought uncharacteristic. Sam stood knee deep in the surf and massaged the fish until it came out of its daze and eventually swam away. "He'll be alright. I'll get him tomorrow."

On the ride home Tommy told Sam how Jack said he had known Tommy's father after all.

"Was he drunk?"

"I don't think so. I mean not any more than usual. He said he could tell by my eyes and my brow."

"That doesn't sound like him," said Sam. "He usually doesn't remember shit like that. I think he must really like you. I wouldn't put too much stock in it though. To be honest he seems a bit off his game these days. I don't know what's got into him but I'm a little worried. Ever since he fell off his woodpile he's kind of loopy. I mean he always drank and cut a lot of wood but now he really drinks and cuts a lot of wood, if you know what I mean. He's averaging like a fifth of booze and two or three cords a day and I don't see how he can keep it up. Sooner or later he's gonna lose a finger or something. It's good that you're around right now Tommy; it makes me feel better to know that someone I can trust is keeping an eye on things."

"Thanks, I appreciate that Sam. I really do. And thanks for all you've done for me lately. I was in a bad way when I met you guys but now I feel like things are starting to happen for me. I have a job and I met a girl and I'm thinking I might even be able to start painting well again."

"Oh you'll paint good Tommy. You'll paint really fucking good believe me. I'll see to that. I've got some ideas. I've been thinking about it. Next time we paint in the woods. You know? Let's do it soon, ok? I haven't painted the trees and the dunes in a long while but I think we should do it. We'll get fucked up and paint some crazy shit out there whataya think?"

"Sure," said Tommy. "I'm up for that, I guess. I mean I'll give it a try."

"Fuck that," said Sam. You gotta stop having that pussy attitude about it Tommy. I mean you did paint those pictures from the slides right?"

"Yeah," said Tommy.

"So I know you're good. Better than me right? Except I don't need inspiration to paint. I mean that's the difference between us and that's gotta be worth something."

"It's worth a lot," said Tommy.

"So then you gotta let me teach you how to do that Tommy. That's what I can show you. You think I wait around for inspiration? I don't. Inspiration is overrated. No offense Tommy but you got this attitude about the whole thing, like it's supposed to be mysterious and temperamental and all that."

"No, I understand what you're saying," said Tommy.

"Yeah well you gotta let go of that shit as soon as possible. Did you finish your fish painting at least?"

"No not yet," said Tommy apologetically. "I guess seeing yours kind of threw me off. Yours was awesome."

"Yeah well that's what I do, but maybe fish aren't your thing. We'll keep trying. I got an idea to maybe get you a little inspired. Tomorrow night they're having a reception for some guy at the Truro dump so we'll go and check it out. Some of the major players will be there. It'll be fun. You can see how lame our local competition is."

"At the dump?"

"Yeah they do it once or twice a year at the swap shack. It's like a wine and cheese kind of thing. It's supposed to be ironic. They usually get a good mix of rich posers and maybe a few real artists show up. You might make some connections. I'll introduce you to the local literati. Who knows maybe I'll get you laid?"

"I don't know about that."

"Oh right 'cause you're still waiting for your Harvard teasock?"

"She might pan out. You never know."

"Tommy you gotta let that one go. Girls like that don't pan out."

"I don't know why you have to be so negative about it."

"I told you why," said Sam. "I hate everyone that went to college. Especially women."

"Some people would say you might be intimidated by them."

"Ok," said Sam. "As soon as I meet a college girl smarter than me, then I'll be intimidated. As for now I'm still waiting." Tommy thought about this carefully. Sam was pretty smart.

"Fair enough," he said. "But Apple just might give you a run for your money. She told me Jack looks like Samuel Becket." Sam considered that and laughed. He seemed to agree. Tommy knew Sam would appreciate that more than he did.

It was getting very late and the fish were no longer biting so they decided to pack it in and head for Wellfleet. Once at Goody's Sam got her out of bed to cook the bass. Tommy felt badly about it but knew better than to put up a fight. Goody didn't seem to mind, she was indeed the perfect girlfriend and Sam was damn lucky to have her. Goody seasoned the bass with bay leaves, fennel and rosemary, wrapped it in aluminum foil and baked it for half an hour. She laid it out with potatoes and sweet port wine. Tommy was pretty sure he had never had such a good meal. "It's a little over cooked," said Sam. "And I don't know why she has to dick it up with herbs. I just use butter and pepper." Tommy wanted Goody to sit with them, but as soon as she cooked she went back to bed. "We'll save her a piece," said Sam. When they were done Tommy began to wash the dishes. "Goody will get that in the morning, don't worry about it."

Sam went out on the front porch for a smoke while Tommy continued with the dishes. When he finished he went out on the porch and found Sam asleep in his chair with a cigarette burning between his fingers. Tommy put out the cigarette, polished off his glass of port, and headed back to Jack's.

The following evening Tommy, Sam and Pablo arrived at the Truro dump swap shack around seven o'clock. The Truro dump swap shack was an interesting local phenomenon. It was like a free thrift store for the cliquey working-class tribe of Truro and north Wellfleet year-rounders. You had to have a dump sticker to get in and believe it or not they weren't that easy to come by. Like the cute post office in Truro proper (the less cute north branch was added to accommodate the overflow of yuppies and "wash-ashores") if one hung around there in the off season long enough one was sure to rub elbows with real-life fisherman, artists and local "color" . Jack had a low number box for instance. Sam and Goody each had their own. Even Pablo couldn't get one. If Tommy were to hang around long enough he'd be relegated to the north Truro office. The real Truro P.O. boxes were no longer issued and only handed down to the worthy. Like getting season tickets to the Red Sox you didn't even try but sometimes they just fell in your lap. Like Jack's Gas and the post office, the dump was one of the last prestigious institutions remaining in Truro.

The idea of the swap shack was that you were supposed to bring things that you were going to throw out but that were actually good and that somebody else would want to have. Mostly it had a lot of books, dishes, vintage clothing and half broken appliances and the occasional TV or stereo. Sometimes you could find decent antique furniture and smart books if you knew what to look for. Sam knew what to look for, but that stuff got snatched up quickly so he had to pop in whenever he could. For him it was like fishing. As any fisherman will attest it isn't the catch that gets you, it's the pursuit. Sam found it downright exhilarating. There were a lot of rich people on the lower Cape — seasonal types who were always moving in and out and so they had a lot of good stuff they had to get rid of, especially in the fall. True to form Sam subverted the altruistic spirit of the swap shack in that he never brought anything of value there himself but he scored all kinds of good stuff there fairly regularly. "I got every book I ever read out of this dump," he told Tommy and

Pablo. "Good stuff too. People down here used to read literature, not bullshit pulp like they do now. I once got a nineteen fifties hard cover of Finnegan's Wake in there. It took me like three years to get through it. I scored a complete set of the nineteen eighties Harvey Pekar American Splendors for Christ sake!" Tommy and Pablo had no idea about either of those things but they trusted Sam and were confident of their historical relevance. "Goody decked out her whole place with shit from the Truro dump. Retro ashtrays, tiger maple coffee tables, all that shit." Sam was getting worked up. He was never far from nostalgia. "I used to fucking love it! Of course it's not what it once was. The yuppies dicked it all over. Now it's all People magazines and Ikia furniture and chipped lamps." With Sam it always came back to the yuppies. The gentrification of the lower Cape was clearly his lament.

They just finished a joint as they pulled in but Tommy had opted out. He didn't like being high in a mixed crowd. It made him feel self-conscious. He respected men like Sam, men who were confident and not critical of themselves. Sam wasn't about to bust balls about that. He was used to it. He wanted to smoke it all himself anyway. Tommy wondered how he could do it. No matter how much Sam smoked he never appeared even the slightest bit high. It was as if he loved to smoke pot all the time even though apparently it had no effect on him whatsoever. In actual fact Sam was never not high and so basically he smoked to stay normal. When they were done Sam snubbed it out on the dash and then pocketed the roach.

As they approached the scene Pablo tucked his latest notebook under his arm. "It's not an open mike," said Sam. "They're not going to let you read."

"You never know," said Pablo. "Last year Norman Mailer came out of the woodwork."

"Like a Pulitzer Prize winner wants to be subjected to your scribbling? Just let me know before you try anything so I can duck out and take a piss. On second thought I would like to see an eighty year old guy kick your ass all over the Truro dump."

"Dude that would be awesome," said Pablo. "Besides, Tommy liked my poem." Tommy nodded.

"No he didn't," said Sam.

It was a clear warm night and there was a decent crowd milling around, maybe fifty people outside and another twenty or so inside. They had tables and easels with paintings on them set up under paper lanterns which were hung along a chain-link fence and then over the entrance of the swap shack itself which was like a converted trailer with a small modular home addition built off the back. Sam made a bee-line toward the table with the free wine in little plastic cups. He took one red and one white and poured them together. There were five or six local artist's displays outside and then the featured artist of the night, an older guy by the name of Arnie Charnick, showcased inside. There was one particularly good artist outside by the name of Carl Tasha. Sam explained to Tommy how the Tasha's were an old art family on the outer Cape and that they had a compound of cool artist shacks tucked away in one of the few remaining secluded and wooded areas left in P'town. Also they also owned some of the original dune shacks in Truro. These shacks where, for the most part, secret and highly coveted by certain locals and yet ironically they were left dilapidated and empty most of the time, except when they were temporarily inhabited by the occasional privileged artist, or, better yet, by one of the local, in-the-know, teenagers who went there, without permission, to drink and make out in the middle of the night. It was in one of those Tasha dune shacks that Sam had first slept with Goody. Over the past twenty years or so the Tasha's had become something of an art dynasty on the lower Cape and Carl, one of the featured artists at the dump, was its current Patriarch. Lately he did mostly jewelry and sculpture. Among other things, he was an expert welder, carpenter and mason. Sam wore one of Tasha's rings. It was a cluster of melted silver blobs cut to look like an octopus. "Dude you like this ring?"

"It's awesome," said Tommy.

"It's worth like a thousand bucks," said Sam.

Once inside Tommy was astounded by the Arnie Charnick paintings. Each one was better than the last. At once he was exhilarated and oddly disappointed with himself. This is what he should have been doing. He rarely got that feeling when encountering a new artist. The only consolation he had was that Charnick was older than he was and that reminded him that he better get moving before it was too late. Sam came up and stood beside Tommy. "Holy shit Sam. Have you seen this stuff?"

"I didn't want to color your judgment," said Sam. "I wanted to see what you said first. Call it a test."

"Well I like it," said Tommy.

"You passed,"

"I like it too," said Pablo.

"Fuck you," said Sam. "What do you know?" The paintings had a kind of vibrant cartoonish quality but not dark and angular like one of the better comic book illustrators but lighter and sinewy, maybe like William Blake or Thomas Hart Benton. He dealt in lower Cape images and pathos. Most of the paintings were of local old-timers and boats and beaches. "This is what we need to do Tommy. Shit like this. You don't have to worry about ripping off guys like him. That shit is open game. Charnick is too good not to cop. The true artist is the guy who knows what's fair game and what isn't. You see what I mean? I'm sure he stole it too, from someone even better than him no doubt." Tommy knew what Sam meant. He had already stolen quite a few ideas from these paintings in the few seconds before Sam even spoke. There was one painting in particular that Tommy liked. It depicted some kind of beast (perhaps a lamb or a doe) skewered roasting over an open fire. The animal had raised its head and was feasting on its own roasted haunch. A ribbon underneath had an old fashioned ornate penmanship (reminiscent of a Frieda Kalo painting) which read: "I have been given to wonder whether the reticence toward the ready consumption of a truly savory flesh was nothing more than the revulsion of taking into one's body that which is closer to one's own self." This quote seemed to Tommy to be deep on multiple layers, first because it seemed to anticipate his own desire to rip off Charnick's technique, and then more literally in that it seemed to be saying to both carnivores and vegetarians simultaneously that the other was perhaps being a bit shallow. In other words if you were a vegetarian it seemed to be supporting your argument, at least superficially, but then on the other hand, a carnivore might read it as a rebuke of the vegetarian's short-sightedness — after all a fish, or even a plant, is still a living thing, if just a little farther from one's own immediate experience of consciousness. The comic ambiguity of the quote hinted at its slippery insight (that perhaps issues of sustainability and cruelty may be, in the end, crucially perspectival). The price tag was a mere twelve hundred and it already had a red dot sticker placed beside it, meaning it was sold. It was worth every penny. One of the few sculptures in the room was an old black cast iron typewriter where the letters on the keys had been rearranged in the middle to read "writers block" . Brilliant, thought Tommy. Fucking brilliant.

And he hadn't even smoked any pot. He went outside to have a plastic glass of wine and a cigarette.

Pablo was milling around having a good time while Tommy and Sam stood off away from the crowd taking it in. "See that guy over there?" Sam gestured toward a sad little fellow in the mist of the crowd. He was actually fifty but looked only about thirty-five owing to the fact that he had never had a drink or a smoke or a good lay in his life. He was slightly overweight with horn-rimmed glasses, a tragically humped back, a pony tail and a douche bag pencil thin mustache and goatee. He wore a tight black polyester turtleneck shirt, even though it was the height of the summer, and he had a 35 millimeter camera around his neck. "That's Paul Howard Squidda the third, God love'm. And yes that's his real name. He's at every arts happening on the outer Cape — never misses a thing. He writes a stupid newsletter about all of it. He always shows up with his mother. I kid you not. She drives him if you can believe it. Everyone thinks he has like a Norman Baits thing going on with her. Some people say she even bathes him every Saturday night." Sam gestured toward a ridiculous old woman standing alone in the crowd daintily holding a piece of aged Gouda in a napkin. She looked to be in her eighties and had plucked eyebrows that were then drawn back in in a way that made her look as if she were in a perpetual state of surprise. "She's a piece of work huh?" Tommy laughed quietly. "The poor thing," Sam continued. She's been at every totally cool art opening in the past ten years and yet she has no idea. She just drives Paul. Granted she's been at every other lame arts thing as well. He tries to get things going by himself by reserving a conference room in the library every couple of weeks for some kind of art appreciation meeting but it's always just him and his mom that show up. He never gets discouraged. That's his strength, the guy has no shame. You gotta respect that a little." They looked back over at Paul who was now trying to photograph a group of giggling under-aged girls teasing him. "That's his M.O.," said Sam. It's totally innocent, that's the funny part. It's just copy for his Xeroxed fanzine/newsletter that nobody ever reads. Honestly he has no idea that he's a creepy middle-aged guy taking pictures of local teenagers. He doesn't even get off on them I'll bet, that's how clueless he is. Still he always manages to find the girls who want their picture taken, I'll give him that. That's the only thing I like about him."

"Those girls are kind of cute," said Tommy.

"Yeah if you're like a sixteen year old skateboard punk," said Sam. "Squidda started this thing that he heads up called the Upwardian Art Society. Whatever you do, don't let him rope you into that. At first it seems innocent enough but believe me it's worse than death for an artist down here to even stand beside him."

"Aren't you laying it on a bit thick?" asked Tommy. Just then Pablo walked up and noticed they were looking at Paul.

"I'm a proud Upwardian" said Pablo. "He was one of the first to publish my poetry. If you ask me he takes some real chances. We're all about moving "upward" you know? He saw that and embraced it."

"See what I mean?" said Sam.

"I like the newsletter," continued Pablo. "I especially appreciate the photography."

"Teenage girls," said Sam to Tommy.

"You know something?" said Pablo to Tommy. "You have the exact same hairstyle as Charles Bukowski." Tommy looked at Sam and he nodded. Tommy ran his fingers through his hair. He was genuinely pleased to hear that.

"See that guy over there?" Asked Sam. The guy was tall and old and wearing a colorful dyed wool Guatemalan sweater, clearly he wore it solely for artistic impact as it was nearly seventy degrees out. "That's Merlin. He's a Mormon from Utah but now he's a history professor at Cape Cod Community College. God help you if he ropes you into a conversation. He talks slower than Abraham Lincoln. Just to bust his balls about Mormonism I once asked him if he thought it was possible for a Catholic to get into heaven and he honestly took a long pause and said, without a drop of irony: 'Well in order to answer that we have to go all the way back to the French and Indian War'. He was all ready to give me a lecture on it. No shit."

"Merlin's a good guy," added Pablo.

"Anyway," said Sam. "He heads up the Provincetown Art Association. They're the ones who probably put this together tonight. He's one of the major players in the art scene down here. Sad isn't it? See those women over there?" Tommy saw four very old women in loose-fitting sexy old lady flowery dresses handing out pamphlets. One of them wasn't half bad and she had an ostentatious handmade silver and amethyst crystal pendant obviously crafted by Carl Tasha perched between her sexy old lady cleavage. "Those are his groupies," said Sam. Apparently in honor of his Utah heritage, Merlin sported a pale blue cowboy shirt and a matching turquoise bolo tie under his Guatemalan sweater.

"Don't tell me you don't think that old lady isn't hot," said Pablo.

"She's not bad," agreed Tommy.

"Merlin's gonna want to meet you," said Sam. "I already told him about you but you gotta play cool and act like you don't give a fuck." Merlin was in fact glancing over at Tommy apparently trying to seem nonchalant about it. The old lady groupies were looking at him as well.

"Maybe we'll get laid tonight after all," said Pablo.

"He can make or break a new painter in Truro as sad as that is," said Sam. "He got me my first show."

"Fuck him," said Tommy.

"That's the spirit," said Sam. "We'll make him beg for it."

"And then there's The Outer Cape Art Alliance and the Five-Zero-Eight, Art Collective," said Pablo gesturing toward a group of young trendy looking guys hanging around a display of violent and sexually suggestive drawings and paintings.

"Five-Zero-Eight as in the 508 area code," Pablo explained to Tommy.

"You figured that out all by yourself did you?" Asked Sam.

"Actually I didn't. Paul Squidda told me."

"Of course he did," said Sam. "You realize he's gay for you? I'm just saying."

"No," said Pablo. "You don't give him enough credit. You know he wrote a novel. Everybody loves to make fun of him but he's got a few tricks up his sleeve."

"A novel nobody will ever read," said Sam. "Have you read it?"

"Like I know what's a good novel," said Pablo.

"I guarantee you it has dragons in it," said Sam.

"The Alliance and the Five-Zero-Eight people are headed up by Chris Franz and those tattoo chicks," said Pablo. "That's where you want to be Tommy. They're definitely the coolest artists here besides us."

"Fuck that," said Sam. They looked over at Chris and the tattoo girls. Chris was about Tommy's age and he had slicked back hair and double full length sleeve tattoos. He had stars tattooed on the backs of both his hands. Aside from the tattoos and the slicked back hair he looked pretty normal. He didn't have any piercings or unusual clothing. His look was definitely understated but he was among a group of enthusiasts who were anything but. They were heavily tattooed and pierced neo-rockabilly type hangers on who looked like they should be loitering outside a nineteen fifties bowling alley. The girls were slightly older, alternative, tragically hip, roller derby types.

"They try too hard," said Sam.

"I'd try hard to," said Pablo. "If I could go home with those chicks, they're totally artistic!" Tommy couldn't disagree. He had come across the type in New York. They weren't teasocks — no, in fact they were complete anti teasocks, a type nearly as compelling though usually not half as smart. They were the girls that seemed clever until you got to know them, teasocks on the other hand really were smart. They sported Betty page haircuts with bangs and ponytails and hung out with guys with classic cars and modern day D.A. type hair cuts only without the grease. One of these Betty Page girls in particular was Chris Franz's date and she was unusually tall and fabulous. She had a low cut blouse where you could see that she had two bar-bell piercings on the tight flat skin between her small but perfectly formed breasts. She could have been nineteen or she could have been thirty-five, a woman like that was beyond age. Tommy assumed she had nipple piercings and tattoos on her privates.

"A woman like that would inspire me to do a masterpiece," said Tommy.

"True," said Sam. "But then she'd never let you get around to painting it." Tommy laughed.

"You know that's a really profound observation on the artistic process," said Pablo.

"I know it is," said Sam. "Fortunately you'll never have to worry about it."

"Still," said Pablo. "Those chicks are fucking killer." Sam and Tommy sized them up and nodded. Tommy was way overdue to get laid.

"Not one of those chicks is as cool as Goody when you really think about it," said Sam. Tommy and Pablo thought about it and looked at each other cautiously. They both agreed but said nothing. Everybody loved Goody. Tommy thought it a shame that she hadn't come out. Apparently Goody never went to these sorts of things. She was too cool for school. Apparently she had her own thing going on and didn't like making friends or seeing people. Tommy understood that. If he had been around long enough he'd be the same way.

They went over to Franz's table to get a closer look. It was all sexy comic anime art. Dark stuff. Tattoo art and fantasy type stuff. They were all about snakes and dragons and naked chicks and zombies. Clearly they could draw but their taste was questionable.

"Have you seen this stuff?" Tommy asked Sam.

"I've seen it." He barely gave it a second look.

"Kind of adolescent no?"

"Definitely," said Sam. "You'd think they were all fourteen forever. Personally I don't get it. I mean some of these guys are in their thirties and even their forties and they're still painting barbed-wire and razor-blades, I mean give me a break. Sooner or later it gets old."

"That's just a certain style," said Pablo. "It's not necessarily teen angst; it's like a legitimate genre these days. People like it."

"People are idiots," said Sam.

"It is cheesy," said Tommy.

"How many zombies can you paint?" Asked Sam. "I mean come on. After a while it's just stupid. This whole nerd delusion of making comics into the new American mythology is sad and totally overly ambitious. I'm sorry but I refuse to accept the premise. We already have a mythology and it took thousands of years to evolve. Superheroes and zombies are just a substitute pantheon for geeks who can't get with actual history." Franz approached. He half heard their comments, or at least read the disdain on their faces, but decided to just ignore it and roll with his standard pap anyway.

"Bellamy!" he said. "How's it hanging? Not a bad turn out this year huh?" Sam shook his hand. He then greeted Pablo before Sam introduced him to Tommy. "He's from New York," said Sam. "He's a painter. You're gonna hear about this guy. I figured I'd better show him around before somebody else does."

"Yeah huh? Well you're in good hands," said Franz. "This guy is one of the last impresarios down here. I hope you haven't sold him anything yet? Sam knows all the angles." He laughed and put his hand on Sam's shoulder. Sam sneered at him.

"No, not yet," said Tommy.

"Well then we should work together," said Franz. He handed Tommy the Five-Zero- Eight sign-up sheet clipboard from his display table. "We're putting together a co-op collective of like-minded artists and let me tell you things are really starting to pop. Not like these other art groups who are all about the profits. We're in it for the community. We do mostly charity and public service type stuff." Sam shook his head and smirked. He made a beating off gesture with his hand.

"For the community?" Asked Sam. "The community is the problem. I disdain the community. That's just code for touchy-feely socialism isn't it?"

"Actually it is," said Pablo to Tommy under his breath. Franz wasn't phased.

"No really guys. Don't get me wrong. Don't tell my girlfriend but I'm a closet right-winger! My father is one of the original high ranking Cape Cod literati, so believe me when I tell you I don't take that shit lightly."

"What is he like in the Masons or something?" Asked Pablo.

"This shit is for real," Franz continued. "We're taking it to the streets. We're giving the finger to committees, sub-committees, art associations, councils and art foundations and everyone else that's a tentacle of the man! We're all about art for the people. We have to take it back, you know? We have all kinds of local involvement coming up. We're doing interactive multimedia sidewalk shows — you know real radical stuff. It's time we real artists join together and do something. Sam you of all people should be with us. I know you're one of us; you don't like these Kinkade print people from Jersey and Connecticut any more than we do. You want Merlin the Mormon and his old timey Art Association types running everything down here? Cause that's what's gonna happen if we don't step up!"

"Sounds like you guys have got it under control without us," said Sam.

"Look at him over there," Franz continued on his anti-Merlin tirade. "That asshole can't even paint. Have you seen what he does? He paints birds on pieces of slate! You know like that shit people hang on their doors? His wife is better than he is. Have you seen what she paints? It's like a calendar spread for Hallmark."

"She's got a fairly tight ass for an older woman," said Sam.

"Or maybe you just wanna go with that hunch-backed pedophile Paul Squidda over there? What has he ever done? He doesn't even make art himself does he?" Pablo was about to defend Paul but Sam beat him to the punch.

"He's an art enthusiast," said Sam. Pablo smiled. "I mean sure he's a hunched back weirdo but at least he means well. He's not cynical like you guys."

"Cynical?"

"Yeah we don't paint zombies and comic book stuff," said Sam. "Somebody's got to paint for adults around here."

"You underestimate us." Said Franz. Sam took the clipboard sign-up sheet from Tommy's hands and tossed it on the table before had a chance to sign it.

"Tell you what," said Sam. "You guys put together a show that doesn't look like it came off of the back of some high school freshman's notebook and we'll think about it."

Chris Franz gestured toward the art spread across his display area. "Haven't you ever heard of Frank Frazetta? He brought this style into the realm of fine art!"

"If you had one guy who could paint like Frazetta you could get away with all the snakes wrapped around naked chicks that you wanted. That's what they call transcending the genre. I don't see any transcendence happening here." Sam looked at Tommy and continued. "He's gonna bring up Frazetta? Can you believe that?" He then directed his comments back toward Chris. "That's like saying Merlin's wife should keep painting dune shacks and light houses because Richard Cobb could pull it off!"

"If you ask me Richard Cobb was overrated anyway," said Chris. This last comment was almost too much to bear. Sam would have punched Chris in the face if Tommy hadn't put his hand on Sam's shoulder to calm him.

"Let it go," said Tommy. "He's entitled to his opinion. Come on, let's take a look around."

Chris Franz tried to laugh it off and back down and so they walked away. Chris gathered himself and went back to his beautiful girlfriend. Within moments he was peddling his "let's shake things up" line on another group of people.

Tommy and the guys moved on to the next table and already Sam and Pablo were looking for the first opportunity to slip away into the background to smoke some more pot. By now Tommy was getting buzzed on the wine and feeling a little less self conscious. They found a dark out of the way spot behind a pile of garbage where they could watch from a distance and smoke. There was a microphone and a podium and Merlin began a tedious talk about the importance of the arts on the lower Cape. At one point he actually said: "supporting the arts on the outer Cape is our civic responsibility." It was all Sam could do to keep from heckling him.

"Why is his name Merlin anyway?" Asked Sam. The few stoners who had followed Sam to have a smoke giggled at this. "Really, who the hell is named Merlin? I mean look at him. It's not like he changed his name to be cool or anything. That's really his name."

"Have you guys seen his wife?" Asked Sam. "She's twenty years younger than him. What's up with that?" Tommy was beginning to sense a trend. Sam seemed to have a thing for Merlin's wife. "He must have a big dick or something," said Sam. "Otherwise I don't get it."

"It's probably the money and the power," offered Pablo.

"Right," said Sam. "Cause everyone knows being the head of the Provincetown Art Association makes you a big wheel."

"It sort of does," said Pablo.

"Anyway," said Sam. "I'd throw her a bone." All the guys giggled at this as they passed the joint around. Eventually Merlin wrapped it up and introduced the next speaker, a well meaning guy by the name of Pierre Lachaise. Sam explained that he was a real dip-shit. Eventually Tommy would come to learn that Pierre was one of the coolest guys on the Cape. One couldn't go by what Sam said all the time.

"Here we go," said Sam. Pierre got up to the mike. He was a deadly serious "spiritual" old hippie type guy who clearly spoke for the old guard artists on the lower Cape. Pierre waxed sentimental on all the joys of the spiritual transcendence of the artistic process, without even the slightest hint of irony, and at one point he started to get all choked up and he said: "You know I'm really feeling the love in this community tonight."

One of the local kids standing beside Sam, waiting for his turn to hit on the joint, tried to get in on Sam's sardonic cynicism when he commented: "This guy really needs to grow a set." Then another kid, who was apparently with that kid, added: "He thinks he's a human be-in in Madison Wisconsin."

"Madison?" Asked another confused stoner in the group.

"Madison is the Berkeley of the midwest," explained Pablo who was quite impressed with himself for knowing that (he heard somebody say that at Community College).

"No," said Sam. "Pierre LaChaise is alright in my book. You know why Tommy?" Tommy had no idea. "Because he's the best damn harmonica player on Cape Cod. He's like Satchmo on the blues harp, no shit. Ask anyone." They all agreed. "How many people are really that good at anything?" Once again Tommy was moved by Sam's unusual generosity at times. It always seemed to come out when it was least expected. That was the thing about Sam. He loved to take the opportunity to bust balls whenever it was justified but then on the other hand he never failed to give a guy his due when it was justified. "Besides, look at him," Sam continued. "Who else could pull off that look and really mean it?" Pierre was skinny and he had long hair and a pointed goatee. He sported a classic black French beret. "He owns that look," said Sam. "I'll bet not one of you has ever seen Pierre without his beret?" They all nodded. No one ever had.

Pierre was now talking about his "deep spiritual connection" to the Cape Cod art scene.

"Madison Wisconsin," said one of the stoners to Pablo. Pablo nodded in agreement.

"Ok," said Sam. "Maybe he is a little too sincere for this crowd. I'll give you that." Pierre wrapped it up with a quote from the poem 'Death to Van Gough's Ear' by Allen Ginsburg.

"Poet is Priest." Said Pierre, as he wiped a tear from his eye and removed himself from the podium.

"See?" Said Sam to Pablo.

"You know that poem you wrote was really good," Tommy told him.

"Thanks Tommy."

When the guys were done smoking they got more wine and mixed back into the crowd. Chris Franz ended up talking with Tommy again. Now he had a chip on his shoulder and was clearly pushing his luck when he brought up the relative merits of Richard Cobb and the Ash Can school. Tommy reassured him that he had no real connection to his father and completely understood Chris's reservations about the extent of Cobb's contribution. Tommy actually welcomed the opportunity to prove to himself his own artistic impartiality. Sam on the other hand wasn't feeling as magnanimous. "It was all a little too reactionary if you ask me," said Chris. "I mean don't you think they were just a little too defensive about the whole idea of regionalism? What was that Shakespeare quote, methinks the lady doth protest too much? Like maybe they were a little too quick to deconstruct abstract expressionism ya know?"

"Your mother was reactionary, she deconstructed my dick," said Sam. "And she liked it."

"Nice." Said Franz. He tried to ignore Sam's attempt to provoke him. "Besides," he said to Tommy. "I'm not even convinced that Jack's was the original model for "GAS" anyhow. As I'm sure you're aware there's a lot of contradictory evidence regarding that."

"Is there?"

"Shit yeah. It's never really been settled definitively one way or the other. Have you ever seen those old photos of the gas station that used to be in Newcomb Hollow? It burned down in the fifties but in the old days it looked just like your father's painting. People say he used multiple sources for a given scene anyway."

"I really think it was Jack's," said Tommy.

"Is there any provenance to that effect?" Asked Chris. "I mean besides your hunch?" By now there were a lot of people gathering around. This was in fact a well known long standing controversy in the local art community.

"I can settle it once and for all right here!" Said Sam. He pulled out the now wrinkled and folded-up "Gas" postcard from his pocket, showing it to everyone in the crowd.

"I was looking for that," said Tommy.

"Look at this guy!" Sam grabbed Tommy under his chin and held his face steady so they could see the obvious family resemblance to the man in the painting. "Tommy's face is my provenance!" Chris laughed at Sam dismissively.

"It's pronounced '*provenance*' (Chris said it with the accent on the last syllable like an Englishman would say).

At that point all bets were off and Sam went in swinging. He clocked Chris in the face hard and the crowd exploded into a frenzied mob scene. A couple of guys on either side attempted to pull Sam and Chris apart which led to even more guys jumping into the fray. Within seconds they had a full scale Truro dump art riot on their hands. Tommy even found himself fighting with a guy he had never met. Pablo grabbed Chris by the back of the shirt and tried to pull him off Sam and then Chris's girlfriend came up behind Pablo and got him in a head-lock. Seeing Pablo in trouble was too much for Paul Squidda and so he jumped in, clawing at Chris's girlfriend. Merlin and the old ladies ran for cover and Pierre LaChaise shrieked hysterically. When the melee subsided someone said the cops were on their way and so Tommy and Pablo jumped into the truck and shouted for Sam to follow. Sam, who had now gotten the better of Chris, hit him a couple more times before jumping into the truck. They peeled out and several cars followed but apparently everyone had their own places they wanted to escape to and so Tommy soon lost them on the winding roads between the dump and bay. Sam had it in mind to escape to Whydah but once Tommy screeched into the parking lot at Pamet harbor and saw that they were alone Sam thought better and changed his mind. He didn't have any beer on the boat. They ended up at the Bomb Shelter. They took a booth in the back where they laughed and licked their wounds for a while.

"I think I knocked out his front tooth," said Sam.

"I think I broke some guy's nose," said Tommy as he examined his bloodied and bruised knuckles. "I think I messed up my painting hand."

"Nah," said Sam. "Suck it up."

"That totally hot tattoo chick broke a nail on my face," said Pablo. Tommy laughed. Pablo had a big scratch across the bridge of his nose. "Did you see Paul Squidda when that chick jumped on me? He was all business. I thought he was going to take that chick apart!"

"What did I tell you?" Said Sam. "Squidda really likes poetry. I guess he took Pierre's words to heart. Poet *is* Priest! He put his money where his mouth is tonight, I gotta give it to him. That hunched back pervert can really move when he wants to can't he? I guarantee you he's home writing about it right now."

"He's a true lover of the arts." Said Pablo and they all had a good laugh.

"I guess I'm kind of fucked with the art scene down here now," said Tommy.

"Are you kidding me?" Said Sam. "You're like in like Flynn now. Tonight was the best thing that could ever happen for your rep. Squidda will write all about it. Shit they'll probably even pick it up

162

in the real paper. We couldn't have planned it any better. You don't want to be affiliated with any of those nerd art gangs anyway. You know what we have to do? We have to start our own art group. It's perfect. Everyone will be asking about us now. In fact tonight Pablo should call Paul and tell him we're starting our own new art association because of what happened. Think about it. It's the perfect beginning. We strike while the iron's hot. We'll call it "The Ash Can Collective " and we'll play up the fact that Franz tried to dispute the Cobb Ash Can School connection to Jack's. It's a totally commercial gimmick. I'll put together a show in P-town and get Mailer and Chomsky and all those rich fucks to show up and we'll make a bundle.``

"I don't know about that," said Tommy. "You know I don't want to cash in on my father's fame."

"Fuck that," said Sam. "We'll have a blast. I'll be skipper if you want to remain impartial or whatever. You can be the artistic director and first mate, and Pablo can be the secretary."

"I can be the Poetry Editor in Chief," said Pablo.

"We'll put that in the maybe pile," said Sam.

"Or I could be the treasurer," offered Pablo.

"No, I'll handle that."

"Of course," said Tommy. Sam looked at Tommy a little surprised.

"You don't think it's about that do you? Hell you can be the treasurer if you feel that way. I'm just looking at the big picture here. I know you don't like to get your hands dirty, since you're a pure artist and all that."

"No I didn't mean that," said Tommy. Sam raised his glass and made a toast.

"To the Ash Can Collective!" They clinked their glasses and patted each other on the back.

"This is gonna be righteous," said Sam.

Chapter Eighteen

Over the next week or so Tommy stayed close to Jacks and awaited the call from Apple that never came. He was beginning to lose faith in the whole thing but he couldn't figure out what went wrong. Their date had seemed to go so well. He hadn't done or said anything that could have blown it. Maybe she was sick or she had a boyfriend? Tommy hoped she was sick. A few more days went by and not much happened, other than Jack cutting and splitting a lot more wood. Sam came by a couple of times to "help Jack with the books' '. This seemed dubious to Tommy. Usually Sam ended up changing the figures Jack recorded in his gas log book before pocketing as much money and cigarettes as he could get away with. Sometimes he would come late at night after Jack was asleep to hang out with Tommy. Sometimes he would fill Goody's truck up with wood before he left. Tommy noticed the wood never seemed to end up at Goody's cottage. Jack continued to drink heavily and he kept on drinking the smelly water as well and Tommy was beginning to suspect that it may have been having a negative effect on his health. He seemed to be getting more and more wobbly and disoriented all the time and one night Tommy saw Jack out in his woodlot talking to himself. He carried on an entire conversation with some invisible person in the darkness. Tommy realized that whatever was going on with Jack wasn't getting any better and he decided he would try to get Jack to go back to the doctor. Obviously he would have to be subtle. Tommy had come to see that Jack's laid-back demeanor was actually a front. In reality Jack was quite proud and stubborn.

A couple weeks passed and Tommy heard nothing from Apple. He had now given up and decided to take Sam up on his offer to get him laid. He also decided to push Jack a little. "So are you gonna show me how to split firewood or what?"

Jack went to his utility room and grabbed two truck tires stacked in the corner. The tires were bolted together through holes drilled in their sides. Jack put the tires over a tree stump which doubled as a chopping block beside a pile of cut logs and a wide wedge splitting mall. Tommy grabbed the mall and threw it over his shoulder. "Knock yourself out," said Jack. "You know about our employee health plan?"

"What's that?" Asked Tommy.

"If you get hurt we don't know you."

"Fair enough." Tommy grabbed a log and placed it inside the tires on the chopping block. He took a good swing and a miss and bounced the mall off the tires. "This thing works."

"There are some gloves and glasses in the utility room," said Jack and then he went back to his cutting. Tommy got on a roll. Over the course of a few hours with the occasional break to man the gas pumps he ended up splitting a half a cord of wood. He wanted to impress Jack. Jack was pleased. "That's a hundred and ten bucks right there, if we deliver it. After my costs and not counting your hourly wage that's about forty bucks profit. I'll give you twenty-five," said Jack. Tommy decided to split some more and this time he took the tires off the block. He took a swing and split the log perfectly. Jack smiled.

"Don't get cocky. And you should probably get some proper shoes." Tommy had on an old pair of work shoes. Jack had only flip-flops. By the end of the day, using his gas splitter and saw, Jack had cut, split and stacked three cords. Tommy split another quarter cord by hand (another twelve dollars on top of his regular pay). Jack probably had about a hundred cord on hand which seemed like an amazing amount to Tommy. "We only need about three or four hundred more," said Jack. At dinner time Tommy asked Jack about his father again.

"Was he an asshole or what? A lot of people say he was grumpy. I got the impression from my Mom that he was kind of mean."

"He wasn't bad," said Jack. "He was one of those guys who deserved to be that way. I mean if he was grumpy you felt like he earned it. I guess sometimes he gave the impression he was just kind of putting up with the rest of us you know? He wanted to be left alone I suppose. If you didn't bother him he wasn't bad. At the time I didn't understand, but now that I'm old I can see why he would be that way."

"I think I know the type," said Tommy. "He was a brooding artist. Maybe that's my problem. I'm too nice. Maybe I need to be more brooding?"

"No," said Jack. "It doesn't suit you. There's more than one way to skin a cat. You just need to find your own way."

"Did he paint very fast?" Asked Tommy.

"No," said Jack. He painted very slowly. Apparently that was a problem for him. He would sit and look at his painting all day sometimes, and then, maybe he'd paint for a few hours before going to bed. It wasn't a very good way to work I don't think but I never claimed to understand art. I think he was dealing with a lot of demons from his past, but that was something he never talked about, not with me anyway."

"What do you think it was?" Asked Tommy.

"I don't know," said Jack. "Women, or maybe it was just art. Now that I think about it I remember he used to get all worked up about certain influential writers and critics and art dealers, guys from New York whose opinions he put a lot of weight behind. I suppose they were in a position to make his work more valuable if they choose, I mean on the price tag anyway. He certainly didn't think anybody knew any better than him about what made a painting valuable, but still he had to think about money and that bothered him."

"The critics didn't like him?" Tommy sat on the edge of his seat across from Jack in the sitting room. He balanced his slice of pizza on his knee but he was too excited to eat. This was exactly the kind of thing he was hoping to get out of Jack. Jack ate his pizza for a moment and he glanced at his newspaper before putting it off to the side. He could see that Tommy wasn't going to let him eat in peace. He looked at his cup on the little table beside the couch. It was empty. Tommy jumped up. "Let me get that for you." He went to the cabinet and poured out some vodka and then filled it the rest of the way with water from the tap. Jack took the cup and took a sip. He didn't say anything. "They didn't like him," Tommy reminded him.

"Something about flatness," said Jack.

"Flatness?" Tommy sat back down on the edge of his seat and took a bite of his pizza.

"Apparently a painting was supposed to be flat," said Jack. "And this really got his goat, I guess because his paintings weren't all that flat, or he didn't think they were flat enough. I had no idea what he was talking about. It had to do with a new theory of painting that was coming out of New York at the time, this idea of flatness. All the abstract expressionists were very flat and they were making big bucks and getting lots of attention and unfortunately your father was anything but flat or so they claimed. To tell you the truth I thought it was all just a bunch of silliness. A painting is flat either way isn't it? I never understood why you would want it to look even more flat. As far as I could tell most of those flat paintings were primitive and ugly. They weren't as good as what your father was doing."

"I've heard of that," said Tommy. "I don't think my paintings are flat."

"That's probably a good thing," said Jack.

"Maybe," said Tommy.

"In the end it was all a tempest in a teapot," said Jack. "He made a lot of good paintings and he made a lot of money."

"So I guess he got the last laugh," said Tommy.

"True," said Jack. "He did. But he never felt he got the recognition he deserved, and he let that get the better of him."

Chapter Nineteen

The tourists were back and the summer season was well under way and business was picking up at Jack's. Tommy was now completely into the routine of running the gas station and Jack spent all of his time on the woodpile. Sam and Jack took care of the inventory and the money and the occasional gas delivery but aside from that Tommy was running the gas pumps and the other miscellaneous sales entirely. As far as Tommy could tell Jack wasn't getting any better but this wasn't something Jack was willing to talk about. Jack knew the water was bad but apparently he was determined to suffer and drink it as penance. He was determined to go down with his ship. Still one couldn't argue with results, and the fact of the matter was that Jack was getting a lot of work done. There was no way around the fact that he was cutting and splitting a ridiculous amount of firewood and this was the one thing that kept Jack's spirits up. Tommy couldn't see how Jack could ever sell as much as he was cutting and splitting but he understood that for Jack that was the last thing on his mind. Tommy felt there couldn't possibly be that many people around in the winter to burn all that wood, and he thought maybe it would just sit there until it rotted away. Even with Sam stealing as much of it as he could, the piles were getting ridiculously big. Jack assured him it was only maybe less than three hundred cord and that actually he still needed a good deal more.

By mid July Tommy had managed to finish his fish painting and it was quite good and he had done a couple of other small landscapes as well, but still he really wasn't painting, not by his own standards. Sam was always pushing him and telling him he had a big show lined up if only Tommy could rise to the occasion and get some good work done.

Tommy was still blocked. Apple had never called or come back. He had all but given up on her and was beginning to think about how he should just give up on the whole Cape Cod thing, admit failure and go back to Antonio ashamed and defeated when he finally saw Apple. As cynical as he had become about the whole thing he could never have anticipated just how bad their next meeting would be. He expected it to go badly but really he had no idea.

It was early in the morning when she arrived. Jack was in his utility room sharpening his saws and Tommy was out front unlocking the pumps when three, gray, government- issued, Crown Victorias, with fed plates and tinted windows, pulled in. Out stepped Apple with her hair tied back tight. She wore some kind of strange business suit, Tommy barely recognized her. She was accompanied by Frank in a lab coat, two guys in suits and sunglasses, and two armed National SeaShore cops. Tommy stood dumbfounded. Jack stood beside Tommy.

"Good morning Jack," said Apple. She then nodded at Tommy.

"My name is Robert Bellamy," said Jack.

"You're the proprietor?" Asked Frank.

"I am." Jack shook Frank's hand.

"What the fuck?" Said Tommy to Apple.

"Relax," said one of the cops to Tommy.

"It's ok," said Apple. "He's a friend."

"Am I?"

Frank handed Jack a packet of papers.

"Take your time and look at those," said Frank. "We're from the Environmental Protection Agency. My colleagues here are from the National Seashore. We have a warrant to inspect your property."

"What for?" Asked Jack.

"We have reason to believe your tanks are leaking," said Frank. "Do you have any knowledge of this?"

"Before you answer," said one of the cops, "I'm required to advise you that you have the right to legal representation."

"No I don't have any knowledge of that," said Jack. "I can assure you we've been in compliance with all the recommended procedures."

"That remains to be seen," said Frank. Jack took off his hat and stuffed it in his back pocket.

"I'm sorry if I seem agitated," said Jack. "But are you calling me a liar?"

"No he isn't," said Apple. "We're just doing our job Mr. Bellamy. Please just let us look around and take some pictures and we'll try to make this as easy on you as possible."

"On what basis do you think the tanks are leaking?" Asked Tommy.

"Sir you're going to just need to step aside and keep out of it," said one of the cops.

"It's a fair question," said Jack.

"It's ok," said Frank to the cop. "Ms. Piehl here is our primary investigator overseeing lower Cape ground water. In an unofficial capacity she happened to be allowed into your rest room merely as a public patron when she had the opportunity to observe what appeared to her to be a likely contamination of the well water first hand, at which time she procured a sample which subsequently we have verified as being beyond acceptable limits. I'm sorry Mr. Bellamy but on that basis we were able to procure a warrant. I can assure you it was legally obtained."

"But we don't have a public restroom," said Jack.

"It seems an employee of yours," Frank looked at Tommy, "invited Ms. Piehl in. She was not legally required at that time to disclose her affiliation with the agency. I'm afraid it was just a coincidence."

"I told you I was a scientist," said Apple to Tommy. "I'm sorry, really. We'll get this all straightened out. It will be no big deal really."

"But she kissed me!" Tommy protested. "What the hell? !" One of the cops pulled Tommy aside and spoke to him privately.

"Look, I feel for you but you need to think about yourself now. We know you just started here. None of this can come back at you. Don't put your neck out for this guy. I'm talking off the record here but if there is any kind of culpability here it has nothing to do with you. You're not in trouble. You need to just let us do our job. Maybe the old man had no idea and he'll be fine, but that's our job to determine, not yours. There's nothing you can do now."

"He didn't know," said Tommy.

"Good," said the cop. "Then he has nothing to worry about."

Apple and Frank and the cops were all over the place. They confiscated Jack's files and photographed the pumps and everything else they could think of and they took samples of water from the sink in his sitting room. Tommy put the 'closed' sign in the door and he sat on the bench out front and waited. Jack went back to work on his woodpile before they were even gone. Apple took close up photographs of the duct taped gas pump handle and the rusty pumps and Tommy approached her. "So that's what your nice camera is for huh?"

"It's not like that Tommy. They pushed me into this. I didn't know it was going to be this way."

"So that's it then? You didn't even really want to hang out?"

"I'm sorry Tommy. Don't make this personal. I didn't plan this."

Within hours they had a backhoe and a big drilling truck. By the early afternoon they had the tanks dug up and a hundred foot monitoring well dug out front. The local newspaper people were there and the cops. The whole place was taped off with crime scene tape. Sam and Goody arrived and Goody was crying on Sam's shoulder as they loaded the enormous unearthed rusty tanks on flatbed trucks and took them away, apparently for some kind of forensic analysis. Jack stayed on his woodpile until dark when everyone else was gone.

Tommy was alone in Jack's sitting room with the TV on waiting for Jack to come in and say something. Jack came in. He put a frozen pizza in the microwave and poured himself a drink. He sat on the couch with his newspaper. "Tastes alright to me," he said and smiled.

"It does smell like gas," said Tommy. "I guess the vodka kills the taste."

"I knew it was coming to an end," said Jack. "I just didn't realize it would be so soon."

"I'm sorry Jack. I don't know what to say."

"I told you not to let anyone use the restroom."

"She kissed me."

"She is pretty," said Jack. Jack ate his pizza and read the paper. He seemed way too calm given what had just happened but there really wasn't anything either of them could say or do about it anyway. Tommy sat quietly for a long time and finally Jack spoke.

"I hope it was a good kiss." Jack smiled at him.

"It was."

"You're young," said Jack.

"I guess so."

"Do you know what really happened to your father Tommy?"

"You mean that he offed himself?" Jacked nodded.

"It was my fault."

"No," said Tommy. "I don't believe that."

"I was your age at the time," said Jack. "And I kissed your mother. It shouldn't have been a big deal but I guess, like you, I found out the hard way just how much damage a little thing like that can actually do."

"But that's not why he did it," said Tommy.

"Maybe not," said Jack. "But he didn't take it well. After that it was all downhill. I tried to make it up to him but it just didn't work out."

"I'm sure there was more to it," said Tommy.

"There's always more to it," said Jack. "But my kissing her certainly didn't help matters. Anyway I guess now you'll have to find another place to work?"

"Are you firing me?"

"I thought you'd quit when I told you."

"I guess maybe I should," said Tommy.

"Besides," said Jack. "You pretty much finished me off by letting that scientist girl in the bathroom."

"I wish you didn't see it that way Jack. It was an accident."

"It's alright Tommy. God knows I deserve it. Payback is a bitch, besides there's really nothing left for you to do around here now anyway."

"So that's it?" Asked Tommy.

"Sorry," said Jack. "I guess I've got to work this out for myself."

Chapter Twenty

Apple had a lot on her mind and the last thing she wanted to do was go out on a date with Oliver from her Dad's yacht club but she had made a commitment and decided to stick to it. She did it to save face for her parents more than anything. Her mother really seemed to like him. She drove in her own car and met Oliver at the restaurant. That was her dating M.O. Getting picked up was so cliché. She wore her hair down with a cute outfit and, of course, no make-up. Oliver was well dressed. He was a good-looking guy. He wore a blazer over a tee-shirt with ironed slacks and a pair of impeccably clean retro-style canvas converse sneakers which Apple thought was kind of trying too hard to look casual. He was obviously kind of rich. He drove a late model BMW. It wasn't as cool as Kalesin but then few cars were. She couldn't hold that against him. He was tall and dark and had short hair with a mustache but no beard which was unusual. Few men could pull that look off but maybe that was a good thing? Maybe he didn't care that a mustache with no beard was totally dated? Maybe he was bold that way? Either that or he was just totally clueless. She was already thinking about whether or not she could kiss a man like that but she decided it was best not to think about it.

The restaurant was a cute little seafood place on the water close to the Pamet in Truro. She wished it hadn't been there by the Pamet. All she could think about was her work. Tomorrow she'd be over-seeing the installation of monitoring wells along the Pamet to determine whether or not Jack's gas contamination had reached the bay yet. She computed in her mind that at an average groundwater flow rate of about a thousand feet per year, taking into account the sandy soil in Truro, with its highly absorptive potential, and that it was a good five thousand feet down gradient from the source area, the traces of toluene and benzene might not have made it into the Pamet River basin just yet. If they had that would be bad, as it was the nearest point of any meaningful contact with the wildlife or human populations.

"You seem a bit distracted," said Oliver. "Is everything ok?"

"Tough day at the office," said Apple. "I'm definitely ready for a Cosmo."

Oliver ordered drinks and appetizers. Apple wanted edamame but they didn't have it. "Maybe next time I'll take you to a hippie place," said Oliver. Apple smirked. They got their drinks and some coconut shrimp and jalapeño poppers. Oliver made a gallant effort but the conversation did not come easily. At one point he actually said: "So, tell me about your interests Apple?" Apple honestly couldn't think of any. She almost said photography but then thought better of it and laughed. "I know," said Oliver. "That was a lame question. To tell you the truth I haven't done this in awhile. But in my defense, interesting people usually do have interests." As soon as he said it he realized that could be construed as an insult. "I mean I didn't mean it that way."

"No, of course," said Apple. "What are your interests Oliver?" He thought for a moment and laughed nervously. He couldn't think of anything either. After some more awkward conversation for what seemed like an eternity the waiter returned and took their orders. Apple ordered pan-seared sesame encrusted yellowtail — very rare — with wasabi glaze, pickled ginger and rice pilaf and another Cosmo. Oliver was glad she wanted another drink. He ordered another beer and a chicken parm. How lame, thought Apple. She remembered how Frank liked the chicken parm at Olive Garden. At this point she almost wished she were out with Frank instead. Still Oliver was rich and a lot better looking and he didn't smell like Lysol. "What is it that you do again?" Asked Apple. "Real estate?"

"I flip houses." Apple laughed.

"What is that funny?" Oliver was actually pleased that Apple laughed even though it was at his expense. "Somebody's gotta do it."

"You must be very strong," said Apple.

"Ha ha. I buy houses, fix them up and sell them again for a lot more. It's quite lucrative, especially on the lower Cape. There are a lot of rich people down here that don't have a clue. Actually I think it's a lot of fun. You have to have a creative side to do it well. I really get into the whole remodeling aspect of it. You have to be able to look at a property and imagine what kind of changes would make it more desirable. You have to know what kinds of changes would have the biggest impact with the least amount of expense. You have to wear a lot of hats. Like interior and exterior design, landscaping, carpentry, and masonry, all that sort of thing. And above all you have to know real estate law, and people, and what motivates a sale."

"And you do all that stuff?"

"Well no. I visualize it and pay other people to do it. I enjoy taking the macro view you know? I'm all about the big picture. I mean all these contractors and craftsmen are great at what they do individually but you rarely find someone who seems to reign it all in into a single package you know?"

"That does sound like fun," said Apple. "So you're kind of like an artist?"

"I wouldn't say that," said Oliver. "When it's all said and done I still have to think about the bottom line. I'm a businessman after all."

"Right," said Apple. "The bottom line. That's kind of insightful. Artists don't ever consider the bottom line do they?"

"I suppose that's why they starve," said Oliver. "I'm just too practical for that."

"Yeah me too," said Apple. She was thinking of Tommy. Their dinners arrived and they dug in. Apple enjoyed her tuna and suddenly realized she was having a good time after all. Oliver wasn't such a bad guy. Maybe she would give him a chance. "How's that chicken parm treating you?"

"It's awesome. I'm glad we came." Oliver smiled at her and lifted his glass. She clinked hers against his.

"One of my interests is yoga." She decided he was worth the effort.

"Yoga huh? That's cool. I try to stay in shape."

"I can see that."

"I lift."

"Yeah huh?"

"I can bench like two-fifty." Oliver shoved a forkful of pasta in his mouth grinning. He had some sauce on his chin. Maybe he wasn't worth the effort after all.

"That's a lot I guess huh?" Apple carefully wiped her mouth with her napkin.

"More than my own body weight." After two beers Oliver was now losing up.

"Impressive."

"Yeah well I'm not there yet. I've got a personal trainer. He wants me to do three hundred, but we'll see."

"You'll make it," said Apple.

"Yeah I hope you're right."

"I usually am," said Apple. Oliver laughed.

"You're funny Apple, you know that? I like your attitude. You remind me of your father."

"My father says I'm a barrel of laughs."

"You are. You totally are." Oliver raised his glass again. Apple clinked it, but this time it was totally perfunctory. "I had a friend who was into yoga."

"Really?"

"Yeah he was kind of a wingnut though. I think maybe yoga is more of a woman's thing."

"I don't know," said Apple. She knew it was but still his pointing that out kind of bothered her.

"I mean I can see how it's great exercise and everything," continued Oliver. "I'm all about that but as I'm sure you know a lot of people take it into a philosophical or even a quasi-religious sort of a thing. I mean as a scientist I'm sure you get what I'm saying."

"I do, but science is not incompatible with spirituality."

"Not all of it," said Oliver. "But a lot of it is. Like the whole thing with chakras and power points and all that. As a biologist in particular I'm sure you understand that most of the philosophical stuff related to yoga is kind of silly. I mean think about it. Why would anyone expect a medical science theory from three thousand years ago to still hold water today? I'm sure you know that better than I do being a biologist. Exercise is always good no matter what. I just don't see why they have to get all high-handed on you when it comes to the spiritual aspects of it."

"I don't know," said Apple. "Sometimes there's more to life than what is scientifically proven."

"Right," said Oliver. "Like leprechauns. After all, you can't prove they don't exist." Apple didn't appreciate this last bit of sarcasm and she changed the subject. As they finished their dinner Oliver tried to get back into the easy flow of their previous conversation but Apple was now convinced that he was not a good fit for her after all.

On the way home Oliver insisted on following Apple just to make sure she got home all right. She didn't object since it was on his way and he already knew where she lived anyway. Once at home he followed her up to her doorway to say goodnight. Did he really have to try to kiss her in the doorway? It was so cliché. She let him kiss her on the cheek and only with great effort suppressed a physical shutter. Oliver was so clueless he practically skipped back to his car.

Once inside Apple fed her cats and took a long hot shower. She decided it would be the perfect night to take Goody's advice and try her homeopathic remedy. She boiled a large pot of water, added the tea tree oil and echinacea, and put her face over the steaming mixture with a damp towel over her head. She inhaled deeply and tried to put the events of the day out of her mind. Her date was easily forgettable but the events at Jack's were anything but. The steam rushed over her and completely cleared her sinuses. She couldn't believe how wonderful it made her feel. She boiled the water again and went for a second round. She would definitely have to remember to thank Goody, she couldn't remember the last time her breathing was so easy. Just before she fell asleep she thought about Tommy. He said Krishna wasn't nearly as hokey as most people thought. Oliver on the other hand, would have thought it was hokey. He was definitely a tool.

Chapter Twenty-One

The day after the visit from Apple and the EPA, and Jack's subsequent attempt to clear his conscience, Tommy packed up his truck and drove into Provincetown to brood. He had no immediate plans other than to sleep in his truck and maybe try to find a job washing dishes after all. He couldn't stay with Jack. He wasn't sure if it was because he felt like an ass for letting Apple into the restroom or if he was angry about Jack's revelation about his father, but either way he needed some time to think. He drove out to the beach. Sam was right. It was a lot nicer when there weren't a lot of people around but at least there were girls around in their bathing suits. He never even got to see Apple in hers.

That same morning Sam arrived at the station to take Jack out to talk with Ben Horegold from the gas company. When Sam arrived at the station the place was a flurry of activity. There were maybe a half a dozen cars and trucks and a backhoe. They had the whole place dug up and they were all running around with clipboards and briefcases. Apple nodded hello to Sam as he approached. "Go fuck yourself," he said and walked right past. Jack wore dress shoes and a button shirt and was all business.

"Let's get this over with," he said and followed Sam to the truck. He had hung a sign on the door that said 'Gone Fishing'. For most of the way to Hyannis they rode in silence.

"They're not going to pin this on us Pop. The tanks were less than fifteen years old. Did you contact the manufacturer?"

"They're no longer in business. I'm not sure where that leaves us but we certainly can't pay for the damages. They say it could run upwards of a quarter million just to dig it all up and replace it with clean fill. And that doesn't even include the cost to get new tanks and pumps."

"So that's it then? The business is gone?"

"I'm afraid so Sam. I'm sorry if I let you down. It must have been a very slow leak. I never even noticed the discrepancy in what I was buying compared to the sales. To tell you the truth I don't know how it could have got passed me."

"You never were too good at keeping records Pop."

"I suppose," said Jack.

"Anyway you can't get blood from a stone," said Sam. "I mean what can they really do? The only thing left to do is see what we can get for the land and the name of the business. That's still worth a lot you know."

"Is it?"

"Sure it is Pop. I've been researching this possibility all along you know. You should have taken my advice before this happened and we would have made out a lot better but we still have options."

"How is that possible?"

"Pop we have one of the only businesses on the National Seashore in Truro. It's grandfathered in and they can't take it away as long as you're still alive. If you sell it and the purchaser intends to keep the same business going then they can't do anything about it. You've got one last chance to cash out but if you let it go under then that's it. It's the oldest gas station on the Cape and that goes a long way with people in this community. You know how all these yuppie's are down here. Nostalgia is all they've got. Without that what have they got? Otherwise we might as well be on the Jersey shore. You want the place to continue on don't you? I mean that's important to you isn't it? Even if it's not with you owning it officially?"

"What do you mean officially?"

"Well just wait and see what Horegold says but you may be able to stay on running the place if we sell out."

"You think so?" Jack hadn't considered that possibility. He was slightly encouraged.

"See Pop I'm looking out for you. I already took a meeting with this guy but I knew you'd worry so I kept it under my hat, but somebody's gotta look at the long term eventualities here. They'd buy you out and pick up the costs of refitting the place and of course they'd reap all the profits but at least you wouldn't be out on the street, not yet anyway."

"What profits? I barely make ends meet."

"No offense Pop but you're not exactly a savvy business man. These guys own thousands of gas stations all over the country. They know how to turn a buck. They'll whip the place into shape in no time."

"I'd like to see that," said Jack.

"Well if you play your cards right you will. Just remember what I said. This is our last chance. After this we're done for." They drove the rest of the way in silence. Just as they pulled into the parking lot Jack spoke.

"I told Tommy why his father killed himself. I figured you should know that." Jack lowered his head in shame. Sam nodded as if he agreed it was the right thing to do.

"You're a sentimental guy, you know that? Why couldn't you just let sleeping dogs lie?"

"I'm not myself lately," said Jack apologetically.

"The hell you aren't. Don't worry about Tommy. We're tight."

"He's a good kid Sam. Leave him alone, ok?"

"You don't understand artists, remember?"

Jack sat across from Mr. Horegold behind the desk and Sam stood looking at the bad paintings on his office walls. "You've got to be kidding me," he said. "I'll lend you something if that's what it takes. Seriously I mean this stuff is embarrassing."

"Kids," said Jack to Mr. Horegold. In fact Mr. Horegold was probably younger than Sam but he was the kind of guy who seemed older. Jack nervously thumbed through the contracts in front of him.

"Take your time," said Mr. Horegold. Sam read the papers over Jack's shoulder.

"It's all just standard boilerplate am I right?" Mr. Horegold nodded at Sam almost imperceptibly and winked.

"Admittedly we had to modify the agreement in light of recent developments but essentially it's the same as I told you the last time. We buy you out and take control but you stay on as a kind of figurehead proprietor if you'll forgive the term."

"Of course," said Sam.

"Of course we'll have to make some changes Mr. Bellamy and you'll have to roll with the punches. It may not be easy on you. I mean you're used to having things your own way but you'd have to concede to certain small changes. We'd try to make it as easy on you as possible."

"We understand that," said Sam.

"What kinds of changes?" Asked Jack.

"Well we'd have above-ground storage and modernized pumps of course."

"Of course," said Sam.

"And we'd deck the place out with new signage and asphalt and vinyl siding and that sort of thing."

"And the wood?" Asked Jack.

"We'll work something out with that," said Sam. "The old man loves his wood. It's no big deal right?" Mr. Horegold fidgeted around with his papers and his pen. He opened a drawer and removed a box of cigars.

"Do you like a good cigar Mr. Bellamy? I know I do." Sam took one and smelled it. He nodded his approval to Horegold as he put one in his pocket and one in his mouth. He bit off the end and lit it up. Sam handed another to Jack but he took it and put it in his shirt pocket.

"We may have to get rid of the wood," said Mr. Horegold. "And we usually don't smoke in here," he said to Sam. Sam took a deep puff on the cigar and blew a smoke across his desk.

"It's cool though huh? We're wrapping this up right Pop?"

"No wood?" Jack put the pen down. "I'm going to have to think about it. I'm sure you understand. This is a lot to think about."

"Of course," said Mr. Horegold.

"Just sign the papers Pop and let's get it over with." Jack thumbed through the papers and shook his head.

"This is a lot to take in. I assure you I'll give it my utmost attention." Jack stood up and so did Mr. Horegold and they shook hands. Sam took a plastic bottle of whisky out of his pocket and opened it.

"So we don't get to do shots?"

"I'm afraid not," said Jack. "Not yet."

"Screw that," said Sam and he took a swig.

Chapter Twenty-Two

It was a rainy weekday afternoon when Tommy sat in a dank hole in the wall on the harbor in Provincetown, a place called the Old Colony Tap. The O.C. was the perfect place to reflect Tommy's mood. Not because it was a shitty dive, but because like Tommy even in its gloominess it had a spark of something hopeful below the surface. The patrons were local, not tourists, and though they didn't say much he could tell they appreciated each other's company. They played Keno, watched baseball and talked about the weather. He found their comradery comforting. Like this old dive, even in his gloomy state he was never far from nostalgia. And he was never far from romanticized melancholy, a feeling which is not bad. He reveled in that feeling and, given that he did enjoy it, how then could he call it depressing? Nonetheless it was, kind of. Tommy thought about this and decided that no two people really had the same idea in their minds when they thought about the meaning of words like 'depression' or 'melancholy' anyway. His gloominess was the good kind, like Van Gogh's. It always came back to Van Gogh for Tommy. But he killed himself when he was only a few years older than Tommy. This brought to mind what Jack had told him about his father. Now that *was* depressing. Still, he wasn't sure if he believed Jack. The more he thought about it the more he knew there was only one thing to do, something he was avoiding all spring and summer. They had a pay phone in the back. He was pretty broke so he would have to call collect.

"Hey Mom, how's it going?"

"Tommy, I'm glad you called. I've been thinking about you."

"I know. I'm sorry. I wanted to get my shit together before I called."

"You know you always say that, and I always say it doesn't matter."

"I know Mom. I'm doing ok now but for a while there I was kind of depressed. Did you get my post cards?"

"I did." There was a pause. Tommy knew the post cards would give her a lot to think about. They were written on pictures of his father's paintings. "Did you find what you were looking for?" Her voice was pensive.

"I did. And I made some good friends too."

"Well that's good. You need some more friends Tommy. You were getting to be a little too isolated in your New York studio. I worry you know."

"Mom, you wouldn't believe how social I've been down here. I have lots of new friends out here and I even went on a date."

"That's great honey. I'm really happy to hear that. How did it go?"

"Good. I even kissed her."

"Well I'm glad you're making an effort."

"Yeah it was fun but I don't think anything will come of it."

"Why do you say that?"

"I don't know, artistic differences I guess."

"Oh Tommy you shouldn't be so picky! Just relax and have a good time with it. It doesn't have to be some big thing. You always put too much weight behind romance and try to make it too serious. You need to just let it happen."

"Yeah I know. Anyway Mom I have this one friend and he's showing me around. He's helping me with my painting too. He has connections in the art scene."

"I'd love to see what you've been doing. Are you getting much done?"

"Some." He knew that didn't sound very convincing. "Anyway Mom, this guy, well his father's name is Jack, and he owns the old gas station in Truro where Dad made that great old painting "Gas" can you believe it?"

"Really?" She sounded concerned.

"Well some of us call him Jack but his real name is Robert Bellamy. Do you remember him?" There was a long pause.

"What did he say?"

"He said he knew you, but I wasn't sure. Apparently his memory isn't all that reliable, but anyway he's a nice guy."

"I can't believe he's still at that gas station."

"So you know him?"

"I did."

"Why didn't you ever tell me?"

"I don't know, I guess I didn't want to think about it. You know I never liked to talk about your father or his friends. It brings up a lot of painful memories."

"I know Mom. I'm sorry."

"He and your father were friends. Your father knew him a lot better than I did."

A flood of questions rushed into Tommy's head and he didn't know where to begin so he just blurted it out. "Jack said he kissed you and that was why Dad ended up doing it. Is that true? Is that why he did it?"

"Your father had problems Tommy. Nobody ever knows why. But I will say this, he was a selfish man. It was selfish what he did and he was wrong to do it. He hurt a lot of people. All of us."

"I know Mom. I know you're right about that."

"Jack was a sweet man."

"So it's true then?"

"Tommy I'm going to tell you something but you have to promises never to tell anyone, especially not your new friends"

"I won't, Mom I promise."

"Obviously your father and I had an unconventional relationship. He had his wife and a whole other thing going on in New York and I was just a summer fling I suppose but then things changed and we started to fall in love. After you were born I hoped things would change, that he would get a divorce and that for your sake we would be together. But that was unrealistic. I was young. He couldn't be close to anyone, not us or his real family for that matter. He had his art and that was all he needed. I knew we would always be in the background waiting for him to do something. I was so sad and vulnerable when I met Jack and he cheered me up. I wasn't thinking clearly Tommy, I'm sorry. I always loved you dearly, from the moment you were born."

"I know Mom. I love you too. You never have to apologize to me about anything." Tommy could hear that his mother was crying quietly.

"Jack was already married and had a son when we fell in love and it was so stupid."

"Both Jack and Dad were married and all three of you had babies?"

"I know, it's terrible, but it was the sixties and we were artists. It was a very different time then. I suppose that's why I never got married myself. After all that I could never take the idea seriously. But you shouldn't feel that way Tommy. I'd love to see you get married someday. There are a lot of people who do it for the right reasons and they make it work."

"You loved Jack?"

"I did. Your father and I were having our problems and Jack was closer to my own age and he was so sweet. It seemed the right thing to do at the time but now I realize it was a mistake. It just wasn't meant to be. I was younger than you are now and I felt lost and lonely. Your father was always painting, besides he had his family to worry about. I know he loved you Tommy but he didn't know how to be a father. He admitted that to me. He said it was because he never had a father of his own. Your grandfather wasn't around. Like you he had to grow up without a father."

"I guess it's a family curse," said Tommy.

"No Tommy, you're different. You're not like your father. I know someday if you had a child you'd be a wonderful father. Anybody who knows you can see that."

"And so Dad found out?"

"He didn't take it well. To tell you the truth I was shocked because I didn't think he loved me anyway, in fact now I'm sure he didn't. Back then I was a much different person. We were all crushed. It was a blow to his ego and he wanted to punish me. I was devastated and almost had a nervous breakdown and maybe I deserved it, but you didn't Tommy, and I'll never forgive him for that. You deserved better from him."

"What happened to Jack?"

"He took it even worse than I did. He looked up to your father and he blamed himself. He seemed to just shut down. He left his wife and me. I was totally heart broken. It was the saddest time in my life."

"I'm sorry Mom. I shouldn't have brought it up."

"No you probably shouldn't have Tommy, but I love you."

Chapter Twenty-Three

Within a day or two of the gas spill being made public word had spread all over the five towns of the lower Cape. Everybody was talking about it. People wanted to know how bad it was or who's fault it was. Several newspaper articles and TV spots were done and Jack was beginning to become a local celebrity. True it was based on what he felt was nothing more than a kind of shameful infamy. He half expected to be the focus of a local lynch mob or at the very least to be taken to task by the local press. As it happened he was quite surprised to find that the local community rallied behind him for the most part and the press coverage was mostly sympathetic. After all, his story did fit the media template perfectly. He was an underdog, a little guy, the last of a dying breed. Everybody knew the idea of a real service station where they washed your windshield and let you run a tab was a dying piece of Americana and Jack's Gas was one of the only ones left that hadn't gone under. Articles were written about how during the eighties federal legislation had severely cracked down on underground tanks and how that had wiped out ninety percent of the independent old time gas stations. The independence angle was a big one and of course the papers loved to bring that up. Modern gas stations are never independent, they are franchised, but still under the thumb of massive international chains, and therefore they are standardized. The mere fact that Jacks was actually a separate company was quite unusual. And then the fact that Jack was so clearly an example of "local color" himself made the story even better. One front page article in Cape Cod's biggest newspaper even referred to him as the "Paul Bunyan of the Cape." He particularly enjoyed that one, but he wasn't as folksy and naive as they painted him to be. He knew they would gladly turn on him and eat him alive when they had run out of good stuff to say about him, especially if it could be shown that he had any kind of foreknowledge of the spill, or worse if it was somehow partly his fault. Already there was a hint of suspicion just below the surface, which was to be expected. Especially from certain wealthy homeowners who lived directly downstream. Obviously they were particularly interested in just how extensive the contamination might be, but as for now the facts were not in and the facts that were in were kept secret. For the time being Jack enjoyed the feeling that the community was totally behind him.

This fact was brought home by a couple of very concrete examples, the first of which was the old flag pole out front. Jack had a very tall, very old rusty steel flag pole out front. It was at least thirty-five feet tall and he had always flown an American flag but during the previous winter during one particularly violent nor'easter it had bent over at a forty-five degree angle ten feet from the top. It was much too dangerous to get to with a ladder and so Jack was unable to use his flag for the past six months. Shortly after all the publicity from the spill Jack awoke one morning to find that the pole had been mysteriously repaired in the middle of the night. The repair obviously required extensive measures such as the use of boom lift and a welder. Jack assumed it was the local municipal utility guys working covertly. He promptly raised the flag which definitely lifted everyone's spirits.

Then there was the beeping campaign. Shortly after the first few news articles appeared, occasionally cars beeped their horns whenever they drove by, they would wave to Jack and he understood it was a show of support. Soon others picked up on the trend until it got to the point where nearly everyone in town beeped whenever they drove past. All day long cars drove past and beeped. Never before had Jack been so aware that he was indeed steward to a historical legacy. It was no longer about him, but what he represented to the community. The encouragement this gave him was always tinged with bittersweet regret; He was pretty sure he wasn't up to it. Sooner or later reality would win out. All of the community support could not overcome the fact that he was in ill health and financially broke and that Jack's Gas was about to disappear forever. He still hadn't signed Mr. Horegold's papers. He knew that to do so would be to betray their trust. Clearly it would have been better for Jack to go out with its boots on. He imagined what the place would be like if it were paved over and covered in vinyl siding, and worst of all he imagined it without the firewood. It was nothing short of tragic. Still he wasn't sure he had the strength to sacrifice his only option, his only reasonable out, in order to satisfy the community's desire for nostalgia. He never really considered Sam's opinion on the matter. He had written that off years ago. Still if he did sell out he'd give Sam half the money just to be done with his responsibility to him once and for all, if not for Sam than for his mother's sake. He would have liked to honor her memory.

Apple arranged for a meeting with Jack. When she arrived he was obviously distracted by the men excavating out front as well as by all the cars driving by honking their horns and waving. He looked to his woodpile out back and she knew that was where he wanted to be and so she suggested they go down the street to a local dinner, her treat. Jack agreed reluctantly, he had a lot of work to do. Jack ordered only coffee but Apple called his bluff and ordered an egg white omelet with artichoke hearts, home fries and rye toast. "You want my toast?" she offered.

"I do prefer rye." She laughed. He hadn't intended the double meaning.

"We have to go over the technical stuff but first Mr. Bellamy let me just say that I want things to work out as well as possible for you and I really think I can make that happen if you let me."

"You can call me Jack."

"Cause you've been called worse?" She smiled.

"Exactly," said Jack.

"Well only if you call me Apple."

"Yes Ma'am." Jack sipped his coffee and she smiled at him. "Apple," he added.

"The main thing now is to find out the precise extent of the contamination and to put into place a plan to proceed with the clean-up. If we're lucky it won't be that bad. I'll keep you updated on our findings as soon as possible. I'll be overseeing the whole process and so any questions or concerns you have in that regard should go through me first, do you understand?" Jack nodded. "You have my number," she continued. "Now a lot of people are going to be asking you a lot of questions and the important thing to remember is to not over communicate. We've got to keep everything in house for your own good. Do you understand?"

"Don't over communicate," said Jack.

"Exactly," said Apple. "Loose lips sink ships. We've got to contain this thing, both literally and figuratively."

"You mean contain it in the soil and groundwater as well as in the media."

"I know you're clever Jack. I can see that."

"Well if it does sink I'm going down with it."

"It doesn't have to go that way Jack. I've got a few tricks up my sleeve yet. You're just going to have to trust me. Can you do that?"

"Tommy trusted you Apple. Was he right to?" Before she could answer, the waitress arrived with Apple's omelet. Apple cut up the dish and gave half to Jack. He took a bite.

"You ok?" She asked and he took a bite and nodded.

"I've never had an artichoke heart egg white omelet," he admitted. "I'm afraid I'm probably a bit more provincial than the folks you're used to dealing with. It's not bad though." He took another bite.

"You're not half as provincial as you think," said Apple. "Maybe you can fool the tourists but not me."

"Well I've come this far without eating artichokes," said Jack. "That's gotta be worth something." They sat in silence awhile before Apple spoke.

"Well I never meant to hurt his feelings," she said.

"That's not good enough," said Jack. Apple knew such informality was not something Jack took lightly.

"I didn't see him this morning."

"He's gone," said Jack. "He was pretty shaken up."

"Where'd he go?" Apple tried to seem as unphased as possible but Jack sensed her concern. He simply shrugged his shoulders and let it go at that.

"So tell me what I'm in for," said Jack. "What are the costs of the clean up and am I supposed to pay for it?"

"Well," said Apple. "It's a lot. Several hundred thousand I should think. It will depend on which method we decide to use, which will have to be determined by the type and extent of the contamination which has not yet been precisely determined."

"Several hundred thousand you say?" Jack nearly choked on his eggs. "There's quite a bit of difference between four hundred and eight hundred."

"Of course," said Apple. I don't mean to be so cavalier about it. In any event I assume it's way beyond your means either way."

"Precisely," said Jack.

"Believe it or not that can work in your favor."

"How so?"

"Well Jack I'd like to speak frankly if you don't mind and whatever I tell you you're going to have to afford me some latitude.

We're just thinking out loud right now and of course you're going to have to nail down the actual details with your legal representation."

"Of course," said Jack.

"Well it's kind of like when someone without insurance shows up at an emergency room with a severe injury, which is to say we can't simply turn you away. I mean we can't not clean it up just because you don't have the money. The EPA has funds for these kinds of clean up procedures provided you meet certain guidelines."

"Certain guidelines?"

"Well provided that the spill isn't your fault and provided you don't have any sizable assets which can be seized. You don't own a home or have any real money do you?"

"No I don't," said Jack. "But how would they determine whether or not it was my fault?"

"Well the tanks were in fact under warranty were they not?"

"Yes they are," said Jack. "But it seems the company that installed them is no longer in business. I'm not sure how that works but I've been informed that because they're no longer in business I won't be able to recover any costs from them. You'll have to forgive my naiveté but I don't quite understand how that could be. I mean either the tanks are under warranty or they aren't. I understood that my tanks were. Otherwise I wouldn't have been issued a license to operate, which obviously I was. It doesn't seem right to me."

"We get that a lot," said Apple. "The company who installed the tanks likely went bankrupt in the past few years trying to keep up with the onslaught of claims and lawsuits after the more stringent legislation went into effect about ten years ago. As you know there are very few underground storage tanks left these days."

"So I've been told," said Jack. "So then I may qualify?"

"Probably," said Apple. "But then there's still the question of your own culpability. We have to take that into consideration as well."

"And how is that to be determined?"

"Unfortunately you'll be subjected to an investigation. As I say as far as that goes you'll have to be careful not to over-communicate, even with me, though I assure you I'm on your side in all of this. That will be something for your lawyer to advise you on. Unfortunately you'll have to pay for your legal representation yourself. But I can tell you they take into consideration such things as your own foreknowledge of the spill and any kind of duplicity in trying to conceal it from the regulating authorities."

"I would never do that. Honestly I had no idea."

"I believe you Jack. But you're going to want to get all your ducks in a row as far as that goes, and remember what I said, don't over-communicate."

"I've never had a problem with that, I assure you."

"Good," said Apple. "Keep it up." They sat quietly for a few minutes and Jack was becoming more and more depressed as he processed what she had told him.

"I suppose no matter what happens I won't be able to keep the place open will I?" Apple reached across the table and put her hand on his arm.

"I'm sorry about all this Jack, really. It's true that even in the best possible scenario, and if you're exonerated completely, and we secure the funds for the clean-up, I'm afraid it won't cover the cost of your refitting the place to reopen. The emergency fund would only cover the cost of the clean-up but not the additional cost of the new tanks and pumps which of course would be substantial." Jack was visibly distraught as this idea sunk in. He had no idea where he would go. He had nowhere to live and no possible means of supporting himself. "I'm sorry Jack, really. It's all a terrible mess." Jack's hands were trembling. He was embarrassed and ashamed.

"And when will we know the extent of the damage?"

"We're working on it. I'll be getting most of the data I need within a few days. We have the results from monitoring wells drilled on your property already and soon we'll be able to compare them with samples taken from monitoring wells drilled a mile or so away out in the woods in the national seashore out behind your property and also at the Pamet basin where the groundwater reaches the ocean. Once we coordinate those results we'll have a pretty good idea of what's going on. We're using something called the respirometric method. Basically we quantify the contamination of the groundwater by determining hydrocarbon biodegradation levels from O_2 and CO_2 reaction rates. Obviously I don't expect you to deal with the technical stuff but basically what we're doing is we're looking for certain petrol-chemical additives like toluene and benzene so we can see just how concentrated they might be and just how far they might have spread down-gradient from their source. The extent to which these chemicals can migrate is fairly unpredictable, one never knows. In my experience the groundwater flow-rate is pretty slow on the lower Cape, which is good. The sandy soil has a high absorptive potential and as I say all this will contribute to just what kind of clean-up measures we have to put in place. I've already done some very preliminary estimates and I remain optimistic."

"Well that's something," said Jack. "I'm glad I've got you in my corner. You seem like a very competent young woman."

"Thank you," said Apple. "I'm doing my best."

"Ok," said Jack. "Well you'll keep me in the loop?"

"Of course."

After Apple and Jack had finished their breakfast they sat quietly and sipped their coffee. Jack remembered that he had a small notebook and pen in his shirt pocket. He pulled them out and put them on the table.

"I probably should have taken notes," he admitted. "My memory isn't what it used to be." Apple smiled. She took the small notebook and pen and wrote down two very long and unusual words on it and slid it across the table. He picked it up and read it. The two words she had written were unfamiliar to him, they were: "Supraglottitis" and "Epiglottis" . Jack read them and as he sipped his coffee. His hands were shaking and he seemed to be having trouble breathing. He had no idea what they meant.

"You're not nervous are you, Jack?"

"No, not really."

"Yet your breathing is shallow and you have tremors. How long have you felt that way?"

"It's nothing." He put his hands under the table and steadied himself. He looked at the two words on the paper.

"I want you to ask your doctor about both of those things. They're medical conditions associated with prolonged gasoline ingestion." Jack put the notebook in his pocket.

"I'm sure I'm fine," he said.

"You know Jack, my background is in biology. I'm working in environmental engineering right now just to pay the bills but my real expertise is in toxicology."

"And I'm actually a Reverend," said Jack. He laughed nervously.

"Well then you can give me spiritual advice, God knows I need it. But I really think right now you need to defer to my expertise in toxicology. When was the last time you saw a doctor?"

"I just went," said Jack.

"Well go again," said Apple. "And show them that paper. Sometimes they need a little help. You know these general practitioners aren't always all that good."

"Come to think of it," said Jack. "My doctor is a cute little foreigner girl. She looks like a high school cheerleader but I guess she's probably in her early twenties. She said I was tip top." Apple laughed.

"Yeah well nationality notwithstanding these kids have a lot of stuff on their minds, you might want to get a second opinion."

On the ride back to the gas station Apple had a lot on her mind. Given the fact that she and Jack had seemed to establish a genuine rapport she decided she would cautiously broach the subject of Tommy's whereabouts once again. "So Tommy's gone huh?"

"Well he left," said Jack. "But I'm not sure if he's gone."

"I see," said Apple.

"He told me you kissed him the night you stole the water sample."

"I wouldn't put it that way."

"I'm sure you wouldn't. In any event you shouldn't have kissed him, not if you didn't mean it."

"I'm not like that Jack, really. You have to believe me. You know something — and I'm only telling you this because I think we could actually become friends. I went out on a date the other night with a really good guy, a friend of my parents, a good-looking professional guy who by all accounts could be perfect for me and yet I didn't kiss him. I mean I guess what I'm saying is I didn't kiss this guy and yet I kissed Tommy. Doesn't that say something? I don't take those kinds of things lightly, you know. Why didn't I kiss him?" Jack considered this a moment.

"Maybe," he said "it's because you didn't have anything to gain by it?"

"Oh that's low," said Apple.

"What do I know?" said Jack. "I'm just a broken down old man with an acute case of epiglottitis supraglottitis."

"Yeah right," said Apple. She pulled up to Jack's and he got out. Before she pulled away he put his hand on her own and thanked her.

"I think you're probably a good kid," he said.

Jack went to his woodpile. He cut, split and drank all afternoon and well into the evening until he could barely see straight. He probably split three cords before he passed out from exhaustion. The next day he drove himself to the Wellfleet health clinic where he relayed Apple's concerns to his doctor.

"So you've been drinking and bathing in this water?" Jack admitted that he really didn't bath as regularly as one might expect and that he wasn't that big on drinking water anyway. The doctor took some blood and told him that gasoline intoxication usually presented first with respiratory issues and that in the long term it could have neurobehavioral consequences. "Have you experienced any tremors, hallucinations or abnormalities in visuo-spatial attention?" Asked the doctor.

"I guess I've been seeing things and sometimes having conversations with people that I know have been dead a long time," said Jack. "Is that bad?"

"We'll have to see if we can detect anything in your blood and gastric contents. You should have told me about this possibility sooner. Have you experienced any fainting lately?"

"Well sure I have," said Jack. "But I assumed it was the vodka."

Chapter Twenty-Four

A few days passed since the shit hit the fan at Jack's and Tommy still hadn't spoken to Sam about it. Tommy's tendency to overestimate people along with his apparent need for approval at any cost (a trait no doubt related to his not having had a father) led him to worry about Sam's reaction. He half expected Sam to kick his ass and if he had Tommy would have deserved it. Finally on the third day Sam left a message for Tommy on Jack's machine saying they should meet at Ballston beach and that Tommy should smarten up and bring his gear. By that Tommy knew that Sam meant he should be prepared to paint. As usual he had a way of making art seem like a sport. For Sam making a painting was a physical thing like going fishing or chopping firewood. With the one word "gear" Sam defused any of the pretentious mystique surrounding the making of art. This was encouraging and suggested that he probably wasn't too pissed at Tommy after all. The last time they hung out Sam mentioned they should try working outside just to switch things up a little. Tommy had no problem with that but he wondered how they would get away with drinking and smoking weed out in broad daylight. Of course Sam would have that covered. Even in the height of the season there were places to go if you knew what was what.

Tommy arrived to find Sam sitting in the sand eating a plum. He had a large canvas sack beside him full of beer and plywood and various supplies and he had a boom box, tied to a strap, slung over his shoulder. Tommy decided to get the unpleasantness out of the way as soon as possible.

"That Harvard teasock fucked me huh? And not in a good way." Sam smiled and punched him in the arm.

"It's partly my own fault," said Sam. "I should have gotten you laid sooner. I have some promising leads on that front but you'll have to try to keep an open mind about it."

"I'm not feeling too picky right now, that's for sure."

"That's your problem," said Sam. "You gotta be pickier." He tossed Tommy a plum. Tommy caught it and took a bite. It was good and he nodded his approval. He was now relieved and all too happy to take any shit that Sam wanted to dish out. After all, he felt he deserved it.

"What can I say? I'm an asshole," he said. "I forgot that all the pretty girls were put on the earth just to fuck me up. What's that line from Dorian Gray? Women inspire men to make great art but then they try to keep them from ever doing it?"

"Something like that," said Sam "At least you admit it. Admitting it is half the battle."

"Yeah the easy half," said Tommy. "So what's Jack gonna do now?"

"What does he ever do? He'll probably drink some more and then split as much wood as he can before they throw him out on his ass. By then I'll be long gone anyway."

"That sucks."

"Yeah well you have to look at the good side of things," said Sam. Tommy laughed.

"And what is that exactly?"

"Well none of us have cancer, not that we know of anyway. And it's a beautiful day and we're gonna paint."

Tommy was relieved by Sam's fatalistic attitude. He was a good guy after all, and he was totally right — and not just about Apple. He was right about everything.

Tommy left his truck in a small gravelly lot on the back beach in a place where you weren't supposed to park but Sam told him not to worry about it. He supposedly knew the guy who owned it anyway. They hiked southward along the coast and came to a stretch of pristine coast lined with dunes and cliffs and lots of twisted locust trees. Sam told him this spot was special first because it was the breeding ground of the dreary piping plover, a pathetic little sea bird that everyone who didn't know shit about the area seemed to care about, and secondly because it was known in the old days as the graveyard of the Atlantic. Literally thousands of ships had been wrecked there due to the high winds and unusually powerful currents. "It's pretty mild out here today," said Tommy.

"That's the thing," said Sam. "It's a totally different story just off shore." He explained how the Windowpane Bank was only a couple of miles off shore and that at about half that distance there was a huge and mysterious sand bar that seemed to come up out of nowhere and it was always migrating around so you never knew exactly where it was going to be. In some places there was only ten feet of water over it even in a full sea. Before accurate sonar mapping it constantly surprised even the best of sailors. "That's why in Truro and Wellfleet they call the real dedicated beachcombers like Goody 'wreckers" . Every time a ship would wreck out there they'd come out and gather up all the stuff that washed ashore. That's why this spot has a certain solemnity even to this day," said Sam.

"That and the sad little bird mating grounds," added Tommy.

"Exactly," said Sam. "The dreary Piping Plover."

"Let me know if you see any of those," said Tommy. "I want to know what they look like. I've heard of Plovers, they're like a kind of sand piper that's on the endangered species list, but I didn't know they mated out here or that they were necessarily so dreary."

"Oh they're dreary all right believe me," said Sam. "People don't usually call them that but I got it from a book about Cape Cod in the eighteen hundreds by Henry David Thoreau. They're skinny little sad looking things. He totally nailed it and they weren't even endangered back then. You ever heard of it?"

"I've heard of it. He wrote letters to Emerson from P-town all about the Cape in the old days. That shit is classic."

"It is," said Sam. "But they were gay for each other, did you know that?"

"Oh fuck that!" Said Tommy. "Why do you always have to say shit like that? You have serious issues man."

"I just call'm like I see'm," said Sam. "Read that essay he wrote about the Wellfleet oysterman that he stayed with and then try to tell me he wasn't half a fag."

"I read it," said Tommy. "I didn't get that at all. They just had a different terminology back then. Sometimes things just sound funny when you put them into our modern sensibilities, you know?"

"Whatever," said Sam. "I didn't say he wasn't a great writer."

"Anyway that's bullshit," said Tommy."

"The plover look like little sandpipers," said Sam. "They make their nests out here in the taller grass clumps. You can tell their eggs by the gray speckles on'm. Sometimes I eat them with onion and kale like in a chowder. They're pretty small though. You need like two or three of them to make a mouth full. They're supposed to give you good luck. I don't know about that but they do taste good."

"But they're endangered."

"Whatever," said Sam. "They're all over the place out here."

They continued hiking along the back beach until they reached the Wellfleet breakers.

At one point they saw two women walking a dog along the shore; one of them was topless.

"That's what I'm talking about," said Tommy.

"Dykes," said Sam. "You gotta love'm." Sam explained that this area was considered one of only two nude beaches on Cape Cod (the other was beside Herring Cove in Provincetown). Legally it wasn't really a nude beach but people got away with it since there was no parking lot or easy access to the road. Sometimes gay guys would go out there and hook up for anonymous sexual encounters. Sam warned Tommy to keep an eye out for the so-called 'dune bunnies'.

"I don't know why," said Sam. "But they feel the need to commit crimes against nature in the dunes. It's getting to be a nuisance. I mean I'm as corrupt as the next guy but give me a break. You don't see us out here doing chicks in the bushes do you?"

"That's only because there's no one out here who will let us. If there were girls like that out here I'm sure we'd be all over it."

"I suppose," Sam Admitted. "I guess fags get a good break that way huh?"

"It all evens out," said Tommy. "They catch a lot of shit in other ways."

They hiked a little farther along the trail. They weren't quite on the beach but they could see the water about two hundred yards away. They made their way through the thickets and brambles and found a spot with big rocks by an old fallen down locust tree under the cover of some weathered and twisted maple, scrub oak, and yellow birch. "This is it," said Sam. He threw his pack on the ground. He sat on a flat rock and removed two small primed pieces of plywood from his bag. He handed one to Tommy and leaned his own against a stump making a kind of makeshift easel. Tommy had his fold up back-pack easel and so he began to set it up as well.

"There are some ledges out there about three miles out that are ridiculously good for Halibut," said Sam.

"Halibut is really good," said Tommy. Sam nodded.

"See this," Sam grabbed a piece of a shrub. "This is Wellfleet beach plumb, the good stuff. You stew it with halibut and it's awesome. It tastes kind of like cherry and Apples, only more salty. Goody knows how to cook it."

"You know Sam the more you tell me about all this stuff the more I don't understand why you would want to leave it all behind."

"That's the thing," said Sam. "It's all like that. The whole world is like that. Everything tends to be a lot more interesting than most people realize but people are usually just too lame to see it"

"I see what you're saying but I'm not sure that where I'm from in the suburbs is really all that interesting to tell you the truth."

"No, it is," said Sam. "Believe me, there's a lot to it if you know where to look."

"I should have been paying more attention huh?" Sam nodded.

"The suburbs aren't that old Tommy. The good stuff is right there, just under the surface."

They both set up their easels facing out over the ocean. Sam turned Tommy's around so it was facing back toward the dunes and the forest. "I'll paint this way and you paint that way," he said. "That way we have both views covered. You need to paint the land before you can paint the ocean. The ocean is cliché in a painting anyway. Let's see what you can do with the dunes first — that is if you don't mind I mean." Tommy had a look at the landscape facing away from the sea.

"Well actually if it's all the same to you I was kind of hoping to paint the ocean."

"Nah," said Sam. "I thought you wanted my help? Otherwise what am I even doing here?"

"Ok. No you're right. I'll paint this way if you think I should." Sam waited for Tommy to get set up and then he gave him a beer and hit the play button on his boom-box. The music was rock blues.

"This is Rory Gallager from nineteen-seventy-two, real Irish jam band stuff." Sam started painting. Tommy liked the music but he didn't think it sounded Irish at all. He thought it sounded like Johnny Winter or Stevie Ray Vaughn.

"This is good painting music," said Tommy.

"So paint," said Sam. Sam lit up a joint and started to paint. Tommy jumped in and tried to keep up. They both got a lot done right away and Tommy could tell that Sam was impressed by the fact that he was apparently keeping up with Sam's feverish pace. Tommy painted the dunes and the sky and the trees. Sam painted the ocean and the sky.

"These clouds are looking really cool," said Tommy.

"Clouds are the best," added Sam without even looking up from what he was doing. Now they were really painting. They were both on a roll. The music was good, the weather was good, and everything was clicking. Within an hour they had both nearly completed their paintings.

"Dude I'm kicking ass!" Said Tommy. He had a good feeling about this piece. He had totally captured the landscape and the subtle colors of the dunes and the sky. He was getting reckless. He was using purple and black and doing all kinds of things he didn't usually do. He painted the trees like they were alive and hadn't felt that way in years. There was something about Sam's influence over him that was really getting him going and he wasn't sure what it was but whatever it was it was working. "Dude this is fucking awesome. Look at this tree, am I right?"

"It ain't that good," said Sam. He was looking at his own painting.

"It's pretty good though."

"What's up with that tree over there?" He had zeroed in on the one part of the painting that Tommy had missed.

"I'm on it." Tommy began to fix the tree that didn't look quite right. "Still the rest of it's pretty damn good."

"It's not bad." Sam barely looked at Tommy's work. He was completely absorbed by his own painting which looked great as far as Tommy was concerned. He suspected that Sam was also inspired by their new duo approach to making paintings and he too was maybe painting a little faster, and a little better, than usual.

"The ocean looks pretty damn good," said Tommy.

"Yah think so? You like my pink clouds?"

"I'm all about the pink clouds," said Tommy.

"The pink clouds are bullshit," said Sam. "Too sentimental if you ask me."

"Ok," said Tommy. "I get that. But that wave right there is sweet."

"No, the waves are awesome," said Sam. "I got the wave just right."

"The waves are ridiculous."

"Don't worry about the waves. How are the dunes? How are the trees?"

"Dude these trees are like the best trees I've ever seen."

Within three hours they had both completed better paintings then they had done in months. Sam was skeptical.

"I've seen better."

"Yeah I guess." The sun was starting to set and so they packed up their gear and hiked back to the truck. Tommy drove Sam back to Goody's place. Sam took both the paintings with him and left the rest of the gear in Tommy's truck.

"I need to look at these for a while," he explained and Tommy agreed. "You're all right with Jack for tonight right?" Tommy agreed and reassured Sam that he had a place to go for the night even though he didn't. He ended up driving back out to the Head of the Meadow Beach where he could sleep in his truck. He sat there for a while and looked at the waves while he ate a can of tuna strait out of the can. He was happy and he slept well. When he awoke he was revitalized and ready to talk to Jack, but first he would have some coffee.

Chapter Twenty-Five

The summer was in full swing and though it was nearly eight p.m. there was still plenty of good northern light when Goody parked her truck off a fire road in the dunes in P'town and took Seamus for a walk behind Tasha hill. The moon would be coming up nearly full and she wanted to find something good for her shrine. She was about parallel with the center of town way across from route six facing the back beach where she could walk the fire roads and dirt paths through the woods all the way out to Herring Cove. The first thing she came across was a bit of road-kill not far from the highway; a big raccoon that had his head squashed. Though it looked pretty gross he wasn't that badly decomposed so she averted her eyes while she sawed off its tail with a pocket knife. It was a good tail, definitely worthy of the shrine. It wasn't easy to saw off but once she got started she was determined to get it. After a few minutes of hard work she had it tucked away in her canvas satchel and she felt that was a good find. If she found nothing else at least she wouldn't go home empty handed. Seamus tried to rub the fur on his neck into the remains but she gave him a kick in the butt and he jumped back and then darted off down the trail into the woods. Goody did a small prayer over the raccoon before she pushed it under a bush with a stick and then ran off after Seamus. "Wait up!" He gave a respectful glance over his shoulder but he kept on running. He knew exactly where Goody was headed and was looking forward to running along the shore. The trail wound through the forest past a couple of small ponds, then across a small winding road and then into the dunes out behind Herring Cove. Goody found the small ponds beautiful. People usually regarded them as insignificant since they were only full of frogs, sun fish and turtles. The turtles sat on the rocks sunning themselves until she approached and then they would hear her and slip into the water. They were red-eared sliders, but she liked to call them sun turtles or shank painter turtles, which is what the locals always called them. She knew there were also small-mouth bass in these ponds but she never admitted that because she didn't want anybody coming out there to try to catch them. She cut some of the cat-a-nine tail weeds from the water's edge and shoved them into her satchel and then hurried off to catch up with Seamus. He was already across the streets sniffing around in the dunes behind the beach. The dunes behind Herring Cove were especially good. Out there she always felt like she was in the middle of nowhere. You never knew what you would find out there. Now it was getting dark and the moon was getting good. It came up in the east and she could see it behind the Provincetown monument through the trees. She loved the Provincetown Monument. It was two hundred feet high and said to be the tallest granite structure on the east coast. The reason she loved it was that, way back, when she was new to the Cape, no matter where she wandered in the dunes behind Herring Cove and Race Point she could always tell where she was by looking for it. She could always find her way back to town by following it if she had to. Nowadays she knew every inch of those dunes but she looked back at it anyway because it reminded her of how it used to make her feel so safe.

She decided to take a break and so she sat on some plush green moss with her back against a locust tree and she took out a bag of grapes and her notebook and a pen. She ran her fingers over the moss and thought about how much she loved moss. It was like nature's carpeting. She thought about writing that but then she thought that sounded stupid, even though it was totally true. She wanted to maybe start writing poetry like her new friend, Sam's buddy Pablo Golokovsky, but she could never think of what to write. Pablo was a cool guy. He was a real poet. He never worried about what to write; he just wrote what he thought without questioning it. She ate some of her grapes and wrote in her notebook: "The moss in the dunes is like nature's perfect shag carpet." She thought about this awhile and then scribbled it out. She tried to imagine how Pablo would say it. Pablo was always writing in his notebook. He was an inspiration to her and had encouraged her to write. He assured her that she had a lot of interesting observations, especially about being in the dunes and walking along the shore beachcombing. It was pretty obvious to her that he found her interesting to talk to and that he found her attractive. Goody felt he was attractive as well, even better looking than Sam in fact. She thought about what it would be like to kiss him. He had full lips and nice teeth, and he was tall and lean and had messy hair. She thought he looked like a movie star. Maybe he would help her write? She knew that he would love to but Sam wouldn't be ok with that. After all he was Sam's friend not hers.

Seamus kept running on ahead, and then doubling back to see why she was lingering under the locust trees, but he wanted to keep going toward the ocean. Goody put her notebook away and followed him toward the beach. They went down through a patch of briars and blueberry and then Seamus found something. It was getting dark and Goody wanted to keep moving but Seamus was definitely on to something and so she went to see what he was up to. Seamus scratched at an old piece of rotting plywood under a patch of inkberry shrubs. He was clearly excited. She dug down under one corner and flipped it over and was totally surprised by what she found. It was an old fox's den. There were three perfect skeletons all curled together, a mother fox and two cubs all dead for a few months at least. It was a very sad thing to see. They must have been there since the early spring. The mother had wrapped herself around the cubs but the cold must have been too much for them. It was just a tangle of fur and bones; they had apparently all died in their sleep. Goody took the mother's skull and left the rest as it was. She flipped the plywood over and said a prayer. Seamus wanted to keep moving but Goody had enough for the day. She carefully wrapped the mother fox's skull in a wool scarf and packed it in her satchel. She turned and began to walk back down the trail headed for home. Seamus didn't follow right away, he was hoping to make it down to the shore. "That's it Seamus," said Goody over her shoulder as she headed back down the trail. "We're done for today." She had three good additions to the shrine, the raccoon tail, the cat-a-nine tails, and the skull and she knew that was as good as it gets. "We'll have to go to the beach tomorrow I guess." Seamus agreed, reluctantly.

It was dark by the time Goody got home and Marisa and Spot were waiting out front. Apparently they were famished and couldn't wait to see her. The mysterious pretty black cat was awaiting her arrival as well though she stayed hidden under the trees in the backyard. Goody put out three bowls of food and went inside. She put out a bowl for Seamus when Artemis the ferret came out to greet them. Artemis was getting very old, nearly six or seven, and she easily spent eighteen hours a day half asleep, but whenever Goody came home she'd always make the effort to put in an appearance. She skittered around under foot and as soon as Goody tossed her satchel onto the couch she climbed inside it and then stuck her head out with one of the cat-a-nine tails clamped in her mouth. "Oh you decided to get up," said Goody. Artemis ran off with the cat-nine-tail and hide it under the couch. "That's mine," said Goody. "For the shrine." Goody went to her cabinet above the sink for Artemis' special protein paste. It looked like a large tube of toothpaste. Artemis poked her head out from under the couch. She wanted her protein paste. "Come on then." Goody squirted a little bit on the floor and Artemis ran over and lapped it up. When she was done Goody picked her up and held her close to her face. "What did you do today? Did you get some rest?" Artemis licked her nose and kissed Goody on the cheek. She put her down, flopped on the couch, took off her shoes and began to unpack her satchel. "See what I got?" Goody took out the skull and showed it to her. She wasn't particularly interested but when Goody removed the raccoon tail Artemis jumped back and ran around in circles nervously. "It's ok. Here, take a look." Artemis smelled it and then bit it and tried to drag it off. Goody pulled it away. "No, this is for me." Artemis was disappointed so Goody squeezed out a little more paste on the floor. "Knock yourself out," said Goody. Goody put on some quiet "woman's folk music" , made a pot of chamomile tea and then began to wrap the skull and raccoon tail with copper wire and hang them in her shrine. She stepped back to look at the placement and fiddled around with them until she was satisfied. She then tucked the cat-a-nine tails around them and she thought it looked beautiful. "Now that's nice," she said to Seamus. He looked up at it and sighed with contentment. "Exactly," said Goody.

After Goody had her tea she took her sea salt from the cabinet, made a circle on the floor and then sat down to meditate under her shrine. She made an attempt to contemplate peacefully but she found that she had a lot on her mind. She thought about Sam, and about her college application. She knew she probably wouldn't get in anyway. She knew she was barely smart enough to go to college anyway. She imagined what it would be like if she went to Oregon with Sam in the fall. He said it was like Middle Earth. Maybe she would like it? She really would like to go to Middle Earth but she knew she would miss the Cape. If she got into college she would have a good reason to not go, but she was afraid to go against Sam. He was smarter than her and always had a way of showing her that everything she wanted was wrong. He had an answer for everything, but he was usually right. What did she really have to keep her there? What did she really have going for her? Just her shrine, and Seamus, and the cats and Artemis. This made her sad.

He would be ok with taking Seamus but he definitely wouldn't let her take Artemis or the cats. If she did go she would have to find a home for Artemis at least. Maybe Jack would take the cats? The thought of leaving Artemis broke her heart. Suddenly she felt lonely and hoped that Sam would come over and hold her until she fell asleep.

Sam had been out painting all day with Tommy and then he went to the Bomb Shelter and had a few more beers before he showed up at Goody's. By then he was pretty drunk. Goody was already in bed. She heard him come in so she got up and they sat outside on the front porch while Sam smoked a joint. Goody didn't usually smoke but she had a couple of hits and they began to talk. "What'd you do today?"

"What didn't I do?" Said Sam. "Tommy and I painted out at Balston and we totally kicked ass."

"Tommy's a good artist. I can tell you guys are really getting each other going."

"You don't know the half of it," said Sam and then he got up and went to his truck and brought back the two paintings they had done. He leaned them up against the wall under the porch light. Goody had a look at them.

"This one is yours," she said and Sam nodded. "I like the pink clouds," she said.

"Tommy is a good kid. I mean he's got a lot to learn but I'm making some real progress with him you know? I should be able to sell this one for like a grand easy." Sam took a long drag and melted into his chair.

"That much? Really? Well it's really very nice."

"Shit I could get two grand probably. And he's just getting started."

"Yours is nice too honey. I think maybe you're doing better now that you're inspired by Tommy."

"You think?" Sam kissed Goody on the cheek.

"Definitely. I mean look at these waves. They're ridiculous. I can totally tell it's Truro on the back beach. I mean the way these waves are breaking ya know?" Sam looked closely at the painting and put his hand on Goody's head.

"Yeah well you know that sort of thing, but you gotta look at it the way somebody else would see it. It's not bad though is it?"

"It's really good honey. It's even better than Tommy's really when you think about it." Goody kissed Sam on the cheek.

"Yeah you're probably right. But I've been painting a long time. After all he's just a kid, but he's got a spark. I should be able to get him straightened out. Did I tell you he wants me to be his manager?"

"But you're not going to screw him over or anything, I mean 'cause he's a nice guy and everything." For Goody to say something like that she had to be in rare form. Sam wasn't a mean drunk. If anything he was much more likely to snap at Goody when he was sober. At the moment he was pretty buzzed.

"I probably won't fuck him over," he said and laughed. "Not yet anyway."

"You really shouldn't."

"I don't know why but I feel like I need to protect him and teach him ya know? I just met him but for some reason I see him like a little brother or something. "

"Like how you used to be with Pablo."

"Yeah except he's smart." Goody didn't agree.

"I think Pablo is smart. I mean you have to be pretty smart to be a poet don't you?" Sam shook his head.

"You have to be smart to be a good one," said Sam. "Anyone with a pencil can be a mediocre one."

"I don't know," said Goody. "I think it takes a certain kind of person to do it. Even to write bad poetry you have to be committed and have a certain confidence to keep it up." Sam eyed Goody suspiciously for a moment.

"He told me how you gave him that macramé wall hanging. I think you have a thing for him or something."

"No, I just wanted to thank him for getting me that college application that's all." This was the first time Apple admitted that Pablo got her the application. She was feeling reckless and suspected that Pablo must have told Sam about it anyway. "I'm sure he told you about that didn't he?"

"That's not the point," said Sam. "You should have told me. Since when do we keep secrets?"

"I know," admitted Goody. "I'm sorry. He just wanted to help me because he looks up to you so much. I'm sure that's why he did it."

"Yeah I never got around to kicking his ass for that one," said Sam. "I must be slipping"

"It doesn't matter anyway," said Goody. "I never even heard anything from them. I must have sent it in too late. Or maybe my application was so bad they didn't even think it deserved a response?" Sam didn't say anything but he shifted around in his chair and spat over the porch rail. The subject clearly agitated him. "Maybe I should give them a call," she added. Sam flicked his cigarette into the woods.

"We're going to Oregon in the fall. You know that. I mean what are we talking about here?"

"I don't know, I guess I just wanted to see if I could get in, you know? I was curious. Besides how I can just pick up everything and leave? What am I gonna do with the shrine?"

"It's just a bunch of fucking bones! We'll throw them in a box and bring them with us. Come on Goody you really have to start wrapping your head around this thing. I'm going. I already bought the land. It's all set. I'm doing this for us, you know? We have to think about our future. Sooner or later we have to get set up for the long term. We can't just keep fucking around with no plan, I mean we've invested a lot into our relationship over the past few years haven't we? Are we just gonna throw it all away 'cause you don't want to stop collecting your damn seashells? I told you they have a fucking ocean out there anyway."

"And what about Artemis? What am I gonna do with her?" Sam jumped out of his seat and paced around on the deck.

"It's a goddamn rat for Christ's sake! I told you we could bring Seamus, even though I don't know how we're going to drive cross country with a huge dog but we'll make it work, but now you're gonna bust my balls over Artemis? You're gonna throw it all away over a fucking rat?"

"I didn't say that," said Goody. "I'm just saying I don't know what I'm going to do with her, that's all. You know how much I love her."

"You're not the only one making sacrifices you know. I'm selling Whydah to that piece of shit Nate Nickerson for half what she's worth. You know how much I love her and how hard it is for me to sell her don't you?"

"I know," said Goody.

"But I'm doing it for us, Goody. We have to start thinking about our future."

"That's exactly what I'm doing, Sam. You know I have ambitions too. I've been thinking a lot about my future lately. You never ask me about what I want. Do you even know what I want? I want to be a poet and a marine biologist! That's what I want!" Sam had a crazed look in his eye and he couldn't help but smile. Goody knew it wasn't a good smile. "Go ahead and laugh! Don't hold back, but that's what I want." This was the first time Sam had heard she wanted to be a poet.

"A fucking poet now? ! Oh that's rich! You don't even fucking write do you? I knew you had a thing for Pablo! How could I have been so stupid? I'm gonna fucking kill him!"

"It has nothing to do with Pablo Sam. Nothing at all. You would think that wouldn't you?"

"Oh right," said Sam. "You and your fucking macramé wall hanging! I'll bet he loved that huh? He's not even published. Do you know that? That stupid god damn rag that Paul Squidda puts out doesn't count; believe me nobody reads that shit."

"I have no idea what you're talking about Sam."

"Yeah right."

They sat in silence for awhile but they both just stewed in their thoughts until Sam blurted out: "A fucking marine biologist! You barely made it through high school! Give me a break Goody."

"Fuck you Sam!"

"Fuck me? Fuck me! "Sam was mustering all his self control just to keep from slapping her. Goody knew he was capable of it, he had done it once before but she was determined to hold her ground for once and she remained calmly seated as he paced back and forth in front of her. "Ok you be a goddamned marine biologist poet and I'll be an astronaut! You've got it all figured out. I'm glad you're finally planning for the future."

"It's not that crazy Sam. I've got to do something. I just didn't want to work at the health food store forever. Is that so wrong?"

"No it's not crazy," said Sam as he stomped down the stairs into the front yard and into his truck.

"Where are you going? Why can't we just talk about it?" Sam riffled through the papers in his glove compartment and found

Goody's college application that he had stolen from her mailbox. He stormed back up the porch and threw it at her feet.

"There's your damn application! What do you think of that?" He lit a cigarette, cracked open another beer and sat down in his chair. Goody picked it up and saw that it had never been mailed. She was devastated. She fell silent as a tear rolled down her cheek.

"You took it out my mailbox before it went out?"

Sam nodded.

"You can only push me so far Goody. What am I supposed to do?" Goody said nothing. She began to cry. "Come on, let's go to bed." He put his hand on her shoulder and tried to be consoling but she shrugged him off.

"No."

"Come on," he grabbed her arm forcefully and led her sobbing into her bedroom. They undressed silently and got into bed. He tried to be gentle with her but she was distant and in shock. They ended up making love but Goody wasn't into it and it was only a half a step away from rape. When she awoke in the morning Sam was already gone fishing.

Goody got up and went through her morning ritual as if in a trance. She threw her unopened college application into the fire and took Seamus for a walk on the beach. Walking on the beach seemed to cheer her up, as it always did, and she had already begun to internalize Sam's oppression. She blamed herself. She should have got the application done sooner if she was really serious about it. It was an awful lot to spring on him so quickly after he had already made all his plans. He was probably right anyway. How could she be a marine biologist poet? The whole thing was so stupid and unrealistic. Maybe Oregon was the answer? Maybe it really was like Middle Earth? She really would like to live in Middle Earth. She had always wanted to live in a world like that. The fact of the matter was that Sam was always the one with a sense of direction and a plan. He was smarter than her. He could be cruel but he knew what to do and he always seemed to be right in the end. She brought Seamus home and went to work. She spent the day in a kind of foggy haze and she was never far from breaking into tears.

On her lunch break she sat on a bench in front of the Wellfleet library and had a tuna sandwich. She saw Tommy drive by and when he waved she tried to smile but he could tell there was something up. He parked, went into the grocery across the street, and then when he came out he walked over to say hello. They talked for a few minutes but it didn't take long for Goody to reach out to Tommy. "He likes you. Maybe you could talk to him." Goody put her hand on Tommy's arm. Tommy shuffled uncomfortably.

"I don't know what I could say. Are you sure you're ok?"

"Oh I'm fucking great," said Goody. "Never better. I'm awesome can't you tell? But he likes you Tommy. I think he would really care what you had to say. You're a nice guy, you'll think of something."

Tommy reassured her that he would see what he could do and then he was off. Tommy knew he wouldn't say anything to Sam. How could he? He thought about kissing Goody. That was all he could think about. She was very interesting, and pretty. Obviously that was out of the question and so he tried not to think about it.

Chapter Twenty-Six

It was a pleasantly warm afternoon in Truro with the sun sparkling on the bay as Apple and Frank hiked toward Pamet harbor. Apple was all business with her hair tied up and her clipboard under her arm but Frank looked like he was on vacation with his partially unbuttoned shirt, sunglasses and floppy canvas hat. Frank took an exaggerated breath of the fresh air and smiled. "Man we really gotta get out like this more often ya know?" Apple smirked at him and said nothing. Frank was unphased. "Do you like my hat? I sent away for it from an L.L. Bean catalog. I wear it whenever I do field work. It just kind of puts me in the mood I guess. I think it's important to look the part. It's not stupid looking is it? I mean I like it but you know sometimes women have a better grasp on those kinds of things." Apple looked at the hat more carefully.

"I guess it's not that stupid looking." Frank was encouraged.

"Maybe I could find like a feather hat pin for it or something?"

"Don't push your luck."

They followed the trail as it wound down beside the Pamet River until they reached the picturesque brackish marshes and then the tidal flats where the river emptied into the harbor. The tide was nearly out and off in the distance they saw an old man wading among the flats with a bucket and a small rake. He was collecting clams. "I don't know if I'd want to eat any of those just now," said Frank. "And that's what really pisses me off about this whole thing."

"I'm sure they're fine," said Apple.

"You like a little benzene with your cherry stones do you?" Apple opened her briefcase and removed a small plastic vial. She squatted at the edge of the marsh and filled the vial with a sample of the brackish water.

"We're over six thousand feet north east of the site boundary here. I can't imagine we'd pick up anything." She capped the vial and placed it in her briefcase.

"No huh? What makes you so sure? Have you done any preliminary calculations?"

"Of course I have. What did you think I was doing all week?"

"Same as always," said Frank. "Fiddling around with your pig eyes."

"Actually I wish. Ever since you dragged me into this whole mess I haven't done a single assay and it's really starting to bug me Frank. Remember you promised me I'd still get a chance to publish by the fall?"

"And you will Apple, trust me. In fact I have some good news on that front."

"Really?"

"Yes but we'll talk about that later. Let's stay focused. The sooner we get this whole mess cleaned up the sooner you can get back to your eyes."

"Anyway I'm optimistic."

"About the eyes?"

"No, the groundwater flow rate. I ran the solute-transport numbers all last week."

"Well I hope you're right but we'll find out one way or another," said Frank.

"The groundwater flow rate from the source area is relatively slow."

"Relatively?"

"Precisely," said Apple. "Provided we get the soil excavation going on site as quickly as possible. What the hell are you guys waiting for anyway?"

"I'm on it. You know that sort of thing takes a lot of local coordination and resources to get underway. These National Seashore bureaucrats are in a whole other world, not to mention the excavation guys, they got their own language. You have to grease a lot of palms to get something like this going in a hurry. I think these guys with the backhoes and trucks might be connected with the syndicate out of Providence."

"Don't be so dramatic."

"You ivory tower scientists don't get what we administrators have to go through sometimes."

"I thought you were a scientist Frank?"

"Nah, who am I kidding? I didn't get here 'cause of my S.A.T.s or anything like you did Apple. You know that." Apple put her hand on Frank's arm and smiled.

"I'm just kidding Frank. I have to admit we make a good team. I could never put up with the crap you have to deal with. What did you get on your S.A.T.s by the way? I'm just curious."

"I didn't have to take them on account of my attention deficit disorder." Apple laughed.

"You know all the angles I'll give you that."

"It's a legitimate disorder recognized by the American Medical Association, and believe me it has no bearing on one's intellectual aptitude."

"Of course not."

"It's nothing to be ashamed of. And as long as we're sharing I also have a touch of dyslexia."

"I'm sure you do," said Apple.

"Sometimes I see Rs and Ks backwards."

"That must be really annoying."

"You don't know the half of it." Apple removed a small baggie and a plastic spoon from her briefcase and handed them to Frank.

"We can ascertain a preliminary hydrocarbon biodegradation level from the o2 and co2 reaction rates in the mud but you have to get way out there." Frank took the baggie and the spoon.

"What do you want me to do?"

"You didn't get that L.L. Bean field study hat for nothing did you?" Frank reluctantly trudged out into the muddy marsh.

"You're employing a respirometric assay?" Frank was knee deep in mud. Apple laughed.

"See you're a scientist after all Frank." After he had done it Frank was actually glad to get his hands dirty. As they walked back to the car he was feeling accomplished and ambitious.

"We're really gonna bring this guy down. That's for sure. You really came through Apple. I knew you would."

"I don't look at it that way Frank. I want to help Jack. He's really sweet. He bought me pancakes the other day. I honestly believe he's a good guy."

"Whatever. In any event Jack's Gas is going down. By this time next year it will be an empty lot enveloped by the National Seashore and he'll be retired."

"I don't know, maybe he'll pull through. I think I'd like to see him work something out. He's such a nice guy Frank. You should get to know him a little."

"Get to know him? Apple get serious. He might be a nice guy but we're going to bring him down and the sooner you get used to that the better. I mean that's what this is all about. That place is finished. Clearly he doesn't have the means to pay for the clean up and to rebuild the place or he would have done it already. Short of him selling out to a big gas company there's no way. And nobody wants that to happen, not even Jack himself. You want to see him sell out to some corporate jackals and turn Jack's into another blight on the National Seashore? Even he doesn't want that. Better to go out with dignity. I'm sure you're right about him. He's an old time Cape Codder and the kind of guy who would rather go down with the ship than sell out and that's exactly what we want. Don't lose sight of the end game here Apple. The guys upstairs want Jack's to go out with dignity and that's what we've been tasked to do. If you feel guilty about it you need to suck it up. You're better off positioning yourself to benefit from it. You've provided a great service and the E.P.A. won't forget that. Believe me I won't let them. My ass is on the line too, you know."

Frank drove Apple back to the Lab parking lot. He parked beside Apple's smart little Audi. As Apple got out Frank handed her a manila envelope. "This is what I was talking about with the pig eyes. You're gonna love it. Look it over and call me if you want to talk. Otherwise I'll see you on Monday." Apple took the envelope and jumped into Kalessin.

"Thanks Frank," she waved and he was gone.

She thought about driving home before opening it but she couldn't wait. She tore open the packet. Inside there were a couple of clippings of articles published in leading American biology journals referring to Apple's work in the measurement of microtubule nucleation as well as a two recent papers published in England from scientists from the University at Eton regarding Apple's work in the organization and dynamics of growing microtubule plus ends during early mitosis. And finally, and most importantly, there was an article about new legislation proposed in Europe which heralded the inevitability of an eventual ban on certain laboratory assays including among others the Draize rabbit eye tests for nearly all cosmetics and household cleansers. The article went on to suggest that American standards and practices were likely to follow the European model. Apple understood that this was huge. If tests such as the Draize rabbit eye assay were banned on the basis of animal cruelty then her own assays on non-living pig eyes would become a logical alternative. She would stand to make a fortune. She couldn't believe that Frank was so on top of these developments. He really was looking out for her. Finally there was a letter to the department of biological sciences of the EPA in which Frank suggested that Apple be a delegate at the biological science conference regarding these developments to be held in London in the fall. This news really cheered her up. If she could get her paper done on time she could present it to some of the most influential people working in the field, and she could likely tour London for a couple of days on the EPA's dime. She drove home elated. Rather than take Route Six, which she usually did, she opted for the longer, more scenic route Route Six A, which wound along the shore overlooking the bay through Truro, Wellfleet and Eastham. In Wellfleet she stopped at Lemba's Health Food to pick up a couple of things. She thought she might like to say hello to Goody and thank her for her homeopathic remedies which she felt were clearly working. She hadn't had a single asthma episode since she started using the echinacea and the tea tree oil. She had learned from her conversation with Jack at the diner that Apple's boyfriend was Samuel Bellamy, Jack's son, and this made her a little reluctant to follow up on her new friendship with Apple. It probably wasn't such a good idea to get any more involved with Jack or his family on a more personal level but she decided that since Goody really had nothing to do with the gas station it might not be too big of a deal. Still from what she had gleaned from her conversations with Apple, Tommy, and Jack, she knew that Sam was probably going to be a problem and she would rather not bump into him if she could help it. Still, in her current state of elation, she decided to go for it anyway. She parked in Wellfleet Center and went into the shop. She didn't see Goody and so she bought some soy milk and protein powder and headed back toward her car when she noticed Goody across the street sitting on a bench in front of the old Congregational church. She walked over and said hello. She could tell that Goody was in a sad mood and so she sat down beside her. "I was hoping to see you," said Apple. "I just wanted to thank you for your advice last week. The echinacea and tea tree oil are really working out for me."

"Glad to hear it," said Goody. "Tea tree oil in particular is one of my favorites. I use it for everything." She seemed distracted. She looked over her shoulder and shuffled around uncomfortably.

"Yeah," said Apple. "I did some research on it in my lab and you were totally right. It's high in vitamin E and has all kinds of healing and restorative properties. It totally has an antifungal effect. Just about any hair or skin issues are usually nine times out of ten because of some kind of fungus or bacteria."

"Yeah huh? I guess there's a lot of invisible stuff? Things you can't see?" Goody smiled. What a cute way of putting it Apple thought.

"Definitely."

"You know my boyfriend Sam doesn't believe in cellular biology. I told him that's what you do and he said it was a scam made up by scientists and the liberal media. But he doesn't believe in anything he can't see you know? That's what he said. I do though. I totally believe in it." Apple laughed.

"That's silly. Cells aren't even that small."

"Aren't they?"

"Well it's not like atoms and molecules and quantum physics and that sort of thing. That stuff is very small and I sometimes think half of it might really be made up. He may be on to something actually."

"He usually is," said Goody.

"But with plant cells you can sometimes see them with just a regular magnifying glass. They're not that small."

"I don't need to see a thing to believe in it," said Goody. They sat for a while in silence watching the cars drive by.

"So how are you doing?" Said Apple. "What's new?"

"Just enjoying the beautiful sunny weather. I found a nice fox skull yesterday out in the dunes by Herring Cove."

"That's great," said Apple. "I'm not too familiar with the trails out there."

"Oh they're good," said Goody. "I always find something out there."

"Maybe we could take a hike out there sometime?" Asked Apple. "You could show me around a little."

"Ok."

"I'll give you my phone number and maybe you could give me yours?" Goody told Apple that she didn't have a phone but she could call her from a pay phone in town.

"Really? You don't have a phone? That's so cool."

"It's not that great," said Goody. "But the price is right." Goody handed Apple her poetry notebook and a pen and Apple scribbled her number on the back.

"Make sure you call me. We should definitely hang out. You said you wanted to do some yoga. Maybe we could do that?"

"Ok."

"Ok well I've got to go but make sure you call me ok? Do you need a ride or anything? It's no problem. Come on, I'll give you a ride." Goody shook her head.

"I'm good. I'm gonna sit here for a while anyway. I just feel like sitting here.

"Ok then I'll see ya," and with that Apple was off.

When Apple got home saw that she had a message from Oliver on her answering machine. He was a nice enough guy but he just didn't do it for her, she wasn't sure why. Obviously he had a great time and was looking forward to going out again. She thought that maybe Oliver's expertise in real estate law would be helpful to Jack but she decided to put that idea on a back burner because she really didn't want to have to go out with him again. Eventually he would try to kiss her and she knew that just wasn't right. She fed her cats, had a cup of chamomile tea, took a shower, rubbed Goody's tea tree oil all over her body and then got into bed with her notebooks and papers to do a little work. She reread her two papers on centrosome maturation and growing microtubules during early mitosis and she was even further convinced than usual about just how awesome and groundbreaking they really were. She scribbled notes in the margins and thought about how she was going to get her pig eye assay totally ready for the conference in London, and though she was very excited about it all she found that her thoughts inevitably wandered to other things, namely to Goody and the gas station and how she might be able to maybe help Jack if she were willing to stick her neck out at the agency. She knew that there were certain new approaches to cleaning up large scale gas spills that were regarded as experimental, but she might like to suggest them for Jack's. She knew that Frank and his lackey advisors would no doubt think they were a bit too radical. That was where her unique expertise in biology and toxicology could really make a difference. Why not use this opportunity to do some real science? If it worked out she could publish a paper on it. This was the kind of thing that

Frank and the rest of the EPA bureaucratic guys had no clue about but that was supposedly why they liked her. She was a scientific rogue and a loose cannon. They didn't know the half of it. Their idea of a clean-up was to excavate as much of the soil around a spill as possible and just hope for the best. It was so primitive! Specifically what Apple had in mind was something called bioremediation which was the use of certain microbial degradation processes to detoxify the groundwater system. She thought about how Goody said that Sam didn't believe in microbes. "What a jerk! He'd probably get along great with Frank." She would propose adding selected oxidants and nutrients to enhance biodegradation in the affected soil — little known techniques such as air sparging, hydrogen peroxide addition and bioslurping. Some of the cutting edge research suggested that there were certain laboratory-selected microbes that specifically consumed gasoline and turned it into relatively harmless carbon residue. Furthermore, and now she was really getting ahead of herself, she was aware of certain radical new studies which suggested that it was possible to genetically engineer new hitherto unheard of cultures of a uniquely aggressive hydro-carbon-degrading bacteria. She jotted down some notes on the subject and decided she would have to run it by Frank as soon as possible. She was so worked up about it she got out of bed and made a cup of warm soy milk and echinacea before finally going to sleep. She had already stayed up an hour past her bed-time but eventually she slept well and in the morning she had another particularly vivid dream about Krishna. Once again he was beautiful and shirtless, playing his golden flute, and he had a small ferret sitting on his shoulder kissing his cheek.

Apple awoke refreshed and ready to get to work. In a blender she mixed frozen raspberries, frozen blueberries, protein powder, and soy milk and had a tremendous smoothie and then had a good cardio workout on her treadmill while listening to the final chapter of her Dad's lecture series on Goethe's Faust. Now she totally got it. How could her father have been so right on? Of course he was clever but this was ridiculously apropos and she assumed it had to be a coincidence. She was indeed Faust; there was no way around that. It was supposed to be a cautionary tale about why one shouldn't be like him but she was too far gone to even care about that, otherwise she wouldn't be like Faust anyway. One thing, however, that did give her cause to reflect was something that the satanic demon character

Mestophanies said to Faust. He said: "I am the deity who always denies. Mine is the philosophy of repudiation!" This struck a cord with Apple. She knew that the prevailing corporate culture at the EPA and more specifically Frank's attitude toward Jack's Gas was a philosophy of repudiation. She liked to think that her own motives could be something beyond that. She decided that she would make an effort to go against that. When others said "no we can't" she would resist with a resounding: "yes we can!"

Chapter Twenty-Seven

It was a drizzly afternoon in early august when Tommy drove down route six in Truro and saw Jack out in front of the gas station. He beeped and Jacked waved as he drove past and kept going. Tommy hadn't spoken to Jack for a few weeks and he still hadn't found another job. He had been sleeping in the back of his truck and was pretty much at the end of his rope and was beginning to think about going back to New York. He drove about a mile past the gas station before he pulled a u-turn and headed back. If nothing else he just wanted to see how Jack was doing and apologize for the way things had gone down.

As he pulled in the first thing he noticed was how much Jack's woodpile had grown. He must have had a few hundred cord by now. He saw that the whole front of the place was all dug up and the tanks and pumps were now gone and Jack was apparently no longer open for business. Jack smiled and seemed genuinely pleased to see Tommy. "How's your summer going kid?" Tommy told him things were kind of tough but that he was hanging in there. "You and me both," said Jack.

"Looks like you're getting some wood done anyway." Jack looked at the huge piles out back which were now a good deal higher than the roof of the gas station. Still he shook his head in disapproval.

"I've been distracted lately. I should have had three hundred cord by now. At this rate I'll be out of wood by Christmas."

"How much would you say that is?"

"Maybe two hundred and fifty if I'm lucky, I need at least five."

"I'm sure you'll make it. You've got some time."

"Just barely," said Jack. "We'll see."

"Actually Jack I was hoping you'd let me split some. I'd do it for free. I just feel like I could really go for some hard work you know? I've been lying around far too much lately and I'm starting to feel like a bum." Jack thought about it and then walked into his garage utility room. Tommy followed him inside. Jack handed Tommy a chainsaw and a thin round file.

"Here, take these. I'll show you how to sharpen the chain. This rasp is called a rat tail."

"Sweet," said Tommy. Jack took the saw back. "The blade is called a bar. You clamp the bar in the vice so the saw floats above the bench like so. You have to do it so the chain still moves freely. If you move the chain manually and watch the teeth you'll see that there's one spot where there's two teeth in a row on a single link. That's where the chain starts and ends."

"Like on a bicycle chain," said Tommy.

"Precisely. That's where you start. You take the rat-tail and you give it one or two passes at a thirty-three degree angle like this. You can go for a third maybe if you don't feel you had just the right angle but definitely no more than that. And don't ever drag it backward either; it's all forward strokes." Jack pushed the rat-tail forward over the tooth at a thirty-three degree angle. Then you push the chain forward, skip a tooth, and do the next one and so on. When you get to the end you start on the other side and do all the teeth facing the other direction. Got it?"

"Got it."

"Ok then, there's that one and those other two." Jack took another saw and went out back. Tommy could hear Jack cutting as he sharpened the saws. He was careful and took his time and so it took him about forty minutes to do all three saws. When he was finished he went out back and split some wood by hand. He decided not to use the tire jig and found that he could definitely manage without it. Later Jack showed him how to use the gas splitter and Tommy did that for a couple of hours while Jack used the chain saws. Tommy really enjoyed using the splitter and loved the way it felt. He knew that if he put his hand in front of the log it would take it right off easily. Still it wasn't dangerous; you would really have to be good and drunk to cut your hand off with a log splitter. When Tommy quit he thought he had a good size pile. He figured it was at least a cord. The sun was getting down into the trees and Jack was now pretty buzzed and so he put his saws away in the utility room. When he came back to check on Tommy he had two plastic cups, very full, with cheap white wine. He handed one to Tommy.

"Ok that's enough." Tommy shut down the splitter and took the plastic cup. Jack picked up a piece of split wood and smelled it. He handed it to Tommy and Tommy smelled it. "You know what that is?" Tommy shook his head. "Elm," said Jack. "It's shit. I mean it's hard wood but it's basically shit. It's hard to split, it's smoky, and it burns as cold as a churchyard." Jack tossed it aside and picked up another piece and handed it to Tommy.

"Oak," said Tommy.

"Red oak," Jack corrected him. "Very good stuff. It smells a little like dog shit but it also smells kind of good for some reason." Tommy smelled it.

"I see what you mean. It does kind of smell shitty and good at the same time."

"It's dense and it burns well. The white oak is even better." Jack handed him a piece. Tommy smelled it.

"It smells salty."

"Chicken soup," said Jack.

"Totally." Jack handed Tommy a piece of maple.

"Now that's good firewood. It seasons up twice as fast as the oak and it's just as hot, but it burns up a little faster. You want to use maple to get a fire started in a hurry."

"I love maple," said Tommy.

"This here is poplar."

"Good stuff?"

"Nah," Jack tossed it aside. "Has a bitter smell and burns like shit. Now ash looks like poplar but it's a whole other ball of wax." Jack picked through the pile and found a piece of ash. "Ash puts off more heat than oak or maple and it will burn soaking wet. I'd make my whole wood pile ash if I could afford it."

"They make hockey sticks out of it," Tommy offered as he sipped his wine.

"Indeed?" Asked Jack. "Well then hockey sticks make good firewood."

Jack gestured for Tommy to follow him around front. "I've got to bail the well awhile if you want to keep me company." Tommy followed Jack to a newly dug well just under where the gas pumps used to be. The National Seashore guys had drilled a hole six inches in diameter and a hundred feet deep and then jammed a pvc pipe all the way down to the water table under the station. Jack showed Tommy how he was supposed to bail the well a few times a day. He had a long hollow plastic tube tied to about a hundred feet of clothesline. It was maybe four feet long and had a small hole in both ends and kind of looked like a plastic wiffle-ball bat attached to a rope. The idea was to drop it all the way down until it submerged in the water table and filled up. Once it was good and heavy you had to pull it up quickly before all the water drained out of it which wasn't easy given that you were pulling on a hundred feet of rope and all the way up the well the water was slowly running back out of the bottom of the tube. If done correctly the tube would still have a foot or two of water in it by the time you quickly pulled it out of the hole, and at the top of the tube there was a layer of gasoline a few inches deep because gasoline separates itself from water and it floats. He'd empty the tube into a five gallon plastic bucket, drop the tube back down the well, and then start over again. It took nearly forty five minutes to fill the bucket, which was then emptied into a much larger specially designed bio-hazardous waste drum. It took maybe twenty five buckets to fill the drum and Jack had two such drums. Once a week an EPA guy would be by to pump them out and Jack made it his personal mission to make sure they were always full and ready to go. "I gotta pay them to tote this stuff away," said Jack. "And it's not cheap. But anyway I'm trying to get as much up as possible. It's got to be done."

"Let me do it for a while." Jack went inside and Tommy bailed the well for hours. He was really getting into it and filled several buckets. By the time he had enough his clothes reeked of gasoline and Jack had gone to bed and so Tommy climbed into the back of his truck and fell asleep.

Over the next couple of weeks they cut and split twenty cord and bailed at least five drums of gassy water. Jack decided to pay Tommy ten bucks an hour. At one point the EPA guys told Jack they might be able to get their hands on a special automated pump which could probably suck up as much, or more, as he was managing to manually bail from the well. That only encouraged him to bail even more. Tommy knew that Jack wanted to bail that well by hand as much as possible. He was doing it as a form of penance and Tommy was all too happy to bail the well as much as possible himself. He too felt he had a certain penance he needed to pay back to Jack.

One morning as Tommy was sharpening the saws and Jack was mixing the 2c oil with gas for the saws Jack decided to share something with Tommy. "You know I'm pretty sure that Sam is just trying to screw me with this deal he's got cooking to sell the place. I don't know, what do you think Tommy? You think Sam's right or what? I'm sure he's told you he wants me to sell the place."

"He told me. But he told me not to tell anyone. He wants to sell Whydah and move out west. It sounds pretty crazy to me but what do I know? Don't tell him I told you."

"Oregon," said Jack. "He's been talking about that for years. What the hell does he know about Oregon? Still, I know one of these days he's gonna do it. Maybe he's right? Maybe I should retire?"

"Well do you want to? That's the only question. I mean don't do it if you don't want to."

"To tell you the truth Tommy, I really don't want to retire."

"No?"

"I mean what am I gonna do? I just want to keep going. I'm too young to retire. I just want to keep cutting wood. That's the only reason I want to keep this place. I don't know what I would do if I couldn't keep splitting firewood."

"Well then do that," said Tommy. "Hang on to the place as long as you can and just keep cutting firewood."

"Sam can be persuasive."

"I know," said Tommy. "But it's your gas station."

"Maybe you could talk to him," said Jack. "I think he'd listen to you."

"I don't know about that. This is you guy's deal."

"Just talk to him, trust me. Give it a shot anyway." How could Tommy turn Jack down? Obviously he owed him a lot. Still he couldn't imagine giving Sam advice on what to do with the gas station or his father.

"You know Jack, I talked to my mother about you. She told me she was once in love with you."

"I'm sure she didn't put it that way."

"No, she did. That's what she said. I don't take that lightly."

"She was exaggerating, I'm sure. I only kissed her a couple of times."

"A couple of times? You told me you kissed her once."

"We may have kissed a few times. It was the sixties after all." Jack gassed up his saw and went out back. Tommy followed behind with a gas can and began to fuel up the splitter. He could hear the occasional horn beeping in solidarity as the cars whizzed by out front. Despite the unfortunate circumstances that made it possible, Tommy realized how much better he felt about this new arrangement. He wasn't nearly as comfortable out front pumping gas and talking with customers as he was now out in the woodlot. He knew that processing firewood was the perfect job for him. It was physical and outside in the fresh air in the woods, and it was relatively mindless and involved absolutely no responsibilities. Because Tommy identified so strongly with being an artist he felt that, unlike most other people, he didn't need to feel intellectually stimulated by his job. He just wanted to be left alone and daydream all day, besides he found that he did feel a real sense of accomplishment when he saw how much wood he could split in a day when he put his mind to it. Also he felt really good about being able to help a guy like Jack who was so clearly appreciative and worthy of his help.

Jack did not like to speak that often, certainly not about personal matters, but at the end of the day he surprised Tommy with this question: "So how is your mother anyway?"

"She's fine."

"Married?" Tommy shook his head.

"I'd like to see her some time. Do you think she'd ever go for anything like that?"

"I don't know," said Tommy. Tommy didn't want to hurt Jack's feelings but he knew there was no way in Hell she'd do anything like that.

Chapter Twenty-Eight

Eventually Apple got a hold of Goody on a Saturday afternoon when they were both off and so they decided to meet at an outdoor café in Provincetown at a place beside the public library called The Café Blaze. The public library was a cool old building on the east end of Commercial Street and out front it had an old oak tree with a bench that was built in a circle right around the trunk of the tree. Apple sat there under the old oak and watched the tourists and locals pass by. It was fairly easy to tell the locals from the tourists. The locals walked differently. They walked faster and had a sense of purpose as to where they were going, often eschewing the sidewalk for a path out in the street where one could cut through the crowd more easily. Also the locals tended to have bicycles or the occasional skateboard and they dressed differently. P'town fashion was definitely a bit more European and avant-garde, you saw lots of scarves and expensive shoes and big shiny Dolce Gabbana sunglasses, and, as in any tourist community, the locals carried themselves with a certain air of superiority. Apple checked out The Café Blaze. It seemed a bit swanky for Goody's taste but she had suggested it and so Apple thought Goody had probably done so in her honor. Apple decided she had better pick up the tab. Goody arrived wearing a flowing black silk blouse and her messy hair was tied up on the top of her head like a palm tree. She wore lots of chunky costume jewelry and a silk scarf. She was definitely a local. "Hey now," she said and hugged Apple without restraint and Apple enjoyed Goody's warm and enthusiastic informality. "Nice place huh? You ever been here?" Apple told her she hadn't but it seemed great. "You want to get some lunch or just have tea?" Asked Apple.

"I could eat. What are you in the mood for?"

"I like everything," said Goody. "But I'm a pescatarian."

"A pescatarian?"

"Yeah I eat any kind of vegetarian food and seafood, but no meat."

"Well then I'm a pescatarian too," said Apple. "And I didn't even know it."

They ordered chamomile tea and then shared a tomato, basil and mozzarella salad and an appetizer plate of tiny triangular cucumber and crab sandwiches. The sandwiches were excellent.

"Cucumber sandwiches are big in England," said Apple. "They serve them with onions and cheese." Apple explained to Goody how she was planning to go to England in the fall for her big pig eye conference.

"That's totally awesome," said Goody. "That must be so great to have a good job. I mean not because of the money or anything like that. I just mean it must feel good to know you're doing something important for the world."

"It does feel good," said Apple. "But I just started and you're younger than I am. I'm sure you could do it if you really wanted to."

"You think so?"

"Oh I know so. Most people don't even start getting their shit together until they're at least your age." Goody looked down and blushed.

"I suppose"

"I didn't mean you don't have your shit together Goody. I didn't mean it like that."

"I just meant you're so young, we both are. We're certainly too young to start settling for less than we deserve and having regrets about it. You know what I mean don't you?"

"I do," said Goody. "I definitely have dreams. And not just dreams but real plans you know?"

"I'd like to hear about them," said Apple. "I mean if you don't mind my asking." Goody sat quietly for a few moments.

"Maybe later." Goody sipped her tea.

"Of course." Apple had another tiny cucumber sandwich and watched the crowd as they passed. "This is a great spot for people watching." Goody nodded.

"So pig eyes huh?"

"Yeah, they're actually quite fascinating."

"I've often thought," Goody mused, "that pig eyes are a true window into a pig's soul." They both laughed.

"That's true."

"But seriously," added Goody. "Pigs are really smart, and you can totally tell when you look into their eyes."

"Indeed," said Apple. "I think all animals are pretty smart in their own way."

"I don't know," said Goody. "What about jellyfish? Do you think jellyfish are smart?"

"Well maybe not. Not like a pig is smart. But jellyfish are probably smart in their own totally alien perspective of the world if you know what I mean."

"They're smart at being jellyfish," said Goody.

"Precisely," said Apple. "I think that's where philosophy and science kind of get all mixed together. We just measure intelligence by how close an animal thinks like a human which of course is totally unfair."

"That's because men have written most of the science instead of women isn't it?" They both laughed.

"You may be on to something there."

Apple and Goody sat there talking for a good long time, longer in fact than it usually took to turn over a table at lunchtime and their server, who was clearly a nice guy, was getting a little impatient. They told each other a little about their backgrounds and their families and where they had grown up and gone to high school. Goody had grown up in a trailer in a farming community in western Massachusetts and had gone to a high school that only had about twenty-five kids in her graduating class. Though Apple and Goody had very different backgrounds they seemed to understand each other, and trust each other easily. And though it was an unusual feeling, both understood that that's how it goes when you do meet someone who could potentially become a good friend. Of course Apple played down her privileged background as much as possible. What else could she do?

"So you're a wash-ashore," Apple teased her.

"Yeah it's true," said Goody. "But I'm a year-rounder and that's what really matters down here."

"I can see that. I've never lived on the outer Cape in the winter. It must be nice. I mean I've driven down here in the winter so I know what it's like but it must be really peaceful and everything."

"Oh I love it," said Goody. "It's way better than in the summer. There's nobody at the beach and when you go into town to go to the post office and the market you know everyone you bump into. It's like being from a really small town but I don't even think being from a small town is the same really because we look at it differently ya know? We look at it differently because we only have a small town for like five or six months at a time. It's kind of special that way."

"I'll bet."

"Sometimes I think I'd like to live in a place that's like P'town in the winter year round, but I don't know if anyplace is like that," said Goody.

"Maybe like Maine or Oregon," said Apple.

"Oregon? You don't say?"

"Yeah but I don't like the West Coast," said Apple. "I don't know why but it just feels so different. It's like a whole other country out there. It's just too far away or something."

"Yeah," said Goody. "Sam likes Oregon but I don't know if he's ever really been there." Apple laughed.

"You're so funny! Do you know that? You're really funny."

"No I'm not," said Goody.

"All right well I told you about my pig eyes Goody so you have to tell me about something you're into. Tell me. What are you into these days? What makes you tick?" Goody laughed nervously.

"Now I feel like I'm on a date or something."

"Oh screw that!" said Apple. "Interesting people have interests, and I know you're an interesting person so what are you into?" Goody told Apple how she had been trying her hand at writing poems lately and that she might like to go to a local open-mike reading in the basement of the Surf Club that evening and that maybe if she could get the courage up she might like to read one. "Oh we have to go," said Apple. "I'm totally down with that."

"Ya think?"

"Oh I'm totally down," said Apple. "Let's just go, no pressure or anything, we'll just check it out and if you're feeling it, then maybe you'll read. Either way I'd like to check it out. You can see what kind of stuff other people are writing. It'll be fun." Goody was glad that Apple was pushing her to go. That way she'd have an excuse. She knew that Pablo would probably be there.

"If I'm gonna read we're going to have to go out and have some cocktails first."

"Whatever it takes," said Apple.

When they finished their lunch Goody suggested they go back to Wellfleet to take Seamus for a walk.

"I'm open for anything." Goody wanted to pay for lunch and, though Apple would have rather paid, she graciously acquiesced. She did however insist on taking care of the tip. She went a little overboard and left forty percent. They walked around town awhile and did some window shopping by the galleries on the east end before heading out to a small residential neighborhood off Bradford Street where Goody left her truck.

"The cool people never pay for parking in P'town," she quipped.

"I left mine in a free spot between the fire station and the supermarket on the other side of town," said Apple.

"Exactly. It will be no problem over there." They jumped in Goody's truck and headed for her cottage in Wellfleet to pick up Seamus and her poetry notebook.

At home Goody introduced Apple to Spot, Marissa, Seamus and Artemis. Apple was amazed that Goody had a ferret. Artemis scurried around Apple's feet and darted off. "That's so cool that you have a ferret. You know I've been thinking a lot about ferrets lately for some reason."

"Me too," said Goody.

"She's beautiful."

"You can tell she's a girl. That's good. Usually people think her name is a boy's because of Artemis Pyle from Lynyrd Skynyrd or this other guy that was a vaudevillian comedian apparently."

"No Artemis is the Greek goddess of the hunt," said Apple. "I totally get it."

"She sure is," said Goody. She took out Artemis' protein paste tube and squeezed a little bit at her feet. Artemis quickly lapped it up. She handed the tube to Apple and Artemis sat at her feet fidgeting. "See, she likes you. But she's not much of a hunter I'm afraid. Not unless you count my dirty socks. She's all over hunting those guys. She drags them under the couch and eats them up. I'm lucky to get two or three uses out of a pair." Apple crouched down and fed Artemis some paste.

"Do you know the story of Artemus and Actaeon?" Goody shook her head. "Well as you know Artemis was a huntress, and known to be beautiful but fierce. She was also known to be very modest. She was perhaps modest to a fault. One day Actaeon accidentally saw Artemis bathing in a stream. He saw that her body was muscular and fit but also subtle and feminine and he was very much impressed with her beauty. Artemis was shocked and embarrassed to see him hiding in the reeds leering at her like that and she became so angry that she threw water on him, turning him into a stag. He was then chased down and killed by his most trusted dog." Goody laughed and took Seamus around the neck and hugged him.

"You wouldn't do that to me would you? Even if I was turned into a stag?" Seamus licked her face and wagged his tail. "I wouldn't put it past him. He's not too bright."

Apple stood before Goody's shrine and soaked it all in. "This thing is amazing!"

"You like it?"

"Like it? Goody, it's amazing. I'm blown away by it. This thing is like the coolest thing I've ever seen."

"Sam says it's not really art. You know because it's all found stuff."

"Oh it's art," said Apple. "It's art and it's more. It's science. Look at these shells. You've got everything in here." Apple pointed to a small colorful shell and looked at Goody.

"That's a slipper," said Goody. Apple pointed to another. "That's a hoof shell."

"And these?" Apple fondled the shells hung on copper wire under the skulls.

"That pretty one is abalone and these are key-hole limpets and regular limpets and that one there is a chinese hat shell, or a turban shell." Apple pointed to another.

"That's a dog whelk right?" Goody nodded. "And this is a triton?"

"A hairy triton," Goody corrected her.

"And you've got periwinkles, moon shells, cone shells, scallop and auger shells."

"And what about this one?" Goody took a lumpy little ugly shell off the wall and handed it to Apple.

"I don't know what this is," said Apple. "Some kind of oyster?" Goody nodded.

"It's a winged thorny oyster. These guys make great big silvery pearls."

"It's beautiful," said Apple.

"And they taste really good," said Goody.

Goody, Apple and Seamus drove out to the secret ponds in Wellfleet. They were clear and sandy and good for swimming but only the locals knew about them. The only way to get to them was off the slightly illegal fire roads that ran through the south Wellfleet woods on the ocean side off route six. Apple was glad they hadn't taken Kalessin. Goody's little old truck cleared the trees by mere inches as they bumped and jostled along on the narrow winding path that would barely qualify as a road. Goody drove right over a bunch of saplings and shrubs and parked in the middle of the woods. They got out and trudged through a patch of briar just to get down to the water's edge. "Pretty huh?" Goody was obviously proud of her secret spot.

"I love it." Seamus was already off into the woods.

"I'm gonna take a dip." Goody took off all her clothes and jumped into the water. "Oh it feels so good! Don't worry, there's no one around." Apple wasn't usually the skinny dipping type.

"When in Rome," she said as she stripped down and jumped in and swam underwater. When she popped her head up she howled with delight. "Oh that's so good!" Seamus jumped in; he was looking for turtles. Goody got out of the pond and climbed out on the edge of a boulder that jutted out over the water. As she prepared to jump she yelled to Apple: "Watch out for the snapping turtles!" And then she did a cannonball. Seamus understood the word "turtle" and got all excited. Apple was a little concerned and dog paddled around afraid to put her feet down in the muck.

"I don't like snapping turtles!"

"They're not all bad," said Goody. "Just because they're not cute they get a bad rap."

"Oh that's true," said Apple, still treading furiously though she was in barely four feet of water. "They're definitely not cute!" Apple made her way over to Goody's jumping rock and climbed up. She stood there completely naked overlooking the beautiful pond and the surrounding forest and for a moment, before her modesty got the better of her, she felt completely refreshed and exhilarated. Goody swam over, climbed up, and stood beside her. Goody's body was lean and muscular and Apple felt a little embarrassed by her own slightly chunkier physique. Apple looked her in the eye and smiled.

"It's kind of nice to swim out here without men leering at you like they do at the beach."

"Yeah," said Apple and she looked at Apple's tattoos and her belly button ring. It was a silver hoop with a purple gemstone. "That's an amethyst isn't it?" Goody fondled her belly piercing.

"Yeah," she said. "Amethyst is the stone of alchemy and spiritual cleansing. It's a very simple and common gem but it has amazing healing potential. I guess I don't have to tell you since you're a scientist."

"Actually I really don't know about that but it sounds fascinating."

"Oh it is," said Goody. "Being in the ultraviolet spectrum, amethyst works with ultrasonic wavelengths as a spiritual stimulant to disinfect certain conditions of the central nervous system."

"Really?" said Apple. "That sounds like the sort of thing we do down at the lab but I've never heard of it. Still I know I need to be more open to new ideas. After all, you were right about the echinacea and the tea tree oil."

"Remember how I told you Sam doesn't believe in your cellular biology stuff? Well don't feel bad because he doesn't believe in the therapeutic use of amethyst either."

"No huh?" Said Apple.

"Nope. He doesn't think scientifically. I think that's maybe why we get along so well Apple, because we both think scientifically you know? I mean I'm not a scientist but I'm interested in science."

"Yes I agree." Apple looked closely at Goody's belly piercing. "Wow, that goes in really deep. Did it hurt?" Goody shook her head and she was a little embarrassed by Apple looking so closely at her belly. She jumped into the water.

The poetry reading was in a little basement bar on Commercial Street in Provincetown. It had a small stage with a microphone, colored lights, plush red couches, and little black cocktail tables. Apple had been to an open mic poetry reading in college (just one) and she felt she knew what to expect. Actually this one was quite a bit better. They had a decent crowd and a bar and the occasional singer/songwriter to break it up between the poets. The poetry was a little hard to take, not just for Apple, but for almost everyone there, but obviously that was the whole point. It wasn't supposed to be easy to take but for all of its goofy earnestness there was the occasional person who actually got up there and bared their soul and that is always inspiring (or so Apple convinced herself after two Grey Goose Cosmos and an afternoon of skinny dipping). Goody also had a Cosmo, and though she had never had one before, she quite enjoyed it. By the time Pablo showed up she was completely elated and she knew that she would have to read. He came over to say hello and Goody introduced him to Apple. Pablo surmised that she was the woman investigating Jack's who kissed Tommy but he didn't say anything about it. He sat with them for only a few minutes and then he politely excused himself and was off. Given that he was about to read he was nervous and not really in the mood to socialize.

"He's really cute wouldn't you say?" Said Apple. Goody nodded and blushed. They chatted awhile before the first poet took the stage. She was a pretty young woman who wore a Russian fur hat and a fox stole over her shoulders. She had a French Canadian accent and a low gravelly voice and though Apple could not really make out what she was saying she knew that it was interesting. At one point she said: "Obsessions are power. Eyebrow ring women, Bookstore Witch women, Spy women and the Sun Princess. These are the women haunting me. Women I name because I don't know their names. Eyebrow Ring Woman I would die for you! Writers are great lovers, our details matter! The stupid little things that happen to us! The conversations that we overhear, that old woman that I watched push a dead squirrel out of the road with a stick! Why did she do that? You tell me. Attachment equals vulnerability and that equals contingency! Love requires intense interest, hence the need to write." The Canadian girl then paused dramatically to smoke her cigarette. "Collected here are some of the poems and poesy of our lovely little one cow town. At their best they don't completely suck." She mock curtsied and left the stage. Everyone knew she would be a tough act to follow.

"That chick is hot," said Goody.

"For some reason I want to kiss her," said Apple and then she laughed and sipped her drink.

"No, I completely get that," said Goody. "That girl is so Canadian. She's a French Canadian like Leonard Cohen and Jack Kerouac. That's what makes them so cool, being French Canadian. Those guys really know their poetry."

"I didn't know that," said Apple.

"Oh definitely," said Goody. "These Canadian lesbians are like on the cutting edge of something."

A couple of not so good local poets followed. Mostly it was adolescent and angry but at certain points it was definitely mature and morose. A young scruffy guy with half a beard sang Jim Croce's "Time in a Bottle".

"Normally I'd rather slit my wrists than listen to a song like that but I don't know; I think he kind of transcended the genre," said Apple.

"Yeah? Really? I wouldn't know." It was late by the time Pablo got up and the crowd was getting pretty lively. "Ok here he goes!" Goody perked up in her seat. Pablo had an unlit cigarette in one hand and a glass of beer in the other but no notebook or papers. He paced in front of the mike for a while pretending to gather his thoughts. The room got quiet but still he said nothing. He put his lips to the mike and was about to speak but then he stepped back a few feet, put his drink on the floor and lit his cigarette, took a long dramatic puff, and then cleared his throat. He waited another moment, until the silence was almost painful, and then he began.

"Strindberg, Dostoyevsky and Jean-Paul Sartre walk into a bar..." (the smart people in the room chuckle).

"The bar keep is like: Why the long face?" A few more people laugh but they're not sure why.

"A buddy of mine told me that Hank Bukowski had severe acne all over his body and that that actually helped him to become such a great poet. That may be so but I still say he got a lucky break in life. Sure he was abused as a kid, had a dead end job, and was ugly as hell but other than that he was born lucky. The man had honey in his veins and he knew what was what. Me I'd rather be ugly and smart any day, but look at me, I'm like fucking Brad Pitt over here." (Again the crowd laughs). "Besides he had good hair and one can never underestimate the impact that has on a man." Pablo ran his fingers and threw his own good hair. "Oh he had a good head of slicked back hair and a chin like Kirk Douglass. He had a head of hair like Herman Melville. And that chin! You could back a semi into that dimple for Christ's sake! With that head of hair and that chin he looked like Henry Wadsworth Longfellow. You ever see that painting of Longfellow hanging in the Portland Maine public library? That's what he looks like and that's no joke. He was like Kirk Douglass with acne. And he had those crazy pissed-off eyes like Nietzsche had after he got syphilis. Oh he had severe acne all right but any of us should be so lucky to look like that. He looked like how Vincent Minnelli thought Van Gogh looked when he was beating off thinking of him." The crowd hooted and hollered. "Vinnie Minnelli I mean," Pablo continued. "Van Gogh didn't beat off — of that I am comfortably certain. There are some things you just know. He was quite a pious and monastic fellow, that's common knowledge.

Now this same friend of mine who told me about Bukowski's debilitatingly severe acne threatened to kick my ass for talking smack about the great Garry Cooper. But how could I not?" Again the crowd laughed. "Seriously," said Pablo. "Now Garry Cooper was a handsome man — as they say he was classically handsome. He was slow and sure, not like Vincent, more like Spencer Tracy. Though like Van Gogh, Cooper was actually a genius with a pencil and a brush — a draftsman and an astute observer of the effects of light. It's a little known fact that Cooper originally went out to Hollywood to be an illustrator, but, as usual, his good looks got in the way. As the story goes one night he found himself at a party at Vinnie Minnelli and Judy Garland's weekend slumming cottage in Topanga Canyon and before you know it he ended up screwing Grace Kelly in the hot tub under the eucalyptus trees." (The crowd cheers). "Anyway one thing led to another and the next thing you know he's fucking Kate Hepburn and swapping pre-production nightmare anecdotes with Lenny Glick on the red carpet outside Grahman's Chinese for the premier of "High Noon" . Which proves my point — good looks are a fucking curse! The man was born to be a painter but the world just couldn't leave him alone! If he had had severe chronic acne all over his body like Bukowski who knows? He could have been the next Henry Darger." There was a confused giggle from the crowd. "What?" Asked Pablo. "Never heard of him? That's my point. Henry Darger was a hell of an American illustrator out of Chicago and nobody ever accused him of being good looking. The man had a face that would make a freight train take a left turn up a dirt road, but man was he a draftsman and nobody ever bothered him. He had the time to sit alone in his divy little Chicago apartment where, among other things, he had the persistence, and the luxury, to be the first man in the world to accurately draw every single facet on the eye of a nearly microscopic Cuban tsetse fly. Now maybe this doesn't seem like such an accomplishment to you or me, but I like to think that Garry Cooper would have begged to differ." There was some hesitant and confused comments and applause as Pablo paused to drag on his cigarette and sip his drink, and then he stepped back up to the microphone. "And so," Pablo continued. "I'll leave you now with this final thought: I'd rather be ugly and smart any day, but, unfortunately, I'm just really fucking handsome!" With that

Pablo took a bow and the crowd went wild. Pablo jumped back into the crowd where people were patting him on the back and insisting on buying him a drink. Some people began to chant for an encore and they pushed him back up in front of the mike. Pablo grabbed the microphone and said: "You'll all have to forgive me. If I had had more time I would have written it shorter. But to quote Rudyard Kipling, there comes a night, when even the best, get a little tight!" Pablo held his drink up to the crowd and then he was off.

Goody and Apple enthusiastically cheered and clapped. "What did I tell you?" Said Goody.

"I'm still processing it," said Apple. "I'm not sure what to think."

"No doubt," said Goody. "Pablo was on fire tonight!"

A few more poets and songwriters took the stage. The singers were timid and too quiet and the poets were loud and so graphically sexual as to make a P'town audience slightly uncomfortable. They had pretty much run the gamut and were about to wrap it up when Pablo told the French Canadian emcee girl that Goody said she wanted to read. He whispered into her ear how she should introduce her.

"Ok," said the girl, into the microphone, with her gravely sexy voice and French Canadian accent. "We have one more poet. I'm sure at least half of you know her, the cool half. I give you Goody Hallet the Witch of Wellfleet!"

Goody was surprised and began to shuffle through her notebook. Her hands were shaking. Apple put her hand on Goody's shoulder. "You'll be fine. Go for it." Goody took the stage for the first time in her life. Once she got in front of the mike she didn't appear nervous. She paused dramatically before beginning and took a sip of her drink. "I should probably light a cigarette now right?" She said to Pablo and a few people hooted. "But seriously I feel kind of silly since I'm the only one tonight with a poem that rhymes but here goes. It's called The Nantucket Sleigh Ride." As Goody began the room went silent. She read very slowly, and carefully, and everyone hung on her every word.

"The ocean doesn't want to die,
It wants to laugh and cry,
And play and sing all day.
The ocean doesn't want to be abused,
It wants to be amused,

And it wants to have its own way.
Black Sam dressed in red.
A brass bell rang above his head,
And the devil's apron he wore around his waist.
Sam always ate the core and he always ate the rind,
He'd swallow the pit whole leaving nothing behind.
Black Sam was mean and Black Sam was bad,
Black Sam bullied every friend that he ever had.
But he loved the mist and the breaker's roar,
So he made the sea his watery whore.
Every night she kissed his lips of stone,
And then ebbed away just to be alone.
He'd love her forever, he'd always warn.
Which would have been true, but for that faithful morn,
When the sky was green over a crimson tide,
And Black Sam left on a Nantucket sleigh-ride.
She dashed him hard, to and fro, and then pulled him down,
Down below.
Soon the sea was calm and no one asked why.
Everyone knows. . .
The ocean doesn't want to die."

Goody smiled and waved and then ran back to her seat. The crowd clapped and hooted. Goody was clearly a hit. Apple smiled and nodded and Pablo came over to join them. "Oh man, that was some deep shit Goody! I felt it. You totally had them."

"No," Goody blushed. "It was stupid."

"Fuck that. You know it wasn't."

"I felt it too," said Apple. "He's right." Pablo smiled at Apple. After they had talked a little bit, and congratulated Goody, a girl came over and started talking to Goody. Pablo took the opportunity to speak privately with Apple. He shimmied his chair closer to hers.

"So Apple how are you?" She laughed nervously.

"I'm good."

"Tommy told me about you ya know?"

"Did he? What did he say?"

"He told me he really liked you, and kissed you, but then you just totally played him to get the dirt on Jack's. What's up with that? I mean, what really happened?" Pablo laughed and put his hand on Apple's forearm very briefly just long enough to let her know that he wasn't trying to be too mean or anything. "He's a good guy. He doesn't deserve that."

"No it's not like that," said Apple. "I don't know, maybe it was, but I do feel bad about it Pablo, really. We kind of hit it off, that's for sure, but there were a lot of extenuating circumstances. I'm under a lot of pressure at work — you don't even know!"

"Oh that is so weak!" Said Pablo and now Goody was listening in.

"It is what it is," said Apple. "Maybe you could talk to him for me? I'd like to make it up to him somehow. I'm not that bad of a person really. Goody will vouch for me." Pablo turned to Goody.

"Oh she's cool." Goody was clearly a little drunk.

"Make it up to him?" Said Pablo. "What, like buy him dinner?"

"It's a start," said Goody. "I happen to know he's not eating well with Jack."

"I don't know," said Pablo. "Tommy's a sensitive guy. I mean we all want to be artists but he really is an artist. He's got it in his blood. The man has honey in his veins!"

"Yeah well maybe you could talk to him and just tell him how sorry I am."

"Well since you're a friend of Goody's and you got her to read tonight. That goes a long way in my book." He put his hand on Goody's shoulder and gave a squeeze which sent a warm feeling all through her body. She smiled, and he winked and told her how good her poem was, and then he was off, back into the crowd.

"What a sweet guy," said Goody after he had walked away.

"Seems a little cocky," said Apple.

"But he totally isn't," said Goody. "That's the funny thing. He's usually too unsure of himself. Something's come over him lately. Ever since he got into college he's been really coming out of his shell."

"Higher education is really empowering. Have you thought any more about going?" Goody nodded but suddenly looked saddened. "I've heard good things about Cape Cod Community College," said Apple. "They say it's one of the best junior colleges in the country since there are so many over qualified professors around here who would normally want to teach at big universities but we don't have any and they just can't bring themselves to move away from the Cape."

"This place definitely seems to have a certain hold on the people down here," said Goody. "I mean for those that get it, ya know?"

"You get it don't you Goody?" Goody smiled and nodded. "What about Wood's Hole in Falmouth? That's a good school too isn't it?"

"One of the best," said Apple. "Actually I did a summer internship there when I was an under-grad. That place is ridiculously awesome. That's where they made the deep sea robots that found the Titanic. They have like one of the leading marine biology departments in the whole world there. Actually, when I was there I worked on a cloning project with a really cool professor who ended up being the first person in the world to successfully clone horseshoe crabs, Dr. Big Dan McCullough. He was awesome. He was a big Hemingwayesque sort of guy and he really got me going on my pig eyes too. That's the thing about college Goody. If you're open to it you get into these mentor type relationships that just send your life off on this whole other trajectory. That's something I'd love to see you get into."

"Wow cloning! I really envy you Apple. The things you've accomplished at your age are amazing. I mean they're amazing at any age."

"Yeah well thank you," said Apple. "But I only helped him with the busy work in the lab. Besides, cloning horseshoe crabs isn't like cloning most animals. They have like fifty thousand babies at a time. They practically clone themselves really."

"Well I love horseshoe crabs," said Goody and she raised her pineapple-cranberry Cosmo. Apple raised her glass and they toasted to the beauty of horseshoe crabs. They ended up staying until last call.

Apple and Goody window-shopped as they walked from the far east end of Commercial Street to the west end. Occasionally they would stop and comment on the things they would like to have but would never buy, like the trendy purses and shoes and the stained glass lamps and beautiful oil paintings. Apple wasn't even the slightest bit spooked by wandering around the empty streets at two in the morning. Goody was clearly in her element. "We'll go for a slice before we go home ok?"

Spiritus Pizza was the place to go in P'town at that time of night. Obviously the crowd was a little bit motley, there were drag queens and tipsy tourists and the occasional old salty dog looking for a cigarette. Apple and Goody got a couple of slices and sat on a bench in the back yard beside a sand bocce ball court. "You know your poem kind of made me cry a little Goody. Is that how you really feel?"

"It's just a poem. I wrote it quickly. Sam isn't that bad I don't think but I was just saying those things to make it rhyme I guess." Apple laughed.

"I think a lot of other things would have rhymed just as easily don't you? I think you have some serious issues with Sam. I mean I'm sorry for being so blunt about it Goody but I'm just saying."

"No, you're right," Goody admitted. They sat and ate their pizza slices quietly for a while enjoying the trees and the fresh air. Goody decided she could really trust Apple enough to tell her anything and she began to ramble. She admitted to her serious difficulties with school when she was a kid and her painful and difficult upbringing and she expressed her fears of not being able to read and write well enough to go back to school.

"No," said Apple and she hugged Goody. "Believe me you're way smarter than half the kids I went to school with, seriously." Goody wiped the tears away from her eyes and told Apple about how Sam had intercepted her financial aid application.

"That is so fucking wrong!" Said Apple. "You've got to be kidding me. That's a felony. You can't take someone's mail, that's a serious crime!" They finished their slices and then walked back out into town to look for Apple's car. "I know I left her around here somewhere." Apple tried to lighten the mood but Goody now seemed kind of glum.

"Well I guess the application didn't really even matter anyway because Sam is taking me to Oregon in the fall."

"He's taking you to Oregon!" Apple stopped walking. "What are you talking about, he's taking you?"

"Well I mean I'll probably go. He says it's like Middle Earth in Oregon."

"Well maybe it is Goody but still I don't know. That's a big decision. It's really far from the Cape."

"Sam says that's the whole point."

Chapter Twenty-Nine

Two weeks later, outside the Truro post office, Sam saw Apple. Pablo had given him a detailed description, including Apple's wide round face, small pointed nose, and her little red car. Sam waited outside. "Hey Apple how's it goin? I'm Sam Bellemy out of Wellfleet."

"Hello," said Apple. She felt a little ambushed.

"You're EPA right? Working with my Pop? I guess your reputation precedes you." Sam extended his hand and Apple grasped it reluctantly and almost shuttered.

"I've heard of you as well Sam."

"Right. From Tommy?" Goody was a little put off by that.

"No from Goody." She laughed nervously. "Goody is so cool Sam. Tell her I said hello."

"Oh She's the best," said Sam. "She's a little screwy but she's still the best. So anyway, how's it going at Jack's? How bad is it really?"

"It's going fine. You know we're still digging it out and bailing the wells. We'll be doing that for a while."

"Yes? So can you just tell me off the record, like in your own opinion, how bad it is really?" Apple had to think about this.

"Well no I can't tell you anything off the record Sam. Sorry but that would compromise the serious legal precautions in a touchy project such as this, but I will tell you on the record however that in my opinion it's pretty bad."

"Yes?" Sam laughed. "That sucks. Well we're gonna do whatever it takes, seriously."

"As will we," said Apple.

"Will you? I don't know if you will. You should though. Not for me but for Jack. He trusts you Apple. I know he does, so don't take that lightly."

"No, I don't take it lightly. I don't know why you have to put it like that."

"Well I know how you played Tommy," said Sam. "He's an artist and he's sensitive. You can't mess with his head like that. It's just not... — "He paused, searching for the right word.

"Ethical?" Offered Apple.

"Exactly," said Sam. "It's not ethical. Tommy told me how you kissed him that night in Jack's sitting room."

"Yeah Pablo mentioned that to me the other night too. You guys are worse than a bunch of teenage girls," said Apple. "Just tell Tommy I said hello." Apple started to get into her car.

"Tell him yourself. I'm not going to tell him anything. Anyway I think you should let me buy you a drink. I need to pick your brain about a few things. What do you say?"

"No," said Apple. "I wouldn't feel right about that with Goody and everything. I'm sure you can understand."

"That's weak," said Sam. "Just don't tell her. I won't if you don't."

"And would that be ethical?" Asked Apple.

"Hey I'm not the one trying to crush an old man's dreams."

"That's low," said Apple. "You know why I'm doing it."

"What, to save the environment or something like that?"

"Isn't that enough?"

"If you say so," said Sam. "So you don't want to go out some time?"

"Maybe we could all go out together? You know, like you and Goody and Tommy and me?"

"Forget it," said Sam.

Chapter Thirty

Apple was hoping to reach out to Tommy eventually. Whenever she would stop by Jack would talk with her and Tommy would stay out back on the woodpile. Usually Apple would comment on how much wood he had and Jack would balk and explain that it wasn't nearly enough. "Well I love the smell of wood and it smells really good around here lately."

"That it does."

One morning Apple managed to pin Tommy down. "Hey, how are you?"

"I'm all right," said Tommy. "Kind of busy, ya know?" He shuffled around and walked off. Apple followed him into Jack's utility room where Tommy set up his bench vise and began to sharpen Jack's saws.

"Been painting at all?"

"A little bit," said Tommy. "I've been thinking about it a lot though."

"And does that help?" Asked Apple.

"Sometimes," said Tommy. "Sometimes the longer you wait and think about it the better it is when you finally do it."

"Sounds like sex."

"I wouldn't know," said Tommy. Apple laughed.

"Oh I'm sure you do fine."

"Yeah right." Tommy pushed the rat tail rasp across the tiny metal teeth carefully. "How are your pictures coming?"

"Pictures?" Apple had almost forgotten her lie about being an artistic photographer. "Oh well I guess I represent the other side of that coin. Sometimes you take so long to prepare and think about it that you end up not doing it at all."

"That sucks," said Tommy.

"Not really," said Apple. "People like that deserve what they get. Perhaps they just don't have sufficient commitment to be an artist after all?"

"Oh they definitely don't," said Tommy. "But it's still kind of sad to think about."

Tommy turned away from Apple and went back to Jack's saw. She could tell that he really didn't want to talk but she knew this was the best chance she was going to get.

"You know Tommy I'm sorry about how it went with us. I mean you know that at least don't you?"

"Yeah you told me before."

"All right then." Apple turned to go and then she stopped and said: "You're not the only one trying to help Jack you know?" Tommy thought about this for a moment but didn't say anything. "You know I bumped into Sam. He said we should all hang out sometime."

"That doesn't sound like something he'd say."

"Yeah well he's right," said Apple. "We should."

"I don't know," said Tommy. "I guess I'm just not into making any new friends right now."

"Too late," said Apple and with that she walked off. She felt good about saying that. After all, how hard was she supposed to try? She wasn't in the habit of chasing after guys. The ball was in his court. Screw him if he couldn't take a hint.

Over the next couple of weeks Apple became more and more obsessed with Jack's Gas and the possibility that maybe there was indeed something more that she should be doing. She knew that Sam was a total jerk and yet she was still haunted by what he had implied, that perhaps it *was* her ambition as a scientist driving her, and not what was really best for Jack. It was that whole Goethe Faustian theme from her father's lecture tapes that kept coming back — that and her yoga vision of Krishna. But what did she really have to offer Jack? What was her strength? Obviously it was her unique understanding of cellular biology. Somehow that was the key. She began to think a lot about microbes. She reminded herself that Sam didn't even believe in them and this only strengthened her resolve. That was indeed a specifically Faustian and Krishna like approach — that the person you were most in opposition to, and most repelled by, would end up being the one to suggest the most elegant solution. If it was ironically or accidentally suggested that was even better, so long as she was open-minded and receptive. And so it went. Microbes were likely the answer. The very microbes that Sam claimed not to believe in could be employed to remediate the gas contamination in Jack's soil. Sam was right about one thing. It was time to take drastic measures. Forget about everyone else, she owed it to Jack, and to herself, to give it a shot. Of course Jack had never heard of bioremediation. Frank hadn't even heard of it.

Apple sat across the desk from Frank in his nearly empty, shabby little office. "Sounds expensive," said Frank.

"We can't afford not to do it," said Apple.

"Spare me the clichés," said Frank.

Apple thought about this for a moment and then added: "It will pay for itself!"

"Very funny," said Frank. "But seriously Apple I think you might be overthinking this whole thing."

"That's what you're paying me for Frank. You never over think anything. Somebody has to overthink it."

"Fair enough," said Frank. "But then someone has to try to rein you in now and again. That, on the other hand, is what they're paying me for."

"Remember Frank you said you wanted me in on this because of my unique biological and toxicological approach? Well I'm telling you that microbial degradation and bioremediation is the only way to go. It's the cutting edge in this sort of project. If it works we'll be on the cutting edge and you'll get the credit for being innovative and forward thinking. I'm telling you Frank this is like the avant-garde of clean-up techniques. We could get out in front of this and really get noticed. I'll publish a paper on it and you'll get half the credit. I mean I don't want to be too frank with you Frank. But when are you gonna get published in any way that can really help you in the future? We have a unique opportunity here to be pioneers in this sort of thing." Frank thought about this for a moment.

"What about the pig eyes? I still got that going for me don't I? You're not gonna forget me when that takes off are you Apple?" Apple smiled. It was only at that precise moment when Apple realized for the first time that the tables had finally turned in her favor and that Frank was actually admitting to himself, and her, that he intended to ride her coattails to success within the agency. She tried to keep a straight face but she was suddenly elated about the prospects of her pig eye assay. Frank was privy to certain info on that front which he had, at least until now, managed to play down and keep to himself.

"I'm not going to forget you Frank. Really, we're in this together."

"Can I get that in writing?" He laughed nervously.

"No," said Apple. "You're going to have to trust me."

"Ok," said Frank. "So what if it doesn't work?"

"The pig eye assay?"

"No. Of course I know that works. It better. But what if the bioremediation doesn't work? What then?"

"It'll work Frank believe me. We'll set it up so they won't even know if it doesn't work anyway. We do like a double redundancy by employing all the standard clean-up procedures as well. That way we hedge our bets. In the end we're the only ones qualified to ascertain whether or not it works anyway. After all, what the hell do they know? We can't lose either way Frank." Frank nodded and took up his pen and notebook.

"All right, so what are we looking at?"

"First off air sparging," said Apple.

"Air sparging?"

"We pump hydrogen peroxide into the contaminated soil." Frank raised his eyebrows.

"Why the hell not!" He jotted it down in his notebook.

"Then we add nitrates."

"Nitrates?" He jotted this down as well.

"Precisely," said Apple. "We add nitrates. Now here's the tricky part. You'll have to send off a letter to Pepperdine University in Los Angeles requesting certain laboratory selected or genetically engineered cultures of hydrocarbon-degrading bacteria."

"Pepperdine?"

"Precisely," said Apple. "Don't worry about the request. I'll write it, you just have to sign off on it and send it."

"I've heard of them," said Frank. "That's a laid-back surfer dude school for rich kids."

"Precisely," said Apple. "They also have a hell of a biology department. We intend to employ these cultures along with our nitrate and hydrogen peroxide sparging regime in a cutting edge experimental procedure known as bioslurping."

"Bioslurping!" Said Frank. He jotted it down in his notebook. "Sounds expensive."

"We can't afford not to do it Frank."

"Because it pays for itself?" Frank put his notebook down and nervously chewed the end of his pen.

"Precisely," said Apple.

Chapter Thirty-One

Technically Jack's Gas was open, but only for firewood, cigarettes and frozen Milkyways. For a month now it had been dug up and over-run with EPA and assorted government hacks and Tommy spent his time sleeping in Jack's bunkhouse in the woodlot and cutting and splitting hardwood (Jack now trusted Tommy with the chainsaws) and also Tommy made firewood deliveries all over the four towns of the lower Cape in Jack's rusty and banged-up old red Dodge Ram pick-up truck. He loved tooling around in Jack's old truck. He had even taken to wearing heavy steel toe boots and torn oil stained canvas Carhartt and Dickies work clothes, which is what all the cool old-time Cape Cod tradesmen and fisherman guys wore. Tommy was gradually being initiated into the exclusive clan of working class guys on the lower Cape. He learned all the back roads and out of the way places. Most of the deliveries were to year-rounders and local artisans and some were old timers who had known Jack all of their lives and many lived in salt box relics tucked away on sandy wooded paths in Truro, Wellfleet and Eastham. When Tommy pulled up with the wood they would want to talk and invite him in. He loved these old houses; they had real paintings and dusty old books. Sam wasn't exaggerating when he told Tommy that he had the hook-up with old time Cape Cod artists and celebrities. He delivered firewood to Norman Mailer and soon he would be delivering to Noam Chomsky. Tommy got a Provincetown library card and began reading Mailer's "Deer Park " and "The Naked and the Dead" and a book on Chomsky's linguistics. He was pleased when he found that he could read those books and understand them since he knew they were regarded as both literary and complex. He was particularly impressed with himself for being able to follow Chomsky and he had discussed linguistic philosophy at length with Sam who also seemed to get it and now Tommy couldn't wait until he could drive out to Chomsky's place where he hoped to meet him and engage him in conversation if possible.

Now when one drove down route six and approached Jack's all you saw was several small mountains of firewood and then the tiny little white clapboard cottage shack among them. Jack's woodpile was enormous. He got up early every morning and went right at it and worked all day. His difficult situation and the well publicized tragedy of the spill actually did wonders for the firewood sales and everybody wanted to see how he was holding up and show their support by purchasing his slightly overpriced and under seasoned firewood. This only made Jack more anxious. As he saw his wood going out he was further convinced that there wouldn't be enough and that he had better pick up his production. He had even tried to convince Sam to put in a day or two on the pile but that never seemed to pan out and so it was left to Tommy and Jack to try to keep up. Jack's health was still in question. He suffered the occasional hallucinations and fainting spells but he insisted on drinking and bathing in the contaminated water. He and Tommy continued to bail the contaminated well by hand. Eventually, toward the end of the summer, Apple arranged for the automated pumping system to be installed, which Jack didn't seem too happy about but he conceded to it, given Apple's strenuous recommendation. Ultimately he knew he had better give the impression that he was doing everything possible to cooperate with whatever was in the best interest of the clean-up process. The one up-shot at least was that the automatic pump freed up more time for him to spend on his woodpile.

As the days grew cooler and shorter and the season began to wind down Tommy and Jack were now really becoming friends and though it wasn't in Jack's nature to talk much Tommy could tell Jack had begun to trust him. One day when they were taking a breather in Jack's sitting room Jack finally decided to broach the subject of Tommy's father once again. "I see you've set up your easel and paints out behind the bunkhouse. Are they going to be ok out there in the rain? You know you can paint in here if you like. I don't mind." Tommy was a bit surprised by Jack's suggestion as he had never really mentioned his painting before.

"No, I'm fine out there Jack. But thanks. I'm just fooling around on an old piece of plywood anyway so it really won't be affected by the elements or anything. Sam said I should try working on plywood instead of canvas. You know, to toughen me up a little I guess."

"And you take his advice do you?"

"Sure. Why not?" Jack smiled and let it go. "Besides, it's cheaper than a stretched canvas. And you don't have much room here anyway. I mean I really appreciate your letting me stay here

Jack. I don't want to inconvenience you any more than is necessary."

"Well you could paint in the laundry room out back," said Jack. "Or even in the utility room if you like. Just clean up after yourself. I think I'd like to see you get something done around here besides helping me all the time. That kind of thing is important. I wouldn't want you to forget why you came to Cape Cod in the first place."

"Ok Jack. Maybe I will."

"Forget maybe," said Jack. "Just do it. Consider it a favor to me." Tommy laughed.

"All right," said Tommy. "I'm good outside, but when it rains I'll set up in the utility room." Jack nodded his approval and took his wallet out of his back pocket. He handed Tommy a fifty. "No," said Tommy. "I'm alright."

"Take it. I want you to take the rest of the day off and go to P'town and get a good canvas and whatever else you might need to work. Forget about plywood. What the hell does Sam know anyway?" Tommy took the money.

"Thanks Jack."

"Make me a drink," said Jack. "And then get the hell out of here." Tommy jumped out of his seat and went to Jack's kitchenette where he filled a chipped coffee mug with gassy water and whisky.

Tommy was in his truck and just about to pull out when Jack came outside with his drink and gestured for Tommy to hold on. "Let me see those postcards," said Jack. Tommy fumbled through his glove compartment and then handed the stack of his father's paintings to Jack. Jack sipped his drink and took his time flipping through the cards until he found one that interested him. "Yeah," said Jack. "I remember this one. I think I was probably your age the last time I saw it." He handed it to Tommy. It was a painting of a little pale blue house under a big golden oak tree on a dirt road. It was entitled "1830's Farmhouse" . "Did you find that one yet?" Tommy looked at it closely and shook his head. "I'm pretty sure that's on the vineyards in north Truro about a mile past Dutra's on Six A," said Jack.

"Really?" Said Tommy. "I thought maybe that was burned down or something."

"No," said Jack. "I'm pretty sure it's still there."

"Thanks Jack!"

"All right then," said Jack. "Knock yourself out. The deliveries will wait until tomorrow." He winked at Tommy, sipped his mug and then went back to his utility room to get his saw.

Tommy knew where Dutra's market was in north Truro. It was at the crossroads of Six A and Highland Road. The vineyards were another mile or so up on the right set back on a winding dirt road. Sure enough he found the old blue farmhouse in the picture. The big oak tree was gone but he could tell as soon as he pulled up that it was the place. He could tell by the architecture and by his own intuition and the feel of the place. It was a beautifully serene spread with a windmill and a water reservoir atop a wooden derrick structure made from a huge wine cask. Behind the house there were several acres of vineyards on rolling green hills enclosed in a winding white picket fence that went up and down over the hills and valleys and the whole thing overlooked the bay and then Provincetown across the water. He wandered around for an hour or so and at one point he saw a woman walking her dog under the trees and he expected her to question him and maybe throw him out but instead she only smiled and waved him on. Tommy thought he might like to paint this scene just as his father had and he could hardly wait to get into town and buy a canvas. He wandered back to his truck and was about to leave when he noticed a small folk art gallery across the street. It was set up in a kind of a residential home where the gallery began in the front porch of an old house and then extended into a garage and barn out back. Tommy went inside and was immediately taken by the charm of the paintings, which were inexpensive and almost exclusively done on wooden planks and plywood panels and driftwood and antique furniture. All of the works were done by a single artist, who also apparently lived in the house — a woman by the name of Susan Baker, though no one greeted him and so he browsed around for a half hour or so alone. It struck him that he could have easily walked out with a painting at any time and nobody would have even noticed. He saw that there was a self portrait of the artist on the wall and a short bio on a plaque beside it. She was a kind looking older woman and he supposed that she had been there in that barn gallery her whole life and he wouldn't have been the least bit surprised to find that she had known his father way back when he had painted the vineyard across the street. She was clearly prolific, and had been at it a long time. Her paintings were primitive yet lively and compelling and most were illustrative and had comic captions incorporated into the picture. Some of the more comical illustrations were reproduced on tee-shirts, beach towels and coffee mugs. One particularly compelling painting was entitled "The Real Elvis Stamp" which was a plywood panel cut and painted to look like a large postage stamp which depicted a fat old Elvis laying beside a toilet, the tiled bathroom floor was littered with spilled pill vials and hypodermic needles. Another large plywood panel was entitled "Our Evacuation Plan" and depicted a map of Cape Cod with a mushroom cloud over Provincetown. You could see all the people in the bay frantically swimming toward Boston. Tommy took a "Real Elvis Stamp" coffee mug, put a five dollar bill under a paper weight on the counter, and then left for P'town. After seeing the Truro vineyard farmhouse and Susan Baker's collection he could hardly wait to get a big empty canvas and get started.

Only in Provincetown could one get art supplies at a hardware store. Tommy went to the hardware store and got the biggest canvas they had — thirty-five bucks for a three and a half foot by six foot museum quality primed stretched canvas. He barely fit it in the back of his 4runner. He spent the rest of Jack's fifty on a six pack of Newcastle Brown Ale, a pack of Midnight Special rolling tobacco, and a piece of beef jerky. He had barely enough gas to get back to Jack's but that was all he needed. He couldn't wait to get started.

On the way home Tommy was excited and his mind wandered. He thought about his father. Of course it wasn't Jack's fault what had happened. Suicide was selfish and passive aggressive. If anything it was just as much his Mom's decision. She admitted it. She kissed Jack. What was Jack supposed to think? Tommy thought about what Jack had told him — how he said sometimes a kiss can mean a lot. Then he thought about Apple. Tommy wasn't sure what to think about that.

Tommy spent the next couple of days painting his new canvas and working with Jack. He decided he would do a painting of Jack working on his woodpile. Jack wasn't crazy about the idea but once Tommy had it in his head there was no use trying to discourage him. Since he had such a nice big canvas to work on he was especially careful and did very little actual painting but instead spent his time doing sketches and studies on paper in preparation. It was obvious to Tommy that it was the perfect thing for him to paint but at the same time he knew it was also dangerous for him to tackle such a meaningful and ambitious subject. It was easy to paint a landscape out in the dunes with Sam in that it was spontaneous and irrelevant. This painting, on the other hand, was far more crucial and could really be a drag if he couldn't pull it off. In such times of self doubt he tried to remind himself of Sam's technique of artistic recklessness and abandon. It was in just such a moment of doubt that he called Sam and told him what he was attempting. Of course Sam was prepared to offer help. "I'll come by and pick you up tonight. Don't paint another stroke until I get there. I got some ideas that will straighten you out no problem."

Sam took Tommy out to sea once more but this time Whydah was off the Pamet rather than in Wellfleet and Tommy was now wise to Sam's plan. If he could keep moving her around all the time he could avoid paying for a legal mooring. Also this time Sam had a small plastic kayak instead of a dingy. It was barely big enough for the both of them and they were both wet by the time they got out to the boat. "Where'd you score this thing anyway?"

"I got it somewhere," said Sam. "I don't remember. It does the trick though huh?" It was small enough that once they got on board Sam pulled it up and tossed it on deck. The sun was low and the sea calm when Sam fired up the engine.

"Where we headed Skipper?" Sam handed him a large knife and a rainbow hued, tiger stripped, fish which Tommy now knew, thanks to Sam's influence, as a mackerel bait fish.

"The Sternman don't gotta worry about that," said Sam. "Just cut bait." Tommy went to his cutting board and bench and gutted the mackerel and then cubed it up the way Sam had taught him. He was happy to be able to do this without the need for any more instruction while Sam quietly and intently rolled a very large joint. "We got enough gas to get to Race point and back I think," said Sam in an act of apparent generosity. Tommy smiled and nodded and kept working.

"That's your deal," he said. "I don't gotta know that." Sam nodded.

"You ready for a beer?"

"Sure. But I got a little surprise," said Tommy. He pulled a half pint of blackberry brandy out of his pocket.

"I thought you were starting to smell like my Pop." Sam opened the bottle and took a sip. "Now we're fishing!"

They drank and smoked awhile and headed for P'town but before they got there Sam had to check his traps. "Mother Fucker!" Sam exclaimed as he pulled the first of his buoy lines on deck. "Those pieces of shit P'town smackmen better watch themselves, seriously." He pulled the empty trap on deck. It was empty and the bait was gone.``

"What's wrong?" Asked Tommy.

"Someone's messin' with me," said Sam. "And I think I know who it is."

"Who?" Sam just shook his head.

"Someone who's gonna get a serious ass kicking."

"How do you know?"

"See this here?" Sam showed Tommy a knot tied into his buoy line. "That's a half-hitch on the line and that's a very serious old time Cape Smackman message."

"Really?"

"You know in the Godfather when Tessio brings Sonny the package with two fish wrapped in a vest?"

"Lou Gabrassi sleeps with the fishes," said Tommy.

"Exactly," said Sam. "A half-hitch on a buoy line is like that. It's a message to warn off interlopers. But I ain't no chump. Not by a long shot."

"I don't want to get into trouble Sam."

"Don't worry about it." Sam baited his trap and threw it back into the water. "I was born in Wellfleet. I'll straighten these guys out." Sam and Tommy hauled up the rest of Sam's traps with a hand winch. One of them had a big three pound flounder in it. "So now we can eat." Within fifteen minutes Sam had dressed the fish and fried it up on his little propane single burner with butter, pepper and a can of string beans and they were eating it as they arrived at Race Point. It was delicious and it had turned their mood around for the better. "And that's what it's all about," said Sam as he put his feet up, wiped his mouth on his sleeve, and lit a cigarette. Tommy agreed as he put a chunk of mackerel on his hook and tossed it into the waves. It was getting dark and he put his feet up on the gunwale and looked at the dark green waves and the stars on the horizon. He lit a cigarette and sighed.

"This is awesome," he said. Sam cast into the sea and said nothing. They sat awhile and looked at the stars and enjoyed the sound of the gulls and the waves gently lapping against Whydah when Sam decided to tell Tommy that he had sold his recent painting of the dunes out at Ballston Beach in Truro. He handed Tommy three soggy fifty dollar bills. Tommy took the money.

"I sold it to an old art fag in town for seven hundred dollars. I figured I'd take half. It wasn't that good, you know that."

"Half?" Tommy looked at the three sea soaked fifty dollar bills.

"Well he didn't pay in full just yet, but what the hell? A bird in the hand, am I right? He only gave me three hundred. You have to finish it before he gives us the other half; basically he just wants you to sign it."

"You told him who my father was? I told you how I felt about that Sam. You should have told me about it first. It wasn't even done yet. I don't want you doing that sort of thing without telling me. I'd rather not sell anything unless I know it's good."

"What? So you can't sign it for another three hundred bucks? Hey fuck it then." Sam held his hand out for Tommy to give him the money back. "I'll tell him no deal." Tommy put the money in his pocket.

"I'm just saying. You could have asked me first."

"Yeah well these sorts of things just come up and you have to go for it. You said I could be your agent."

"I guess," said Tommy. Sam seemed a bit put off by Tommy's attitude but he sat quietly and said nothing. They fished and drank for a while in silence. They got a few bites but nothing serious and then finally Tommy spoke. "A fifty percent finder's fee? That's a little steep no?"

"I got you a job and a place to live didn't I? And I offered to get you laid. What the hell more do you want?"

"No. That's all right," said Tommy. "I appreciate your help."

"Jack tells me you're working pretty good on the woodpile."

"He said that?"

"Sure why not? So you're painting something good finally? A portrait of Pop? How's that working out?"

"It's nothing," said Tommy. "Not yet anyway."

"Just crank it out man. Don't sweat the details. Just get it done. I'll sell it no problem."

"I don't know about that. You know how it is. I want to make sure it's good."

"Don't overthink it," said Sam. "Van Gogh used to paint a new picture every day."

"Yeah I know. "

"Don't say it like that. You don't know shit. Just fucking do it. Van Gogh wasn't even that good, you know. Not really." Tommy laughed.

"No he was pretty fucking excellent come to think of it." Sam laughed as he baited his hook and tossed it out.

"Yeah but he never made a dime you know that. I mean we gotta eat, am I right?"

"No you're right. I know what you're saying."

"Yeah and he never got laid either, not that much anyway. That's a well established historical fact. I mean you don't want to model your life after a guy that never made a dime or got laid. I got this book from the P'town library recently. It's called 'The Psychoanalyst and the Artist' and it takes the case histories of certain great painters like Chagall, Picasso and Van Gogh and then applies an old school psycho-analytical approach to understanding their work and their lives. It's pretty interesting. You should read it."

"Definitely," said Tommy. "That sounds great."

"Oh it is. Basically what I got out of it is that if anything you want to model yourself on a Picasso method rather than a Van Gogh one — not on what the pictures look like or anything like that but on how he went about accomplishing it all."

"Picasso had a more fun way of looking at things didn't he?"

"No doubt, way more!" Said Sam. "And he painted way more too, and he made a lot of money and got laid all over the place. Basically he proved that the whole starving artist lifestyle really isn't all it's cracked up to be. It certainly isn't necessary, or even advisable for that matter. All things being equal it's way better to have fun and be well-fed when you're an artist."

"No, I get that," said Tommy. "But I like Van Gogh's pictures better."

"Me too," said Sam. "But that's beside the point. Picasso knew how to live."

"You know I've read that my father supposedly subscribed to a similar theory, though I'm not sure that he was able to actually put it into practice in his own life. He once wrote an introduction to a book on the New York art scene where he claimed that contrary to popular opinion art is not born out of suffering but rather it's born out of healing and coming to a strong sense of being grounded in everyday life. The way he put it was that the flowering of fruit requires firm roots."

"That's it," said Sam. "That's what I believe. Suffering in art is way overrated. That was Nietzsche's theory on art too. In his first book 'The Birth of Tragedy' he said that the impulse to make art starts out as Dionysian but it has to eventually evolve into the Apollonian before it can ever become truly great art."

"Is that the same thing?" Asked Tommy.

"Totally," said Sam. "Right now you're like Dionysius, but you have to get more like Apollo."

"That shouldn't be too difficult," said Tommy.

"Well maybe it is," said Sam. "But you gotta have high ideals to shoot for. All I'm saying is don't hang your hat on a sexually frustrated religious fanatic like Van Gogh — there are plenty of other role models."

"No," said Tommy. "He was cool though, you have to admit it."

"You know he was half a fag don't you? That's common knowledge."

"I've heard that," said Tommy. "But I don't buy it."

"Supposedly that's where all the repression and self destructive tendencies came from in the first place. He wanted to suck dick but all his Christian superstitious bullshit wouldn't let him admit it even to himself. That's what these modern art psycho-historians concluded anyway."

"That's bullshit," said Tommy. "He had epilepsy." Sam hit on the joint and laughed.

"And you think that can explain all of it?"

"Sure, why not?" Said Tommy. They didn't even know what epilepsy was back in those days. There's even a special kind of epilepsy that makes you want to mutilate yourself when you're having a fit. That's why he cut off his ear. That's why he shot himself in the stomach. Think about it, nobody shoots themselves in the stomach to commit suicide; it took him like three weeks to die from it. If he lived fifty years later, when they had penicillin, he wouldn't even have died. That's why he liked absinth so much. Did you know there's a certain chemical in wormwood — one of the key ingredients in absinth—which is effective in suppressing epileptic seizures? Basically he was intuitively self-medicating!"

"Yeah, or he just liked to trip out on wormwood. His buddy's Toulouse-Lautrec and Louis Anquetin turned him on to drinking absinthe in art school and they didn't have epilepsy, they just wanted to get high."

"Either way," said Tommy. "Besides, if he was gay why did he have that prostitute girlfriend that he took so much shit for?"

"Well she did model for him for free," said Sam.

"You've got an answer for everything."

"I'm just saying. Prior to her he had to pay the local peasant girls to model and he caught a lot of shit from his brother for that since he clearly couldn't afford it."

"And then there was that girl he fell in love with," said Tommy. "She jilted him and broke his heart."

"Kee Vos-Stricker," said Sam. "She was his first cousin."

"But in those days that was totally common," said Tommy. "Right around the same time Edgar Allen Poe married his twelve-year-old first cousin and they were madly in love."

"I've got a few cousins I wouldn't mind throwing a bone at," said Sam.

After a while Tommy got a bite. It was a strong hit and he leapt into action. Sam jumped out of his seat and grabbed his flashlight and hung over the side. Tommy started reeling it in and his rod was bending way over. It was clearly pretty big and he was totally psyched. Sam stood beside him and coached him along.

"Give it some play. Let him take it. Relax. He's on there. Just take him in easy. You got it!" Tommy reeled it in until it was flipping around on the side of the boat. "It's either a striper or a shark." Tommy pulled it thrashing onto the deck. There was no moon and it was dark and he had no idea what he had. Sam put his boot over the fish and whacked it with his flashlight. "It's a shark!" Yelled Sam as he shoved his steel toe boot into its mouth just for fun. It bit into Sam's boot and thrashed about as Sam hit it a few more times with his flashlight before he cut the line and picked it up and quickly drop-kicked it over the side. "That's a mako," said Sam. "How did it feel?"

"It felt awesome!" Tommy was ecstatic. Sam told him it was only a baby but it was easily twenty-five pounds or more. Sam gave Tommy a beer and patted him on the back.

"Now we're fishing!"

"That hook was huge and way down in his throat," said Tommy. "You think he'll be alright?"

"He won't even notice it," said Sam. "Makos are made out of rubber."

"I see." Tommy tied another big hook on his line and he grabbed another chunk of bloody mackerel.

"Now we can relax," said Sam. "We got a good one. Anything else is a bonus." Sam took a shot of blackberry brandy and handed it to Tommy. He decided to roll another joint. Tommy cast out onto the darkness and sat back down, put his feet up on the side, and looked at the stars. He could see Venus bright on the horizon and the constellation Orion overhead.

"I always thought Orion looked like a kite," said Tommy as he sipped the blackberry brandy.

"It does," said Sam. They sat quietly and fished and smoked for a while.

Tommy was now very high. "You know the ocean is so black right now."

"I know," said Sam, and then after a while he added: "Being at sea is the closest you can get to really feeling empty. It's the closest you can get... you know, to feeling eternal.

"Yes," said Tommy. "I get that."

And then, out of the blue, Sam caught a really good fish, a black sea bass, a real keeper. Maybe it was just dumb luck, but somehow Tommy suspected it wasn't. Sam had the secrets and he wasn't about to give them up to Tommy or anyone else. "Now that's a fish," said Sam. "We'll eat that bastard for a week!" They stayed in the same spot for another forty minutes just to make sure, but that was it and they never got another bite and so Sam fired up the engine and headed back for Truro. He didn't even want to catch another fish. That was as good as it gets.

It was very late as they cruised back across the harbor toward the Pamet. "You hear anything from Apple?"

"Not really," said Tommy.

"She's not bad looking," said Sam. "I bumped into her a few days ago."

"How'd that go?"

"Yeah she kind of suggested that I take her out sometime but I shot that down right away."

"Really? I'm surprised 'cause I wouldn't think you were her type."

"Nah, but you know how it goes. Chicks dig me," said Sam. "But I wouldn't do that to you, just in case you want to take another shot at her or whatever." Tommy didn't say anything. The idea that Apple would make a play for Sam bugged him a little. "Come here for a minute. I want to show you something. Sam headed straight for a small yacht moored way off shore in North Truro. At about a hundred yards away he killed the engine and turned off the lights. He told Tommy to douse the lantern on deck. "Now come over here." Tommy stood beside Sam in Whydah's wheelhouse. "I want to show you how to do this." Sam pointed to the key down under the seat. "This is how you start her back up. And see this here? That's your throttle. You only want it at about half way when you turn her over. This here's a choke, you pull it up and once she goes over you gotta put it back down real quick, but you probably won't need that 'cause she's already warmed up. You see these two levers here, that's your steering. You ever operated a big commercial lawn mower like an Ex-Mark Navigator or a Walker? Cause it's just like that."

"No not really," said Tommy.

"Well anyway it doesn't matter but it's just like that. You put one hand on the throttle like so, and then you just slightly fuck with these two like this to steer. Don't push'em forward or you'll bog it. You just pull back on either of these slightly for port or starboard like this. You got it?"

"Not really," said Tommy.

"Don't fuck with me," said Sam. "Now you're making me nervous."

"Ok, I got it." Tommy went for the ignition under the seat but Tommy shoved him away.

"No not yet! Just sit here and wait. You probably won't have to do anything but if I get into trouble I'll holler and then you fire it up ok?" Sam then went on deck and tossed the kayak into the sea.

"What are you doing Sam?" Sam grabbed his oar and climbed overboard into the kayak.

"Keep your voice down," Sam whispered as he rowed toward the yacht. "I'll be right back." Tommy went and sat in Sam's seat at the helm and then looked over his shoulder and quickly stood up. He remembered that Sam told him to never, ever, sit there. He paced around and was getting a little pissed. After about ten minutes he saw Sam making his way back toward Whydah. The tide was against him and he could see that Sam was having a hard time. Sam put his arms over his head and made a whirling motion with his hands and so Tommy rushed into the wheelhouse, pulled the throttle back and turned the key. Whydah sputtered and coughed but didn't start up. Tommy's hands were shaking as he pulled up the choke and tried again and she rumbled and turned over. Carefully he inched the throttle and felt Whydah start to move forward. He pulled back a little on one of the steering levers and started to get his bearings. He headed straight for Sam who was now about thirty-five yards away, slightly to Whydah's starboard. When Sam got close Tommy pulled the throttle all the way back and drifted right up beside him. Tommy leaned over the side to greet him. "You did good," Sam whispered. "Here, take these." He handed up to Tommy two small, very heavy, electronic devices of some sort. Once Tommy had them safely on deck Sam climbed on board and pulled the kayak up behind him. "All right, let's get the hell out of here." Tommy just stood there dumbfounded. "What the fuck are you waiting for?" Tommy jumped back into action. He pulled back on the throttle and repositioned Whydah in what he thought was the direction toward Wellfleet.

"I don't know where I'm going!"

"You got it," said Sam. "See that orange light on the water tower way the fuck over there? That's Eastham. Head for that. And don't run over any buoys." Tommy was exhilarated to be at the helm.

"I'm on it, Skipper." Sam lit up a cigarette, handed it to Tommy and then slapped him on the back hard.

"You did damn good Sternman. Fucking aye! Where's that brandy?"

"I knew you were crazy Sam but why did you have to get me mixed up in this kind of shit? Seriously, I'm kind of pissed."

"Relax," said Sam. "I wouldn't have done it if I thought it was risky. That was 'Bonita', Ducky McGuire's rig out of Nantucket. He's worse than I am. That piece of shit has owed me for three years now. Payback's a bitch. He knows it's his own fault if he's cocky enough to leave 'Bonita' a sittin' duck like that right in my own backyard. Shit he should know better. Besides I happen to know he jacked that epirb box off this rich stiff's rig, the 'Tanner' out of North Carolina. He won't even be able to report it stolen. That's the beauty of it. It's a victimless crime. And I never liked him anyway. He's a real piece of work this guy. He's got like a pencil thin mustache that makes you just want to smack him in the face every time you see it. And he wears all these gold rings and he has long fingernails. I get the creeps just thinking about it."

"Bob Dylan has long fingernails," Tommy offered.

"Be that as it may," Sam continued. "But this guy's probably at the A House right now takin' it the hard way from some bus boy who drives to work on a Vesper."

"I'm gonna assume that's a gay slur," said Tommy. "Still I don't see why you have to drag me into it." Sam reached over Tommy's shoulder and dropped the throttle way down.

"Here, come on and take a look at this stuff, Sternman. I don't think you fully comprehend just how ridiculously we just scored. We're talkin' thousands of dollars here. Tax free — for like ten minutes work." Sam held the lantern over the two black boxes. "This here is what's known as an epirb, and it's a good one. Epirb stands for emergency position radio beacon. All the nice rigs have them. Basically it's like the black box on an airplane. When the shit hits the fan and your rig goes down deep this thing goes off and lets everyone know precisely where you met your watery end. Legally all the deep sea equipped vessels are supposed to have them but I always figured what the hell? I mean if I'm feeding the crabs in the abyss what the hell do I really care at that point anyway you know? Now a good one like this is pricey, like a grand easy and it's fairly easy to unload." Sam held the lantern over the other black box which had a video monitor built in and looked like a small computer. "Now this is the real score. This here is a state of the art digitech multi-beam sonar real-time seafloor profiling unit. These things cost like three grand. You can use it for all kinds of stuff. Mainly it's a fathom meter and a fish finder for rich hacks who don't know where they're going or where the shoals are. We could have some real fun with this thing but I'm thinking I'll unload it quick for like eighteen hundred bucks and somebody will think they're damn lucky to get it for that. Overall with this haul, and our tasty flounder dinner, not to mention your kick ass mako shark, and my big ass rock bass, I'd say we had a pretty damn good night of fishing tonight whataya think?"

Tommy thought about this awhile and then he said: "I don't think of myself as a criminal Skipper. I'm not cut out for it." Sam smiled and shook his head. He was rolling another joint.

"You said you wanted me to teach you to be a real Outer Cape artist?"

"I did."

"Recklessness and balls is way important as far as that goes."

"If you say so."

"If you get anything from me artistically that's it. That and another five hundred bucks for tonight's haul if you want it."

"No shit?"

"I'll give you five hundred bucks next week. But you have to sign that painting."

"I knew there'd be a catch. Let's just get home without getting arrested and I'll think about it."

"Deal," said Sam and he went into the wheelhouse and opened Whydah's throttle full on. "You know she'll do thirteen knots all the way to Nauset Harbor from here if we don't run out of gas."

"I have no idea what that means," said Tommy.

"Well it's pretty fucking fast," said Sam.

Sam moored Whydah two hundred yards off Pamet and then dropped Tommy off by the river in the kayak. "You gotta do me a solid," he said.

"What's that?"

"Jack's got a meeting in Hyannis with Ben Horegold from the gas company in a couple of days. Do me a favor and make sure he makes it would ya? Maybe you could go with him or something? He might resist the idea of you going with him at first but you gotta insist. Believe me I know he'll feel a lot better with you there. He really needs moral support on this one Tommy, and he really needs to make this meeting. I'd go but I think he thinks I'm trying to force him to sell out or something and I just want him to go and hear the guy out."

Tommy told Sam he would try to convince Jack to take him along. "You better drive," said Sam. "I don't want him driving all the way to Hyannis in his condition. He hasn't driven further than ten miles from the gas station in like five years."

"I'll try," said Tommy.

"Don't try. Just do it." And with that Sam headed for Wellfleet.

Chapter Thirty-Two

Having been out all night with Sam Tommy slept in and awoke to the sound of Jack's chain saw rattling in the woodlot. He got dressed, made some coffee and went into the office to find Jack's clipboard sitting on the counter with a list of the new orders and deliveries for the day. One particular item jumped right out at him: One cord to be delivered to an address in Wellfleet by the name of Chomsky. Was that Noam? It had to be. Tommy was psyched. He had been reading Chomsky's book and discussing it with Sam for the past couple of weeks. He wasn't even sure if he'd have the courage to say anything to him but he was excited just to knock on his door and pick up a check. Tommy backed Jack's truck up to the pile and began tossing the firewood into the bed quickly. Jack stopped cutting to nod good morning. Tommy held up the clipboard and gestured toward the truck and Jack waved him on and then resumed cutting. Once Tommy had the truck loaded he pulled around out front and just as he was about to pull out Jack came around out front to take a breather. Tommy held up the clipboard and asked Jack: "Is this Noam Chomsky's place?" Jack shrugged.

"It was a woman who placed the order. She seemed nice enough. Make sure you get paid." Tommy began to pull out. "You know where you're going?"

"I'll find it!" And with that he hit the road. As it happened Tommy had to drive around aimlessly for quite a while before he found it. It was in a very out of the way part of south Wellfleet on the back beach, way out in the woods by the ponds out behind Newcomb Hollow. Though Tommy didn't know it at the time it was quite close to the little secret pond where Goody had taken Apple skinny dipping only a few weeks earlier. Tommy arrived at a modest house at the end of a long winding dirt road and an old woman came out to greet him. He said hello and asked where she wanted the wood. She said out back would be better if he could manage to get it out there. After much repositioning he was able to get the truck behind the house where he then dumped the wood. She handed him a check and thanked him. Tommy thanked her as well and then pretended to be pleasantly surprised by the name on the check. He commented that she had a lovely little place out there in the woods and asked her if by any chance she was related to the philosopher

Noam Chomsky. She smiled and said he was her husband. "Wow," said Tommy. "That's awesome. It's really a great honor that you guys are burning our wood since I've always been sort of an amateur student of American philosophers and coincidentally I've been recently enjoying one of his books."

"How sweet," she said. "He's writing in his study right now. Let me go see if he'll come out and say hello."

Noam came out and shook Tommy's hand and they stood on his backyard deck overlooking the pond. Not knowing what to say Tommy told him that he had just read one of his books on linguistics and that he was a big fan. Noam seemed amused and smiled at his wife who was now standing close beside him. Tommy could sense how in love they were by the way they looked at each other knowingly and how she put her hand on his arm as he quietly spoke to Tommy. He enquired as to what it was about that book that Tommy enjoyed. Tommy summarized what he thought the main point of the book was and Noam seemed to agree, which was quite gratifying to Tommy since Tommy was aware of how difficult Noam's theories on linguistics were. Tommy was reminded of what Antonio Azule had taught him about Noam Chomsky's controversial political philosophy and before he knew what he was doing he found himself echoing Antonio's erudite and radical opinions on the matter, and to make matters worse he was suddenly charged up with a healthy dose of Sam's brash confidence and his likely unqualified, or unearned, philosophical arrogance. It was probably all these factors together, along with just a general sense of giddiness, which prompted Tommy to make the ill-advised attempt to confront Noam on his radical critique of American political philosophy. Tommy told him that he was aware of his reputation for speaking on the immorality of American foreign policy. Noam smiled and shrugged his shoulders. Tommy explained that like all the young men of his generation he grew up hating Reagan and Bush but that since then he had come to realize that maybe he had been duped by the European-style democratic socialist left after all. Still smiling, Noam shook his head as if to say that Tommy was maybe on the wrong track. Tommy told him that since he was so committed to being an artist he had come around to the idea that he wanted to be able to skip through the cracks and that he thought only with a kind of pure capitalism and minimalized government could he be free to do what he wanted.

"No, no, no," said Noam. He objected very quietly and was still smiling. He had the disposition of a Buddhist. Noam explained that it was the capitalist corporations which would bully him more than the government. Tommy protested and said that even though he had no money to speak of, his life was easy and free and that he found it easy to make a buck and move around without interference. Noam, somewhat patronizingly, told Tommy that the corporations actually do control him. "Take your truck for instance," said Noam. "You choose what one you want but really the whole industry is set up so that they only let you buy one from one of a few corporations, all of which are in bed together."

"So it's the totalitarian impulse then?" Tommy asked. "In other words I should be afraid of the totalitarian impulse in capitalism as well as socialism?" Noam agreed but he wasn't exactly buying it. He felt that government in the form of unions and cooperatives could be less totalitarian than corporations gone unchecked. Basically he disagreed with the premise that the market is ever free anyway. He implied that Tommy mistakenly thought the market was free but really it, and by extension, our lives, are controlled by rich corporate bosses. Tommy protested by offering his own life as an example, reiterating that he had always been free to bounce around outside the system while finding it easy to make a buck whenever he wanted. Tommy told Noam that the idea of responsibility to a community was utterly unfathomable to him. Noam smiled because he did not believe him. Tommy said that their transaction was a perfect example, that he had cut, split and transported the firewood with his own hands. It was pure capitalism. He gave him firewood and Noam gave him money and there was no need for a middle man to mediate or to protect either of them. Noam reiterated that Tommy had to use a truck and that he could only buy one of a specific type which was determined by the big corporations. He also explained that Tommy had used public roads to get the wood to him. Tommy pointed out that American-style anti socialist philosophy still allows for society to collectively pay for things like roads and infrastructure since everyone but anarchists agree that that is one of the few legitimate functions of government and that as far as what truck he buys the real point is that no one is making him buy it. "I don't have to buy it if I don't want to." Again Noam just shook his head.

Tommy Told Noam that he was a painter and that the great thing about being an artist was the idea that it was so crucially individualist and pure. "If I can make a cool painting then somebody will want to give me money for it. What could be more righteous?"

"No," said Noam. "It's only because some rich guy wants to make himself look good with your paintings."

"So what? We both get what we want in the deal."

"He's exploiting you in a sense."

"No," said Tommy. "I'm unexploitable." Noam laughed, again he didn't believe Tommy. "Seriously! I challenge anybody to exploit me. It can't be done." Now they both laughed.

"Well perhaps in this instance you exploited him?"

"Nah," said Tommy. "Besides, if he lets me then he deserves it. 'Caveat emptor' ain't it?"

"Well one should have a certain sense of responsibility," said Noam.

"Nah," said Tommy. "I don't see how responsibility is necessary."

"But you are responsible," said Noam. "You came here with the wood exactly when you said you would."

"Because I wanted to sell it to you."

"You could have dumped it out front where it was easier for you but less convenient for us but instead you asked my wife as a courtesy."

"But that's just it," said Tommy. "I want to be nice when it's not required. As soon as it's required I resist it."

"But that's silly," said Noam.

"But doesn't organized and enforced responsibility lose it's moral worth?"

"No," said Noam. "Not really."

"Sure it does," said Tommy. "Like forced sharing is not real sharing at all." Noam only shook his head and smiled. "But what about someone like me?" Asked Tommy. "I'm a good person and I just want to be left alone."

"Anybody can go live in a cabin in Montana and be a libertarian," said Noam. "But in a society you have to take on responsibilities beyond what is best for yourself. Besides it's not capitalism that allows you to be alone; you could just as easily skip through the cracks in Siberia."

"But I'm talking about skipping through the cracks right here with my friends around me."

"No," said Noam. He was growing tired of Tommy.

"But what about space colonization?" Tommy asked quickly. He sensed that he could only get in a couple more questions. "I mean don't you think that space colonization will inevitably be libertarian since it will be such a vast, multifaceted and uncontrolled type of expansionism and entrepreneurialism?"

"No," said Noam. "Nothing gets done in space other than by big government or big corporations. Take the moon landing. To think that the Apollo program had anything to do with actual research is a joke." Now Tommy only shook *his* head. He had meant that libertarianism would flourish in the future when lots of people were up in space anyway, that technology would likely get to a point where free people would explore and exploit the infinite resources of space. Tommy was disappointed by Noam's lack of enthusiasm for having put men on the moon. Of course it was a publicity stunt and a function of the cold war but how could anyone disregard the great spirit and achievement of Apollo? The simple fact that people actually walked on the moon was enough. The Soviet Union was a government which was committed to restricting the individual in the name of the collective and they didn't make it. American philosophy was committed to dynamic and blatant individualism and they got there first. Of course Tommy didn't say this to Noam since he knew he could only test his patience just so far. Noam started to say something about getting back to work and that it was nice to meet him when Tommy hit him with one last question. Tommy had saved his best question for last.

"What about Nietzsche?" He blurted out.

Apparently Noam had also saved his best answer for last. He said: "Nietzsche had a lot of rich friends." And with that Noam thanked Tommy for the wood and went inside. Tommy felt that was ironic since Noam no doubt had lots of rich friends, whereas Tommy didn't have any.

As Tommy drove away he was giddy with having had the opportunity to butt heads with a world famous member of the philosophical intelligentsia and he couldn't wait to tell Antonio and Sam about it, and yet oddly he felt slightly disappointed as well. Somehow he had thought that Noam would set him straight and bestow upon him some crucial insight that he had been missing. As it happened it only reinforced in him the scary thought that perhaps guys like Antonio and Sam were right after all. Sam, after a few anti semitic comments, informed Tomy that Noam had called Venezuela a model for other South American countries, and that he had been an early denialist/apologist for Pol Pot and the Khmer Rouge. In other words Noam was pretty clearly wrong about those two things. Sam was an iconoclast, and he was good at arguing.

Over the next couple of days Tommy kept mulling over his conversation with Noam. One of the things that struck him was that the more he thought about it the more he realized just how apropos their discussion had been given the meeting that he and Jack were about to have with Ben Horegold. If Tommy came away with nothing else from his conversation with Noam Chomsky it was that one should be wary of being enveloped by the big national, or even multinational, corporation, and now here was Jack, facing just that situation. And, echoing Sam, Tommy had defended the corporations in the name of freedom and laissez-faire capitalism, which is just what Sam wanted Jack to do. He wanted him to cash out before it was too late. Tommy could sense that Jack wasn't so sure, but he felt as though he really had no choice.

Jack wanted Tommy to stay behind while he went to his meeting so they could stay open for the day, in case any wood orders came in, but Tommy was insistent and he contrived an excuse about how he needed to see if the art store in Hyannis had a better selection of oil paints than the hardware store in Provincetown, and so Jack conceded to lock the place up for the day. They took one of Jack's trucks but Tommy drove. They drove for a half hour or so before Jack spoke. "Well I guess we owe it to them to go and at least see what they have to offer," said Jack.

"That sounds reasonable," offered Tommy.

"The fact of the matter is," said Jack, "we don't have enough funds to keep the place going without their help. We're zoned as a gas station and as a condition of our temporary suspension of condemnation with the National Seashore we have to replace the tanks and pumps and get back into the game within a reasonable amount of time, otherwise we're going to go belly-up and the National Seashore can take back the whole lot and I'll be out on the street. If I sell out I can get a nice chunk of change and they'll pay for the new tanks and let me keep my job. At least that's what I think they're offering. Today we'll find out for sure."

"That might not be such a bad way to go," said Tommy.

"I suppose," said Jack. "Short of my qualifying for another mortgage and doing the repairs myself I don't see how we can keep it going."

"And that's not an option?" Asked Tommy.

"I'd be dead before the interest was even paid off," said Jack. "Do you think Sam would make the payments?" Tommy decided to let that one go.

They arrived at a small corporate park facility behind the West Barnstable courthouse. Ben Horegold greeted them and offered Tommy a seat outside while he directed Jack to follow him inside. "Do you mind if Tommy joins us?" Asked Jack. "He's a good kid and we're pretty tight these days." Tommy blushed.

"Fine with me," said Ben. "How's Sam?" Jack shrugged.

"He had to go fishing," offered Tommy.

"Just as well," said Ben. "The last time we met I thought he was going to follow me out to the parking lot and rough me up a little." Ben winked at Tommy and laughed.

"Sam's bark is worse than his bite," said Jack.

"What do you think of my art?" Ben asked Tommy, referring to the cheesy framed prints adorning his office walls.

"They're all right," said Tommy.

"Well he's definitely more diplomatic," said Ben to Jack. Jack agreed. After some more meaningless small talk Ben laid out the paperwork and contracts across his desk and went through the minute details with Jack, explaining them line by line. "Ultimately this is what we're prepared to offer." He pointed with his pen to a very large number at the bottom of the page. "And that's what you net after we pick up all the cost of the repairs of course," said Ben. Jack looked at the figure and maintained his poker face. It was a considerable sum, more than he had anticipated.

"I see," said Jack. Jack pushed the paper over so Tommy could read the figure. Tommy kept quiet. He knew it wasn't his place to offer a comment. "What do you think Tommy?" Asked Jack. Tommy tried to scan the documents as quickly as possible.

"So Mr. Horegold," he began.

"Call me Ben," Mr. Horegold interjected.

"Ben," said Tommy. "So if I understand all this what you're offering is to buy Jack out, do all the repairs and get the place operating again, and then let Jack stay on as the proprietor to operate the station?"

"Exactly," said Ben. "Though of course Jack you would then be an employee of our corporation technically and therefore not the proprietor in all the ways in which he had been previously. I don't want you guys to go into this with any kind of misconceptions. The fact of the matter is there would have to be any number of changes to the day to day operation of the station, all of which would be entirely at our discretion. In fact I can't even promise you that Jack would always be able to run the place exactly as he wanted to." And then he said to Jack: "In fact I'm afraid I can't even promise you that you would always have your job at the station, since like any employee of a company your continuing employment would be contingent on satisfying your employer's requirements. But having said that, let me assure you that I fully intend on having you continue to run the place more or less as you always have and barring any unforeseen circumstances we want nothing more than to continue the local brand as you have established it. We are fully aware of your branding and reputation in the community and we want to continue on in that tradition. That is definitely our intention as a marketing strategy. We understand the unique niche that your gas station serves in the community and we want nothing more than to continue in that tradition. After all, it's in our best interests as a corporation. We don't want to be perceived as some faceless corporate entity bowling over a local tradition which you have so clearly symbolized and embodied for all of these years. Our hope is to transition as seamlessly as possible into a new Jack's Gas while making only those changes which will enable the station to become a more profitable entity in the community." Jack nodded and smiled insincerely.

"We appreciate that," said Tommy. "Seriously. But can you be a little more specific about the kinds of changes you might make?" Ben eyed Tommy suspiciously but tried to play it off like he was perfectly at ease.

"Well of course there's the price structure and the inventory to begin with. At the very least we'd have to take control of that. Of course we'd be bringing our own product to the table and we wouldn't be dealing with whatever distributors you had been dealing with previously, not unless they were competitive with what we can find elsewhere, which I'll be honest with you, they probably won't be, not by a long shot, but that doesn't have to be a big deal, I don't think."

"Of course," said Jack. "To be honest with you I think I've been raked over the coals for years now anyway."

"Precisely," said Ben. "And we'll be making some upgrades to the physical plant aspects as well. They'll have to pave the place over and put in new signage and things like that. I mean we all love the dirt lot and the cedar clapboard shack, and the hand painted signs and all that, but I'm afraid they're just not going to be practical going forward." Jack was now clearly a little put off.

"So you'll tear down the whole structure then? I mean that's kind of the whole point to the place isn't it?"

"I don't think we'll have to go that far," said Ben. "Though it's a possibility going forward. You'll have to keep an open mind about it. For now I'd like to see some improvements and additions on the existing structure. Like maybe a new roof and some vinyl siding, that sort of thing."

"Vinyl siding?" Jack was clearly displeased.

"I can assure you we want to maintain the original flavor of the place," said Ben. "I mean, after all, keeping the rustic charm that you bring to the table is crucial to our business model for the future. That's our whole strategy."

"Is it?" Asked Jack.

"Sure," said Ben. "I mean, we want you to keep your tee-shirts and your hats and you're your frozen milky ways and all that stuff. We definitely want that. That's the whole point, believe me."

"I appreciate that," said Jack.

"I know you do," said Ben as he shuffled the papers together and handed them to Jack. "So then that's it really. Are you prepared to make a decision today? You just have to sign a few things and we can get started." Jack noticed that Tommy seemed a bit uneasy and so he decided to not sign anything just yet. Instead he just put the papers under his arm and stood up.

"If you don't mind I'm going to have to take this home and read it." Tommy was relieved and Ben was clearly disappointed.

"Of course," said Ben. "In fact I insist. But keep in mind we're on a timetable here. We only have a certain window of opportunity before the National Seashore decides to take action. Once that happens I'm afraid it will be out of our hands."

"I understand," said Jack. "You'll have your decision within a week." Ben looked at his calendar.

"Friday then?" Friday was less than a full week away but Jack nodded and they shook hands. "There's one other thing," said Ben. "I know the firewood business is important to you Jack."

"It is," said Jack.

"I'm not sure you'll be able to continue with that once we take over."

"No?" Jack tried to conceal his concern but he was clearly rocked.

"I'm afraid I can't guarantee anything either way on that front," said Ben. "But I just want to make sure we're clear on that before you sign anything." Jack knew that meant the wood was definitely out if he signed, and that threw him into despair. He remained silent as Tommy shook Ben's hand and thanked him.

On the way out of town they hit the local art store and Tommy, though he had barely a penny to spare, bought a small bottle of dammar varnish and a tiny, five dollar, tube of titanium white paint. Jack stayed in the car and when Tommy returned he showed Jack what he had purchased. "This is the good stuff," he told Jack. "I haven't had art supplies this good since I left New York in the spring." Jack smiled.

"Well then," he said. "At least driving out here wasn't a total waste. On the ride back they were silent for the most part.

"I'll bet we got a few good wood orders on the machine while we were out," said Jack.

"No doubt," said Tommy. Tommy waited a few more minutes and as they were driving into Truro he said: "I guess no firewood is kind of a deal breaker for you huh Jack?" Jack shook his head.

"That and the vinyl siding." Tommy laughed nervously.

"And paving over the woodlot," Tommy added. "What the hell?"

"I'll be honest," said Jack. "It's a goddamn nightmare." Tommy felt the tears well up in his eyes. He tried to wipe them away without Jack noticing. It was the first and only time he would hear Jack curse in anger.

"We'll get through this Jack one way or another." Jack put his hand on Tommy's shoulder. "Thanks for coming with me today."

"Sam made me do it," said Tommy.

"He should have come," said Jack. "But I'm glad it was you instead."

"He's not that bad."

"No, he is," said Jack. "But that's my fault. I accept that now." Tommy put his hand on Jack's arm as he pulled into the dirt lot behind the station. "You know I really loved your mother Tommy. I hope you'll tell her that for me some day." Tommy nodded.

"I will."

"And you're going to have to read all those papers for me if you don't mind. I can't read all that stuff." Tommy laughed.

"Of course," said Tommy. Jack got out of the truck and left the pile of papers on the seat as if they had no importance to him whatsoever. He surveyed his woodpile as though he had never seen it before. He looked at it and smiled and took a deep breath.

"Smell that? It smells good doesn't it? What do you think that is like four or five hundred cord?"

"It's a lot," said Tommy. "I've never seen so much wood."

"Nah," said Jack. "It's probably only three hundred and seventy five I'll bet — if that. I've got a week left. How much can we do in a week?"

"Ten cord," offered Tommy. "Maybe fifteen."

"We can do twenty," said Jack. "I'll be in the utility room. Make me a drink." Tommy was inspired by Jack's enthusiasm and after he made Jack, and himself, a drink they went at it feverishly and soon he made them each a couple of more drinks until finally they had split two or three cords. Finally Tommy gave it up when he could barely see the hand in front of his face. Jack kept at it until ten o'clock and then he went to bed. They hadn't eaten anything all day.

"We'll eat tomorrow," said Tommy, and then he went to bed.

Chapter Thirty-Three

Things were going pretty well for Apple. She had always loved the fall. It was her favorite season by far, and though autumn hadn't quite arrived just yet the humidity had fallen and the sweet smell of fruit, nuts, and dried weeds was on the wind. Everywhere she could smell the aroma of Jack's firewood on the breeze and all of it promised a new beginning. Already she was nostalgic for the coming holiday season and all of the successes it portended for her burgeoning career. Like most Cape Codders, Apple now associated the coming of fall with the impending satisfaction and relief of another tourist season winding down and she felt that soon all the pay-off of her hectic summer would be waiting for her. Her innovative air sparging and bioslurping initiatives were now well underway. She had recently overseen the application of a modified hydrogen peroxide bioremediation culture at Jacks, and also she had applied an innovative and hitherto untested genetically engineered nitrate into the contaminated soil, and so, having done all this, and having received enthusiastic interest and support from her colleagues in the EPA biology lab she had to admit that Frank's letters and recommendations on her behalf had indeed been a total success. The beauty of it all was that whether or not they were effective was not really the point — after all, disproving such an approach had scientific value as well. Either way, once she had compiled and analyzed the data, she was in the unique position to publish a compelling case study. Still, of course, she hoped it would work. The more she got to know Jack and Goody, and the more she thought about how she may have treated Tommy unfairly the more she became convinced that regardless of whether or not it was in her best interests with the agency she wanted to do what was right and she wanted to help Jack's Gas survive. Like everybody else she knew how unlikely that was, but still she had a nagging doubt, that just maybe there was a way, and the more emphatically Frank insisted that Jack's needed to be enveloped by the National Seashore the more she felt that maybe there could be another way. She had, after all, now become accustomed to the idea that Frank was usually wrong about such things and so she decided that if indeed Frank were right about Jack's it would actually be sort of disturbing to her worldview and personal philosophy. She therefore owed it to herself to at least try to prove him wrong.

The first thing she had to do was make sure Goody knew that she would in fact adopt Artemis gladly if that was indeed what Goody wanted. The more Apple thought about it the more inevitable such a decision seemed but since Goody had no phone Apple decided she had better go to the health food store in Wellfleet and tell her in person, which is exactly what she did. Goody seemed relieved. "Are you sure?" Asked Goody. "She's quite a handful."

"Oh I'm sure," Apple assured her. "I think that's exactly what my Krishna yoga vision was about." Goody thanked her profusely but then almost apologetically added that Apple would have to come by to visit a couple more times so that Artemis could get used to her a little more before the move. "Of course," said Apple. "Oh man this is gonna be awesome, Thank you so much Goody. I can't wait."

"Yeah," said Goody. She tried to smile.

"You're sure you want to do this?" Asked Apple. Goody nodded.

"If not I totally understand. I only want to do this if it helps you out."

"I do," said Goody. "I need to lighten my load a little right now. And Artemis needs a change as well. I can sense that."

"Well you can still visit with her as much as you like," said Apple. Goody seemed contemplative and quiet.

"Did you hear anything back from Cape Cod Community College?" Asked Apple.

"No," said Goody. "It's too late now."

"It's never too late. You've gotta do it Goody. You can get in for the January semester if it's too late for the fall."

"I suppose," said Goody. Apple stamped her foot down and flipped back her hair.

"Screw that! You can't let Sam get away with it Goody. You can't! You can't let him do that to you. You're a good writer. I loved your poem, everybody did. You were the best poet that night hands down. Everyone there thought so. You have to do it Goody. I know it's not my place but I just have to say it, I'm sorry but I have to. You need to dump that man right away. You're too good for him."

"I'm working on it."

"Are you really? Well I'm glad to hear it. But that's not the sort of thing one works on ya know?"

"But he loves me. I mean sometimes I question whether or not I actually love him but I never question whether or not he really loves me. And that's got to be worth something doesn't it? Nobody else has ever loved me you know?" Apple was about to tell Goody that Sam was more than likely a narcissist and not capable of real love, but then she thought better of it. She didn't want to suggest to Goody that she had never been loved at all.

"Oh honey," Apple wrapped her arms around Goody and hugged her tight. "You're such a sweet and caring person and you deserve so much more. And you're going to get it all someday too. I just know it. I see how caring you are with your animals, and they love you. I can definitely see that." Goody wiped a tear from her cheek and smiled.

"That's true," said Goody.

"Sure," said Apple. "And their judgments are much more insightful and pure."

"That's true," said Goody. "Unlike men they look right into your soul and they don't care what you look like or anything like that."

"That's true. Not that you should have to worry about anything like that. I mean look at you, you're so cute." Apple stroked Goody's wild and unkempt hair. "You're very pretty, you know. I can't believe you don't see that."

"No," said Goody. "You're much prettier than I am."

"Are you kidding me? I'm twenty pounds overweight and my teeth are cooked. I'd much rather look like you Goody. Look at you. You don't have an ounce of fat and your eyes are dark and piercing — they're like Cleopatra's or something."

"I've heard of her," said Goody and Apple laughed though she knew Goody wasn't making a joke. "Do you think I wear too much eye-liner?"

"Not at all," said Apple. "I could put on eye-liner all day and never have eyes like yours. That's your thing and believe me it's working. You just assume that I'm pretty because of my confidence and my attitude, that's my thing, and that's what you need to learn Apple. It's all about attitude."

"But you really are prettier than me Apple. You have that little up-turned nose and those high cheekbones like an elf from The Lord of the Rings." Apple laughed and blushed a little.

"Let's just say we're both unusually good looking and leave it at that," said Apple as she wiped the tear from Goody's face, hugged her again, and then without thinking about it she gave Goody a soft slow kiss on the cheek. Now Goody blushed and Apple stepped back and regained her composure.

"That wasn't like a real kiss was it?"

"No," said Apple. "I mean not unless you wanted it to be." Goody kissed Apple back, on her cheek, and they both laughed. "We're just a little emotional right now," said Apple.

On the ride home Apple found that she was indeed worked up emotionally and at one point, as she drove over the highlands in north Wellfleet, she decided to pull over, get out of the car, and watch the sunset over the bay. When she got home she decided to call her mother. During a pleasant conversation with her mother Apple was reminded of what Goody had told her — that she had never been loved by anybody. Apple was now poignantly aware of just how appreciative she was to have such a loving and close bond with her family and how that fact alone was the sole reason she was the person she was. Pebbles was going on about her plans for the weekend and about the family and about her idea that they should have a clambake get together before the season was over and how they hadn't had champagne and steamers and lobster in awhile when Apple interrupted her mother to tell her just how much she loved her and to tell her how much she appreciated all that she and her father had done for her. She told her mother how much she loved everything about their strong family ties and how much she valued their family traditions like getting together for an end of the season clambake at the club in Yarmouth Port.

"Well that's so sweet Honey. I know you do, and it's so nice to hear you say that. We love you very much as well. You know that."

"I know Mom."

"Is everything ok Apple? I mean I don't know where this is coming from. It's no secret that you aren't too crazy about parties at the club these days."

"I don't mind the club. I guess I've just been so busy lately and I lost track of what really mattered to me, but I want to change that Mom."

"Well that's fabulous Honey, but you don't even eat clambake do you?"

"Actually I've been thinking about becoming a pescatarian anyway." Pebbles laughed.

"Do I even want to know what that is?"

"Well I met this really cool woman in Wellfleet and she told me about it. It means that you're a vegetarian except with good fresh seafood too."

"Well that sounds great Honey. Your father will certainly be happy to hear about that one."

"Well I haven't tried it yet but I think it's something I should be open minded about."

"Well we'll put you down for a lobster then. It's going to be a great time Apple. Listen, speaking of the club, your father and I were wondering how it went with you and Oliver. He mentioned to us that you guys went out to dinner in Wellfleet at a seedy little place that you recommended and had a nice time and all but that you never called him back. What happened if you don't mind my asking?" Apple was a bit perturbed.

"He told you that? Did he tell you what I had to drink as well?"

"Oh don't hold it against him Honey. He's a perfect gentleman. We had to practically drag it out of him."

"Oh I'm sure," said Apple.

"I know you're busy but you could have at least called him back to thank him."

"No you're right Mom. I should have done at least that."

"You should have Honey, but I don't have to tell you that. I guess you had your reasons."

"And what's that supposed to mean Mom?"

"Nothing. Nothing at all, really. I mean unless you've met someone else. I don't know what you're doing these days half the time. Your father said something about your going out with some starving artist guy who works at a gas station but I knew that probably wasn't true."

"What are you talking about? Are Dad's spies following me or something?"

"Don't be so dramatic," said Pebbles. "You know your father has friends in the agency. You know I don't put much stock in their gossip."

"I take that back about what I said about the club. I'll go to the clambake 'cause I value keeping up the family traditions with you and Dad like I said, but those old men at the club are worse than a bunch of schoolgirls! And it's not true by the way. I went out with this guy a couple of times and that's it."

"Ok," said Pebbles. "Don't let it bother you Honey. I told you I didn't put any stock in it. But what about Oliver? I don't know why you wouldn't like him. He's tall and handsome and polite and he has lots of money."

"I can't believe you would say that Mom!"

"Ok, you're right. That was wrong. I take that back. But even if he weren't rich he'd still be tall and handsome."

"Mom I've got to be honest, your obvious sexual attraction to this guy is kind of creeping me out a little."

"Don't be fresh," said Pebbles.

"He's got a little mustache with no beard!"

"And?"

"And you don't find anything smarmy about that?"

"No, not really. In fact I'm not even quite sure what you mean."

"You wouldn't," said Apple.

"He kind of reminds me of Clark Gable," said Pebbles.

"If you must know Mom, that's not a very hip contemporary look. I mean what is he like a nineteenth century oil barren or something?"

"I don't know," said Pebbles. "I think he kind of pulls it off with the mustache. I thought you liked men who aren't afraid to be iconoclastic?"

"Iconoclastic?"

"It means — ," Pebbles began but Apple interrupted her.

"I know what it means Mom. But since when do you use terms like that?"

"Why can't I use a term like that? I read you know. In fact I happen to be reading Andre Gide's 'The Immoralist' for my book club right now."

"Are you really? And how do you find it?"

"To tell you the truth it's a little too French for my taste, though it is fancy and literary and I like that." Apple laughed.

"Ok then," said Apple. "You won this round Mom. Oliver's mustache is indeed iconoclastic and he does sort of bring to mind a young Clark Gable."

"I just think you should have called him back either way just as a courtesy at the very least," said Pebbles.

"Of course you're right Mom, and I will, I promise."

"Well don't bother now. It's been too long and he's going to think you want to go out with him again."

"No," said Apple. "Believe me I can handle it."

Apple spent the rest of the evening doing yoga and meditating and as usual it led her into a state of heightened relaxation, and she ended up getting some insight as to what to do next, but rather than acting rashly she decided to go to bed, and she hoped that she would dream about it. After sleeping on it she knew that she would feel more secure in what she should do next, and she usually did. Ever since Apple began practicing yoga she found that she was becoming what was sometimes called a "vivid dreamer" . This was something she was now very interested in, and she decided to pay closer attention to her dreams as well to research and read up on the matter in scientific and psychological journals. She was not aware that she had this in common with Tommy, who was also, as fate would have it — though not through yoga — a vivid dreamer. Though in Tommy's case, as was previously mentioned, this had more to do with the fact that he was "into avoidance" and would often sleep more than ten hours a day (not to mention, during those rare periods when he was in a phase of high artistic output he often liked to take a well-timed mid day nap). Apple's dream life had always been unusually active but now, with yoga, she had begun the more specific discipline of trying to dream productively and with a purpose. The first insight on this front was her realization that dreaming vividly was actually a skill that one could cultivate with practice if one put her mind to it. Purposeful and productive dreaming is a phenomenon which is probably only experienced by a relatively small percentage of people and it is therefore usually denied if not at least totally underestimated. Nonetheless it exists and Apple was a vivid dreamer as was Tommy, which in itself is even rarer given that they happened to cross paths. Many people have the sensation of having a particularly compelling dream, but then when they awake, usually in the morning, they then have a sense of disappointment, realizing that it was only a dream after all. This is like the feeling one has when one is enjoying a particularly engrossing story that has suddenly ended and one wishes it would go on. The first real achievement of the "vivid dreamer" is that unique ability to go back to sleep and then go back into that same dream, which is often surprising, but it is in fact possible with practice. This is the first radical achievement of the vivid dreamer, and it is, in and of itself, quite satisfying and compelling. The next level of achievement of the vivid dreamer, which only even fewer people realize, is that rare ability to then know that one is in fact back in that dream, and experience this feeling while one is actually still engaged in observing the dream first hand, and when this happens it is a strange and wonderful experience. Now, thanks to having studied up on the subject, and having thought a lot about it, along with having had a satisfying and productive yoga session just before bedtime, Apple had, on this particular evening, achieved this second and highest level of vivid dreaming. And so on this night she dreamt of hanging out with Frank, Tommy and Oliver through a series of odd and confusing adventures, all the while she intermittently went in and out of an acute awareness that she was in fact still dreaming — Apple realized that this was the catch in vivid dreaming — an unfortunate stipulation which kept it from being totally within her control (that no sooner had she realized that she was actually in a dream, she would then get caught up in the myriad details of the dream and then find herself back in the usual state of dreaming wherein one is convinced, however erroneously, that one is actually experiencing a normal waking state). Still, the mere fact that one could intermittently realize one was dreaming without waking up was in itself a huge achievement of purposeful and productive dreaming. During a particularly vivid dream on this evening was the prevailing oddity that she was somehow experiencing a series of adventures with Frank, Tommy and Oliver in such a way that they were all occupying a single body, which is to say the very different qualities of these three men were seamlessly co-mingled into a single personality in which any clear differentiation between them seemed not only unnecessary but irrelevant. Upon reflection, once she was clearly awake (or was she?) Apple concluded that perhaps this strange amalgamation represented all those whom for whatever reason had recently wanted to control and possess her, both sexually and otherwise? This was her first and easiest insight and so of course she would seize upon it, but, upon further, and perhaps more honest reflection, she considered that maybe this strange hybrid creature of her imagination represented an amalgamation of those poor souls of whom she had wanted to somehow possess and control toward her own selfish purposes? It seemed to her that this was an equally viable hypothesis. Still, in the end, being as she was a scientist, she magnanimously opted for a synthesis of both of these views admitting to herself that while it was true that all three of these men clearly wanted to get into her pants, she also wasn't above capitalizing on that fact to get at what she ultimately saw as furthering her own raw ambition. Once Apple had a short workout, a shower, and a cup of tea she knew what she should do next and she tried in vain to suppress the knowledge that this action would seem to confirm the latter of her hypotheses. She would call Oliver, though not for the reason her mother had suggested.

As is so often the case with dreams, the original impression, which only a few moments before seemed starkly delineated and brimming with conviction now seemed hazy and timid, and so even as she dialed Oliver's number she knew she would have to forget about her dream and instead she would wing it on pure intuition.

"So Oliver, how's it hanging?" Even as Apple spoke the words she couldn't believe she had said it. She had never used such a crude phrase before, not with someone with whom she barely knew. Oliver laughed and responded generously. He told her that he was well and that he had wondered why she had never called him back, but then he quickly qualified this admission by explaining that he understood just how busy Apple probably was, what with her important biological research and science and everything. Apple tried to take his comments as non-sarcastically as possible, which wasn't easy at first.

"Yeah I know it probably does sound funny but the pig eyes are really a handful and I sometimes lose track of my social life."

"I'll bet," said Oliver. "I've been really busy myself."

"Flipping houses?"

"They don't flip themselves," said Oliver. "But I enjoy it. Like you said Apple, somebody has to do it."

"I did say that, didn't I? I can be such a snob sometimes."

"I don't look at it that way," said Oliver.

"You don't? Good I'm glad, 'cause I didn't mean it that way."

"Why would I?" said Oliver. "I may not have gone to Harvard or anything like you but I still make a lot of money."

"Yeah huh?" Apple was suddenly reminded of why she thought Oliver was such a tool. "Exactly," she said and then added: "You know my mom thinks you look like Clark Gable."

"Yeah huh? He's dead isn't he?" Apple laughed at this. Apparently, even for a tool, Oliver wasn't without a certain confident and self-effacing wit, which was, she had to admit, somewhat charming.

"Anyway I just wanted to thank you for the dinner and tell you that I felt bad about never calling you back."

"You're welcome," said Oliver. "And I think I understand why you didn't call me back and believe me it's no problem, really." Apple was definitely curious and not a little put off by precisely what Oliver may have meant by such a statement, but she also knew that for now it was better to just let it go.

"Well anyway Oliver I should have called you back but I've been so busy with the clean-up at Jack's Gas and that was the other reason I called you. I think that maybe with your particular expertise you might be able to help me with some questions I have regarding lower Cape real estate laws and regulations. Now Jack does have court appointed representation but I'm not sure just how thorough they really have been. I can tell you off the record that I suspect that the prevailing attitude has been to simply push through whatever procedures will lead to the EPA's best interests, which in this case is really nothing short of putting the clean-up completely in the hands of the state's default exegesis, with the inevitable outcome being to shut down Jack's once and for all and for the land to be officially enveloped into the National Seashore property."

"Well you are EPA aren't you Apple? Aren't your aims theirs?"

"Well not exactly," said Apple. "That's why I say off the record. My aim is to do the right thing Oliver. I want to get the place cleaned up of course, but I want to do it in a way, if at all possible, which takes into account Jack's best options as well." Oliver laughed.

"You are a real firecracker aren't you? Just like your Dad."

"I'd rather you didn't bring him into it," said Apple. "Or anyone else for that matter. All I'm asking for is an outside, and impartial, opinion. I'd hate to think that Jack maybe had other options that hadn't been explored. You know the ins and outs of lower Cape real estate law. You've dealt with these people before. You know how they operate."

"That I do," said Oliver."

"What I'm interested in is an outside and impartial opinion, such as your own, on just what options may be available, that's all."

"I see," said Oliver. "And that's all?"

"Well for starters. I was also thinking we could maybe look into the possibility of getting Jack's listed in the National Register of Historic places. You've had some experiences with that haven't you?"

"I have."

"They say it's one of the oldest gas stations in the country, and likely the oldest one on Cape Cod," said Apple. "And they have all kinds of ties with the original Outer Cape art colony — they have Jack Kerouac's hat hanging over the cash register, I've seen it myself. Jack's was even the subject of a painting by Richard Cobb from fifty years ago, which is worth millions and regarded as an American masterpiece. It's hanging right now in the Guggenheim collection at the Museum of Modern Art in New York."

"And we've got provenance for all this?" Asked Oliver.

"Right now Richard Cobb's son is painting Jack, splitting firewood, and sleeping out back in a truck in Jack's woodlot."

"Well that's pretty cool," said Oliver.

"So you see what I'm saying?" Said Apple.

"I sure do. I'll look into it, I promise."

Chapter Thirty-Four

Tommy had a little table, stool, and field easel set up beside the woodpile. He had no intention of trying to get Jack to pose and so he would just have to be content with capturing an impression of him while he worked. Even by Tommy's own humble appraisal the painting was coming along well. Once in a while Jack would take a breather and stand beside Tommy allowing Tommy to look more closely at Jack's features or his clothing or whatever. All this was done nonchalantly as possible given that Jack was not comfortable with being the subject of artistic inspiration, but of course he'd put up with a little discomfort to support Tommy's ambition. Being well aware of this generosity Tommy was unobtrusive. On rare occasions Jack would even offer commentary. "I like the way you have the trees and the sky in there."

"Oh that's the easy part," said Tommy. "You think the sky's too blue?" Jack nodded.

"But you're probably doing that on purpose," he offered.

"No," said Tommy. "For some reason I've always been a little heavy handed with the blue."

"Well that's your style," said Jack.

"That's true," said Tommy. "I'm all about the blue. Especially Phthalocyanine Blue, that stuff's downright addictive."

"Now you lost me," said Jack. "You know just seeing you working out here makes me feel good. It reminds me of your father — and your mother for that matter."

"Really?"

"It does. You know Tommy I would appreciate it if you could tell your mother that I sometimes think of her. Maybe you could tell her that. I did love her and I regret that we never got a chance to talk things out." Tommy knew that for Jack to tell him this was a big deal. He was obviously in an unusually nostalgic and contemplative state of mind, no doubt brought on by the difficult decision he was facing.

"She knows," said Tommy. "But I'll remind her if you like."

"I would like that."

"Sure."

"You know with my imminent retirement and all." Tommy waited awhile and let that sink in.

"So you do want to retire?"

"I'm tired, and I'm old. Obviously you can see that Tommy. But I guess I'd always thought that when the time came I could do it on my own terms and in a way that was best for the gas station. I shouldn't think about it in terms of what would be best for me, which is to cash out and wash my hands of the whole mess. Obviously that's what Mr. Horegold and Sam would like, but as I'm sure you know by now their motives may be somewhat suspect. Being steward to a place with such a history is actually quite a responsibility."

"I can see that," said Tommy. Jack went back to work and Tommy continued to paint until the light was almost completely gone. At one point Sam called on the office phone and wanted to talk to Tommy.

"So how'd the meeting go? Did you go with him?"

"I did. It went fine. Jack didn't sign anything just. He brought the papers home so he could read them more carefully but based on the way he was talking tonight I'm pretty sure he's ready to go through with it."

"Oh that's great news Tommy. Thank you. Good work man."

"Well I don't know about that Sam. He seems pretty bummed about it to tell you the truth. I gotta tell ya if he does sign the place over it seems kind of tragic to me."

"What the hell are you talking about? That's as good of a deal as we're gonna get. Don't make him feel any worse than he has to about it."

"I didn't say anything," said Tommy.

"Yeah well don't. Just do me a favor and stay the fuck out of it if you feel that way."

"Hey I brought him out there didn't I?"

"All right Tommy. But just don't make him feel bad about it."

"I won't. I'm just trying to be supportive and help him through it. You know that Sam."

"Ok that's cool. Thanks man. But maybe you could lean on him a little to hurry up and sign the fucking thing already? Can you do that for me?"

"I'll do my best."

"Well I guess that's all I can ask. Just keep me informed ok?"

"Sure," said Tommy. "No problem."

Later, after Tommy had drank, smoked, and painted himself into a state of exhaustion he packed up his paints and joined Jack in the sitting room for some microwaved frozen dinners. After they had eaten Jack poured them both a drink, put on his reading glasses and spread Mr. Horegold's papers across the coffee table. "Let's see if we can make heads or tails of this before I go to sleep." Tommy told him that maybe they shouldn't get so totally rocked on vodka before they went over the contracts. Jack agreed, ostensibly, but then admitted he couldn't bear to face the situation any other way and so Tommy pulled it together and summarized them as best he could. Jack listened carefully to Tommy's synopsis and he thought long and hard about every detail. In the end he seemed defeated as he signed all the papers and then suggested that maybe in the morning Tommy could drive them out to Hyannis. Tommy agreed and went outside for a smoke while Jack went to bed. After sitting alone for a while under the stars, Tommy climbed into the back of his truck and went to sleep.

At about three o'clock in the morning Jack awoke and went into his sitting room. He was barely awake and in a semi-trance state as he made himself another drink. Though he was shirtless, and only in his underwear, he put on his boots, his hat, and his glasses, and he went outside to his woodlot. He fired up his favorite splitter. The engine rumbled loudly through the dark empty forest. Jack surveyed his enormous woodpile partially obscured in the pre-dawn mist and said to himself: "Well that's just about five hundred cord." He then got down on his knees in front of the splitter and removed his hat and glasses, tossing them off into the darkness. He took one last look at his woodpile. "Definitely four hundred and seventy-five cord anyway." He then laid his head tight against the sharp, cold steel wedge of the wood splitter and sighed. "Ok, maybe not four hundred and seventy-five, but it's definitely a strong four hundred and fifty." He then closed his eyes, clenched his jaw, and pulled down on the lever. The massive hydraulic wedge came down fast and hard on Jack's head, and remarkably, other than a twinge of regret, he felt very little.

Tommy awoke to the sound of Jack's splitter. At first he assumed Jack was probably just getting an early start, but as he lay there in the total darkness he realized that this was way too early, even for Jack. He was half asleep as he stumbled out back, but then what he found shocked him into a state of utter hysteria. Jack lay slumped across the splitter over a massive puddle of blood. Tommy let out a yell of horror before he killed the engine and then wrapped his arms around Jack and pulled him free of the splitter and laid him down on his back in the blood soaked wood chips and pine needles. Jack was completely unresponsive and most likely already dead. The left side of his face was a mangled and bloody mess. He had a massive gaping wound across his jaw and cheek. His ear was completely detached and dangling from the wood splitter. Tommy paced back and forth and shouted at himself for a few short moments before he decided to get Jack into his truck and race to the hospital. He picked him up and was half way to his truck when he realized that the hospital was at least an hour away and so he laid Jack back down in the dirt and ran inside to call the cops. Three cruisers arrived, one of which promptly sped off with Jack laid out in a bloody mess across the back seat, and Tommy quickly surmised that he was now the primary suspect in a homicide investigation.

Chapter Thirty-Five

Given that Oliver was interested in making an impression on Apple he promptly gathered as much information as possible regarding what he thought might be some of Jack's options. He then called and suggested they get together to discuss the details. Though Apple was eager to see what he had come up with, she was determined to not give him the impression that their meeting could be construed as another date, and so she suggested that they meet in the morning for coffee. Oliver was a little disappointed but he was all too happy to take whatever he could get and he assumed if things went well he'd then be in a better position to take her out on a proper date shortly thereafter. They met at little diner in Orleans just off Route Six, a place in a strip mall without even a hint of charm or atmosphere which is exactly what Apple wanted and she thought the place suited the occasion perfectly. To further drive home the point she wore glasses, a pony tail, no make up, a sweatshirt, and jeans. "Wow you look great," said Oliver with complete sincerity since he had not seen her dressed this way before and indeed found it quite compelling.

"Thanks." Apple was a little bit annoyed that he felt it necessary to comment on her appearance at all and she was reminded of the paradox that most men find a woman dressed down far more attractive anyway — but if she he taken the time to get dolled-up, even slightly, he would have taken that as a sign as well. Either way she couldn't win. For his own part Oliver was dressed casual but decidedly smart in the way all preppie Cape Cod guys dressed to signify the weekend. He had a bright yellow, short-sleeved golf shirt, ironed khaki slacks, and impeccably clean tennis shoes. Apple had to give him points for wearing a bright yellow shirt, perhaps he was indeed slightly fashion forward after all (if not quite "iconoclastic" as her mother had suggested).

Apple started with a cup of blueberry herbal tea and Oliver had coffee. They talked comfortably for a while and then Apple ordered eggs benedict — Oliver gladly took this as a sign that all bets were off. He somewhat brazenly opted for a meat lovers omelet with a side of sausage. "I hope you don't mind?" He quipped sarcastically.

"Knock yourself out," said Apple. Before the food arrived Oliver produced some notes and Xeroxed papers from his casual, brown canvas, "weekend attire" L.L. Bean attaché case and spread them across the table.

"I went to the Barnstable Hall of Records and dug up, and made copies of, all the original titles and deeds of Jack's land dating all the way back to the late seventeen hundreds if you can believe it."

"Wow really, that far back?"

"It's really quite fascinating," said Oliver. "Likely there was some activity on his particular lot even before that but there was a fire in the Hall of Records in the seventeen-nineties and so nothing can be definitively documented prior to that point. The first owner on record was a one Joseph Stocker in eighteen o'four. He had a little farm house on Holsberry Road down by the Pamet and his land included about twenty-five acres which, at its farthest point, extended to just beyond where Jack's currently resides." Oliver showed Apple a Xeroxed copy of the handwritten documents and a crudely drawn map addendum which attested to that fact. It was written in the very neat and ornate script characteristic of that period.

"Wow, people had ridiculously good penmanship back in those days didn't they?"

"That's cool isn't it? Apparently Jack's was some sort of old hunting cabin which ended up being put to use as a way station for the whaling industry. They may have used that spot to process the whale blubber into oil, to be sold to the local inhabitants as a source of fuel."

"And that's how it came to be designated as a kind of fuel depot in the early nineteenth century," said Apple.

"Precisely. And at the time the Outer Cape was the leading producer in the entire world of lamp oil and other such related whale products and so that went on for nearly seventy five years. Over that time the place changed ownership many times but it always stayed within the circle of the Stocker family or its close associates and then in the early nineteen hundreds the land, now considerably smaller in area, was purchased by a legendary figure in the history of Truro by the name of Jack Snow." Oliver showed Apple a copy of the original deed of ownership when Jack Snow purchased the six acres of land which included Jack's lot for eighteen hundred dollars. Oliver continued to explain that at that time, that was a fortune, but Jack

Snow was among the youngest of the heirs of the highly regarded Nickerson family out of Wellfleet, many of whom to this day still own some of the most prized properties in Wellfleet, Truro and Provincetown.

"That's fascinating," said Apple.

"I know," said Oliver. "And Jack Snow kept the place, apparently as nothing more than a rustic hunting lodge, until nineteen twenty-eight, when in his old age he decided to make the radical and, at the time, thoroughly modern move of converting the place into a gasoline filling and service station."

"I've heard of Old Pop Snow," said Apple. "He's supposed to be one of the original founding fathers of Truro."

"He's the original Jack of Jack's Gas." Oliver showed Apple a copy of the nineteen twenty-eight deed which officially incorporated the business under the name: Jack's Discount Fuel. "As you probably know your "Jack" was once ' Robert Bellemy', Pop Snow'sfirst employee at the gas station and his unofficial protégé. But do you know the story of just why Old Pop Snow was so infamous?"

"No," said Apple. "But I have heard whispers from my Dad and his older friends at the club."

"Exactly," said Oliver. "That's all I have to go on as well. Evidentially, back in the thirties, Pop Snow had a business partner in Jack's by the name of Richard Aiken. Aiken was a local smackman and skipper on the now notorious boat out of Wellfleet known as "Whydah" . The story goes that one night Pop Snow and Richard Aiken had a disagreement, apparently about the way in which they should proceed in their current business venture at Jack's Gas and one thing led to another and next thing you know Aiken was lost at sea and Old Pop Snow was the new skipper of the Whydah."

"I don't know about that," said Apple. "That sounds somewhat apocryphal."

"It does at that," Oliver admitted. "But that's how the story goes, and we do now have Samuel Bellemy, Jack's son, the notorious Wellfleetian rogue, as Whydah's current skipper to sort of add credence to the myth."

"True," said Apple. "I can attest firsthand to that. He's definitely a rogue, but that could just be a total coincidence."

"Maybe so," said Oliver. "But it's almost too perfect. You had better be careful if you ever run into him."

"Oh I have, and I was decidedly careful I would say."

"Well that's good," said Oliver. The food arrived and they both ate heartily. "So your Mom tells me you're a pescatarian now? How's that working out for you?" Apple knew that now Oliver was just teasing her a little, she didn't mind.

"And you knew what that was?" Oliver shook his head.

"She filled me in. What about your eggs? Why should baby chickens have to die? Not to gross you out while you're eating or anything."

"Biologists don't get grossed out," said Apple as she took another bite. "Besides, edible chicken eggs are unfertilized."

"I don't know," said Oliver. "That sounds like a semantic loophole to me."

"Maybe so," said Apple. "But I never claimed my decision to not eat meat was for ethical reasons anyway. I just think it's kind of unappealing if you know what I mean."

"So it's on primarily aesthetic grounds then is it?" Oliver took a bite of his sausage and smiled, savoring the flavor for a moment, then he continued: "Aesthetic judgments are always pure and beyond reproach. One may as well try to argue why chocolate is better than vanilla, it's pointless."

"I had no idea you were so philosophical," said Apple.

"I have my moments," said Oliver. "Besides, it's obvious that chocolate is way better." Apple laughed. They enjoyed their brunch and Oliver went back into some of the more obscure minutia and myth regarding the early history of Jack's Gas that he had managed to dig up, including reports from certain reliable old-timey Cape Cod literati that Dianne Arbus had once photographed Jack Snow working at the gas station just before he died.

"Now all this is awesome Oliver, really, we've got Cape folk-lore coming out of our ears at this point, but what are we really talking about here? What are Jack's options realistically?"

"It's actually pretty clear cut," said Oliver. "As you know Jack's is operating under a pre-existing temporary suspension of condemnation provision granted by the National Seashore. What that means is that technically he would not be allowed to continue operating except for the fact that his business was founded prior to the National Seashore's rather stringent standards and control. As such, he has been, so far, grandfathered in, every couple of years, whenever the National Seashore opens its books for review. His one saving grace has been that Jack's Gas has been in continual operation since before the National Seashore was officially created."

"So the real point in keeping the land in its private ownership status is to not disrupt or crucially alter the pre existing business?" Asked Apple.

"Precisely," said Oliver. "The way I see it, given the severity of the spill, Jack has only three options: Ideally, he could keep the place going as is — which of course is unlikely. He would have to clean up the spill, replace the tanks, and get it all going again in a reasonable amount of time, or else he could choose to sell out to a big multinational outfit — probably his best option financially — and something which, I understand, he is currently exploring, who would then have to try to make the case in court that they were indeed continuing on with the same business model and plan of the original Jack's Gas (this would be a tough case to make, though not something out of the realm of possibility, given their near infinite resources). And then, finally, Jack's easiest — and perhaps his most noble — recourse, is simply to throw up his hands in defeat and give the land over, once and for all, to the National Seashore Property."

"Is that what you think he should do? 'Asked Apple.

"If I were him I would," said Oliver. "Because he's a righteous old school Cape Codder — but if I were myself, on the other hand — -which I am — I'd sell out to the big gas company, and I'd let them kiss my ass while I faded into the sunset with a nice chunk of change. To be honest that's what I really think he should do."

"Do you really?" Asked Apple.

"Well we all know the National Seashore is the best thing to ever happen to the Outer Cape," said Oliver, "Jack's Gas notwithstanding."

"I see what you mean," said Apple. "I mean I've worked toward that goal all my life."

"I know you have," said Oliver. "Obviously Jack's Gas is the exception to the rule, but let's face it, without the National Seashore we're no better than the Jersey Shore."

"I've been there," said Apple. "It's not a pretty sight."

"And that's all that separates us from them, seriously."

"I know," said Apple. "It's kind of scary."

Apple gathered together all of Oliver's notes and Xerox copies in a manila folder which she then carried outside to stow away in Kalessen's trunk. Oliver followed her out to see her off. He was hoping to grab her and kiss her at the last second. Apple knew he was thinking that (didn't all men always think that?) and for a moment she considered obliging him, after all he had totally come up with the goods, but she couldn't get past the ironed khakis and the mustache (was that hopelessly shallow on her part? — unlike her mother she just wasn't into the Clark Gable type). Instead she offered sincere thanks, hugged him perfunctorily, and then quickly jumped into Kalessin.

It wasn't until well into the evening, when, after relaxing with some yoga, and rereading all of Oliver's notes, that Apple had hit upon the perfect solution to Jack's dilemma. She had discovered a way in which he could keep his business, and his land, without even installing a new gas station. It was so perfect! Utterly elated, she immediately phoned Oliver to get his professional opinion. Oliver was all too happy to hear from Apple so quickly.

"Man you're fired up about this place huh?"

"Consider this," said Apple. "As you say, way back in the late nineteenth century Jack's was a fuel depot for Whale oil, which is why Pop Snow was able to make the easy transition into a filling station in the early twentieth century. He originally incorporated the business under the name of 'Jack's Discount Fuel' because along with gasoline he sold oil, coal and kerosene (which was a big item at the time for lamps and also heating). In fact I happen to know that Jack has the old kerosene tanks in his utility room which he still uses on rare occasions. Over the past twenty-five years or so Jack continued to sell not only gasoline, but home heating oil, kerosene, propane and firewood, all under the original rubric of 'Jack's Discount Fuel'. Now why couldn't he make the case that he intends to continue doing just that with or without the gasoline? If he were still selling coal, propane, kerosene and firewood how is that not providing discount fuel to the community? I happen to know that for the past few years hasn't made a dime on the gas anyway and everyone says that the only reason he kept the gas station was because it gave him a place to split firewood. He probably made fifty thousand on firewood last year alone, though I doubt if he pays any attention to that at all. In fact I know he doesn't. He already has over four hundred cord on the place right now, which at two hundred a cord delivered, which is what he gets, is over eighty thousand dollars worth and he shows little sign of letting up. Clearly he's poised to be the primary source of wood fuel in Provincetown and Truro this winter."

"I think you're right," said Oliver. "You may be onto something. We're going to have to advise Jack's lawyer to take a better look at his options."

"Do you really think so?"

"Sure, why not. It's worth a shot."

"Thank you so much Oliver. I knew you'd come through."

"Clearly it's all you," said Oliver. "I'm impressed."

Apple knew Jack didn't like to talk about important matters over the phone so she decided to drive over and have a chat with him right away, but first she thought it advisable to call up Frank and at least give him a heads up before she talked to Jack. Of course Frank would advise her against giving Jack any legal advice, especially since he wasn't privy to Jack's talks with Ben Horegold and he assumed the inevitability of the National Seashore's plans to take control of the land. Still Apple was determined to do whatever she could to help. As far as her commitment to the EPA went Apple felt that she had performed admirably, first by going way above and beyond her normal responsibilities in single-handedly exposing the spill and then furthermore by taking a radical and innovative approach to both containing and mitigating the contamination. What more could they possibly expect?

"I see you're still determined to work on Saturdays," said Frank. "Don't you check your messages? I called you shortly after you left the lab yesterday."

"Sorry Frank, I'm so busy lately."

"I know," said Frank. "Friday night yoga. Anyway — "Apple interrupted him.

"Listen Frank I think I figured out a way that Jack can keep his business going after all. I mean I'm not sure but I got some advice from a friend who has a lot of experience with creative Outer Cape real estate deals and I just wanted to give you the heads up before I talk to Jack about it. The long and short of it is that he may well be able to legally continue with his temporary suspension of condemnation as long as he keeps his firewood business going."

"Well that sounds promising," said Frank. "But haven't you heard the news? It may be too late."

"What news?"

"I'm sorry Apple. I thought you knew. Jack tried to commit suicide last night." Apple was silent for a moment. "Are you alright?"

"What happened? ! Is he all right?"

"We don't know yet," said Frank. "The details are pretty grim. Apparently he got whacked out on codeine and vodka and stuck his head in the wood splitter. I don't even know if he's dead or not. I'm really sorry Apple. I was thinking maybe you should go and —"

Apple hung up before Frank could even finish his sentence.

Chapter Thirty-Six

When Apple arrived at the Hospital in Hyannis she found Tommy, Sam and Goody in the waiting room. Tommy nodded and smiled at her. Goody gave her a big hug. "Thanks for coming," said Goody.

"Of course," said Apple. "How's he doing?"

"He looks really bad right now but the doctor says he's going to be ok."

"Thank God," said Apple. "I feel terrible that this had to happen. I really had no idea that he was so distraught. Did you guys get a chance to speak to him yet?"

"We did," said Goody. "But he was pretty out of it. Obviously they've got him on a lot of meds right now. He seemed to be in fairly good spirits when we spoke to him earlier."

"People on morphine usually are," said Sam.

"I'm so sorry Sam," Apple put her hand on Sam's arm. "You must be so relieved that he's going to be ok."

"That's a matter of interpretation," said Sam. "He hasn't been ok for a long time."

"We have to think positively right now," said Goody. "At least he's out of the woods right now." Sam smirked at Goody's choice of words.

"Yeah he's out of the woods tonight." Sam took Apple's hand and squeezed it gently. "We appreciate your concern though, really." A chill ran down Apple's spine as she pulled her hand away.

"Of course," said Apple.

"Don't feel bad," said Sam. "It's not your fault, not really." Apple cringed and backed away. Adrenaline surged in her chest and ran down into her limbs until she felt a distinct tingling in her hands and feet. Ordinarily she would have defended herself and maybe even told him off (surely he deserved it), but, for some reason, inexplicable to her at that moment, she remained silent, and then, to her own amazement, she began to cry.

"I'm so sorry Sam, really." Goody took her by the arm and led her down the hall.

"He didn't mean that," said Goody. "He's just emotional right now. We all are." Goody and Apple walked down the hall toward Jack's room when a nurse suddenly intercepted them. "She's family," Goody assured the nurse. "It's ok. We won't go inside." The nurse backed down, and so they stood there, arm and arm, comforting each other in the hall peering at Jack through the Plexiglas window. He lay peacefully, with his eyes closed, and his head wrapped in bandages.

"He doesn't look so bad does he?" Said Apple as she wiped the tears from her eyes. Goody nodded and gave Apple a hug.

"He'll be fine. I'm sure of it," said Goody and then she added: "But they had to amputate his left ear."

Tommy and Sam were alone in the waiting room. "That's twice now that you saved Pop's life."

"I guess. I only wish I went out back when I first heard him fire up the splitter. I could have stopped him."

"You know if he had died I could have unloaded the place with no strings attached and gone out to Oregon with a shit load of money."

"Still you're glad he didn't die," said Tommy. "I know you are. I saw the look on your face when you came in. You can't deny it."

"Yeah. He is my blood after all. I guess some things are pretty hard to get past."

"You shouldn't want to get past that Sam. He's a good man. Anybody would be proud to have him as a father."

"You wish he was your father don't you? But he isn't Tommy. He's my father, not yours. Don't forget that. You don't know what he and I have been through."

"I know that."

"Do you?"

"Sure I do Sam. I can respect that. I'm not going to interfere with your plans for the place if that's what you're saying."

"I know you won't," said Sam. "Besides, I'm leaving soon either way. I already sold Whydah to Nate Nickerson. He's a solid guy — a skipper in south Wellfleet."

"No shit. How soon?"

"Soon," said Sam. "Don't tell anybody though. I might have to burn a few bridges before I go. You know how it is, but I trust you Tommy. So far you and Goody are the only ones that know."

"Is Goody going with you?"

"Yeah I'm taking her," said Sam. Tommy didn't like the sound of that. He knew Goody was ambivalent about Oregon at best. "Did Jack sign Horegold's papers or what?"

Tommy decided to lie to Sam. "I don't know. I don't think so. To tell you the truth I think that's what got him all worked up last night."

"Fuck it," said Sam. "It doesn't even matter. I'm going to talk to his lawyer and get power of attorney and then it won't even be up to him anymore anyway. He's not fit to make decisions. Shit two months ago that doctor in Wellfleet said he had acute gasoline intoxication, which supposedly causes permanent brain damage, but I thought maybe she was just full of shit. Obviously now with this stunt we all know better."

"I don't know," said Tommy. "I have to say he seemed pretty normal to me. Once the spill clean-up got underway he seemed to get a lot better."

"Yeah," said Sam. "Other than occasionally sticking his head in a wood splitter he's totally fine."

Sam then went down the hall to get Goody and tell her it was time to go home. After more handshakes and hugs Tommy and Apple suddenly found themselves alone. They stood around for a few minutes, understandably feeling somewhat strange, exchanging what little small talk was possible given the awkward circumstances. Tommy kept looking at Apple's hair and her tight muscular neck and he was reminded of why he liked her in the first place (she had a good neck). "Look," said Apple. "I really think we need to get together as soon as possible. There's a lot of stuff I need to talk to you about. I've come up with some ideas — some really exciting and potentially important ideas regarding Jack's land and his future and I really don't know who else to talk about them with. What do you say?" Tommy acquiesced, explaining that he was glad to hear that, given that he had ideas for Jack's as well, and that he too had no one with whom to talk about them.

"I have to say, Apple, I'm impressed by the effect you've had on Goody. She can really benefit from a positive role model." Apple blushed.

"She's awesome," said Apple. "I love her."

Apple and Tommy decided they would meet early the next night, for dinner, at the Wicked Oyster in Wellfleet. They walked out to the parking lot, and, as they said goodnight, Apple hugged

Tommy and then kissed him, softly, on the cheek. On the ride home Tommy was elated; he would have to go for it with Apple after all.

Once home Tommy found that it was a little chilly. The autumn nip was now in the air and so he lit up the wood stove in Jack's sitting room. Given that Jack wouldn't be around for a good while Tommy was reckless and he broke out Jack's vodka; he even had a cigarette right there in the sitting room on the couch with his feet up on the coffee table. He kept drinking, and smoking, and thinking about what Sam had said, and about how Apple had kissed him softly on the cheek, and then he knew just what to do. In Jack's office he found Ben Horegold's papers, the papers which Jack had indeed signed, and he kissed them, as if to pay proper respects, before he shoved them without hesitation into the fire of Jack's pot-belly stove.

Chapter Thirty-Seven

Once the cops had a chance to talk with Jack, and consult with the hospital psychologist, they determined that Jack's wounds were in fact self-inflicted. They informed Tommy, by way of the answering machine at the gas station, that he was no longer a "person of interest" and they apologized and said he was free to resume work in the woodlot. They went on to say that they had completed their on site investigation and that he, or anybody else, was free to disturb the scene as was necessary. Tommy understood this was meant to be a subtle suggestion. Somebody had to do it. He went out back with rags, sponges, and a bucket of soapy bleach water and scrubbed down Jack's splitter. He raked and shoveled the coagulated stain into a wheelbarrow and took it into the woods where he dumped it behind a maple tree. He kicked leaves over it and sprinkled the ground with wood chips and sawdust. He didn't find the clean-up gruesome. The intimacy of it reminded him that he was Jack's right hand man.

Taking full advantage of Jack's absence Tommy slept in Jack's rickety homemade plywood bed and he slept very well indeed. It was the first time that he had slept in a proper bed in almost five months and so he awoke refreshed and ready to cut and split, and maybe he'd even make a few deliveries. He was in the utility room having his coffee and sharpening Jack's saw's when Sam arrived. Sam wanted to get Tommy high but Tommy passed and told him he wanted to get some work done. "Suit yourself," said Sam and then he went inside to rifle through Jack's office to look for Ben Horegold's papers. After about ten minutes he joined Tommy again in the utility room. "Where the hell did he put them?" Tommy shrugged and continued sharpening the saws.

"I don't know what he did with them," said Tommy. "He was in a crazy mood that night." Sam went back inside to look a little more. Eventually he gave up; slamming the door behind him he sped off without even saying goodbye. Tommy suspected that Sam knew he hadn't been completely honest with him. "Fuck him," Tommy said aloud to himself. Sam still hadn't paid Tommy for that painting — he sold it without his permission no less — not to mention the money from the other night on Whydah, which Tommy now realized he would never see.

After a few hours of hard labor on the woodpile, which was paradoxically very relaxing (he now completely understood Jack's obsession), he decided to make a couple of quick deliveries to some regulars. At one place an old woman came out and expressed her concern for Jack and demanded to know what was going on. Tommy told her that Jack would be ok, and (since she, like everyone else in town, had heard rumors of Jack's plight) he assured her that what had happened was merely an accident. The old woman shook her head, squinted and smiled at Tommy with incredulity and said: "I know you're a good kid."

"Thank you," said Tommy.

"Just take care of him for us will you?"

"I will," said Tommy as he dumped the wood, collected the check, and drove away. With each such encounter Tommy became increasingly aware of the solemnity and gravity drawing him in. It wasn't about Jack (Jack was the first to admit that), rather it was about a certain, now almost forgotten, Cape Cod attitude and aesthetic. For those that were already initiated, such as this old woman, and Jack, it was now more crucial than ever that there be some new younger people to take up that torch and carry it into the future.

Later that day Tommy went into Wellfleet to hit the library and to get some groceries. He stopped by Lembas Health Food and found Goody in the back stocking shelves. "Hey there."

"Hey you." As usual Goody looked pensive and lost.

"How are you holding up?"

"You know," said Goody. "I'm good." Tommy could tell that she was barely keeping it together.

"Goody," Tommy put his hand on her shoulder. "I know what Sam is planning with Oregon and everything."

"He told you?"

"Yeah but don't tell him I told you."

"I know," said Goody. "I won't."

"Listen," said Tommy. "Apple and I are concerned for you."

"That's so embarrassing," said Goody.

"No, don't feel that way. We're your friends. We understand what you're going through. We want you to know that we're here for you and we want to help. Just make sure you don't let him force you into doing something that you don't want to do."

"But he probably knows what's best I suppose," said Goody. Tommy shook his head.

"No I don't think he does."

"I thought you were such good friends?"

"We are. Maybe that's why I'm telling you this. Seriously, don't go with him unless you really want to Goody. Apple and I will help you, no matter what it takes."

"Will you?" Goody seemed relieved. She put her hand on Tommy's arm.

"Definitely Goody. Just do me a favor and think about it."

"But he does love me Tommy. I know he does."

"Ok," said Tommy. "I'm sure that's true, but just keep in mind that love isn't everything. And there are lots of different kinds of love and some of them are destructive and dangerous. I know I'm not that much older than you but one thing I have learned in the past few years is that love, the good kind, isn't so painful. It shouldn't make a person do something so wrong."

"I know what you're saying," said Goody. "Apple thinks I should break up with Sam. She already told me that, but I'm just not so sure."

"Apple can definitely be a little too sure of herself at times," said Tommy. "But I have to admit she's really smart."

"So is Sam," said Goody.

"That's true," admitted Tommy. "When it comes to art and history and stuff like that."

"But when it really matters?"

"Exactly," said Tommy. "You know what I'm saying. Just do me a favor and don't tell him I told you that I don't think you should go."

"But that's what you think?" Tommy nodded apologetically.

"You're afraid of him aren't you?" Asked Goody.

"Maybe a little bit."

"Me too."

"And that's my point," said Tommy. "It shouldn't have to be like that."

Chapter Thirty-Eight

Tommy didn't take his date with Apple lightly; in fact he spent all day getting ready. He cleaned out his truck and got an air freshener, and then he bought a nice bottle of merlot and a rose. He did his laundry and prepared an outfit (a button down plaid shirt and a new pair of jeans). He even gave himself a haircut and trimmed his beard. They met at the Wicked Oyster in Wellfleet around six thirty but rather than have dinner they decided to just have a drink and then head to P'town to check out some art in the east end galleries. Tommy parked his truck on a side street right by Norman Mailer's house, and they walked along, happily, both slightly buzzed and giddy. Being one of the first nights in autumn it was windy and cool and the back streets of Provincetown were quiet and charming and adorned with pumpkins and red and gold leaves blowing around along the narrow sidewalks and the little paths leading into town. Apple wore a flowing silk scarf, tight jeans, really cool red and white Puma sneakers, and an earth-toned wool sweater. She wore her glasses, which Tommy really enjoyed. He thought she seemed artistic and intellectual in her thick red-framed glasses (which was, incidentally, exactly the effect she hoped to achieve). At one point, when they were both clearly feeling the ambiance of the cozy, little, tree-lined streets, Apple took Tommy's hand in her own and she sort of skipped along for a moment and smiled warmly at him. From that moment on Tommy was relieved and relaxed; this date was now totally in the bag. He squeezed her warm soft hand and knew that he would likely sleep with Apple that night. Perhaps this seemed crass or superficial? It wasn't. Nothing could be as meaningful, or romantic to Tommy, as far as he was concerned, at that moment, she was the most beautiful woman he had ever met.

They walked past Mailer's big brick house overlooking the bay and they tried to look into the windows without being too obvious. They couldn't see anything. Tommy explained that he had been quite impressed by Mailer's novels "Deer Park" and "The Naked and The Dead" . Apple expressed the usual feminist concerns that perhaps Mailer was a bit misogynistic. "I guess," said Tommy. "But still he's pretty awesome if you ask me." They walked a little farther until they passed the little blue house where John Dos Passos had once lived.

"I've never heard of him," said Apple.

"Oh he was huge," said Tommy echoing what Sam had told him. "He had the "USA Trilogy" which was like a tour de force exposé of the socially progressive novel back in the thirties. He was chummy with Hemingway and he was one of Gertrude Stein's expatriot lost generation guys. He wrote like forty-two classic American novels which nobody ever reads anymore for some reason. But the coolest thing about him was that he was friends with Picasso and he was a great Provincetown painter on top of everything else. He was one of the first cubist expressionists. The only bad thing is they say he was kind of a closet case communist supposedly, but I don't know about that. Besides, all the avant garde artists were commies back then anyway. I mean it's easy for us now, in retrospect, to criticize that, but way back then who knew? Apparently most of them even supported Stalin, philosophically, for a while, but eventually they conceded that Stalinism was bullshit and so they all claimed to be Trotskyites instead. In the end even Trotsky was too far left and so they all had to claim a kind of quasi-socialist, A-political, mysticism by default, which was I guess the only alternative. But that's why pencils have erasers, am I right?"

"You know Tommy, it's nice to hang out with someone like you. You're different. You challenge me." Tommy smiled and squeezed Apple's hand. He knew he had better quit while he was ahead.

They stopped at a few more galleries along the way and Tommy tried very hard to not bully the conversation and let Apple give her own opinions on the paintings, but when they stood in front of a particularly showy impressionistic seascape done in purple and pink hues he found it difficult to keep quiet.

"What do you think? Is this cool or what?" Tommy shook his head.

"Oh come on," said Apple. "I know you have an opinion." Tommy shook his head and kept quiet. "Oh come on!" said Apple.

"It's crap," said Tommy. Apple laughed. She wasn't put off. She wanted to provoke him.

"It's not that bad is it?"

"No it definitely sucks," said Tommy.

"Does it?"

"Well look at it," said Tommy. "It's not even a real painting. It's like something you'd see in a hotel room. It's totally lame. It's too purple, and it's too pink. And the composition is sentimental and generic. First of all it has the fan brush trees which are a dead give away. Nobody paints trees with a fan brush like that — it's like a Bob Ross painting or something. It's like a Kincade print — totally cookie-cutter, and then you've got like the black gesso background with the liquid-clear alizarin crimson clouds. It might as well be on black velvet! The only thing missing is the snow-capped mountains done with a pallet knife, and like the little broken down barn in the foreground for Christ's sake!"

"No, I see what you mean," said Apple. "I was only testing you." She then moved on to another painting. "But this one I really like. I was only kidding about that one but this one really moves me." Apple stood before a small, simple brown and gold painting of the dunes. "Seriously, I like this one." Tommy took a few moments to look at this next painting.

"Now that's it," said Tommy. "I mean look at it. That's a real painting. You can just tell as soon as you look at it. That's worth a thousand bucks easy." Apple read the small label beside it.

"It's twelve fifty," she said.

"And worth every penny," said Tommy. "In fact it's worth thirteen hundred if it's worth a dime." Apple laughed and took Tommy's hand. "I wish I could paint one that good. That's a painting."

"It doesn't have any purple in it," said Apple.

"Exactly," said Tommy. "Nobody uses purple. Purple is for suckers. It's too easy."

"Van Gogh used purple," said Apple.

"That's different," said Tommy. "He earned it."

Apple and Tommy walked west on Commercial Street and stopped in several small galleries along the way as they headed toward the center of town. In one gallery they looked at some stark and beautiful black and white photographs of fishing boats, the dunes and the ocean, and some of the local architecture. "What do you think of these?" Asked Tommy.

"I like them."

"Yeah, me too. You still have to show me some of your own work," said Tommy. Apple grinned and nodded. She hadn't been able to bring herself to come clean on that one. Now she hoped that maybe she could actually become a photographer before he ever found out.

"Well getting to know you has kind of inspired me to get back into it," she explained.

"Really? How so?"

"You know, just seeing someone who is so into being an artist and all. You inspire me."

"I like to think everyone is an artist in a way," said Tommy.

"No, some people definitely aren't." She laughed nervously.

"So what kind of photography do you do?"

Apple then remembered what Oliver had told her. "Are you familiar with Diane Arbus?"

"Sure," said Tommy. "Pictures of freaks and fringe people and Social Realism and all that right? She ended up committing suicide didn't she? Boy that's some heady stuff. I should have known you'd be into that kind of photography."

"Yeah she was pretty cool," said Apple. "Did you know she did a portrait of old Jack Snow, the original Jack, working outside the station?"

"No. I hadn't heard that. That's totally cool. I'd love to see that. Have you seen it?"

"No I haven't," admitted Apple. "My friend Oliver told me about it just the other day. We definitely have to get our hands on a copy of it."

"You have a friend named Oliver?" Tommy laughed.

"What's so funny about that?"

"Nothing I guess. I just never knew anybody named that, other than that kid from the Brady Bunch."

"Yeah I suppose it is a little funny. Remember what I told you about my embarrassing waspy background?"

"Right," said Tommy. "Scooter and Pebbles from the yacht club at Yarmouth Port." Tommy laughed and Apple poked him in his side.

"Don't make fun."

"No, of course," said Tommy. "And what about Oliver? What's his deal?" Apple knew what Tommy was getting at.

"Oh he's just some tall handsome rich guy who wants to be my boyfriend, but don't worry I don't go for that type."

"Well," said Tommy. "I only hope I'm short, ugly and poor enough for you."

"Oh I'm sure you do all right for yourself."

"You know some people think my pointy beard and choppy hair make me look a little like Van Gogh." Apple pushed Tommy playfully.

"You'd like that wouldn't you? Actually you're much cuter but don't get ahead of yourself. I'll hold anyone's hand after a couple of cosmos."

"Ok," said Tommy. "I'll settle for being cuter than Van Gogh. Incidentally, did I show you my tattoo?" Tommy began to unbutton his shirt.

"You did! Please don't pull that thing out again."

"Suit yourself." Tommy buttoned his shirt.

They continued along Commercial Street in silence for a while, holding hands, and then Apple said: "You know speaking of my friend Oliver, he happens to be quite knowledgeable in outer Cape real estate and he and I had some ideas about some options that Jack might like to hear about."

"You know," said Tommy. "I'm having such a good time right now not thinking about Jack's for once. If it's all the same to you I'd rather not talk shop tonight."

"No you're right," said Apple. "Let's just have fun."

Chapter Thirty-Nine

Sam started drinking early. He had a lot on his mind. Goody told him about Tommy's date with Apple, which rubbed him the wrong way. He resented her sticking her nose into his business and he knew Tommy was being played for a fool yet again. And if that wasn't bad enough he was now aware of Apple's influence over Goody. If there was one thing Sam disliked it was a strong independent woman, especially an Ivy League, Yarmouth Port type. Sure, she was good-looking, but what the hell was Tommy thinking? It was as if he hadn't learned anything from him after all.

Sam was supposed to meet with Nate Nickerson in the afternoon at the Bomb Shelter to hand over the keys and title to Whydah. This, of course, was emotionally unsettling for him, but on this front he was pretty much in complete denial. As far as he was concerned all he wanted was the fourteen grand, and once he had that he knew he would likely hit the road for Oregon within a day or two. He could work out the details of the sale of the gas station over the phone or through the mail. He just needed that extra cash to put him over the top and then he'd be gone once and for all. He intended to take Goody, whether she wanted to go or not, and drive her rig out west, knowing full well that his own truck would be damn lucky to make it across the Mississippi. Given all this he was quite worked up and already half in the bag when he arrived at Goody's cottage in the early afternoon.

Goody was kicked back on the sofa with a cup of tea when Sam stormed in with a wild look in his eyes. "It's happening, Goody. Pack your bags. We're leaving tomorrow."

"What are you talking about? Tomorrow? I'm not ready."

"So get ready." Sam tore through the cabinet over the sink looking for his bottle of rum. "There's no time like the present right? I'm off to see Nickerson tonight and if he has the cash, which he better, there'll be nothing left holding us back." He poured a glass of rum and took a huge slug.

"What about the animals?"

"We're taking Seamus. That's what you said right? You can drop Artemis off at Jack's. Tommy will take care of her until your friend picks her up. She said she wanted to take her, didn't she?"

"And the cats?"

"Fuck the cats. They don't even live here half the time anyway, you know that. The whole Cape is full of stray cats. Who's gonna notice a couple more? They'll live on mice until someone picks them up. You know they're up to it."

"You're scaring me Sam. How drunk are you?" Sam took another swig of rum.

"Seriously Goody. I've never been more sober in my life." She stood up and he took both of her hands in his own. He calmed himself and spoke softly. "We're leaving tomorrow morning, just deal with it. Do you want to work at the health food store for the rest of your life? Where's your sense of adventure? You know I love you Goody. Don't you love me?" Goody began to cry.

"I do Sam. You know that." Sam kissed Goody on the cheek.

"You're gonna love it out there. Remember what we talked about? It's just like Middle Earth. I promise." He then rushed into Goody's bedroom and returned with one of his better paintings. "I'm gonna sell this for short money to some art fag in P'town and then I'm done. Seriously Goody pack your bags tonight." Sam took his painting under his arm, and his bottle of rum, and stormed out. Goody rushed after him and shouted from the front porch.

"Can't we talk about this?" Sam jumped in his truck.

"I'll be back later after I see Nate. We'll talk then." And with that he sped off. Goody went back inside and cried on the sofa. Seamus, sensing something was wrong, jumped up beside her (he wasn't usually allowed on the couch) and nuzzled his head under her arm.

"What do you think about Oregon Seamus? They say it's like Middle Earth." Seamus flopped his snout on Goody's lap and sighed deeply. As far as Goody was concerned that said it all.

Sam polished off his bottle of rum in the parking lot outside the Bomb Shelter and by now he was clearly getting a little drunk, even by his own standards. He then went inside and sat alone at the bar and had a few more. Nate Nickerson showed up just before sunset with fourteen thousand dollars in small bills stuffed into a wool sock in his front pocket.

Nate bought a round. "Dude I've got the cake! You got that paperwork?" Sam nodded and slugged down the shot. They talked a while, nearly incoherently, as Sam went into the minutiae of Whydah's specs and history and some of her capabilities and unique mechanical requirements. Nate had heard it all before and realized that Sam, due to the obvious gravity of the situation, was lapsing into what could only be described as a slight case of seller's remorse, along with a healthy dose of nostalgia and drunken ragtime incoherence.

"You know about the brass bell?" Asked Sam.

"You told me about it way back in the day when we used to fish," Nate assured Sam.

"Billy Howl was a full blooded Merganser out of Chatham who drowned in the seventy-eight Nor'easter," Sam told him again anyway. "He stole that bell off Jacob Ryder's rig, 'the Red Night', way back even before Pop Snow had Whydah. Pop won it in a game of chance; it was his good luck charm. That bell never leaves the wheel house."

"I know that Sam. It never leaves the wheelhouse. Shit everybody knows that."

"And the tea pot?"

"The antique silver tea pot you got from Goody," said Nate. "She gave it to you on her birthday. It was her mother's. Under the scup board hold right? You're leaving that?"

"Of course I'm leaving it! What the hell do you think?"

"Right," said Nate. "Thank you. It's a privilege, believe me."

"You ever hock that tea pot — I don't care how much you can get for it — and I'll come back and hunt your ass down. I'm not kidding. You got that?"

"I wouldn't have it any other way," said Nate.

"All right, so let's have it then." Sam gulped his beer and Nate dug into his front pocket to produce the cash but then Sam added: "You know we have to go out fishing one last time tonight before I sign her over." Nate tucked the sock full of bills back into his front pocket and sighed.

"I don't know if I can do that," he said. "I'm pretty buzzed. I gotta go home."

"No, we're going out one last time Nate! That's a deal breaker. I gotta do this. We got a full moon and stripers running at high tide. It's too damn good to pass up. I gotta go out one last time — you understand that don't you? Now let's have it. I want to see some cash!" Sam tried to grab Nate's arm but Nate jumped backwards and sent his bar stool toppling over onto the floor. The whole bar went silent and now every eye in the room was on them.

"I know you're a good deal meaner than me Sam, but for that kind of money you're going to have to kill me." For a moment Sam considered it, he had very little to lose, but then he smiled.

"Relax. Nobody's killing anybody." Nate picked up his stool and sat back down. Sam removed some paperwork from his breast pocket, unfolded it and placed it on the bar in front of Nate. It included Whydah's registration and title as well as a bill of sale, both of which were unsigned. "Here take these. Put them in your pocket."

"You gonna sign them?"

"I'll sign them when I get back," said Sam. Nate stuck the papers in his pocket and Sam got up and prepared to leave. "You sure you don't wanna come out, it's gonna be fun?" Nate shook his head. He knew the rumors of Pop Snow and how things went down the last time Whydah had changed skippers. "Can you at least spot me a few bucks until the morning?" Nate handed Sam a twenty. "What are you serious? That won't get me out of the Pamet." Nate pulled out another fifty which Sam quickly snatched up. He squeezed Nate's shoulder, punched him in the arm and headed out. "You're a good shit," he said over his shoulder. "I'll see you in the morning." Once Sam was gone Nate decided to stay and have one last beer. He was a bit shaken up and needed some time to collect himself. Maybe he just lost seventy bucks, but somehow that didn't matter. He knew, all things considered, he got off easy.

Sam stopped at the Wellfleet packie and grabbed another fifth before heading back to Goody's. He was hoping that she had settled down by then and started to see things more clearly. Obviously they would have to go to Oregon. There was nothing left on the Cape for them now. Though Goody's truck was parked out front he was surprised to find her cottage dark and empty. She must have taken Seamus out for a walk. He went inside and found a note that Goody had left for him by the door. It read simply: "Sam I'm sorry but I don't love you anymore and I'm not going with you." He paced the tiny room for a few minutes and then sat down and opened the rum. As he drank he reread the note and grumbled to himself. How could she do this to him after all he had done for her? He was completely at a loss but thought maybe he could change her mind if only he could talk to her. He sat there drinking and smoking, in the dark, for a long time and then finally he stood up to go. As he put his hand on the door he reminded himself that he intended to never be in that cottage ever again, and so he took one last look around, slowly, and he sighed. He looked at her shrine. "Technically it's not art," he said aloud. He then remembered his foot locker under Goody's bed and laughed. That he had almost walked out and forgotten it was testament to just how drunk (or emotionally distraught?) he really was. This foot locker was now, easily, the most important thing in his life. He reached under her bed and fished it out. It was a small rectangular wooden box. Having once been an ammunition crate in the war it was sturdy and had a heavy brass clasp and a pad-lock. He set it down by the front door, carefully. Until now he had been trying very hard to keep his cool, but, when he looked at Goody's shrine, one last time, he snapped. First he sent a chair hurling into the shrine, then a lamp, and finally the whole kitchen table. He then began to rip down all the bones, driftwood, seashells, feathers and everything else and throw them violently around the room. He crushed the skulls under his boots and even stomped on the horse head before stuffing it into the toilet. He took a hammer out from under the sink and smashed the quartz, amethyst, and seashells into the floorboards. Artemis cowered, trembling, under the couch as Sam grabbed his footlocker and his bottle and stormed out. He sped off in his truck down to the beach looking for Goody. He never found her. She and Seamus had been hiding in the backyard, in the shadows of the trees, the whole time.

Chapter Forty

Tommy and Apple went for pizza slices and ice cream at Spiritus and then went back to Tommy's truck for a ride out to Race Point. They walked along the trails in the dunes overlooking the back beach. "The ocean side of Provincetown is completely different from the bay side," said Apple. It's like a whole different town."

"It's like a whole different planet," said Tommy. Though it was now late, the dunes glowed yellow and white under the stars and the moon illuminated their way along the trail.

"The dunes are totally luminescent," said Apple. "It's like walking in the snowy woods at night."

"Yeah," said Tommy. "It's like that poem by Robert Frost."

"Do we have miles to go before we sleep?" Asked Apple. Tommy laughed.

"Exactly," said Tommy. "I hope we do, really."

"You know that poem is supposedly about suicide?"

"That seems to be coming up a lot lately," said Tommy.

"Yeah." They both went quiet for a moment and then Apple said: "Did you know Dos Passos killed himself after he photographed Jack's Gas?" Tommy knew she was only teasing him.

"Don't you mean Diane Arbus?"

"Right," said Apple. "I knew it was one of those people. Wasn't she a communist or something?"

"You had better stick to science," Tommy pulled Apple close and kissed her.

"No she was a lost generation cubist or something," added Apple. Tommy kissed her again. They leaned up against a tree and made out, enthusiastically, for nearly half an hour. For Tommy it felt like five minutes. Eventually they came up for air and started to stroll again. At one point they stood on a bluff overlooking the ocean. "That's where I'm going in a couple of days. Way over there." Apple pointed out across the sea.

"Are you really?" Apple explained to Tommy about her big pig eye conference in London.

"I am so poised to knock their socks off it's not even funny," said Apple. Tommy was now already so into Apple again that his first impulse was a twinge of concern and regret that she was about to travel so far away from him, but he knew it would be ill advised to admit to anything like that just yet.

"That is so awesome," he said. "You're gonna kick ass over there."

"Yeah," said Apple. Tommy decided to not even ask her how long she would be gone. "I'll only be gone a week," said Apple. Apparently they were on the same page.

"Could you get me something while you're over there?"

"Sure." Apple laughed. "Like what?"

"I don't know. Like an ashtray or something."

"You want an ashtray?"

"Yeah you know. Like one of those souvenir ashtrays from a tacky tourist shop. I've been using an old tuna can. Did I tell you I like to smoke when I paint?"

"I think you like to paint when you smoke."

"Either way. But it would be nice to have one that had sentimental value or whatever."

"That's so sweet."

They walked down out of the forest toward the shore and saw that the tide was starting to come in. The green waves lapped at their feet. They were now way down the beach and it would take the better part of an hour to get back to where they had left the truck. "You know," said Tommy. "If we keep heading this way we'll eventually come to the really secluded part of the dunes behind Pilgrim Lake. That's where the dune shacks are, I've always wanted to check them out. Goody and Sam told me about them. They're supposed to be cool."

"And they're open to the public? '

"Well no, not technically, but they're unlocked and abandoned, especially this late in the season. It's where the cool people go to hang out."

"Are we too old to be cool?" Asked Apple.

"It might be a long walk."

"What was that line from Frost?"

"Through the forest dark and deep," said Tommy. "With miles to go before I sleep."

Sam gave up looking for Goody and decided to take advantage of his last night with Whydah. If this was going to be his last night he would go all out, not for striper, but for cod. Codfish were his first love. True, stripers were tasty and fun to catch, but, if the truth be told, they were flashy and over-rated; they were for the tourist and the weekend warrior — for the real Wellfleetian, when the chips were down, it was all about the lowly codfish. A fat, bearded, codfish would be the only fitting end to his career on a night such as this. Unlike striper, cod weren't discriminating eaters, they'd gladly choke down anything, which was all the better — he hadn't gotten around to procuring proper bait. He did have, however, a bucket of rancid clams and several gruesome mackerel heads, and he had some left over bluefish scraps. You don't need a good jig to land a codfish; a few drop lines would do the trick. Always the optimist, Sam had ridiculously large hooks and heavy sinkers (nearly four ounces a piece) which he dropped at a hundred and twenty feet. He plopped into a rickety lawn chair, kicked up his feet on Whydah's low gunwale and looked at the stars and waited. Tonight was for codfish, but Sam couldn't get Goody off his mind. He smoked and drank and stewed in a contemplative reverie. He got so drunk he began to dream while he was awake. The stars and the sky were vibrant and crackled with violent energy. Sam had always had an unusually high tolerance for alcohol but on this night he reached an all together new plateau. He approached a near psychedelic ecstasy. No matter how much he drank he couldn't get to that point where he felt drunk or sick, or even for that matter even remotely sleepy. He was awake, more awake than he had ever been in his life. If he were to snag a codfish in his present mood he would just as soon jump into the dark abyss and wrestle it into submission right there in the cold water. This desire became utterly irresistible. Even without getting a bite he had to fight off the desire to get up and dive into the cold dark sea. It called out to him. It was then that he spied a darkened forty foot fiberglass New York rig moored seven hundred yards off Herring Cove looking like a ripe peach just waiting to be bitten into, he knew what to do. Those rich yuppies were ruining the Cape. He had no choice. He came up beside her and saw that she was empty. He dropped anchor fifty feet off her starboard, took off his boots and his shirt, emptied his pockets, and then, without even a moment's hesitation, dove in. When he hit the cold water he was exhilarated and immediately felt happy and alive.

Once onboard the yuppie rig he raided her cabin greedily. He found a mesh sack for toting fish and he began to fill it with anything of value he could find. First there was the Epirb radio beacon device, and then there was a sonar depth finder and beautiful antique brass sexton. He riffled the drawers and cabinets and emptied the bar. He scored other miscellaneous items such as an expensive wrist watch and a glass compass. Within moments he slipped back over the side and swam, with the tote bag draw-string clamped in his teeth. Once aboard Whydah he raised anchor and headed around the point. Still no codfish.

Something clicked in Goody's head that night and there was no turning back. Perhaps at some time in the future she could restore the cozy serenity of her cottage and maybe even rebuild her shrine, but not on this night. This dark night was not for rebuilding, it was for destruction, and not only for Sam — Goody was determined to let loose some destructive energy of her own. One thing was for sure, she had no more tears.

She grabbed her canvas beach wrecker sack and packed it with the remains of her shrine, gathering up every last piece of coral, feather, broken bone and seashell, as well as all the crystals, sea glass and driftwood. Now there was nothing left, and for that she felt sad. For the first time her cottage felt barren and lonely. So be it. She took Seamus, tossed the sack into her truck, and headed for the dunes.

She left her truck on the side of the road at the Truro Wellfleet line and hiked into the forest, first down through the wetlands and bogs into the wild blueberry grove. At places the thickets were so dense she had to crawl to get through but then the land rose up and she climbed the hills, taking paths so narrow that usually only deer used them. The harvest moon lit her way. Soon she came to the high ground where it opened up and she could see the ocean. There at the highest point on the hilltop, where there were no trees and the ground was covered with a soft bed of bayberry, lichen, inkberry and primrose, she dropped her pack and rested before heading back into the woods where she gathered dried sea grass, twigs, birch bark, bay leaves and a locust stump. She had only a single book of matches and no paper but Goody had always been good at starting a fire. She ripped up the matchbook cover to get it going and within a half hour it was roaring. Lying on a soft aromatic bed of moss and bay leaves Seamus watched Goody, with his one good eye, as she removed driftwood, sea shells and feathers from her bag and tossed them into the fire. She then danced in the moonlight as they crackled and sparked in the flames. She jumped and twirled and threw her arms around like a mad woman which caused Seamus to get up and pace and wag his tail. He didn't understand what had come over Goody but he knew he liked it. Goody untied her hair and whipped it around wildly and then she looked at Seamus and shouted: "Yes!" Seamus barked and howled and Goody laughed. "What do you think?" She said to Seamus. "I'm tired of looking at life with a sigh! I'm tired of saying no! Tonight we say yes! Yes! Yes! Yes!" She threw some more wood, and some more pieces of her broken shrine, into the fire, and then she continued her wild dance, all the while continuing to shout: "Yes! Yes! Yes!"

Goody danced around the fire for a long time and at one point she peered out across the moon-lit sea and caught sight of Whydah as Sam rounded Race Point and headed off the back beach toward Truro. To be sure it was only the dimmest of silhouettes and a couple of tiny lights, yet there was no doubt. Goody knew Whydah, but more to the point she knew Sam. A northeasterly gale kicked up, shaking the trees all around her and dark heavy clouds began to roll in from off shore. "Yes!" shouted Goody. "Let it rain!" She threw another piece of driftwood onto the fire.

Sam retrieved his empty drop-lines; the crabs had taken his bait. He didn't care and instead he smiled and reveled in the irony that apparently there were no more cod on Cape Cod. This only strengthened his argument that it was indeed time to head out west. He had already robbed three more boats in P'town. Resigned to the fact that in the morning he would be gone forever he was feeling reckless, and now, with the approach of a rain storm, he was further emboldened. He knew that no one would be out on a night such as this. Not with a northeasterly gale, a full moon high tide, and dark rain clouds gathering in the east. So much the better. He'd rob every trap between north Truro and south Wellfleet. The first set which Sam relieved of their catch was set by none other than Lawrence Prince. Prince, the toeless skipper of Sultana who married the Harbor Master's cousin and told Nate Nickerson that Sam was scrubbin' hens in the harbor. "Payback served cold is a bitch," said Sam as he dumped the catch on deck. It was a full load, and no doubt had quite a few keepers, not that Sam was about to cull the chicks from the tinkers on a night like this. Just to bust balls, Sam tied a half-hitch knot in Lawrence's buoy line before he threw it over. The next traps

Sam went for were John Julian's, skipper of The Boneta out of Eastham. Julian, a full-blooded Mashpee Wampanoag, was said to be a distant relative of King Phillip — whether or not that was true he was known to be a formidable man. Sam didn't half-hitch Julian's line, he did, however, steal his lobsters. By half past twelve the rain came down heavily and Sam had already robbed a half a dozen rigs and poached forty pounds of lobster, but as far as he was concerned he had only just begun.

Now the clouds covered up the moon and Tommy and Apple could barely see where they were going as they ran into the wind along the shore. They were drenched and shouting and laughing wildly when they reached the first of the dune shacks. It was a small, and apparently very old, weathered clap-board shingle structure not much bigger than a shed. It had only one door, one window and a peaked roof with a thin black stove pipe sticking out on top. Though it was set back in the woods a couple of hundred yards off shore it was nearly buried in the sand. The dunes were all around it and on one side a huge dune had formed up against the wall and it looked as though eventually the dunes would swallow up the tiny shack completely. Once inside they took off their wet sweaters and shook the rain out of their hair like a couple of shaggy dogs. The interior was sparse, but dry and comfortable. There was a kitchen table with a wood bench, some empty cabinets, a half sized cast iron wood stove, and a small cot with a wool army blanket. There were no lamps or electricity but there was a candle, a small pile of firewood, and a stack of old newspapers. "Oh we have to have a fire!" Said Apple. "Nobody will mind will they?"
"Who's gonna know?" Said Tommy and he began ripping up newspapers and breaking up some kindling. "This place is great isn't it?"
"Who's is it anyway?"
"I've heard they're owned by the Tasha family in Provincetown but they just kind of left them out here for everyone to enjoy. Have you heard of them?" Apple shook her head.
"I don't think I have."
"Goody and Sam told me about them. I guess it's a big family and they go way back in the art scene down here. Apparently they have a whole network of cool old art studios all over P'town. Their current patriarch is this old artist named Carl. Sam introduced

me to him at the Truro Dump Dance in the spring when I first arrived. I got a chance to see his work. He's a welder and he does like brass and silver sculptures and he makes a lot of jewelry that's really popular with the locals. Goody and Sam both have Tasha rings."

"I think I know which one," said Apple. "Goody has this one ring that looks like a bunch of little brass balls that are cut in half kind of so they look like a flower."

"That's the one," said Tommy. "Sam's got one too. I want to get one but I guess they're pretty hard to come by." Tommy got the fire started and then sat beside Apple on the bench.

"Did you say the Truro Dump Dance?"

"Yeah it's like an artist's Gala held at the dump down the street from Jack's. They have it every spring."

"Oh we have to go to that next time. I mean if you're still around by then."

"Ok?" Tommy was encouraged that Apple would think of him in such a long term way. She seemed to be picking up on what he was thinking when she added:

"You know I'm not necessarily going to sleep with you tonight or anything."

"I know that." Tommy answered quickly and nonchalantly without looking disappointed at all, but technically he didn't believe her anyway. That she had said "not necessarily" was all that he had to hear to put him in an even better mood than he already was, if that were even possible. He was just about as content as it gets by that point.

"You know I brought a little surprise." He fished through his soggy backpack and pulled out a bottle of Merlot.

"You're good," said Apple, smiling. "Let me see that." Tommy was relieved that he had spent the extra ten bucks to buy a good one. Everything was falling into place. He was on fire tonight!

"I hope you don't mind plastic cups." Apple moved closer and kissed him on the cheek.

"Set me up." Outside the wind howled and the heavy squalls pounded the roof.

"It's getting pretty bad out there." Tommy poured the wine. They clicked their plastic cups in a toast.

"Here's to the wind and rain," said Apple.

Goody threw everything she could find into the fire and it burned ten feet high. She threw all of her bones and shells and all of her dead and broken dreams into the flames and it burned hot and smoky, sputtering and choking in the rain but still she, and the fire, kept going. In the violent throws of the storm she persisted. She sang her mournful elegy into the wind as the sea rose up and threatened to swallow up Sam and Whydah in its erratic squall. She danced and sang through bouts of ecstasy and dread, calling up every spirit in the dunes. Every witch, rake and rogue, from under every tree and every rock, she called them all. She called those who lived and died on the waves and in those scraggly forests and in the dunes, and all the while she danced and shouted: "Let it rain! Let it blow!" Seamus paced around the fire wagging his tail and intermittently howling into the storm. Goody saw that Seamus was onto something and so she took off all her clothes and began to howl at the moon.

Now nude and dancing and chanting around the fire as the nor'easter was slamming the coast with full force Goody saw Whydah rounding the rip maybe five hundred yards off south Truro. There was no way Sam could moor Whydah safely off the back beach. She danced around the fire and shouted: "Let it rain! Let it blow!"

Whydah rounded the rip off the Race; she passed the bath houses in the P'town dunes and headed straight into the danger field off the backside of Truro toward Wellfleet. From there Sam saw the fire over Corn Hill against the dark sky and his intuition told him it had to be Goody. He knew she was determined to put up a fight. When the nor' easterly gale kicked up ten foot seas he realized just how formidable Goody was when pushed to her limit. He had always admitted, to himself at least, what she was capable of, and he knew that sometimes her spells did work (especially if she was sufficiently pissed off) but, as usual, his arrogance prevailed. He was, after all, the one man likely to wrangle Goody in a pinch, besides he did love her, and he did understand how her mind worked. Specifically he knew that if Whydah survived the night she would likely concede in the morning and follow him out west. In this respect Sam's intuition was quite accurate, though premature. It was, after all, only one o'clock in the morning and Goody's fire, and the storm, were just getting started. Sam might have underestimated Goody's resolve, and to be sure, he underestimated his own drunkenness and greed.

Had he turned Whydah north just then he could have passed the rip before the tide turned on him, but instead he persisted south where he hoped to poach a few more traps, and maybe rob a few more boats, under the cover of the heavy rain.

The gale force wind and rain pelted the tiny shack relentlessly but Tommy and Apple were safe and warm inside. They sat by the fire enjoying their wine and each other's company. "You know," said Tommy. "Not long ago there was a poet who spent a few months alone in this shack and he wrote a famous book about it, a collection of poems. I don't remember his name but he was known as 'the poet of the dunes'."

"Really?" Said Apple. "I didn't know one could write a famous book of poems anymore."

"Well I guess it wasn't famous, but it is highly regarded — you know, among those who know what's what." Apple laughed.

"It's so cute how you guys around here are kind of snobby in your own way."

"How can a poor man be snobby?" Asked Tommy. "You do realize I'm totally broke don't you?"

"Oh that doesn't affect it," said Apple. "I know you know what I mean. Like how guys like you and Sam and Pablo think all this artist stuff is so important and historical and everything even though nobody else seems to know anything about any of it? I think that's the way you guys like it because it gives you a sense of superiority. It's really kind of elitist in a way."

"So you think I'm pretentious or something?"

"No, not pretentious," said Apple. "Just snobby, but I'm not saying it's a bad thing. I find it endearing." Tommy laughed. He understood that Apple's criticism was actually a veiled self defense. She was the one with the West Newton, Harvard PhD., preppie pedigree, and if she wanted to accuse someone else of being snobby or elitist for a change he was all too happy to oblige her. In fact, for him, it was definitely a compliment (he did, after all, live in the backroom of a gas station).

"Most Americans are Philistines," Tommy threw in for good measure (which only proved Apple's point). "It's really kind of sad, but I guess that doesn't make me an elitist since nearly everyone thinks that these days."

"No," said Apple. "Actually it does. Only snobs accuse people of being 'Philistines'. That went out with the Victorians." Tommy thought about this and then nodded in resignation.

"You know if I could live in any other period in history it would be during the Victorian Age."

"That doesn't surprise me," said Apple. "You've got an old fashioned feel about you I would say."

"I just think that everything should be made out of wood and leather," said Tommy. "Is that so wrong?" Apple poured them some more wine and Tommy put another log on the fire.

"You know Tommy we're not that unalike after all." Tommy sipped his wine and smiled.

"No?"

"I don't think so," said Apple. "I think that superficially one might think that artists and scientists are like opposites, but really, just below the surface, they sort of operate in the same realm, and in that way they're kind of like kindred spirits."

"They're both idealistic and misunderstood," offered Tommy.

"Yes," said Apple. "And often they end up in the fringe of society." Tommy laughed at that last bit.

"I'll certainly cop to that one," he admitted. "But I didn't know you were too."

"I'm here aren't I?"

"That's true," said Tommy. He slowly, and carefully, leaned over and began to kiss her.

Goody had now been dancing around her fire for hours and her bare feet were swollen and raw. She wrapped a small wool blanket around her shoulders and kept going. Her voice was now strained and barely audible but she persisted with her incantations in a low horse whisper. Seamus was now worn out and concerned as he nervously paced the perimeter of the hilltop. He wanted to head back home but apparently Apple wasn't ready to leave and so finally he took refuge in the thickets under a grove of scrub oak and locust. He tried to get some sleep but there was no use. Instead he just lay there and sighed, keeping his one good eye on Goody.

Black Sam stood in the spray on Whydah's pitching deck and braced himself against ten foot swells. The wind and the rain had barely abated when a fog blew in, a dense fog the likes of which he had never seen outside the Nantucket Shoals. He could no longer see where he was headed and would have to rely on dead reckoning, but at this point that hardly mattered. He knew damn well where he was and he had only two choices: To continue south another ten miles to Nauset Harbor, or to swing her directly into the wind and brave the fifteen miles back to Herring Cove. Either way he knew there were roving sand bars that he couldn't predict — some were a mere eight feet below in a full sea (one never knew where when running south on a back side gale). Ultimately his pride and local parochialism won out. If he were to dash Whydah he'd rather have it be known that it was among the Truro dangerfields. A thousand skippers better than he had made that choice. So be it. He swung round and headed north east. Once committed, he could no longer let go of the wheel. For a good while he made progress and he began to think he'd make it back to P'town after all. He held on tight with one hand as he reached down underneath and dug out Goody's silver teapot. No sooner had he pressed it against his lips for good luck when a rogue wave exploded through the plexiglass wheelhouse and sent Sam flying off his seat. With the wind knocked out of him he sloshed around on deck and then finally he got his bearings and found the strength to crawl toward what was left of the wheelhouse. The wheel spun in a violent blur, it spun like a fan, and yet strangely Whydah appeared to be not moving at all. Sam's heart sank. He knew what that meant. Blinded by the fog he had dashed Whydah against the rocks. Now his only hope was to try to grab hold of anything that might float. If he was lucky he was only a couple of hundred yards off shore. Crawling on his hands and knees he tried to make his way toward his kayak lashed in the stern but then another huge wave crashed over the deck and it sent him violently into Whydah's low gunwale. At that point Sam assumed he'd be swept into the sea, yet oddly, he was utterly relaxed. He lay on his back, with his eyes closed peacefully, when, after a minute or so, he opened his eyes and was surprised to find that he was not dead. He sat up and took stock of his situation. Whydah had spilled her scup and a swarm of lobsters flopped around his waist and legs. He couldn't feel his feet, which was very odd, and he saw that he had lost a shoe, and worse his legs seemed to be twisted and laying in an unnatural arrangement. He lay in a tangled mass of oar weed and kelp and for the first time he understood why the old timers called sea-weed 'the devil's apron'. He thought about Jack, and about Goody, and about how he should have had a whole other life out in Oregon. Whydah creaked, snapped, and groaned mournfully, as she rose up and spilled herself over Truro's dangerfield breakers, and it was there, under a full moon, on a high tide, in the autumn of nineteen ninety-six, when Samuel Bellamy, The Black Prince of Wellfleet, bravely met his watery end.

Chapter Forty-One

A few days after the storm, when Sam's demise was not yet firmly established (though there were certain rumors), Apple left for her pig eye conference in London just as Jack, who was now making a remarkable recovery, returned from the hospital and of course, went straight to his woodpile. When Tommy saw Jack, who was now growing a beard (they didn't think it was a good idea to give him a razor in the hospital) with his bandaged ear, the bandage held in place under a wool cap (he had lost the lower portion of his left ear) he couldn't help himself and he said: "You know who you look like don't you?" Jack grinned.

"I told you before," said Jack. "I don't know anything about art."

The sad news came a few days later when nobody had heard from Sam for a week and then, finally, the Coast Guard confirmed they had found Whydah. She was way off the back beach, at the bottom. Ironically it was all the stolen emergency position radio beacons that did the trick. The signal was so strong they thought they were looking for the wreck of the Lucitania, but what they found instead was a little rusty old twenty-nine foot stroller with a dozen or more state of the art Epirb devices on board. Combined these devices were worth way more than the Whydah herself. Apparently Sam had hit every swanky yacht from P'town to Wellfleet in a single night. In the end the Coast Guard and The National Seashore officials agreed to leave Whydah where she lay; apparently she wasn't worth the trouble, though, for a couple of days they sent down several teams of divers. They never found Sam. They did, however, retrieve certain effects, which they solemnly presented to Jack. They were well aware that this went above and beyond protocol, but they did so in deference to Jack's revered status in the community. He was moved by their generosity. These effects included, among other things, Whydah's bell, Sam's footlocker, and Goody's teapot. Jack displayed Whydah's beautiful brass bell in his sitting room and gave the rest to Goody.

Goody lived with the water-logged footlocker sitting in the middle of her cottage for a few days before she finally got up the courage to smash it open. It was padlocked but once she got it in her head there was no stopping her. She beat on the lock a few times with her hammer and when that didn't work, she stormed out and drove to Jack's, where she retrieved a power drill and reciprocating saw from the utility room. Jack was inside reading his paper when he saw Goody taking the tools. He didn't even bother her. He figured if she needed his help she'd ask.

Goody gave up on the lock and cut right through the side of Sam's locker. Inside she found two one way train tickets to Oregon, the deed to a small hunting lodge on ten acres of land, a stack of cash, and an assortment of maps and letters. She also found the rest of her college applications which Sam had stolen. She consoled herself with the idea that if she started right away she could get into Cape Cod Community College for the spring semester.

In London Apple was met with unbridled success. Her pig eye toxicology assay was the toast of the town. She made some invaluable contacts, one of whom was with an influential representative of a multinational cosmetics corporation who had high hopes that her pig eyes could be a viable, and humane, alternative to the ubiquitous Draize rabbit eye test. If such a thing were to happen! Well Apple didn't even want to let herself think about it. Suffice it to say if such a thing were to occur she would never have to worry about "funding" ever again. In any event her paper was accepted by a reputable journal and she was now well on her way.

Apple returned home with Tommy's ashtray; it had a picture of Big Ben on it and needless to say Tommy totally loved it. She spent the rest of the fall overseeing the clean-up at Jacks and getting closer to Tommy. With the help of Oliver she managed to get Jack's Gas listed in the National Registry of Historical Places and they even gave him a nice brass plaque to display out front. Jack played on the tragedy of his son's death, and his own "frail health" and "neurobehavioral abnormalities" (due to the "accidental" ingestion of gasoline) as a way to gracefully back out of his deal with Ben Horegold. Public opinion was now clearly on his side. In the local press he was portrayed as bravely holding out against the predatory practices of the big oil companies, which was hardly the case given that it was Sam who was in fact courting *them*. In any event, since Jack was ultimately cleared of any culpability regarding the spill (due in no small part to Apple's sworn testimony) and furthermore because he clearly didn't have the money, the federal funds eventually kicked in to pay for the clean-up.

Jack decided to retire after all. By Thanksgiving his health had made a near total recovery and so he decided he would like to do something different, something he had always wanted to do but never thought he would be able to. He knew now that life was all too precious and unpredictable and if there was something — anything — that you had always wanted to do, you'd better do it while you still could. Everyone felt it was a fitting tribute to Sam when Jack said goodbye and boarded the train for Oregon.

Tommy got Jack a cell phone before he left, which at that time was something of a novelty (or at least it was for an old salty dog like Jack, this way he could keep track of his business). Tommy would keep the home fires burning and sell Jack's wood. In accordance with Apple's plan they would reinstate the original name of "Jack's Fuel" and along with the firewood he'd sell a limited amount of kerosene, propane, and coal — and then of course there were the frozen Milky Ways and the newly designed "Jack's" tee shirts. Tommy would pay himself eleven bucks an hour (he gave himself a raise) but the rest would go into a bank account for Jack.

Chapter Forty-Two

It was a cold, clear, starry night, just before Christmas, when a crowd of locals gathered outside Jack's. To get a crowd like this in Truro, at night, in the off season, was impressive indeed. Everybody was all smiles, bundled up and cozy, while Goody passed out freshly baked muffins and cups of hot cocoa. All the die-hards from the art scene were there. Paul Howard Squidda showed up with his mother. He took pictures for his Upwardian Society newsletter (which apparently some people other than Pablo had started to read) while Merlin the Mormon, sporting yet another Guatemalan wool ensemble, worked the crowd with his gang of old lady Art Association groupies. Tommy was relieved that apparently there were no hard feelings from the fiasco of the Dump Dance Art Gala when he saw that the Outer Cape Alliance guys turned up — even Chris Franz, the hipster zombie painter extraordinaire, and his tattooed Betty Page girls from the Five Zero Eight Collective, where there.

Pablo read a poem, which very few people were still following by the end (though Goody was impressed) and then Tommy, with Apple standing beside him, stood on the front stoop and addressed the crowd. "Thank you all for coming! Obviously we wouldn't be here right now if it weren't for all of you. I guess what I want for all of you to take away from tonight is that this place is all of ours. We see it as a real community effort and we just want everyone to know that when we conceived of this project we knew that it had to be a genuine outlet for the community. Anyone who's really sincere in their art can show here. We don't want to judge. If there's going to be one prerequisite for showing here it is this: It has to be real, and sincere, and none of that cookie-cutter bullshit." The crowd cheered and clapped. "Short of that we'll hang, and hopefully sell, anything." Again everyone cheered. "Ok then. Let's do it!" Tommy ceremoniously pulled a cord over his head, and a sheet dropped, revealing the huge new hand painted sign over the front door. It was trimmed in Christmas lights and it read: JACK'S DISCOUNT FUEL AND FINE ART. The crowd cheered. "Now come on in and enjoy!"

Inside they had beer, wine, and food, and a fire going and though the space was small they had covered every possible space with art, even the ceilings. Tommy had even converted the bunk house in the back into a gallery. In one corner, over the washer and dryer, Apple displayed her "latest" photography. There were black and white photos of Jack on the woodpile and black and white architectural studies of London, but most impressive were her vibrantly colored blow-ups of her microscopic images of pig eye cells dosed with glowing purple trichloroacetic acid. "They're totally psychedelic," said Pablo.

"Thank you but I don't think I quite like that characterization," said Apple.

"Well they're definitely jazzy," said Pablo.

"I guess I can live with that," said Apple.

"Oh they're jazzy," said Tommy. "No doubt."

Just then Goody pushed her way through the crowd and threw her arms around Apple. "I got the letter this morning! Thank you so much Apple. They said I start in February. I can't believe it. Woods Hole has the best marine biology program in the country!"

"Actually it's the best in the world," said Apple. "We got lucky. I had a friend who helped me pull some strings, but you're going to have to really buckle down and kick ass. If you're up to it I'll totally help you."

"Oh I will! I promise!" Pablo kissed her on the check and gave her a big hug. Tommy raised his wine glass to the crowd.

"Let's hear it for Goody! She's going to be a Wicca poet marine biologist!" Everybody hooted and cheered and drank to her success.

It was quite a night, even Antonio Azule from New York showed up with a few choice examples of Tommy's older stuff. "Tony Blue I love you!" Shouted Tommy as he introduced him to all his new friends. Everyone got a kick out of seeing Tommy's early paintings, which were clearly way different than what he was now doing on the Cape. Tommy was impressed by Antonio's companion, the notorious red-headed potter who had unceremoniously taken his studio. Tommy whispered to Antonio: "Now I see what you meant. You were right to throw me out." Antonio looked around the room, impressed by the scene.

"Clearly I was." Antonio then made his way across the room to Apple. "You know I could definitely sell your stuff in New York." She smiled.

"Talk to my agent," she said. Antonio looked at Tommy's new paintings and shook his head in amazement.

"I can't get over his new stuff. It's like he's a whole new artist now. He should have been doing this all along."

"It's all 'cause of Sam," said Tommy. Tommy's old paintings were good, but in the end they were traditional easel paintings, done slowly, in oil. His new paintings, however, were radical and vibrant, and done in some kind of new orgiastic frenzy. Tommy had now adopted Sam's technique and attitude in art. Basically it was a sort of reckless abandon in acrylics, sharpies, and spray paint, and in so doing Tommy had managed to bang out a dozen or more ground-breaking paintings in the past two months. Whatever he was doing it was clearly working.

"Let's hear it for Black Samuel Bellamy!" Shouted Tommy as he raised his cup. His toast was met with a mixed response. Even posthumously people were a little afraid of Sam. "Well fuck you then!" Said Tommy. "He was one of the best painters I ever met!" Tommy was getting a little drunk. Apple put her arm around him and led him off into a corner where they kissed for a while. Tommy then remembered that he had one last surprise for the evening. He went into the office and held up the phone. "Everyone gather around! We're gonna call Jack!" The room fell silent as Tommy dialed the phone. Jack answered and everyone was quiet as Tommy told him all was well and how they were having a party for their new art opening. Jack was happy to hear about it.

"It's so good to hear your voice Jack. We all miss you."

"And I miss you all as well," said Jack. "Listen Tommy, I know this might seem a little odd to you but ever since I arrived here I've decided to go by my real name, Robert. I've made a couple of friends here and that's what they call me now, and for some reason I really like it. I don't know why but it feels like I'm getting back to who I really am."

"Ok," said Tommy. "That's a little weird but I guess I can see what you mean." Tommy then said to everyone: "He wants to be called Robert now. Everyone says hello." Tommy held up the phone and everyone yelled in unison:

"Hello Robert!"

"Well you sound good," said Tommy.

"I am," said Jack. "I'm taking it easy now."

"Well you should," said Tommy. "Don't worry about us. We've got it all under control here. Just relax and enjoy your retirement ok? We'll be in touch."

"Ok," said Jack. "I will."

Jack hung up and placed the cell phone down beside his coffee mug of vodka on a massive moss covered stump, and he picked up his new thirty-six inch chain saw. All around him two hundred foot sequoia loomed majestically overhead. He had a lot of work to do. He knew he'd better get moving.

As the night wound down, and most of the guests were gone, Tommy almost forgot to give Goody her present. He found her in the woodlot, snuggling with Pablo on a bench under the trees. "It's getting kind of cold out here."

"I hadn't even noticed," said Goody. Tommy handed her a long brown and red feather.

"I found it in the woods."

"It's from a turkey," said Goody.

"I thought you might like it to start your new collection," said Tommy. Goody looked at it for a moment and then handed it to Pablo.

"Thank you Tommy. It's beautiful."

Chapter Forty-Three

Over the next couple of weeks Tommy fell into a rhythm. The wood orders came in as quickly as he could load them into the truck. Every night he sat by the fire and painted.

One Saturday morning, just after Christmas, he was out front loading the truck when a car with out of state plates pulled in. They were a typical young family, just out for the weekend having fun. The kids got out to stretch their legs while Dad bought a map and a couple of frozen Milkyways.

"So you must be Jack?" Said the man.

Tommy paused, smiled, and said: "I've been called worse."